PRAISE FOR BRIAN LUMLEY AND THE NECROSCOPE® NOVELS

"Since reading Lumley's Necroscope series, I know that vampires really do exist!" —H. R. Giger

"Provides plenty of fun in the classic pulp tradition."
—*Publishers Weekly* on *Necroscope: The Touch*

"Lumley has accomplished the impossible by creating a book that will captivate fans of science fiction, horror, and espionage alike." —*Romantic Times BOOKreviews* on *Necroscope: The Touch*

"Lumley combines horror and alien-invasion themes uncommonly deftly." —*Booklist*

"Lumley excels at depicting heroes larger than life and horrors worse than death." —*Publishers Weekly*

"A vampire adventure for the Tom Clancy set."
—*Fangoria* on *Necroscope: Avengers*

"*Necroscope* fans will find themselves reading as fast as Lumley can type."
—*Kirkus Reviews* on *Necroscope: Invaders*

NECROSCOPE:®
THE TOUCH

+ BRIAN LUMLEY +

TOR®

A TOM DOHERTY ASSOCIATES BOOK
NEW YORK

This is a work of fiction. All of the characters, organizations, and events portrayed in this novel are either products of the author's imagination or are used fictitiously.

NECROSCOPE®: THE TOUCH

Necroscope® is a registered trademark of Brian Lumley

Copyright © 2006 by Brian Lumley

A Tor Book
Published by Tom Doherty Associates, LLC
175 Fifth Avenue
New York, NY 10010

www.tor.com

Tor® is a registered trademark of Tom Doherty Associates, LLC.

ISBN-13: 978-0-7653-5521-8
ISBN-10: 0-7653-5521-3

First Edition: June 2006
First Mass Market Edition: September 2007

Printed in the United States of America

0 9 8 7 6 5 4 3 2 1

This one,
with affection, is for
the pair who accompanied me
in my "grave" search for Möbius
in Leipzig: Frank "Uncle" Festa,
and Helmi Sigg; also for all
KeoghConners, past, present,
and future.

NECROSCOPE:®
THE TOUCH

A RÉSUMÉ OF SORTS

At 3:33 A.M. on a wild and rainy Sunday in mid-February, 1990, thirteen members of E-Branch—the strangest, most esoteric of England's several Secret Services—experienced something that astonished even them: the destruction of a man who was once one of their own, but no longer. They experienced, in fact, the death of Harry Keogh, Necroscope, transmitted to E-Branch HQ via some fantastic and unknown psychic medium from a world in a parallel universe, a world known only as Sunside/Starside.

Harry had gone there to escape the persecution and death—though not necessarily *his* death—which must surely follow if he remained in the world of men. For no longer a man, other and far more than a man, ordinary mortals would attempt to hunt him down because of what he had become as a result of his selfless services to mankind: a Great Vampire, a Lord of the Undead, the last of a race of beings who called themselves Wamphyri!

Neither an old wives' tale nor a grotesque myth, since time immemorial these Great Vampires had hidden among us, preying on men and secretly inhabiting our planet—but their source-world was Sunside/Starside. As to how they came here:

Certain Wamphyri Lords—"victims" in their own right, the vanquished of Starside bloodwars—had been banished through a wormhole gate on their world, only to reemerge on

Earth in old Wallachia, the ancient source of all vampire "legends." And for centuries Wallachia, now Romania, was their secret seat.

But when their plague had looked set to explode across the world, inundating mankind, then it had been time for the Necroscope, Harry Keogh—the man who talked to dead people in their graves and used a metaphysical medium known as the Möbius Continuum as an instantaneous means of conveyance—to seek out and destroy them, one by one. But when dealing with the most devious of all Earth's Wamphyri, that Father of Lies, Faethor Ferenczy, Harry had come too close and had been infected.

And so when he left our world for Starside, the Necroscope wasn't simply running for his life, but for ours. E-Branch might kill him, true, but what if they failed? He was by far the most powerful being in creation, and if he should unleash *his* plague on Earth . . . what then? The end of mankind, which he had fought so long and so hard to forestall.

Harry's problems were only just beginning. On Starside the Necroscope discovered that far from being extinct, the Wamphyri had risen again in a new, yet more terrifying form. And Shaitan—the Devil himself—was their leader! Crucified and burned, even as Harry's life force drained from him, he was transferred by the will of Others to the metaphysical Möbius Continuum. And there, hurtling across the centuries of past time, he underwent a final metamorphosis. And this was what those thirteen members of E-Branch witnessed in their HQ on a wild, wet Sunday morning in mid-February, 1990:

A nebulous telepathic projection, a fading 3-D hologram of the Necroscope's smoking corpse, falling or receding faster and faster into unknown depths. But as his twirling figure dwindled to a speck, a mote, and finally nothing, there where it had been, the observers saw an awesome, silently expanding novalike sunburst of pure golden light! And although it existed only in their group mind, still the coven turned away from the blinding intensity of the glare—*and from what flew out of it!*

Only two of them caught the final moment, saw those myriad golden splinters speeding outward from the sunburst—angling this way and that, sentient, seeking, disappearing into as many unknown places—those "pieces" of the Necroscope Harry Keogh. But were those golden shards *all* that remained of him? Perhaps, in a way, they were. While in another way, they were not.

For on Starside, as Harry's incorporeal mind fragmented in that glorious bomb burst, he had been aware that each and every one of those fragments, those golden shards, *were* him! And that wherever they were bound—into whichever time or place—some echo or knowing part of him would go with them.

But at a time some three and a half months *prior* to the Necroscope's passing . . .

PROLOGUE

It was a transit hotel, ten minutes off the M25 and twenty from Gatwick Airport. Ideally situated, it was used by air crews and passengers alike as a sojourn and watering hole before, between, and after flights; a busy place usually. But at 4:30 on a misty November morning, normally it would be fairly quiet.

Not now, however, for the crying of a child—its piteous wailing and intermittent shrieking from one of the rooms—had warranted the night security officer's investigation. Following which, and despite that he was in shock, shaken to his roots by what he'd discovered, he hadn't been able to get to a telephone quickly enough.

Inspector George Samuels of the Metropolitan Police—twenty-seven years old, seventy inches tall, raven-haired, with large ears, piercing grey eyes, and a small cynical mouth; a man who preferred wearing his uniform to casual "civilian" trappings—was referred to caustically by his fellow officers as "a highflyer" and "something of a whizz kid," if not in the detection of crime. His father had "connections," and it was an accepted fact that having risen rapidly through the ranks—by what his peers generally considered suspect means or machinations—the young Inspector still wasn't above blowing the whistle not only on police officers of like or lesser rank but also on his superiors, or taking credit for the work of his juniors, or greasing up to anyone perceived as a possible future rung in the ladder of his ambitions.

As a practical policeman, however, he lacked that certain something and would usually go by "The Book" because his hours on the beat had been drastically curtailed by his accelerated promotions. But as anyone who did it the hard way would surely attest, "The Book" (notoriously long on chapter and verse) is almost by definition short on experience. For example: "blood," probably the most important aspect of evidence, is referred to objectively and clinically, becoming just another word in "The Book." But as a physical, tactile reality blood is sticky, has a disturbing smell, and is invariably terrifying to victims and observers alike when it pulses in dark crimson spurts from the sliced arteries of warm, shuddering bodies . . .

Tonight the Inspector had tasked himself with "visiting" (in fact spying upon) late-shift commanders in various police stations in the city's suburbs and outlying districts, and had conveyed himself in an unmarked police vehicle as far out from the centre as Reigate, where moments after four-thirty he had entered the local station right on cue, albeit inadvertently, as the call for police assistance came in.

The mobile patrols and standby were already busy, dealing with two traffic accidents and a domestic dispute, and so the Inspector was obliged to cover the incident himself. The scene of the problem, whatever the problem was—about which the Desk Sergeant was uncertain, because according to him the telephone message had been badly garbled by the shocked, babbling, almost inarticulate caller; though Samuels suspected that this lack of pertinent information was more likely due to gross inefficiency on the part of the Desk Sergeant himself—was a transit hotel serving Gatwick Airport from a site only a few minutes away.

Since an ambulance had already been called by someone at the hotel, which seemed to suggest that the unknown problem had resolved itself in all but the business of an actual investigation, Samuels returned to his vehicle, clapped a strobing blue light on its roof, and set off into the night.

Should the case turn out to be "awkward"—more problematic than he would wish—he could always call in a Scenes of Crime squad to deal with the messy or intricate details. And finally, however it worked out and if there was anything of profit in it, he would ensure that he received all the kudos worth garnering . . .

At the Tangmore Transit Hotel Samuels found the night security man, a sixteen-stone, thirty-something bruiser in a uniform two sizes too small for him, shivering and wringing his hands where he waited under flickering white neons in the hotel's entrance. That alone—the size and physical presence of the man compared to his state of funk—must surely have alerted most policemen to the likelihood that something was well out of order here . . . but not Samuels, who was checking his white gloves, setting his hat straight, and dusting down his uniform; while wide-eyed and pale as a ghost, the security man introduced himself as Gregory Phipps, and without offering his hand, in something of a hurry, made to usher the Inspector inside.

At which point the blaring klaxon of an ambulance sounded, its lights ceasing to flash and its siren growling into a lower register, then abruptly shutting off as it slewed to a halt at the curb. Two uniformed paramedics got out and threw open doors at the rear of their vehicle. Experienced and proficient, their senior member—a short, mature man with broad shoulders, sharp eyes and features, and a very abrupt manner—wasted no time in addressing the Inspector:

"We must be on the same job, sir. So what's happening?"

"I've only just got here," Samuels replied. "It seems that Mr. Phipps here has called us in to . . . well, to assist in whatever the problem is." And turning again to Phipps: "So then . . . what *is* the problem?"

Phipps licked his lips, ushered the three into the almost empty foyer and toward the elevators, and finally said, "I got some information from reception late yesterday evenin'. Nothin' ter cause concern . . . so I thought. It was just that a nervous, 'arassed-lookin' bloke 'ad checked in wiv an infant—but wiv no wife or other woman—gone up ter his room, 'adn't come darn again. This 'ad been a little arter 4:00 P.M.; I didn't get ter know abart it until ten o'clock just as the girl was goin' orf shift."

The elevator arrived; the four got in; Phipps's finger was shaking as he pressed the button for the second floor.

"Well then, go on," said Samuels, examining his immaculate fingernails and adding, before Phipps could continue, "Oh, and by the way, I'm of the same opinion as you: that there doesn't seem to be too much out of the ordinary in what you were told. Surely it isn't unusual for a man to check in with a child—even an infant—when he could simply be waiting for his wife, a girlfriend, or even a nanny, to arrive from overseas? I mean, he might have been expecting someone off a plane early in the morning. Or he could have made arrangements with a partner to meet up here before catching some outbound flight." Shrugging, he looked to Phipps for an explanation.

Phipps's Adam's apple bobbed as he moistened his throat. "Right, but this girl—I mean the receptionist—she's the observant type, you know? She was worried abart this . . . well, this babe-in-arms, who she said was lookin' pretty sickly. And no wife or woman on the scene, and nothin' 'eard from room 213 right through the arternoon and evenin'. So I thought the same as you: bugger all ter worry abart. So I told myself, 'Greg my lad, don't you go lookin' for trouble. If trouble's in the air, it'll find you.'"

"And did it?" Samuels asked as the elevator halted with a slight jerk on the second floor.

Not entirely with it—having said his piece and then gone back to his own thoughts—Phipps blinked and said, "It?"

"Trouble." The Inspector sighed, doing his best to contain his impatience. "Did it find you?"

Phipps's Adam's apple bobbed again. "Lord, yers!" he said, gruffly but quietly. "Yers it did! Abart 'arf an hour ago, when I figured the kid 'ad been cryin' long enough and banged on the door ter see what was goin' on, got no answer and went in—and then called you lot."

Leaving the elevator, he pointed along the corridor with a scarred, big-knuckled hand that was still trembling like a leaf in a gale. And: "Room 213, yers." He nodded, indicating the way while yet holding back. "It's just along 'ere."

"Lead the way," said Samuels, who was only now beginning to feel or experience something of the security man's anxiety, his trepidation ... his fear? But a big man like Phipps? A man who could obviously take care of himself, as well as manhandle others? He was all that, yet now someone who seemed unmanned.

The receding string of subdued lights in the corridor's narrow ceiling were flickering and buzzing; they seemed on the point of shorting out. It could be the same problem Samuels had noticed in the neons at the hotel's entrance, but it loaned the corridor a surreal, almost alien dynamic where the walls seemed to shift in and out of perspective. It was an eerie strobe-like effect that had the Inspector blinking and feeling confused and dizzy. Moreover, the harsh, oddly wheezing or choked wailing of a child—one who had been crying for quite a long time—was now clearly audible.

The crying got louder as they approached room 213, where Phipps stopped short, handed a duplicate key to the Inspector, and stepped back a pace. "That's it," he said. "This is as far as I goes. It's ... it's all yours now." He shook his head, as if to deny all responsibility from this time forward.

Inspector Samuels, taking him by the elbow and giving him back the key, said, "No, you open it."

But the senior paramedic said, "Hang on, sir! Not so fast. First he must tell us what's in there. We're completely in the dark here!"

Turning on him, Samuels snapped, "What? Are you fundamentally deaf or something? Can't you hear what's in there? It's a stressed child. A child in trouble. And—"

"—And," Phipps at once cut in, his voice shuddering and almost breaking, "there's a lot more than just a kid in there. But don't arsk me, 'cos I can't rightly explain what it is that I saw. And 'avin' seen it the once, well that was quite enough, thanks very much. So I'll just stay out 'ere if you don't mind. But as for openin' 'er up: I should at least be able ter manage that for you, yers."

Reaching out, he turned the key in the lock in the silver metal doorknob, turned the knob, and pushed the door open.

"Wait!" said the senior paramedic a second time. "What do you mean, you can't explain what's in there? Is it dangerous?"

"Dangerous?" Phipps shook his head. "No, I don't think so. Not anymore, if it ever was. But 'orrible? Oh, yers."

"Right," said Samuels with a curt nod. "A crime scene. So in we go. But you two," he spoke to the paramedics, "don't you go touching anything. We may have to call in Scenes of Crime." And he pushed the door all the way open and stepped through it—into darkness.

The paramedics came close on his heels as the Inspector found the light switch to one side of the door just inside the room. A ceiling light flickered into being, but then continued to flicker, while from the corridor Phipps said, "They've been like that for a couple of hours now—the lights I mean. Most of the rooms is okay, but it's really bad in the corridors and just 'ere. Somethin' must 'ave blown out at the mains. There's a 'lectrician darn in the cellar right now tryin' ter find and fix it . . ." His voice trailed into silence.

The main room was L-shaped, with the bathroom on the left and the long leg of the L containing a bed, bedside tables, and a telephone. The infant, a boy no more than fifteen months old, was sitting on the floor with his back to the bed sobbing, but quietly now. He'd filled his diaper and it had leaked onto the floor where crisscross trails told of his wet wanderings. His eyes were sore from crying, his face pink streaked with brown. There was a lot more brown in his hair and on his chubby little body. It looked as if he'd been trying to clean himself up and make himself more comfortable, but had only made things worse. At least he didn't look ill or sickly, just tired, frightened, and very unhappy.

Samuels turned, shot an accusing glare out of the door at Phipps where he'd backed up against the opposite corridor wall, indicated the child, and asked, "Why didn't you take him out of here?"

But the security man only shook his head. "Didn't want to touch anyfing. Reckoned it best to leave fings exactly as they was. Figured you wouldn't be too long gettin' 'ere." And then, with a nod of his head: "You . . . you'll find *it* just round the corner there."

"*Phew!*" said the younger paramedic. "Like, if that's just baby shit, well God bless his poor little arse!"

"I'll see if I can find a woman to see to the kid," Phipps said from the corridor, and made to go off. But:

"No, you'll wait right there!" Samuels snapped. And moving along the foot of the bed—avoiding the dark-stained trails and small brown blobs on the carpet—he turned the corner into the short leg of the L. There he saw a writing desk, a glass-topped table, two chairs . . . and something on the floor in the farthest corner of the room.

The light in that sitting room was even worse than in the long L; flickering and buzzing, it made the room a kaleidoscope of changing shapes and shadows. But as the Inspector came to an abrupt halt, then started forward again around the table, closer to the thing slumped in the corner—and as the light flickered yet more violently before steadying up however briefly—"*Jesus Christ!*" he choked the words out.

The paramedics came to flank him. The junior man carried a torch that he shone into the corner. At which Samuels stepped back on legs that were suddenly rubbery, bumped into the table, and croaked, "What the . . . what the hell is *that!*?"

Down on one knee, the senior paramedic looked closer. "It can only be one thing," he said, gaspingly. And in the light of the torch he stared at but didn't touch a man-sized, *almost* man-shaped mass. "These are human or large animal remains," he went on in little more than a whisper. "But what in God's name . . . I mean, what could have done this to him, or it?"

Pushing the glass table aside, Samuels forced his legs to move him forward again. But as his flinching gaze followed the torch's beam where it moved along the length of the—

body?—so his lips drew back in an involuntary snarl of horror.

Its upper half was propped against the corner walls where they formed a right angle, while its lower half, lying flat to the floor, *radiated* raggedly outward. The walls behind it and the carpet beneath it were soaked black, which would be crimson under more normal lighting conditions. Its skeleton of flensed white bones lay partly hidden in or under it while its innards and viscera in general slumped or dangled externally, hanging there like various lengths of sausage or so many red and purple loaves of meat. The pulp of its brain clung to the empty skull.

"It . . . it's a man!" said Samuels, staggering to and fro, and beginning to breathe faster as his gorge rose. "It's a man, and he . . . he . . . he . . ."

"He's inside out!" breathed the younger paramedic, beating the Inspector to it. "And look! That *pipe* thing is moving!"

The "pipe thing" he was pointing his torch beam at was in fact a convulsing alimentary canal whose puckered anus suddenly opened, voiding itself in a twenty-inch surge across the carpet. At which the heart—it could only be—started up and throbbed six times with a desperate, pounding beat before fluttering to a standstill as the upper half of the mess toppled and slopped sideways down onto the floor.

Hissing their mutual horror, the paramedics literally flew back away from the impossible thing they had witnessed, and the junior man gasped, "That thing—that bloody unnatural fucking mess—it was alive?"

"Well, if it was," the other found the strength to answer, "there was nothing we could have done for it." And backing out of the short L, he tripped on something—in fact on the prone, unconscious figure of Inspector Samuels—and almost fell. And regaining his balance, in more ways than one, he said, "Get on down to the wagon. Take that security bloke with you and bring back a body bag and a stretcher. I'll stay here, use the phone to call out a Scenes of Crime crew, and maybe a policewoman to look after the kid. But until they arrive we won't be touching anything . . . well, except that." And grunting his displeasure, he nudged Samuels's sprawled figure with the toe of his boot.

"Not much of a cop, was he," said the younger man, making it less a question than a statement of fact.

"He was all wind and piss," the other agreed. "The sooner we stretcher him out of here the better. We can just thank God he's not typical of the breed."

Out in the corridor, security man Phipps was well pleased to accompany the young paramedic down to the ambulance. And no one noticed that throughout the hotel the lights were all back to normal.

As for the baby boy: he was fast asleep and snoring . . .

1

3:33—Again!

What the hell was it, Scott St. John wondered, about 3:33? And always in the morning. But actually he knew what it was all about, the reason he'd woken up at this time almost every morning for the last three months and three weeks . . . and yet *again* that bloody number! Three, and sometimes three of them! The top prial in three-card brag—if you were a gambler and incredibly lucky—or the number of a crowd. Or, in Scott St. John's case, his personal version of 666. And he supposed (no, he knew) that it would always be a completely unnecessary reminder of his own very personal hours, days, and weeks of hell. No, he didn't need numbers to remind him, because he simply couldn't forget.

Just for a moment he looked for Kelly on her side of their bed, his bed now. But then again, he always looked for her when he woke up like this . . . even when he woke up unlike this; which is to say, normally. Not that that happened very often, not anymore.

God, he was lonely! He was lonely and lost, and he'd been this way ever since 3:33 A.M. on that terrible Sunday.

Scott's mind immediately shrank away from the memory; and as an automatic reflex, hurriedly, unashamedly, knowing that he couldn't succeed, still he tried to smother the memory and cast it out. But despite his best efforts, he knew he would never be able to cast it far enough. It had its hooks in him . . .

He knew he'd been dreaming again, the dream he'd first had beside her hospital bed as she lay dying. And how he had cursed himself afterward, after Kelly's weak, shrunken little fingers tightened on his, waking him out of one nightmare into another. Cursed himself, yes—in the moment after her fingers slackened off for the last time—because he'd been asleep in his chair, worn out by his three-day vigil. Three: that *bloody* number! But Kelly had been dosed with painkillers; she wasn't aware of his presence there; that sudden tightening of her fingers had been an involuntary spasm, a final constriction induced by . . . well, by what?

Perhaps, in her sedated, subconscious mind, she'd noticed Death's stealthy approach and made one last effort to hang on to something before that grim Old Man stole her away. And feeling the pressure on his fingers, then Scott had woken up. Unthinkably painful now: to know he'd been asleep and hadn't squeezed back to reassure her. But better Kelly's tender-seeming, involuntary, unrequited squeeze than a death rattle. Scott had been an eight-year-old boy when his father died, but he could still remember that final, fluttering gurgle of stale, empty air. It would have been monstrously horrific to wake up to another one of those, this time from Kelly, and know that he'd remember it for the rest of his life!

God, you morbid, maudlin bastard! he thought, meaning himself, not God. Not that Scott had much time for God either, not any longer. For after all, what kind of God would let . . .

. . . But no, he mustn't go there. Not again, and again, and again. Not like he'd been doing. For three months, three weeks, and (he checked his mental calendar) yes, three days! Not only that but three hours and thirty-three minutes, too! Except time had moved on and it was now 3:36.

Scott knew he wouldn't get back to sleep again, and so got out of bed. It wasn't unusual; he'd stopped counting the number of times he'd done this when he hit ninety (three times thirty, of course) because he'd suspected that he was only aggravating matters. If he surrendered to it like that, accepting it as his lot, he might have to suffer it forever. But for goodness' sake, *must* he blame himself for the rest of his life for being asleep when Kelly died? Would he never, *ever* get a decent night's rest again?

And yet it wasn't only memories of Kelly that caused Scott to start awake. It was also the dream, and the hour of darkness when he dreamed it: a time that had significance other than the moment of her death. He felt quite sure of that without knowing why. But occasionally, and always briefly, he would recall some small detail of the dream, only to have it slip away as soon as he was awake, like a word on the tip of his tongue that refused to come. Not that there was ever anything that might indicate a guilty conscience—nothing particularly frightening or morbid, either—and certainly nothing of the so-called supernatural, which in any case he didn't believe in. And so, while he blamed himself for failing to maintain his watch as Kelly passed away, Scott was grateful that he couldn't be censured for the unknown and therefore incurable wasting disease that had taken her from him.

And so his dream—this recurrent yet unremembered dream—wasn't a guilt thing or even a genuine nightmare. But it was something weird, for sure. Weird enough to do this to him, this waking up at 3:33 thing, anyway.

And even as he mulled it over, there it was yet again, or at least a part of it: like that word on the tip of his tongue, or more properly a scene on the rim of his mind:

A splinter or shaft of light—a dart of golden light, yes— speeding through a dark place, the darkest place imaginable, toward . . . what? Was that a face? A clock face, maybe? A clock showing 3:33, just hanging there in a dark void? Or could it be a dartboard, with the dart speeding home to (what else but) the triple three? Ah, but then, in another moment, the dart slowing down—swerving to and fro, this way and that, oddly curious—before finally directing itself toward Scott. Seeking him out, yes, and sentient!

Scott twitched involuntarily, started, and broke the spell. And as quickly as it had come the memory slipped from his mind, leaving him frowning, frustrated, and asking himself, as he had asked so many times before: *Now what the hell is this? A total breakdown of my short-term memory, or what?*

Or was it just that he was still half asleep?

He went into the bathroom, put the light on, stared at his face, all haggard in the mirror. Running the cold water tap, he splashed himself more surely awake, then watched the water drip from his chin into the bowl. And: *Lord, what a mess!* he thought. *Scott, my lad, you're one totally fucked-up mess! You should see a counsellor or a shrink; or, since you never believed in such, you should do it yourself: simply pull yourself together and go back to work while there's still a job waiting for you.*

Well, *if* the job was still waiting for him . . .

The local newsagent opened up at 5:45, so Scott must do without cigarettes until then. Good, because lately he had been smoking far too many. Accepting and yet despising his addiction, it had become a trick of his to string a pack out through the evening, so that he smoked his last one before going to bed. Which meant he couldn't smoke in the morning until he could buy more. Which also meant that he could usually be seen walking the streets at all kinds of ridiculous hours—like now.

He must look like a bum, he thought: bleary-eyed, unwashed and unshaven, his collar turned up and his hands thrust deep in his overcoat pockets, trudging through a North London shopping district, with pages from yesterday's newspapers flapping down the wind tunnel of dreary-looking facades. Worse still, he *felt* like a bum, or what he

imagined bums felt like. Self-pity? Well, probably. But he
hadn't turned to drink yet. Not yet, anyway.

The dawn chorus had started up just as he'd left his house
in a pleasant residential area maybe half a mile farther
north. There were trees, shrubs, and tall hedges there,
where the birds had built their nests in March and raised
their young in April. The newcomers, full grown now, were
as active as the young of whatever species; always first
awake, they were ever hungry. Scott's house (just his now)
had luxuriant ivy clinging to the front wall as high as the
upper windows. Several house sparrow families were in res-
idence, and the young ones had just commenced chirping
themselves awake as he'd shut the door behind him.

Scott and Kelly hadn't had any chicks. She wasn't able and
had blamed herself. It had seemed a real shame at the time,
but it hadn't hurt their love. And as it now turned out . . .

But there he went again. His thoughts had a life all their
own and seemed uncontrollable, venturing where he really
didn't want to go. But it was unavoidable. And damn, he felt
even more like a bum because he'd been thinking how fortunate it was that they'd had no kids! Yet surely it *was* fortunate
because he knew he could never have coped, not without
Kelly. Or maybe he would have coped, knowing they were
parts of her. Of course he would. *God,* how he wished he
could stop thinking!

But suddenly, a welcome distraction: the newsagent's
shop, where Scott the automaton had ended up almost without noticing. And it was open. He entered and found a
frazzled-looking woman, her hair still in curlers, behind the
counter. She was checking accounts while her tubby, bald-
headed husband separated out the morning delivery of magazines and daily newspapers onto shelves that divided the
floor space into twin aisles.

The woman, recognizing Scott and knowing his needs,
had calculated the cost even before he'd picked up a newspaper and named his brand of cigarettes. Of course she
knew him; this was probably his twelfth, or more likely his
thirteenth (that three again), morning in a row. Paying up,

he was about to leave when he noticed another customer in the back of the shop: a smartly dressed young woman who had stepped into view in his aisle.

Scott knew her, at least by sight: he had seen her before, and not only here in this shop. What's more, there was a certain something about her. She had the kind of looks that, before he met Kelly, would have turned his head . . . but that on the other hand would as quickly have caused him to think twice. Because a woman like this was surely not alone in the world. She couldn't be said to be beautiful, but attractive? Oh, yes—albeit in an indefinable way—and there was definitely mystery, and a sort of magnetism, too, in her every movement.

And she was looking at him, at Scott the bum.

Suddenly aware—reminded of his unkempt if not actually disreputable appearance—Scott turned up his collar more yet, sank down into his coat, left the shop, and paused in the street to light a cigarette; where a moment later he felt the touch of a hand on his arm. A very gentle touch that brought with it the merest hint of some unrecognized, subtle perfume. Or perhaps it was simply her breath when she said, "I'm so sorry. I know it's none of my business and I really don't mean to intrude, but . . . she must have been a very wonderful human being."

Scott's jaw fell open; he also dropped his cigarette, felt himself beginning to bend to pick it up, caught himself just in time. That much of a bum he wasn't. But looking at her standing so close, he wondered: was it really that obvious? He had heard about psychics who could read you like that. Your aura or something.

"It's very obvious, yes," she said, as if she were reading his thoughts. "To me it is, anyway. It's very clear, written in your face, your . . . demeanour? You are—how do you say it?—radiating your sorrow. I can feel it washing outward from you."

Finally he found his voice. "Do I . . . do I know you? Maybe you knew Kelly? Have I met you before somewhere? I'm sorry, but I don't seem to remem—"

"No," she quickly, quietly cut him off, then glanced nervously up and down the street. "We've never met face-to-face and shouldn't be speaking even now. But I sensed you from afar, and I found you here and watched you. Your pain has spoken for you; so much pain that I felt I must make myself known, perhaps too soon."

"What?" said Scott, drawing back from her until he came up against the newsagent's window. "What are you saying?"

"We've never met," she said again, "but you do know me, or you should, or you will." And moving closer she whispered, "You are One, I am Two, and soon we'll be Three. Can you understand? I can see in your face that you can't. I don't quite understand myself, so perhaps we both still need time."

A crazy woman! Scott thought.

The early morning traffic was starting to move now. A taxi pulled up at the curb; the driver wound down his window, leaned out, and said, "Miss?"

Scott's crazy woman nodded, half turned away from him, and then turned back. "If anyone asks strange questions, try not to say anything. If you *sense* anything strange, keep your distance but try to explore it. *Do* think about what has happened to you, your loss, but think coldly, without anger, pain, or passion. Do *not* search for me; when it's time, I'll find you. As for Three: it only seems to be a question, but might just as easily be the answer."

Before Scott could say anything in return, she touched his hand, this time his flesh and not just his coat sleeve. He felt an almost electric tingle—static electricity, obviously—at which he jerked a very little and blinked. And still speechless he watched her cross the pavement to the taxi.

But as she seated herself and before closing the door, she looked at him one last time and said, "Scott, promise me you'll be very careful."

With which she closed the door and was gone . . .

His mind a complete blank, a well of astonishment, Scott stayed right where he was, chain-smoked two cigarettes, and might have made it three but that would have meant surrendering to *both* of his bad habits. Finally he snapped to, strode into the shop, and looked for the woman in curlers. She was up on a stepladder behind the counter, replacing a dead bulb in its light socket. As she got down she was grumbling, ". . . That's the fourth time in a *bloody* week! Cheap *bloody* . . . ! I keep putting them in; they keep blowing! And they cost a *bloody* fortune! I—"

"The young woman who was just in here," Scott cut her off. "She left a minute ago, just after me. Would you happen to know who she is, where she lives, or anything about her?" Why he was bothering to ask after a crazy woman he couldn't have said, and especially since she'd asked him not to.

Dusting her hands off on a rag, the woman said, "Eh? That girl you were speaking to outside?" And then, cocking her head on one side and cackling like a crone, "Oh, yes? *Fancy* her, do you? Well, I'm sorry, love, but I can't help you. She's been in here three or four times, but hasn't said very much. Has to be an early bird, though, 'cos I never see her except in the mornings." And after a further bout of cackling, closing one eye in a lewd gargoyle wink, she continued. "But never mind. P'raps if you come in again tomorrow—and chat her up a bit, you know?—maybe you'll get lucky, eh?"

Scott left the shop and headed for home. And for the first time in what felt like a very long time his brain had something to work on other than his misery.

That girl, woman, person, who could be twenty-two going on thirty-five—who the hell was she? And how did she know about Kelly, and about Scott? Well, not so much about him, because it really *must* be obvious. His sorrow was written in his face, and in his demeanour; in fact, it radiated from him. Her words, yes. But what else had she said? And what the hell was it that she'd said about Three, which he'd sensed had a capital T? She'd said he was One, she was Two, and soon they'd be Three . . . also that Three wasn't just a question but could as easily be the answer. Now what was *that* supposed to mean? Or maybe he wasn't hearing things right and it was him who was crazy!

As for her looks: if he had to describe her, how would he go about it? Damn it, he couldn't remember! She never seemed to look the same twice! And now, thinking about it, Scott believed he'd seen her maybe a dozen or more times; not only in the newsagent's but in various places in the city. Her face, mirrored in a shop window; her figure, glimpsed across a busy street or on a crowded tube train; her perfume, lingering in the air, whose fragrance he had forgotten until she touched him. So then, was she some kind of stalker? But whatever, she *had* touched him—the merest touch—and his hand was still tingling.

And he felt . . . he felt *alive* again!

Was she Russian, Italian, American? Maybe a cross between the three? (God, that number!) Scott—whose knowledge of languages, accents, and dialects was way above average; who *had* to know at least something about them, because he was an interpreter—had never before heard anything like hers. But there yet again, maybe it was him. Maybe he really wasn't hearing things right. Yet he felt sure he'd heard her well enough when she spoke his name— *without ever being told it!*

And what about those weird warnings? About people asking strange questions, and him keeping his distance from something unspecified, and not trying to find her? Oh, really? Well, he'd be seeing her again tomorrow morning, that was for sure!

By which time he was home, in through his gate and up the garden path to his porch . . . which was where they were waiting for him: those men in their grey, half-length overcoats, their grave-seeming eyes looking him up and down, sizing him up like so many hungry undertakers—especially the very tall, extremely gaunt, and dour-seeming one—and tucking him away in their individual mental pigeonholes.

And somehow, while Scott was registering his surprise at their presence here, and wondering about their purpose, one of them got behind him and he felt a tiny spider bite on his neck just above his upturned collar. Except that even as he reached up an oddly rubbery hand to slap the thing, he was fairly sure that it hadn't been a spider.

Then, as his legs turned to jelly and their faces began to swim, they grabbed and steadied him, and kept him from falling; one on his left, another on his right, and the third one—the gaunt one—telling the others he'd go fetch the car, his high-pitched voice coming as if from a thousand miles away. Three of them, of course. But then, what else should Scott expect?

Following which there was only the darkness and a sense of floating, drifting, sinking . . .

2

The mind-spies of E-Branch in the heart of London were enjoying "a quiet period." The duties of the agents in that most secret, strangest of all the United Kingdom's Secret Services were just about as routine as they would ever get. Yes, they continued to listen to the minds of others, monitored the suffering planet's ecology, tracked the movements of nuclear vessels and munitions across the world's most remote terrains and beneath her oceans, maintained the status quo and when they could improved upon it, and generally did their utmost to shield humankind from terrors that a majority of the world's inhabitants couldn't conceive of and certainly wouldn't believe in; but all of that was routine, even habitual at E-Branch HQ, and the ESPers were enjoying what was for them a comparatively quiet period.

Ben Trask was the Head of Branch. A mousy-haired, green-eyed man in his middle to late thirties, he was about five feet ten, just a touch overweight and somewhat slope-shouldered, and normally wore what could best be described as a dismal or lugubrious expression. This was as a result of his talent; for in a world where the plain truth was so often hard to find it was no easy thing to be a human lie detector. White lies, half truths, frauds, facsimiles, and utter falsehoods smacked into Trask from all directions, until he frequently felt he wasn't able to take another hit. His team knew this, and while they might sometimes embroider the facts in casual conversations with other E-Branch colleagues, they invariably told the truth, the whole truth, and nothing but the truth to Ben Trask.

This morning, feeling the need to clear up a growing backlog of paperwork, Trask had come into town early. But he wasn't going to be on his own. Despite that it was only a few minutes to 7:00, already there was no lack of activity in E-Branch HQ, on this private and mainly inaccessible top floor of a building that to all intents and purposes was a quality but by no means ostentatious central London hotel. The weary Night-Duty Officer was making ready to hand over his duties, and the members of an early shift of Trask's agents were organizing an interrogation.

In the main corridor, on his way to his office, Trask came to a halt to look down at an unconscious man on a wheeled trolley. The man was maybe thirty-five, blue-eyed, and a very light blond. While he wore his hair unfashionably short, he wasn't at all bad-looking, but at six feet tall he didn't appear to have the weight to go with his height. He was either lithe and athletic or he wasn't looking after himself too well . . . probably a mixture of the two, but more likely the latter. He might well have been sleeping in his clothes; his hair was awry; he hadn't shaved for a day or two, and so looked more than a little worse for wear.

"And who is this?" Trask inquired as one of the three-man team opened the door to the interrogation cell.

Ian Goodly, a very tall, thin, gangly man—but a man with an exceptional talent, his occasionally unruly ability to sense something of future events—paused to blink owlishly at Trask, and said, "Good morning to you, too, Ben. As for him"—he indicated the unconscious man— "you okayed and signed the paperwork yesterday."

Nodding wryly, Trask replied, "Yes, I've been signing

lots of things lately. Which is why I'm in so early this morning: so that the next time I write my name on something I may even have read it first!"

"As always, you're overworked," said the precog, smiling a rare smile. Ian Goodly's expression was usually grave; only his eyes—large, brown, warm, and totally disarming—belied what must otherwise constitute an unfortunate first impression: that of a cadaverous mortician. Sure enough, his smile vanished just as quickly as it had appeared, and he continued:

"This is Scott St. John, who was 'spotted' by one of ours at an OPEC conference in Venezuela . . . he's a freelance interpreter: Arabic dialects, chiefly. We might have checked him out at that time, around three months ago, but since he'd recently lost his wife we allowed him time to recover; not long enough, apparently, for it doesn't look like he's fully recovered even now. In fact, he still looks very much down. He'd contracted for the Venezuelan job months prior to his wife's sudden, terminal illness, and soon after she died he flew out to the conference where he tried to fulfill his commitment. He stuck it out for a day or two, then had to quit. It was then, when he really began to go to pieces, that our man spotted him."

Trask nodded. "And his talent, if indeed he has one?"

"That's why we brought him in," Goodly replied. "Whatever it is he's got, whatever it is he can do, if anything, we can't pin it down. We've been watching him—well, from a distance—but while there's definitely something about him it isn't ringing any bells just yet. So it could well be something we've not seen before. And as I know you'll agree, we can always use new talents. Right, Ben?"

"Scott St. John, eh?" Trask moved aside, allowing Goodly's colleagues to wheel St. John into the interrogation room out of sight. "So why did you knock him out? Do you think he's dangerous or something?"

"It's his curriculum vitae," Goodly answered. "His father, Jeremy St. John, was a diplomat; for some seven years he served as British Ambassador at the embassy in Tokyo.

Divorced, he was also a single parent, but he didn't have much time for the boy. So Scott spent a lot of time with a Japanese minder, a reformed Yakusa-type with a penchant for the martial arts. Result: Scott St. John is a karate black belt, with qualifications in several other lethal oriental, er, pastimes." The precog paused, shrugged, and continued. "Since it seemed possible he might not want to come with us . . . well, we weren't taking any chances."

"Hmmm!" said Trask, frowning. "What do you think, Ian? Are we maybe a little too heavy-handed sometimes?"

"We might occasionally seem to be, I suppose," the precog agreed, "but sometimes we've had to be. I think we get it right more often than we get it wrong."

Trask nodded and said, "You're right, of course. But being in a job like this—more or less autonomous, with the power to do just about anything, right *or* wrong—it occasionally gives me pause. You know what they say about absolute power?"

Goodly's turn to nod, as gravely as always. "But we're not *that* powerful, Ben," he said. "And personally, I've never known a group of individuals less prone to corruption than our people in E-Branch. Which, as you'd know better than any other man, is the plain and simple truth."

Trask smiled wryly and said, "But it wasn't always so, now was it? What about Geoffrey Paxton? Wasn't he one of ours, too? And let's not forget Norman Wellesley—a former Head of Branch and my immediate predecessor!"

Goodly shook his head. "No, I can't entirely agree. Geoffrey Paxton was mainly the Minister Responsible's man, let loose among us to keep an eye on Harry Keogh. As for Norman Wellesley . . . he was the exception that proves the rule. With that closed mind of his we couldn't read him. But being what we are now, we don't need watchers to watch us, Ben. With us it's instinct: we watch each other, and we watch ourselves. And, if I may say so, having got rid of those two we do so quite needlessly. E-Branch and its members, we're just fine, Ben."

Again Trask smiled, and said, "Ian, if you're ever in need

of a job you can be my conscience." And over his shoulder as he started off again along the corridor toward his office, "But do let me know how it goes with St. John, right?"

"Of course," Goodly answered, before following his friends into the interrogation cell . . .

Scott St. John snapped awake to the stinging smell of ammonium carbonate. Seated, he at once tried to get to his feet, only to discover that he was tied down, his wrists manacled to the arms of a chair. Then, all mush-mouthed, he commenced an instinctive response to his situation: "What in the name of . . . ?" And immediately gagged on an acrid bitter-aloes taste, before swallowing sour spittle in order to moisten his bone-dry throat. And still gulping, his eyes watering, he looked dazedly all around.

He was in a grey-carpeted, cell-like room with blank, nonreflective walls, no windows, and a single light in the ceiling behind a long narrow desk where two men sat facing him. A third man, the very tall gaunt-looking one (for Scott had immediately recognized the trio as his abductors), was just now returning to his colleagues, having tossed a used ampoule into a wastepaper basket. And as Scott quickly gathered his senses, so the gaunt one sat down with the others behind the desk.

Though the faces of the three were shaded, silhouetted in the light that shone on them from above and behind, still Scott could feel their eyes on him, watching him closely; so closely, indeed, that he felt they might somehow be probing him, albeit covertly. Which was such a weird, even ridiculous idea that he wondered how he had dreamed it up: this notion that they could be searching him without touching him—almost as if they were in his mind, or trying to be.

As best he could Scott focussed on their faces, something he hadn't had time to do when they'd jumped him. The tall, thin one was the most distinctive of the three; seated to the right of the desk, he now leaned forward a little and began speaking in a high-pitched but by no means threatening voice:

"It seems you're pretty much returned to us, Mr. St. John. Good! Would you like a drink? A glass of water, perhaps?"

Scott stared hard at him. "How do you suggest I drink it?" He coughed the words out, his throat still burning. "Through a straw, maybe?" He shook his trapped wrists against the arms of his chair, grimacing as he ran his tongue around the inside of his foul mouth.

"That's the general idea, yes," the other piped. "Through a straw, to get rid of the bad taste. For we're well aware how that knockout drug of ours can sometimes affect people. And so I'll ask you again: would you like a drink?"

Scott wanted to say yes, but instead he shook his head. He wouldn't give this lanky bastard the satisfaction. "No, I don't want anything to drink!" he growled. "I want to know where I am and why I'm here—and who you people are—and what the hell you think you're doing? I've been attacked, assaulted, drugged, snatched, from right in front of my own house, manacled, and . . . and God only knows what else! And you can bet your life someone will be in serious trouble when all of this is sorted out."

The other nodded, remained unruffled, and replied, "Well, I'll try to answer all of your questions, and then we'd like to ask you some of our own. Meanwhile it would help if you'd calm down and try not to be so angry. A bad or threatening attitude won't improve matters and may only prolong this procedure."

Scott shook his head in disbelief and tried to work things out. There seemed only one possible solution to this thing, one answer. "You've got the wrong man," he said, hoping, *knowing* it must be so. "Whoever you think I am and whatever you think I've done, you're seriously mistaken." But when that made no appreciable impression, and more furiously yet: "Listen, who the hell *are* you people? MI5, the KGB, or the Stasi or something? You're not the police, that's for damn sure!"

"No," said the gaunt one, as calm as ever, "we're not the police. But you may certainly *think* of us as police—well, of a sort, though not the usual sort—and rest assured that what we're doing here isn't illegal, and you won't come to any harm. Also, I want you to know that when we're through here you'll be free to go; we'll return you to where we found you. As for your other questions . . . you want to know who *we* are, where *you* are, and *why* you're here? Well, that's only fair and reasonable, and my colleague here will try to supply you with some answers." He looked at the man next to him, and Scott did the same.

There seemed to be something wrong with this one's face. Granted it was partly shaded and silhouetted, but Scott's eyes were adjusting to the room's lighting now and he'd noticed the stiffness of this second man's features. He believed that he'd already made a mental note on that same subject—probably at his house, when these three first approached him—since when events had moved so speedily that nothing much had fully registered.

Now, however, he saw that he'd been right: there was something wrong with the man's face. For in fact Scott was looking at Paul Garvey, an E-Branch telepath. Garvey was tall and well built, athletic and about the same age as St. John, and until a time some nine months ago he had been a handsome man. Then he'd tackled a murderous, necromantic sex maniac called Johnny Found and lost most of the left side of his face. And despite that he had been subsequently worked on by the best plastic surgeons in England, still the nerves in his rebuilt face didn't connect up too well. He could smile on the right side but not on the left, and so to avoid the travesty he didn't smile at all. Also, his speech had suffered, which meant he must carefully control the formation of his words.

He did so now, and in a very slightly slurred voice said, "You mentioned the KGB and Stasi, Mr. St. John. Well, we're not them; in fact, they're working at a very low level now—'keeping a low profile,' as we like to say—but you also mentioned MI5, which was closer to the mark. We are in fact members of a branch of the UK's security services. This is our headquarters, where you are our guest . . . for a little while, anyway."

Still feeling confused, dehydrated, Scott growled, "Okay, but before we go any further, maybe I'll take that drink now—that's if you'll free my hands. And perhaps you'd also like to explain why I was drugged in the first place?"

As the third man got up and left the room, Garvey nodded and said, "That was unfortunate, yes, but it was deemed necessary. It was partly due to the nature of our work and partly to your CV. You're a karate black belt, Mr. St. John. Outside this building we couldn't tell you who we were; there are no IDs we could have shown you that you would recognize or accept. Also, the location of this headquarters isn't known to the public at large; and last but not least there was a distinct possibility that you would resist us, perhaps violently."

"More than a distinct possibility," Ian Goodly chimed in. "I myself, er, assessed the probability as very high."

"Well, you're right," Scott answered. "I wouldn't have come with you without a damn good reason. In my job I'm occasionally privy to some pretty sensitive stuff, so I'm naturally watchful when it comes to strangers. Once in Riyadh, in Saudi Arabia—"

"We know," said Garvey. "You were approached by, shall we say 'agents of a foreign power' who wanted to know the details of a conversation between the Saudi oil minister and one of the diplomats at a meeting where you were the interpreter. You were offered a large sum of money, turned it down, and then reported the matter. Several Iraqi, er, diplomats were then sent packing back to Iraq. All very correct and laudable."

Staring hard at him, and thinking hard, Scott said, "Maybe you've just this minute verified your credentials. For who else would know all this stuff if not someone in intelligence? Okay, so I'm impressed. Now will you get these manacles off me?"

The third man—a "spotter" called Frank Robinson, a man whose talent was the ability to detect other ESP-endowed people—had reentered the room carrying a can of soft drink. He also had the key to St. John's shackles and looked to Goodly for his okay.

The precog responded with a nod, but warned, "Scott, if we free your hands and you react contrary to our wishes, you'll be shot . . . if only with a tranquillizer dart. In which case we'll have to start over. Is that understood? You won't try anything, well, too hasty?"

When Scott reluctantly nodded his accord, Robinson went to him, put the drink on the floor, and freed his wrists. As he did so, Scott got a good look at him. The spotter was blond, looked young—maybe twenty-one or -two, Scott thought (albeit incorrectly, for his guess was four or five years short of the mark)—and wore an abundance of freckles on his fresh, boyish face. But young or not so young, as soon as he was done with Scott's restraints he moved quickly away; experienced, he was taking no chances.

Scott picked up his drink, took a sip, then refocussed on the men behind the desk. There was now a weapon—a tranquillizer gun, he supposed—in plain view on the desk in front of Goodly. And between sips, Scott growled, "Okay, now that you've established yourselves, can we do away with all this cloak-and-dagger stuff? What are these questions you want to ask me?"

It was Frank Robinson's turn to speak, and as he regained his seat he said, "Scott, we sometimes recruit suitable people into our branch. By suitable I mean gifted people, people with special traits and talents. It has recently come to our attention that you might be just such a person."

"What, because I'm a patriot, take my job seriously, can't be bribed?" Scott shook his head. "There must be a slew of men, British men, with those same qualifications . . . or maybe you're making me the same kind of offer as the Iraqis in Riyadh—only this time I'll be doing it for my country, right? I'll be doing it for 'the cause.'" He made no attempt to hide his scepticism, his sarcasm.

"Scott, we don't know what we may ask you to do." Robinson shook his head. "We've no idea what you *can* do, not yet. That's what we're here to find out. But I should warn you now that our questions might seem rather odd . . . or maybe not. It depends on what you know about yourself,

because we sometimes meet up with people who don't even
know they have these special talents."

Again Scott shook his head. "You've lost me," he said.
And before he could say any more Ian Goodly came in with:

"I think that maybe the best way to proceed is to proceed.
So as strange as these questions might seem, please think
about them before answering, and then try to answer them
truthfully."

And so the questioning began . . .

3

"Are you aware of anything strange in your life?" Goodly
began. "Something you can't explain, either previously or
recently?"

And again Scott felt that inexplicable, eerie sensation of
being observed—or of someone feeling, listening—but on
the inside. Moreover, he was fully awake now, alert, refreshed, not quite so confused. And from nowhere, suddenly he remembered the girl in the newsagent's shop, her
weird warning: *If anyone asks strange questions, try not to
say anything.*

That had been strange in itself: some sort of presentiment
or foreknowledge of things to come? Whatever, Scott immediately shielded his mind . . . then asked himself: *What . . . ?!*
But he knew what, knew instinctively that he had somehow
reinforced his own mental privacy, denied access to his mind!
And across the room, behind the desk, both of the gaunt
one's colleagues had at once straightened in their chairs;
they'd become far more attentive, their gaze rapt upon him,
as if suddenly he'd said something of real importance. But
Scott had said nothing at all. He'd merely thought it, and then
to himself. And once again: *What?!* For now he was thinking
things that even he didn't understand.

"Well?" said Ian Goodly, whose demeanour seemed unchanged.

And Scott answered, "What kind of strange? I've had my ups and downs like anyone else—recently more down than up—but as for strange: no, I don't think so." *A lie! Their first question and he'd lied to them like a criminal who has something to hide! What the hell was going on with him? Why was he accepting and complying with the warnings and advice of a total stranger, a woman he'd never met until this morning? But then, he'd never met these people either; and at least she hadn't stuck a needle in him! She had only touched him—touched his hand—and now, just thinking about it, he could still feel the tingle.*

While Scott was turning these things over in his mind, the three behind the desk had huddled together to converse in whispers. When they drew apart Goodly continued with his questions:

"You appear to be . . . well, a very *private* man, Scott. And we think you could be holding back, resisting us, not answering entirely truthfully. Is that a fact? Are we right to make these assumptions?"

"I like my privacy, yes," Scott answered. "You can definitely take that for a fact. Also this: if or when your questions get to be too intrusive, I'm not going to answer them."

"Oh? And did you consider my question about strangeness in your life intrusive?"

Scott decided to throw them a red herring. He wasn't sure why, but he didn't want to admit to his "three" fixation. Also, there were things he would like to know about his mystery woman before telling anyone else about her—if ever. And so he said:

"Listen—you want to know about strangeness? Okay, I can tell you about strangeness. The whole world is full of scumbags: crazy, murdering, psychotic scumbags. Terrorists, drug-addicted sociopaths, total weirdos, pedophiles, and fanatical fundamentalist fuckups of all kinds who would cut your throat as soon as look at you. They live their lives, and nothing much happens to them. They may be out on the streets, in prison, in hell, or some junky's paradise, but still they're living lives of sorts. And then there are the decent people, like my wife, who caught a freak bug, wasted away, and died just like that. So I ask you, if that isn't strange—that my wonderful Kelly is gone, while all this shit is still floating down our gutters—what is? If that's what you mean by strange, then I'm with you. Other than that, no, there's been nothing strange in my life."

A red herring, perhaps, but at the same time it brought a feeling of relief. It was something he'd wanted to say, to get off his chest, for a long time. And now he'd said it, and with feeling, and it was real because he'd meant it.

Goodly glanced along the desk at Garvey, then at Robinson. Both men shrugged and looked bewildered, and Scott sensed that while they remained attentive they were no longer quite so rapt upon him. Perhaps in some small measure he'd managed to satisfy their curiosity. But Goodly wasn't finished yet.

"Scott," (he was obviously trying to choose his words with care) "we know that you gamble from time to time. You're not a habitual gambler, but—"

"*But*—" Scott cut him short, "sometimes the people I've worked for—Russians, Arabs, various others—sometimes they've wanted to visit casinos, and then I've been called upon to help with the language, or to explain the games, or simply to accompany them. Yes, I've played in London's casinos now and then—always in the course of my work— but I've never lost a fortune and I certainly haven't won one."

And Goodly said, "You're not especially . . . lucky, then?"

Frowning, Scott answered, "No, but neither am I especially unlucky. So what?"

"Let me be more plain-spoken." Goodly sat back a little. "Do you understand the word 'telekinesis'?"

"I'm an interpreter!" Scott replied sourly. "I don't speak Greek, no, but I know how its roots are buried in our language. Are you trying to insult my intelligence? Of course I know the meaning of telekinesis!"

Goodly nodded. "My apologies. But you've never wondered if perhaps you could, er, move something? With your mind?"

"What?" Scott half stood up, sat down again as Goodly took up the dart gun. "What did you say? Move things with my mind? I mean, is this some kind of weird joke?"

But now it was Paul Garvey's turn. "Scott, look at me," he snapped, his face twisting and his tone brooking no denial. And as Scott looked at him he continued. "Now tell me, can you read my mind?" *Can you? Are you doing it even now, Scott?*

Scott tightened his shields—was amazed that he could do so—and thought, *What the hell is happening to me? What in the name of all that's . . . ?*

But he'd kept his thoughts shielded (how, he didn't know!) and now, managing to control himself, out loud he said, "That's it. We're all done." And then, getting to his feet, "I'm out of here!"

Aiming his dart gun, Goodly said, "No, we're not done. And you're not going anywhere, not yet. *Now sit down!*"

Scowling, angry, unsure of his ground but quite certain of the weapon in Goodly's hand, Scott slowly sat down again.

But by now the young-looking, freckle-faced Frank Robinson was on his feet. And leaning forward with his palms flat on the desk, he said, "Scott, we know you can do something. So what is it? Is it mesmerism, telepathy, second sight, clairvoyance, ESP of a sort we don't understand? Maybe you can kill things with a glance: we've come up against that before! Perhaps you can find lost or missing people, locating them with your mind alone. But we know you can do something. Maybe you can wish people lame or even dead. Why, for all we know *you might even have killed your own wife!*"

That last was deliberate, of course, designed to get Scott to react without thinking, perhaps to display his secret talent in an act of blind insensate fury. And again Scott was reminded of his mystery woman's words of advice: *Think coldly, without anger, pain, or passion.*

But too late for that now.

Scott was on his feet, weaving, making for Frank Robinson, reaching for him over the desk and causing Goodly to
reposition himself, redirect his aim. And Robinson's face a
mask, as white as snow with a gaping "O" shaped mouth
and black blob eyes that were fixed on Scott's bunched fist
and craggy knuckles—

—And then the damp-squib *phut!* of Goodly's gun, even
as Scott hauled Robinson across the desk and aimed a crushing blow at his face, but a blow that was never launched. Because out of nowhere, suddenly Scott was floating, drifting,
sinking in this lake of inky darkness that he was sure he'd
known before . . .

The darkness didn't last; or it did but became sleep as opposed to total unconsciousness. "Ordinary sleep." Or in
Scott's case, about as ordinary and as normal as it had ever
got to be in the three months since Kelly's death.

*There were three of them, of course: three black dots on a
vast white plain that was awesome in its immensity, blinding
in its intensity . . . a plain that went on forever. The three
stood out like meteorites on some Antarctic snowfield, one
close, the second near-distant, and the third three-quarters
of the way to the horizon.*

*The closest one was Scott—so close that suddenly he was
in* him, *squinting out across the vast, white, blinding plain
at the other two.*

*At that distance there was no way to tell who or what they
were, only a sure knowledge that they were looking at (or
maybe looking for?) him. He desired to draw closer to them
across the snow, sand, salt—across the brilliant surface of
this place, where- or what-ever it was—but seemed rooted
here, immobile, because he hadn't been enabled. Or he had,
but that had been in another dream, in many dreams, always
unremembered. It was very frustrating.*

*He looked left, right, and over his shoulder on both sides
as far back as he could see. But in every direction except
one, forward, there was only the dazzling white plain. And*

forward there was only the endless glare and the dots, one near-distant and the other far away.

Then it came, a shaft or splinter of light, a dart made of golden light! Usually it came in the dark . . . this was the first time it had come in the light . . . but in the light of what? And Scott thought: It will enable, empower me. It has empowered me! This is a reminder, because it knows I forget. And also because I don't know how to use what it has given me . . .

The darkness was above him—the Darkness of Ignorance—like a black sky over the achingly white Plain of Discovery, of Learning; and Scott knew that his mind was a blackboard waiting to be written upon and that the dart was a stylus. The darkness was his: his ignorance or naivete. And the vast empty plain was a lack of knowledge, a mind unfulfilled. His mind.

Simultaneous with the dart, a word came to Scott. The word was 'allegory'; he was dreaming in allegory, symbolically. And he watched the dart zigzagging in the darkness clouding his mind, searching for him as he knew it had searched before. But all of this was only a reminder, and Scott also knew, remembered, when it had found him: on the day, at the hour, the very second when his wife, his Kelly, had died!

That was what had awakened him—and he suspected in more ways than one.

And here it came again, speeding down out of the darkness, slowing down, swerving to and fro, this way and that, eager and curious, and finally striking for his head, or maybe his heart, or perhaps his soul.

It entered him, melted in him, became a part of him.

There was momentary fear—for after all, he had been invaded—but there was no real sense of shock, no pain, nothing to distinguish the after from the before . . . except . . . perhaps . . . a certain awareness? The knowledge that he was now enabled? But with what? And why? And by whom—or by what?

Scanning the shimmering white plain again, he saw that

*the black dots were no closer but at the same time felt an
ability, a mobility, stirring within himself. He could now
move forward. Again it was allegorical: here, in his dream,
Scott could "move forward" in a linear sense, while in
himself—in his life—he could simply move forward. In both
cases toward his future.*

*Making an immense effort—but of will as opposed to
physical strength—he began slowly to traverse the surface
of the dazzling plain toward the black dots, which now he
saw had only seemed black against their brilliant backdrop.
And as he gained in proficiency, stilling his straining arms
and legs and allowing his mind to drive him, so the dots
drew closer and began to take on more definite shape and
colour.*

*Scott slowed down, approached more carefully, fought the
dazzle to bring the first of the shapes (actually the second of
them, for he had been the first) into clearer perspective. What
he saw was bipedal, upright, vaguely anthropomorphic: man-
like, or more properly womanlike. But by no means a human
female. It looked anything but human, and he slowed more
yet.*

*Or maybe the shape was human after all. It must have
been the glare that had confused him—much like the sun
masking its corona, or any strong light source throwing an
abstract silhouette onto an object to distort its true
outline—for as Scott drew closer he saw that indeed it had
the figure of a woman . . . and what was more, that he knew
which woman.*

*He had seen her before (kaleidoscopic, flashback images
of the newsagent's shop; of walking the night streets of
Highgate, Finsbury Park, Crouch End; of a trip into town
on the tube: all of these scenes incorporating that same—
never quite the same—barely remembered face, and even
now remembered only because of the compassion in its
eyes). Dim, blurred, obscure until now, that face; because he
hadn't been focussed, not then. His mind, fogged by misery,
had too often wandered through happier times, brighter
memories; he could have bumped into friends of a lifetime*

without recognizing them until they spoke to him, and even then couldn't have spoken back with any degree of co-herency.

But she, *this woman, had been there—often and in diverse places—and Scott knew now that while he had only ever caught glimpses of her, she had been watching him.*

As she was now.

He brought himself to a halt and stared at her wide-eyed, mouth agape, incapable of speech. What was she doing here? Had she been waiting for him? Were they in some way connected? And if so, what was the nature of their affinity?

Scott hadn't spoken, and neither did she when she answered him: You are One, and I am Two. *Her lips hadn't moved, not by a fraction! Then, turning her head, she looked toward the horizon at that third spot on the brilliant white surface, and said:* He is Three.

Scott looked where she looked, at that hunched, immo-bile, unhuman *(but by no means alien) shape halfway to the horizon. In that same moment, with his attention diverted, Scott sensed motion and transferred his gaze back to the woman . . . too late, for she was gone! But this time her image—the way she looked—stayed with him. Previously he had failed to remember her or remembered her differently; he could never have described her. But now she was fixed firmly in his mind's eye.*

She (for there was no way he could call her Two) was five-seven or -eight; her hair was a sooty black, like dusk but deep as space; she had eyes as green as a fine jade, slightly tilted without seeming entirely oriental—perhaps Eurasian—though her skin did seem dusted with saffron, or was it a light olive, or possibly something between the two? "Two," yes . . .

She had not *set him afire; there hadn't been anything more than ordinarily sexual; he couldn't have described her breasts, backside, or legs. Her eyes had been his main focus, or perhaps her small, pretty, shell-like ears? . . . Her straight nose, ample mouth? . . . Her slightly parted lips, showing a flash of gleaming teeth? . . . The brightest of stars shining in the pupils of those deep green eyes?*

So all right: he had *been attracted. Sexually? Well, maybe that, too. But wherever she had gone, the sexual excitement had gone with her. Scott felt dismayed, frustrated.*

It was that dream that everyone has known at some time or other, where some object of desire is unattainable, just beyond reach. But no, not sexually, not this time. Scott's only desire had been to talk to her, discover who she was, what she wanted, and why she was watching him. (Or watching over him?)

But she was no longer here, and now other eyes were watching him.

He is Three . . .

Her words returned to lure Scott on, across the shimmering plain to where the third black dot waited. He sped faster now, finally in control of his motion, and as before the inky speck on the blinding white surface became more distinct. A smallish figure, hunched up. Or so he'd thought. But now he saw that he was wrong. It was a large dog seated there, ears erect, tongue lolling; a dog that now stood up, sniffing at Scott as he came closer.

And now the surreal nature of the dream surpassed itself, for as Scott approached to within a few feet the creature gave a small whine from deep in its throat and said, Is it you? Are you The One?

Even dreaming Scott started. The creature's tongue continued to loll; its muzzle hadn't moved, not a fraction. Just like the woman's words, this thing's thoughts were in Scott's mind! Its thoughts, yes!

And: I am not a dog, *it said.* Or a creature, or a thing. I am a wolf, the son of Wolf . . . well, with something of a dog in me, perhaps, which I got from my mother, but even she was a dog of the wild. So then, that is me. But what of you? Again I ask: are you The One?

Scott got down on one knee and tried to say out loud, "You won't bite me?" But the words didn't come, which wasn't unusual for him . . . he had rarely been able to speak in his dreams. The words didn't come, but the thoughts were there, certainly. And:

If you were a hunter I would bite you if I could, *the dog, or wolf, or Three, answered.* But you are not here. You are far, far away. I smell you, I sense you, I hear you, as I have for a long time now. But you are not here. Are you The One? My father has told me that one day there might be someone for me as there is for him. He has his Zek, and I have no one.

Scott sensed loneliness, a longing for companionship, and went down on his other knee, reached out a hand to the animal's head, stroked the soft fur. You're alone?

I am the last of three, *Three answered, flinching a little from Scott's touch.* My mother named us One, Two, and Three. But my mother and my brothers are dead and I am alone. I am Three.

Scott was fascinated. And your father?

He is not alone. He has his Zek, his One. But he has told me that one day there could be someone for me, my One. I sensed you afar and thought that you were him.

Scott nodded. I don't know how, but I think it's possible, just possible, that I may be your . . . well, your One, yes.

Three licked his hand. Two thinks so, too.

Scott jerked back a few inches. Two? The woman, Two?

Three looked startled. She is the joining one. Didn't you know that? You have your dart, and I have mine, but she is the one who will bring us all together—*if* you are my One. If you are The One.

Scott stood up, thought: This is just a crazy dream!

No, it is more than a dream, *said Three, his fur bristling as he backed away.* And I must go. I sense the hunters. They are looking for me. I killed some chickens. Now I must hide! If you are my One—if you are The One—you will find me. *He sprang away, vanishing into thin air, and the dazzling white plain was empty except for Scott.*

Wait! *Scott yelled.* I don't know where you are, so how can I find you? And how do you know about "Two"—I mean the woman? And what's all this about darts?

He went to move after Three—tried to move physically— and felt himself falling.

Mouthing incoherently and jerking his arms and legs, which only served to dislodge him from the backseat of the car where he was stretched full length, Scott fell all of fourteen inches onto the rubber mats between the front and rear passenger seats, and so shocked himself awake . . .

4

Scott got out of the car, a Mercedes, and found himself in the lane outside his house. Since there was no one else in the vehicle to question or vent his anger upon, he aimed a staggering, halfhearted kick at the door panel and almost fell over. Then, dazed and confused, and failing to note the car's registration number, he went tottering through his garden to the front door of the house. Somewhere inside a telephone was ringing.

He entered, let the phone ring, washed out his mouth, and poured himself a drink. Time enough then to answer the persistent clamour of the phone. And:

"Scott St. John," he grunted, choking the words out, his throat still dry despite the stinging brandy-and-coke mix he'd fixed for himself. "What is it?"

"Mr. St. John," came the answer, "if you should ever want to contact, us, here is our number. You'll put the call through directory inquiries and ask for Xavier, or your call won't be answered." Scott recognized the high-pitched voice as that of the tall man, whose name he still didn't know.

"And I suppose you'll be Xavier?" he said, after copying the number onto a pad.

"You may suppose whatever you want to suppose," came the answer. "Though of course Xavier could just as well be a code. But in any case, only the number itself is important. My name is immaterial."

"Oh, really?" Scott snapped. "Well, tell me something,

Mr. Immaterial: what makes you think I'll ever want anything more to do with you and your lot?"

"Well, one never knows," said the other, and Scott sensed his shrug. "But the way I see it the future could be a complex thing . . . for all of us." And with that the phone went dead.

Slamming the phone into its cradle, Scott looked out of the window and saw movement and the gleam of polished bodywork through a gap in the garden hedge. A man with a hat pulled low over his eyes sat at the wheel of the big Mercedes, driving it away. Scott couldn't make out the driver's face and in another moment the car had passed from sight.

Scott went unsteadily into his study, flopped into an easy chair, and finished his drink. And lighting a cigarette he tried to think things through. For the first time in a very long time he remembered the contents of a dream, and a most unusual dream at that, which had probably been prompted by—or had some sort of obscure connection with—his encounter with these peculiar Secret Service types; but in what way connected? Or was it all in his mind, and might he even be losing his mind? Had Kelly's death caused that much damage? he wondered. It had traumatized him, certainly, but was it worse than he'd thought? And if so, how much worse?

He felt odd, changed, no doubt about that . . . but crazy?

Scott shook himself, tried to pull himself together, order his thoughts, think positively. He knew of a way to corroborate at least something of what had happened; which had to be better than nothing, because if some of it was real, then maybe all of it was real. In which case he wasn't mad at all but involved in something way beyond his current understanding, beyond anything he'd previously experienced.

Collecting the notepad from his front room, Scott called directory inquiries from his study and asked for the number on the pad. The operator, a woman, asked him if there was a fault with his telephone—why didn't he call the number direct? To which he patiently replied that it was a special number and he wanted to speak to Xavier.

Then he waited for one minute, two, and was just about to hang up when a male voice he didn't recognize said, "Ah, Mr. Scott St. John! You're either (a) going to give me a hard time over our treatment of you, or (b) you require us to assist you in some way or other, or (c) you're simply testing the system. Well then, which is it?"

Scowling at the phone, Scott said, "How do you know that my solicitor—or perhaps a policeman, or some other respected member of society—isn't standing beside me right now listening to all of this? How do you know I haven't arranged to have your number traced?"

The voice on the line sighed and said, "So then, you are simply testing the system. Well, and now you know it works. As for having the number traced: you're welcome to try, of course . . . but it won't get you anywhere. And so, since we're both of us wasting our time, I bid you good day." The phone went dead in his hand.

"And that's that," Scott told himself, replacing the telephone in its cradle but much less furiously, more thoughtfully this time. "I'm not going crazy after all. But all this cloak-and-dagger stuff, that's only one facet of whatever's going on here, while my 'Three' fixation, and the woman, and the dreams—especially that last one—are something else. But what?"

Then, realizing that he was talking to himself, which was hardly reassuring, he lit another cigarette and fell silent . . .

At E-Branch HQ, the precog Ian Goodly reported to Ben Trask in his office. "We've had St. John taken home," he said, frowning and fingering his long chin thoughtfully where he stood before Trask's desk. "He got, er, more than a trifle upset—in fact, rather aggressive—so we sedated him and called it a day. As for our little chat, interview, or interrogation, call it what you will: I have to say it left me with mixed emotions, and to be frank, more than a little concerned."

It was well past noon and Trask was still engaged with his backlog of paperwork, but knowing Goodly as well as he did, and seeing the look on the precog's face, he put his work aside and invited the other to sit. "All right, so what's bothering you?"

"Well, we worked it between the three of us, as per SOPs," the precog answered. "Each of us in turn framing our questions, while the others listened, probed, did their own things."

Trask nodded, said, "Robinson, Garvey, and you. A spotter, a telepath, and a precog, in that order. In short, an excellent team. So what did you get out of him?"

"I'm not quite sure," said Goodly, shuffling in his chair, and still frowning. "In fact, I'm not at all sure! It's possible we might have done better with you in there. What I'm trying to say: while I'm convinced that St. John has something, I haven't the foggiest idea what it is. And what's more, I don't think he knows either! But in retrospect, if you had been in there—"

"We might have found out that he was pulling the wool over your eyes? Or rather, I might have known if he was lying?"

Goodly nodded. "But . . . those are big 'mights.' "

Trask leaned forward, put his elbows on his desk. "Do you want to explain that?" And Goodly continued:

"Frank Robinson knows—he's absolutely sure—that I'm right and St. John has some weird tricks up his sleeve, even if he doesn't yet know about them himself. Paul Garvey questioned him about telepathy: he sprang it on St. John right out of the blue, asked him if he could read his mind. And if you ask Paul he'll swear that St. John immediately put up shields that were almost as strong as Wamphyri mindsmog. Psychically—or more properly telepathically—he simply disappeared!"

Trask started behind his desk and almost came to his feet. But Goodly put up his hands reassuringly and said, "No, you can rest easy. He isn't Wamphyri. Paul reckons that St. John didn't even know he was doing it; it was a reflex, knee-jerk reaction, entirely instinctive."

Trask sat back again, relaxed a little, took a deep breath,

and said, "So, what are you saying? And anyway, if St. John can shield himself, what difference would my presence have made?"

"Well," said Goodly, "even the best of us have difficulty lying to you!" He offered one of his rare smiles. "We might try occasionally but you usually know. So, if St. John was actually aware of his talent—if he was *deliberately* hiding behind some sort of mental facade—you would probably have known that, too. And if he wasn't, then we could be sure that his gift, whatever it is, really is undeveloped, fetal, and that he doesn't know he has it."

Trask nodded. "You mean if I couldn't read his reaction to any specific question—or if he tried to shield himself before answering—then we'd have reason to suspect he was lying?"

Goodly shrugged, sighed, said, "Something like that, yes." And after a moment's thought: "It can get very difficult, can't it, Ben?"

"The work we do?"

"Knowing the things we know," the precog replied. "Knowing what's possible, and that almost everything is, but only rarely knowing what's coming and never precisely, not even me. I mean, what if St. John has something like poor Darcy Clarke's thing?"

"A guardian angel?" Trask shook his head. "You would never have brought him in. He'd have sensed your intentions and given you a very bad time. Oh, I know Paul Garvey can look after himself, but against Scott St. John? Him being a karate black belt and all?"

"No," the precog answered. "I didn't actually mean Darcy's guardian angel—not precisely—but *something* of that sort. It could be of real benefit to us, or real harm if St. John was on the wrong side. Not that I think he is."

"So, what do you want to do?" Trask frowned and offered an irritable twitch of his shoulders. "Do you want to bring him in again? Why didn't you just keep him here in the first place and pursue it further? Why did you let him go?"

"It was my decision," said Goodly. "And I'll tell you why. If St. John's shields are indeed instinctive—something he has no control over, like Darcy's guardian angel—then putting him under pressure isn't going to work: the moment he decides someone is trying to probe him, his talent will switch on and he'll do a psychic rope trick. But if we can approach him without his knowing . . ."

"Another bout of covert surveillance?"

"Yes, in a way." The precog seemed undecided. "But we've already tried that without any positive result. So I was thinking maybe we could put some obstacles in his way and see how he finds his way around them, how his talent helps him to cope with them. But even before that I was thinking maybe I could team up with Anna Marie English—go in tandem with her, as it were—and see if we can learn something that way."

"Anna Marie?" Trask raised an eyebrow. "In tandem? You and the ecopath? How do you mean?"

"It's what she does," Goodly answered. "She's an ecopath, or as you just pointed out, she's *the* ecopath. *Sui generis:* the only one we know of. Mind and body, her condition parallels the state of the Earth itself. If there's a gas leak from a Russian atomic power station, Anna Marie wilts. If twenty tons of farm slurry leak into some Cornish river, Anna Marie has nightmares about it long before it gets into the newspapers. As the ozone layer thins out, so does her hair. So I was thinking—"

"Yes, I understand," Trask cut in. "Working hand in hand, literally, Anna Marie might be able to tell you how St. John's talent will affect the future. But the whole world's future—the entire planet? I mean, isn't that a bit strong? Aren't you going overboard on this thing? He's just one man, not an army, Ian! And how much harm can one man do?"

"How much harm could Harry Keogh have done?" Goodly countered. "Or Boris Dragosani? Or Yulian Bodescu? Or—"

"Okay, I get the point." Trask held up a hand, and Goodly continued:

"And anyway, I wasn't thinking in terms of how much harm, but more properly how much good."

Now Trask narrowed his eyes, nodding knowingly. "Ian, you haven't told me everything, have you? You've talked about Paul Garvey's and Frank Robinson's opinions but not your own—not entirely. So now let's have them."

Goodly sighed and said, "Ben, you know there are problems with scrying on the future. You're well aware that—"

"That the future's a devious thing?" Trask beat him to it. "I know I've heard you *say* that often enough, yes. But come on: what did you learn about St. John's future?"

Looking very uncomfortable, the precog began to shuffle in his chair again and said, "While Paul and Frank questioned him, doing their thing, I had the opportunity to do mine. I tried to read what was in the cards for him, but all I got was a jumbled set of very vague impressions. He was partly shielded, yes, but his shields were growing stronger all the time. In fact, we were probably initiating all of this resistance—with our questioning, if you see what I mean. Anyway, as for what I saw or felt:

"I felt a lot of violence, a lot of energy expended, a lot of danger. Indeed, incredible danger. Other than that: well, as I've said, it was all very jumbled, didn't make a lot of sense. There was something horrible in there, I'm fairly sure of that, but don't ask me what it was because it was completely alien to anything I've ever experienced. I didn't understand it, and now I can't even remember what it was all about. That's how different it was."

Starting to look bemused, Trask stared hard at the precog. "And you would have kept all this to yourself? I'm sensing that you'd have kept it to yourself! I know you mentioned your 'concern,' but now it's looking much stronger than that, isn't it? So what *is* going on here, Ian? More to the point, what's going on with you?"

"Nothing is 'going on' with me!" Goodly's normally piping voice rose higher still: a sign of his frustration, Trask knew. "It's just that it's like always: when you read the future you only very rarely see everything. The immediate future might be clearer—just a little clearer—but casting a week ahead is like driving through a thick fog. And a month

is like being in a dark cave full of bats: now and then you'll
hear the flutter of wings, or maybe feel the air fan your
cheek, but that's it, that's all. And then, when you *do* see
something, you can never tell if it's the before or the after,
the cause or the effect. But in Scott St. John's case there are
a couple of things I *do* feel fairly certain about. First, that
the horror I sensed was spawned in evil. Well, horror usually
is, but there's evil and there's evil. And something else: St.
John will fight the evil to the end and with everything he's
got—whatever that turns out to be. And finally . . ."

"Well?" Though puzzled and feeling angry and disappointed, still not knowing what to make of Goodly's reticence, Trask was fascinated now. He wanted to know it all,
but *most* of all whatever it was that the precog was still holding back . . . and why.

"Finally"—Goodly was on his feet, tall, thin, and pale—
"finally, I know that St. John won't be fighting this alone.
There'll be others helping him: a woman and—oh, I don't
know—someone else who I couldn't see at all clearly. But I
sensed that all three of them will be, well, talented . . ."

Finished, the precog eased his slender body back down
into his chair. And after a long moment:

"Ah!" Trask said at last, believing he finally understood.
"And St. John's helpers? You wouldn't be talking about
yourself and Anna Marie English, by any chance?"

The precog shrugged his thin shoulders. "I can't say that
it will be us for sure, but if it is—"

"Then you were afraid that I'd say no, keeping you out of
it for your health's sake. Right?"

"No," Goodly answered, very firmly. "Not at all. For *if* I
saw Anna Marie English and myself—which isn't at all
certain—there's no way you could keep us out of it because
that's not how it works. We can't avoid the future, Ben.
What will be will be, and according to certain modern theo-
rists has already been! But on the other hand if it *wasn't* us
that I sensed, then fate will step in to divert us, stop us going down that route."

"Oh, indeed!" Trask sat up straighter. "Absolutely! I can

agree with you there because *that* sounds like fate in the shape of me!"

"But you won't do that," said the precog, hurriedly.

"And why not?"

"Because we'll be fighting evil in a battle that could be of the greatest importance to . . . well, to everything! And anyway, you want to know what this is all about just as badly as I do."

"Hmmm!" said Trask gruffly, chewing his lip. "What's this, Ian, psychology? You're not only my conscience now, but also my psychoanalyst? Well then, let me think it over. *Hmm!*"

And a moment later: "Okay, I've thought it over: go ahead, get on with it. But the moment you sense any kind of danger for you or Anna Marie—the moment you learn who or what this evil, this horror is—then you'll get the hell out of it and report back to me, and we'll turn E-Branch loose on it as a dedicated fighting unit with our gadgets and ghosts and all our resources primed for action. But I feel I should warn you now: working on what little we know— what little you know or have *told* me you know—I'm tempted to activate the entire Branch right now!"

"But you won't," said Goodly once again, shaking his head. "This is mainly St. John's show, Ben. St. John and his helpers, who or whatever they are. Just the three of them."

"The three of *you,* you mean!" said Trask, frowning again.

But the precog wouldn't commit himself. Shrugging, he said, "Maybe, maybe not. I've told you all there is, Ben, all I know: that there'll be three against an unknown, terrible threat. And the rest is . . . well, the rest is for the future."

Goodly waited then, but when Trask just sat there, saying nothing more but simply staring at him, he left and closed the door quietly behind him . . .

As Goodly went looking for Anna Marie English in the Ops Room, the locator David Chung was on his way up in the elevator. And so the two men missed each other by just a few seconds.

Chung, a Cockney born and bred, was returning to E-Branch HQ after helping the Metropolitan Police in their search for a missing child, and his mood was very subdued. With his assistance, his special talent, they had found the girl in a shallow grave under shrubs in one of London's parks. And the only good thing to come out of it: as soon as he'd seen her, touched her, then Chung had been able to lead the police to her murderer. A moment's elation, but too many hours of black gloom, and weeks ahead that would be full of it.

Now in the corridor the locator's steps suddenly faltered, slowed, brought him to a halt. He was alone yet seemed to sense a presence; there was an odd, indefinable quality to the air he breathed; he felt that he walked in the wake of a ghost, and he shivered. He looked back the way he'd come, then forward; there was no one else in the corridor, just the feeling that someone, something, had passed this way. But when, and who?

Chung's eyes scanned long lines of doors on both sides of the corridor. Nothing strange in that; this was once the uppermost floor of a hotel, after all. And it still was, except that now it housed E-Branch. Behind those doors, Chung knew that his fellow agents were at work. But what else was at work here?

Then it dawned on him where he'd paused, and where he was standing: directly opposite a door with a nameplate that read:

> ### HARRY'S ROOM

And once more Chung shivered.

But already the feeling had passed, and he breathed freely again, straightened up and shrugged, and finally grinned at his own weird fancies, the product of a possibly overworked talent. For after all this was E-Branch, wasn't it? And this was or had been Harry's room. How could a man help feeling strange knowing that the Necroscope—the man who talked to the dead, who came and went like a ghost himself—had once stayed here? And Chung was well aware of the fact that residual psychic currents could last for a very long time.

Perhaps it were best he switched off for a while, gave his talent a well-earned rest, went and wrote up his report. And so he carried on to his own room, leaving Harry's Room and a gradually fading something behind him . . .

5

Having sat alone in his office for some time *really* thinking it through, Trask believed he had arrived at a final understanding of Goodly's reticence in respect of what now must be considered "the Scott St. John case." For in the light of Goodly's obvious and very real concerns, Trask knew it would be a dereliction of duty on his part not to follow it through, that he must now let Goodly and Anna Marie English carry out an investigation as per the scheme he'd okayed with the precog.

As to why Trask had been obliged to almost physically drag the entire thing—the fine details—out of Goodly: that was because he'd suspected that the precog wasn't telling the *whole* truth. A partial truth isn't a lie, it's simply incomplete, and Goodly hadn't wanted to alarm the Head of Branch by putting too much stress on the dangers he and the ecopath might be facing.

But Trask hadn't been fooled by the other's half-truth; he completely understood the precog's difficulty in that respect—how he must feel torn between two agencies, two loyalties: that of his singular talent, his ability to read something of future events and then to act on his perceptions as best he could, and on the other hand his respect—an abiding and mutual respect—for the Head of Branch, Trask himself, his friend and colleague for many strange and dangerous years.

As for Trask's abrupt, apparently snap decision to let the precog proceed as prescribed, however:

While it was almost impossible for anyone to lie to Trask, the man himself was not confined to the truth. He didn't relish it, but when he felt justified and believed it was warranted he wasn't averse to telling the odd white lie, or in this case not telling all of the truth.

What? He should simply step aside, letting two of his most valued, uniquely talented agents, not to mention colleagues, go off into uncharted territory against horrors such as the precog had hinted at? Not likely! In his scrying on the future, Goodly had sensed the presence of two ESP-endowed people—presumably E-Branch agents—helping St. John. But what if there was to be a third and fourth that he *hadn't* sensed and wouldn't even know about?

Trask knew that sometimes it was prudent to have a watcher watching the watchers. Goodly wanted to use covert observation? Very well, Trask would have David Chung and a colleague perform a little discreet spying of their own—on Ian Goodly and Anna Marie English!

A stakeout, both mental and physical, on two top E-Branch agents, in order to ensure their safety; in Ben Trask's opinion a sensible, logical precaution. Chung would watch Goodly's back without the precog ever knowing it.

Trask called the Duty Officer and asked if David Chung was back from that job with the police. He was? Good! Then could he please report to Trask's office in . . . say, half an hour?

And between times he would get back to reading through the remaining papers, reports, and requests on his desk, and see if they contained anything requiring the attention of E-Branch . . .

The half hour passed quickly enough, and saw Trask moving paper marked with a tick, a cross, or some curt comment—indicating variously yes, no, or maybe—from

one side of his desk to the other, and from his In Tray to the
Out or Action Tray. E-Branch got the weird stuff, the insol-
uble crimes and inexplicable occurrences that fell outside
the expertise and experience of more orthodox security services, secret or otherwise, and Trask got to choose from
these cases—these frauds, murders, disappearances, freakish incidents, atrocities, political scandals, and suspected
acts of treachery and espionage—any that he might consider within the scope of E-Branch investigation.

This most recent crop of unresolved cases and requests
was typical of the broad spectrum Trask had become used
to, ranging from the murky and mundane to the eerie and
exotic, the odd and obscure, and often the odious.

There was the case of Herr Ernst Stenger, a former leading
light in East Germany's now defunct *Ministerium fur Staat
Sicherheit*—the Ministry for State Security, or simply "the
Stasi"—who had gone missing from his base in Leipzig, suspected of absconding to Switzerland with the key to a bank
vault containing a heap of Kremlin gold; treasure that he had
been squirreling away over the course of two decades, allegedly on behalf of Stasi underlings: a terminal "golden
handshake" between the old Soviet Union and her myriad
East German spy minions.

In his absence, Herr Stenger stood accused of many bru-
talites, including torture, rape, and murder. He had also
been in charge of an East Berlin Stasi cell controlling various German border police (*Grenz Polizei,* or GREPO) officers and units. In addition to the frequent and gratuitous
killing of refugees by these border guards *after* the would-
be escapees had scaled the Wall or Wire to the west—all on
the orders of Stenger—it was also believed that he'd sent
Stasi agents into West Berlin to eliminate members of Allied Military Intelligence, and that he had forged links with
the IRA and other terrorist organizations in order to enable
such operations.

Naturally MI5 and MI6 would be pleased to have words
with Herr Stenger before certain Russian "authorities"
(meaning the remaining die-hard cells of a moribund KGB)

or ex-Stasi "colleagues" caught up with him; wherefore it would be much appreciated if E-Branch was to discover his current whereabouts and inform the relevant agencies of the same . . .

Trask chewed his lip over this one, but not for long. Did anyone really believe he had the sort of manpower required for this kind of job—or the time? What, when Israel's Mossad and a handful of other intelligence agencies worldwide were *still* searching for the last few war criminals from the Second World War? Hell no, it could take forever! He would post the details as restricted information, for E-Branch eyes only, on the slim chance that something would turn up . . . and leave it at that.

Trask scanned the next document, and sighed. A UFO sighting in Wales, coinciding with crop circles in Dorset: typical! While MI5 and the Metropolitan Police recognized E-Branch for its true worth, some educated loon in the Ministry of Agriculture and Fish was getting all steamed up about little green aliens scything cryptic designs, and leaving (probably) very rude messages in Old English cornfields!

Tearing the document in half, he dropped it into File 13: his wastebasket, for shredding.

Next up—

—Something strange and very unpleasant. And despite that Trask already had *some* knowledge of this case—but the barest of bare details (its bare bones?), which he'd read of in newspaper reports at least six months old now—this was the first time it had been brought to his attention in all its grotesque minutiae. He read it twice, slowly.

One of Her Majesty's Government's opposition ministers—Gregory Stamper, a very rich man with shares in several of the planet's most profitable precious-metals mining concerns—had been found dead under what was euphemistically termed "odd and suspicious circumstances": British phlegmatism, Trask supposed. But the forensic pathologist author of an accompanying medical report (someone who was himself quite obviously a pathological abecedarian) had gone one step farther and titled the thing:

A REPORT ON THE EVAGINATION OF
G. STAMPER:
An Operation of Incredible—Albeit
Criminal—Surgical Skill, Which Sight Unseen
I Would Have Pronounced a Medical Impossibility.

Evagination? Even knowing what it meant—at least being able to guess, from the pictures in the file—Trask typed it into his desk dictionary. And the answer came up:

"To evert: to remove from a sheath: to turn outside in."

And he wondered, *Is that different from inside out? How is it different?* But in any case that was it: something he usually did with his socks first thing in the morning, so that he could pull them on more easily. He "evaginated" them, which wasn't at all Trask being facetious . . . in fact it served to paint in his mind a clearer picture or understanding of the word; except, of course, that what he did to his socks didn't damage them.

And reading the rest of the report, despite ignoring the many technical or medical words that failed to register, Trask found that *that* appeared to be precisely what this experienced criminal pathologist was suggesting: that while Stamper's evagination was certainly the cause of death—because a man can't live for long with his internal organs dangling on the outside—still there seemed to have been no actual damage to his soft tissue, his "sheath"?

It made very little sense; only the statement that "sight unseen I would have pronounced (this) a medical impossibility" made any sense at all!

Trask sat back in his chair, pulled at his chin, tried to think back, oh, how long—a thousand years?—to a time when his father had taken the ten-year-old Benjamin out to Malta in a last attempt to heal the rift with the boy's Maltese mother. Sitting alone on the rocky rim of the sea in Valletta while his parents did whatever they were doing in a run-down fisherman's cottage, listening to their shrill, angry voices and trying to shut them out, the boy had been mercifully abstracted from the argument when a sun-bronzed swimmer had come dripping from the sea with an octopus wrapped around each hand and wrist.

What had happened then . . . was that "evagination"? No, not at all, because there *had* been some damage to soft tissues when the swimmer/fisherman had used a knife to cut through a septumlike bridge in the body sacks of his catch to turn them—what? Outside in? No, they'd been turned *inside out*; and in any case, it would have been impossible to evaginate their tentacles. And why had the fisherman turned the creatures inside out? In order to tear off their now *external* organs. Trask remembered how the ink sacks had splattered black dye on the yellow rocks, and how a flock of screaming seagulls had rained from the sky, fighting over eviscerated gills, heart, liver, and other bits floating on the water.

Evisceration then, in the case of the octopuses. But evagination? In poor Gregory Stamper's case it could only have been; because as this long-winded forensic pathologist—the man who had done the postmortem—was careful to point out, there was no sign of any actual "surgery," no cutting except his own upon Stamper's hideous remains, which he had been obliged to perform in order to reverse as best as possible their unique condition and thus complete his examination . . .

For long minutes Trask stared at the photographs—

—And gave a massive start as a knock sounded on his door! This stuff he'd been reading had got to him; hardly surprising, really. Taking just a moment to compose himself, he called out, "Come in," and David Chung entered with his report on the missing—now dead—girl. Speaking quickly, the locator summed it all up, then handed over his typed report.

"And you're sure we got the right man, the right scumbag?" said Trask.

"Oh, yes," Chung answered, with a great deal of satisfaction. "He took a life and now he'll be doing life. It's all over for that bastard!"

"But not for you, eh?" said Trask, knowingly.

"I'll get over it, sir," the other answered as he made for the door. "Don't we always?"

But Trask stopped him, saying, "David, give me a minute or two, will you? Please sit down."

The locator turned and said, "No, it's okay, really—I'm fine . . . sir?" But then, seeing the look on his boss's face and realizing that Trask's request wasn't about him, he sat anyway.

And Trask told him, "Myself, I'm not at all okay or fine—far from it. But since you've already had your regulation sickener for the day, what's there to spoil? So maybe I can ask you to share mine." He pushed the disturbing monochrome photographs across the desk, and the locator's almond eyes at once narrowed as he picked them up and looked at them.

"What . . . ?" he said, his bottom jaw falling open a little.

"David," said Trask, "can you help me with something? Can you tell me how you'd go about evaginating someone?"

"How I'd do what?" Grimacing, Chung continued to stare at the pictures.

"How would you turn someone outside in?"

"What in hell's name am I *looking* at, sir?" The locator's nostrils widened; his lips twitched, drew back in disgust.

"It's what I was talking about," said Trask quietly. "It's what I was asking you. This person is outside in. Now how would you do *that* to someone, David? Well, always assuming you wanted to, of course."

"He's inside out?"

Trask shook his head. "No, he's outside in, evaginated."

"Some kind of sick joke?" Now Chung looked up, and just in case this *was* a very sick joke he decided to add his ten-pence-worth. "Well, maybe I could shove something up his backside all the way . . . say, a broom handle with expanding grappling hooks? And I'd expand them and drag him out through his own, er—"

"No," Trask cut him short, "because that would rupture his anus, split it and him wide open and tear his insides. But with this thing in these photographs, there was none of that kind of damage. No cuts, no incisions. And look at his legs—what used to be his legs—and his arms, and even his head. They've been evaginated, too."

"You were being *serious?*" said Chung, weakly. "And this is a real person: someone who has been . . . outside-inned?"

"Yes." Trask nodded. "As if the flesh has been rolled off his bones—like you would roll off a stocking—then straightened out with the skin inside the tube, and laid out alongside the bare bones. But no cutting, no slicing."

"But blood?"

"Of course blood," said Trask. "It's your skin that keeps the blood in, David! And when flesh parts from bone, naturally you bleed. Or, in this case, unnaturally."

"And somebody somehow did this to whoever this was?"

"The pathologist who performed the postmortem reckons if he hadn't seen it he would have said it was impossible. But in any case—whether someone did it or not, whether it's murder or something else—it happened."

"But how else could it happen if no one did it?" Chung was appalled yet fascinated.

Trask shrugged, but not negligently. "Have you ever looked through Sir Keenan Gormley's cases?" Gormley had been the first Head of Branch in the days when the organization had been known as INTESP, an awkward sort of acronym based on the words 'intelligence' and 'espionage,' or perhaps ESP; Trask had never bothered to ask about it and no longer cared. "Gormley covered two cases of spontaneous human combustion and wrote them up very convincingly . . . which is to say he believed they were genuine. No one had set fire to or murdered the victims, they had simply burned themselves up."

"I've heard of such cases, yes," Chung nodded. "Some

kind of violent, volatile chemical reaction or something. But this?" He shook his head and pushed the pictures back across the desk. "This isn't in any way the same."

"But in a way it is," Trask said. "They're both mysterious and inexplicable occurrences. I suppose that what I'm saying or asking is: if someone—chemically or otherwise—can somehow spontaneously incinerate, is it also possible there's a mechanism for spontaneous evagination?"

But the locator could only frown and shake his head again, answering, "Sir, you've got me."

"Yes," Trask agreed, "and it's got me, too . . . it's got me beat! But I've read this report and you haven't heard the worst of it. When they found this—this *mess*—it, or rather he, was still alive, the poor devil!"

"Jesus!" Chung barely breathed the word. "He was . . . ?"

"Alive, yes." Trask nodded. "A very nightmarish, agonized sort of life, obviously. But he very quickly died—thank God!"

And Chung said nothing but simply sat there . . .

Eventually Trask gave himself a shake, said, "David, see if you can find someone who isn't too busy right now, have him do some research for me. I'm very interested to know if there have ever been any other cases like this here or abroad. It's something I think we should look into."

The locator stood up. "Maybe you'd like me to take it on?" he said, hoping against hope that Trask wouldn't. "It seems I'm free for the time being, so perhaps—"

"No." Trask shook his head, and smiled however wanly. "No, for there's something else I'd like you to do. Something that's not nearly so ghoulish."

"Oh?" Chung tried his best to hide his relief; the less he saw of that sort of thing the more he'd like it.

"Yes," said Trask, then told him about the Scott St. John case, explaining his requirements with regard to Ian Goodly and Anna Marie English. "It's for their own good," he finished off.

"Yes, sir," said Chung stiffly, "I know. But still I won't like it, spying on our own."

"I know, David," said the other. "But what's to like? This is E-Branch, my friend, and there are things no one likes— not you, me, or anyone else—but we deal with them as best we can. And anyway, it isn't spying: you're to be their backup, that's all, even if they don't know they have one. And finally"—Trask narrowed his eyes determinedly— "finally I'm the boss here, and I get to delegate. I've just done that, so now get on with it."

"Yes, sir," said Chung, heading for the door.

Watching the locator leave, Trask felt he'd made the right decision. The task he'd assigned to Chung might well be considered a little dubious, but at least it would take his mind off that poor kid he'd found raped and murdered under a bush . . .

6

When the white executive jet rolled to a halt on the dilapidated airport's heat-hazed runway, and the dust devils stirred up by its vortex settled, then the welcoming committee of six combat-accoutred, armed black soldiers ran out from the shade of the seedy airport building to form up on both sides of the steps where they unfolded from the plane's cabin.

Following them at a far more leisurely pace as the whine of the jet's engine wound down, a handsome black youth of some eighteen years, immaculately clad in a grey silk shirt, an expensive white western suit, and white shoes, made his way to the foot of the steps. Glittering on the breast of the youth's jacket, a triple row of spurious, court-mounted medals hinted however inelegantly of his ranking in this godforsaken, cynical, and sinister autocracy: that as the beloved only son of a ruthless, murderous dictator, he was the next in line.

With the heat bouncing up at him in waves from the runway, the youth flailed a whisk left and right to keep the flies at bay, and only paused when he saw movement in the inky darkness of the airplane's oval hatch. First a face appeared, seemingly hunched forward, in fact ducking low, and then the frame of an abnormally tall, long-necked, stick-thin man in a white, high-collared kaftan and red leather sandals. Pale-skinned, he wore his silvery hair in a comb from three inches above his nose to where it overlapped his high collar at the back. His eyes were dark and deep-seated under ridged, tapering eyebrows; his ears were small and round, and his mouth was no wider than his thin, pointed chin. Had he worn a blue-grey tangled beard, moustaches, and sideburns—if he had smiled, and if his skin had been darker—then he might well have been mistaken for an Indian mystic, the guru of some esoteric order. There was a certain air about him, of forbidden knowledge and learning; visions and powers beyond man's natural scope. But however impressive he might seem with his great height, still he was pallid, clean-shaven, unsmiling.

As he stepped down from the plane with an awkward, stiff-legged gait, the young man paced forward between the soldiers, bowed, held out his hand, and in an expensive, English-school-educated voice said, "Father, I am sent by *my* father, General Wilson Gundawei, to bring you to the palace. The soldiers are an honour guard."

Ignoring the proffered hand, the other said, "Peter, you are well it seems—recovered, and fully—and I am pleased. With *you* I am pleased; but alas, not with your father." While his voice was deep and resonant, with no readily recognizable accent, his thin lips seemed barely to move and his words were oddly stilted, strained, uncertain. And the young man thought: *It was the same on the occasion of our first—and in fact our last—meeting. Perhaps he does not speak too much. Perhaps he is not used to speaking. It could be that among great mystics, thinkers, and healers, speaking is frowned upon.*

The man looked at him, and as if he had heard the other's thoughts—but more likely in order to cut any further formalities short—said, "I have little need for conversation." And then, looking left and right at the soldiers, "Weapons, Peter? Such is your father's greeting? Such is the General's regard?"

"An honour guard," the other said again, his hand falling awkwardly to his side. And with an apologetic shrug: "Or should we simply say . . . a guard? The times are uncertain; the General has enemies, as have all strong men and rulers. He thinks it is best to be cautious and takes care to protect me, that's all—oh, and you, too, father! For if not for you, why, he would have no heir to protect!"

A shining limo flanked by a pair of military vehicles came speeding from behind the airport building. As the car came to a halt, its passenger doors slid open and two uniformed bodyguards bearing light machine guns got out; hard-eyed, alert, they stood facing outward. Meanwhile, the escorting half-tracks had taken up positions facing the airport's perimeter; their canvas roofs had folded back and down to reveal flak-jacketed gunners behind armoured panels.

"Uncertain times," said the stick-thin man, nodding. "Yes, it would appear so." Then, checking the time on his wristwatch, he made some kind of adjustment, and with the black youth leading the way stepped lurchingly toward the waiting limo . . .

In better times, an earlier era, the General's headquarters had indeed been a palace, very splendid and opulent. Then there had been kings, princes, and black courtiers—and sometimes white ones, too—and diplomats in fine clothes, and only very rarely military men: always high-ranking officers in ceremonial dress, wearing medals and ribbons that were real and well earned. Then, too, there had been justice . . . well, of a sort. But not merely the rough justice and injustices of implacable power in corrupt hands.

Such were the thoughts of Peter Gundawei, his father's son but by no means like-minded, as he and the General's tall enigmatic visitor climbed marble steps to the high-arched entrance, and passed through into echoing halls flanked by cool if dusty rooms. On every side black guards came to attention as the pair passed by; in one room a colonel held an O-Group with a platoon of soldiers, used a bamboo cane to punctuate his orders, pointed out locations on various wall charts and maps. Other rooms stood empty, without a stick of furniture; but in the center of the complex behind massive, heavily guarded, gold-banded doors, there General Wilson Gundawei had his private rooms.

The soldiers—six of them, seated on benches—stood up, came to attention, saluted the handsome youth, looked upon the tall man at his side with some suspicion. They had not been on duty during his previous visit, and their orders were to search all strangers. All well and good, but what was there to search? This one was so thin, his kaftan sheer and sheath-like. He wore a watch upon his wrist; no other visible ornamentation. And the young, educated Peter Gundawei—the General's haughty son and heir—was there to brush them and their weapons contemptuously aside.

The officer in charge rapped with his knuckles three times upon the great doors, and in a while an eight-inch-square panel was opened from within. A young female face—pretty, black, a girl in her teens—looked out, quickly withdrew. A key grated; hidden bolts were sprung; the officer and one of his men hauled on huge, polished mahogany handles and the doors cracked in the middle, swinging slowly open. No sooner had the visitor and his escort passed through than the doors ground shut behind them.

The room inside was vast, high-ceilinged, a meeting point for many other rooms and passages that converged on it like so many spokes in a wheel; but it was also well secured. The great doors through which the disparate pair had entered this "inner sanctum" were the only doors, though it seemed likely that the General had arranged a bolt-hole somewhere, just in case. There were no windows so the room was lit by four great chandeliers, and in the very middle of the ceiling an enormous fan beat the air with six broad blades.

Some fifty feet away across an ornate marble-tiled floor, a curtained bed with gold- and ivory-inlaid "posters," or more properly marble columns, occupied a central area against a wall draped with animal-head trophies on a leopard-skin background; the General was known to be a legendary hunter—and not only of big game. To both sides of the bed huge cushions were piled deep on the floor where four unsmiling, mainly naked girls sat huddled together two to a side. The none-too-gentle swaying of the great bed's amber- and gold-beaded, not-quite-opaque curtains suggested that the General might well be "hunting" even now.

And while this hidden activity continued, taking advantage of what looked like his last opportunity, Peter Gundawei turned to the visitor and whispered words of belated warning.

"At the airplane you told me you were not pleased with my father," he said. "I'm in your debt and feel I must advise you: do *not* be so frank with the General himself! While his patience is limited, his rage knows no restrictions whatsoever."

The other merely glanced at him and said nothing, but his almost invisible smile came very close to mocking. And deep in their sockets his eyes gleamed like jet marbles.

In that same moment the great bed's bead curtains swished open and the General beckoned them to attend him. They did so, crossing the marble floor to stand at the foot of the bed. And General Wilson Gundawei adjusted his heavy robe and belted it, and eased himself upright off the bed onto its slightly raised dais. Barefooted, naked but for his robe, he faced them; while behind him—trying to cover herself with strings of precious beads—a beautiful young girl got off her knees, cowering on purple sheets.

"Ah!" said the General. "And so you stick to your guns—your, er, schedule—arriving precisely as planned, if not as *I* planned. For as you can see I am my usual tardy self . . .

and not a little annoyed at being disturbed while enjoying my, er, exercise? Anyway, it is good to see you again, Guyler Schweitzer." Smiling, he held out a pudgy hand. His visitor, ignoring the supposedly "welcoming" hand, instead appeared to study its owner. What he saw was a megalomaniac potentate, a man bloated with greed, power, and lust. And bald and shiny from his sexual exertions—standing there like an ebony Buddha come alive—General Wilson Gundawei looked at his empty hand and the smile melted on his face. He came to the edge of the dais, stuck his hand out farther yet, demandingly, and said, "Guyler, I'm sure you know that it's not polite, and at worst an insult, to—"

"I do not touch others unless it becomes . . . unavoidable," the tall man cut him off. "As for my name: yes, Guyler Schweitzer is my name—my business name, at least—but those in my employ and a majority of others I am pleased to . . . *acknowledge,* and to whom I may on occasion give succour, including your son, Peter, call me father. I greatly prefer to be called father."

The General clenched his fist, dropped his hand, said, "My patience extends only so far, 'father.' But please to enlighten me: shouldn't that be 'Father' with a capital 'F'? Or would you simply prefer to be called 'Our Father'—or God?"

The visitor seemed taken aback, momentarily surprised, then straightened, stood taller yet, and said, "Despite my search for Him, I am not convinced of the existence of any such deity, nor would I emulate Him if He were real. But if there is such a One I would be glad to find Him; indeed, we might even have matters to discuss . . . before one or both of us ceased to function. And if there was time I would ask Him why—why in His omniscience, His omnipotence, His ineffable artistry—why He has made certain of His creations so gross and lacking in grace."

This was the most that the General and his ashen-faced son had ever heard the tall man say at any one time; as a result of which—of *what* he had said—the youth's jaw fell open.

General Wilson Gundawei's face turned slate grey. His eyes bulged and he puffed out his cheeks. He didn't fully understand what the tall man had said, only that it sounded like some kind of insult. *Well, and a good many miles between here and the airport,* the General thought. *Also between this towering, insolent skeleton and his private jet!*

Even as he was thinking these things, however—and as if to deliberately inflame the General more yet—his visitor continued: "I think you know why I am here. A matter of important, unfinished business: an as yet outstanding debt . . ."

But of course I know why you're here! the General thought. *You are here on a fool's errand, and you're an even bigger fool to provoke me. Also, you are now even farther, or might as well be, from your little toy airplane. As for business: no, I think not. There is one final personal matter which I must now attend to, but you shall do no more "business" with me, or with anyone else—"father!"*

That last thought had brought the blood back to Gundawei's face; also the smile, but a grim, slyly sardonic smile now. And in a low soft voice he said, "I have no great desire to discuss business of any kind with you right now—or ever! As to debts: do you know to whom you are speaking? Do you imply that General Wilson Gundawei is in your debt? I cannot recall any contract."

"There was no contract." The tall man sighed and shook his head, then checked his watch and made a small adjustment. "Just a gentleman's agreement. Your son had AIDS, and I cured him. In return you agreed to pay my company ten million dollars in gold in regular shipments, commencing in February. But the initial payment is now some months overdue, and all subsequent attempts to communicate with you have gone unanswered. Now I have come here personally to hear your explanation; also to either accept your excuse and make new, final arrangements with you, or to enforce a penalty. Unfortunately, it looks like being the latter."

Yet again the tall man had spoken at length, and more than ever his words were insulting—it seemed deliberately so.

"A penalty?" Gundawei roared, stepping down from the

dais. "You shall *what?* Enforce a penalty?" He spat the words out. "Do you dare to threaten me, and in my own palace?"

"You have broken your promise." The visitor stepped back a short, jerky pace. "I cured your son. Where is my payment?"

"There *is* no cure for AIDS," the General cried. "You liar, you charlatan! Why, any witch doctor from any one of a hundred mud-hut villages could have done as much, and more!"

"No cure?" said the other, apparently unmoved and utterly unafraid. "But what of your son's arm? I touched him there."

"A touch! *A touch?*" screamed Gundawei. "What's in a touch? I should pay ten million dollars for a single touch? A touch of *madness,* that, Guyler Schweitzer!"

But Peter Gundawei stepped between the two, rolled up the right sleeve of his jacket, dared to show the General the place where his dark flesh was clearly marked with four fingers and a thumb, as if his skin had been bleached there. "Father, look. I bear the mark!"

The General brushed him aside and cried, "Young fool! Now be quiet! Hush! *Hush!* And you, Schweitzer . . . are you a madman? Don't you know how easily I can make you disappear?"

Now the visitor's thin lips cracked in a malevolent smile, displaying tiny, needle-sharp teeth that glinted with an almost mother-of-pearl sheen. "Your son's arm bears my mark," he said, "but I am without payment. Yet when you called I came, and you showed me gold, a great treasure. Where is it now? Hidden away from me?"

"It's gone!" the General screamed. "Just as you shall soon be gone! A hundred thousand enemies are gathered on my borders. My gold has turned to paper: money to pay my soldiers. The gold you see in these rooms is the *only* gold! But even if I had it I would not have paid it. What, for your so-called cure? My son was not eating; he had a malaise, some fever that has passed of its own accord. As for the marks on his arm: you use an acid to scorch, mutilate your victims, and then demand payment for this . . . this so-called miracle, this assault, this sleight of hand! What? Did you think I was simpleminded? *Bah!* And now I am done with you!" He waved his hand dismissively.

"A penalty, then," said the other, still unmoved.

Gundawei thrust his purple, grimacing face up at the tall man and said, "A penalty? By all means, but you are the one who shall pay it." He jumped up on the dais, yanked on a bellpull, cried, "Girl!"

A young woman ran out from the corridor nearest the great doors. The General pointed at the doors and shouted, "Fetch my guards!"

The man called Guyler Schweitzer turned to Peter Gundawei, who was still flustered, and said, "I have to go. But what was given must be taken back." As he bent close the youth saw something in the dark hollows of his eyes, an odd expression, that caused him to back away. The other moved awkwardly yet rapidly closer, reached out a spidery hand, and circled the young man's neck in long fingers. It lasted only a moment—not so much a grip or powerful hold as a touch, almost a caress—before the youth was released, staggered away, tripped on a corner of the dais, and fell on his backside.

The General had seen the incident, the moment of contact, between Schweitzer and his son; he rushed toward the tall man with a thick arm and clenched fist upraised. And meanwhile the dictator's girls were on their feet, fleeing this way and that, anxious to lose themselves in the maze of rooms and corridors; and the great doors were being hauled open, while the shouting of soldiers grew louder where they crowded outside.

"You . . . you . . . *you!*" the General screamed, beginning to froth at the mouth and aiming a blow.

But again his visitor moved: shot out a hand, trapped the falling arm in a vise-like grip and effortlessly held it there, straining in mid-fall, immobilized, impotent. And then he said, "Ah, no, General, not me—you."

Wilson Gundawei felt the touch: his great weight, and all of his strength, held in this strange man's thin fingers—yet it felt like little more than a touch. And it burned—but not with any sort of heat the dictator understood. More a peculiar tingling, an almost electrical current that caused a vibrating, crippling loss of control over his own flesh. First in his arm, then his shoulders, neck, and head, and finally the rest of his trunk and all his limbs.

Pulling free of his enigmatic visitor, the General managed to lurch onto the dais before his legs buckled and he fell into a seated position with his back to the bed.

His son, weary now, and with his white suit hanging loose on him, crawled to Gundawei's feet, staring at him through red-rimmed eyes where the General began to writhe and shriek aloud in some unbearable agony. And terrified now beyond all measure, the youth cried, "Father? . . . *Father!*"

But the General—tearing frenziedly at his robe until it shredded, and clutching at his belly—seemed not to hear him. His navel was stretching, slowly enlarging, opening outward. It formed a sphincter that slowly peeled back on itself, until his stomach looked like a huge black overripe pomegranate splitting in the sun . . . and already its juicy red seeds—its pulp, his guts—were becoming visible.

Peter Gundawei looked to the tall man for help, held out a trembling hand to him; but that one merely shrugged and said, "The penalty, yes." And then, unexpectedly and horrifically, he showed emotion—a form of emotion, at least—rocking on his heels to a chittering, staccato burst of what could only be mad laughter. A moment more and he fell silent, touched a button on what had seemed to be an inexpensive watch, and nodded a final, cynical farewell. Then his tall, slender figure shimmered like a mirage, turned transparent, and was gone.

Gone, vanished as if he had never been there at all . . .

Several of the ornate bulbs in the three great chandeliers had shattered, raining smoking glass and molten filaments onto the marble floor. Electrical connections in the lights and central fan hummed and snapped, showering white-hot sparks everywhere, in all directions, through the now smoky atmosphere of General Gundawei's inner sanctum. The fan itself ran amok, first slowing to the point of stopping, then whirring into frantic activity, rocking on its stem as its blades lashed the ozone-tainted air. A moment later and the entire assembly tore loose from the ceiling and crashed to the floor.

The screams of half-naked girls running this way and that, the whites of their round, frightened eyes strobing on and off, like a swarm of trapped fireflies in the reeking blue smoke and crazily erratic lights. And the soldiers in a tangle, dazed and stumbling, their weapons at the ready with nothing to shoot at. And Peter Gundawei—thin as a rake, with staring, muddy-brown eyes in a suddenly hollow face—straining *away* from his father now, yet unable to *look* away as the General's flesh shrank from his bones and his juices spilled from the dais onto the marble flags.

Then the officer in charge of the guard—an older man, a captain—found his way to the dais and saw what was there: saw Gundawei, his General, *still alive,* his huge eyes blinking furiously . . . even though his brain was emerging from an expanding ear while his upper lip and nose curled upward in a single masklike sheet from his red-dripping skull! And Peter Gundawei, the General's son, gasping his life out with his white western suit all wrinkled and floppy on his diseased, AIDS-shrivelled body!

A moment longer the Captain stared, his eyes scarcely able to accept what they saw. Then—

A girl collided with him, clutched at him, said, "Father! Oh, Father!" His own daughter. And finally he knew what to do.

Ordering his men out of the room, he wrapped his daughter in a purple sheet from the huge bed, told her not to look, and set her aside out of harm's way. Then came the sharp stutter of his automatic gunfire, momentarily drowning the angry snapping and buzzing of shorting electrics, and adding the acrid stench of cordite to the room's other stenches.

And so the pair on the dais died, but mercifully . . .

Not that the Captain was strong on mercy. His daughter was only one of many girls taken by the General, true . . . but still she had been too high a price to pay for her father's miserable rank, despite that he'd been given no choice in the matter. Now he stripped the stars from his epaulettes, tossed them onto the bed, and called his men back into the room.

"Ask no questions," he told them, "but there's been murder here. Now then, search the rooms—and quickly! Gather up every precious thing, anything of value. Our country has been drained to the dregs, so from now on we must help ourselves."

Respecting him, they ran to do his bidding. And in a while when they had stripped even the bead curtains, then he set fire to the bed . . .

At the airport, close to the executive jet itself, the tall man blurred back into being. His pilot saw him from the cockpit and started at his employer's sudden appearance out of nowhere. But at Guyler Schweitzer's signal—the urgent, circular motion of a claw-like hand—he regained his composure and started up the engines.

Seated in the shade of the down-at-heel airport building, the members of General Gundawei's so-called honour guard were taking it easy, smoking and chatting. But as the whining of the engines became a dull roar they looked up to see the tall, thin man boarding the airplane, and as the door closed pneumatically behind him they stubbed their cigarettes, grabbed their weapons, and came to their feet.

The plane was taxiing, turning about to face the length of the neglected runway; while inside the building a telephone was ringing, ringing, ringing. A soldier went inside to answer it—then came running back to his comrades, yelling and gesticulating at the jet, but much too late. For the airplane was already powering along the runway and accelerating to takeoff speed.

Then it was in the air, climbing rapidly, banking steeply, presenting its lone passenger with the opportunity to look down through his window at the straggly group of soldiers where they shielded their eyes from the sun's glare to gaze up at him. From here they were like so many ants . . . but then again, so were all men to the creature that called itself Guyler Schweitzer.

Sitting there, he felt a sudden motion, an eruption in the flesh at the back of his neck under his kaftan, and in a matter of moments something vaguely resembling a second head, a bubble of grey-green, red-tinged stuff like pus from a great boil rose up from his kaftan and crept like a slug onto his shoulder; and he did nothing to suppress it. The thing had small crimson eyes and tiny black nostrils like the pits in a coconut. And for all that for now this familiar had no mouth, still it spoke to him:

My Mordri, you kept me down when I would have been up. Why would you do that to me?

And despite that he didn't need to, Guyler Schweitzer answered out loud. "Because you might have caused a fuss. This was dangerous territory, my Khiff. I did not desire that you should frighten anyone prematurely, and I wished no harm to befall you yourself. You should thank me."

I will thank you, if you will share. And then, avidly: *Did you . . . did you hurt someone?*

"That was the nature of my visit, yes."

And I may absorb your memories?

"Of course, as always!"

Now?

"By all means."

And extending a pseudopod into Schweitzer's ear, the thing shrank *into* him, appearing to deflate like a ruptured balloon.

Then, turning again to the window for a last glance at the dwindling airport, Schweitzer bared his small, sharp mother-of-pearl teeth in something other than a snarl—in fact a sneer—before sitting back, and finally relaxing into his seat.

And in his head the Khiff fed on all that he had seen and done in the palace of General Wilson Gundawei . . .

7

Scott St. John woke up with a headache that had cost him almost half a bottle of fine brandy, which *still* hadn't given him a good night's sleep! Which was probably why he'd done it—spent most of yesterday evening drinking—because he'd hoped it would put him down, free his mind of all its questions, and—if only for a night—stop it chasing its tail in this endless round . . . or so he told himself. But in fact (and now he contradicted himself) he hadn't really noticed he was drinking to that extent, not at the time. It was *because* he'd been trying to work things out—turning things over and over again in his head as he looked for an explanation, a TOE, his own personal "Theory of Everything"—that he'd kept topping up his glass until it had become automatic and, well, sort of repetitive. A sorry excuse . . .

And to think that only twenty-four hours ago he'd been congratulating himself that he hadn't become an alcoholic . . . *yet!* No, and not yet either (he hoped), but he would definitely have to watch it.

He remembered hearing the alarm go off at 6:00, then nothing. So he'd obviously gone back to sleep. And why the hell had he set the alarm for 6:00 anyway? Because he'd wanted to go and talk to that girl, that woman, that who or whatever she was . . .

God! The woman! The only one who might have answers to any of this!

He came out of bed on the double, which only served to set his head throbbing like a tom-tom. And then, cursing his stupidity that he'd let himself sleep in, he dressed, skipped washing and shaving, took three aspirins in water, and rushed out to the garage . . . only to run back inside again for his car keys!

The car: he'd driven it maybe twice since Kelly died—on

one occasion coming close to having an accident, and on another forgetting to pay after filling her up—*and* his insurance must surely have run out by now. Several reasons why he'd been doing so much walking of late. But now, this business with the woman: it was important, and he might already be too late. Only please don't let him get pulled over, not with all this booze in him.

The woman, yes. His mystery woman:

He had dreamed of her again last night, he knew that much, but this hangover was getting in the way of remembering what it had been about. She hadn't actually put in an appearance in the dream (if she had, he thought he would surely remember that), but it had been her *voice:* he'd heard her voice, repeating much the same things that she'd told him yesterday. So then, deep in his subconscious he had obviously put a lot of weight on what she'd told him. Now, driving to the newsagent's, Scott tried to recapture more surely the dream, her words, something of the meaning of the thing, and once again of everything else that had or was still happening. And rightly so because:

"*Do* think about what has happened to you," she'd told him. "Do think about your loss . . ." (The loss of Kelly? It could only be.) "But try to think coldly, without anger, pain, or passion." (Why? Because it was somebody's fault? Kelly's death, someone's fault?) And once again, as before: "If something strikes you as strange, try to explore it but from a safe distance." And, finally: "Don't look for me. When it's time, I shall find you . . ."

Well, to hell with that last! Something—and perhaps more than one something—was most *definitely* happening to him. And if she knew the answers, if she had any idea at all about what was going on, then he simply *must* seek her out!

Parking the car close to the newsagent's shop, Scott went in and picked up his newspaper, scanned the aisles for his mystery woman, and was disappointed. He tried to ignore the annoying, knowing sidelong glances from the *other* woman, the one in hair curlers who was watching him, waiting to serve him; but he hadn't paid for his newspaper yet, and he still had to purchase cigarettes over the counter, where as usual she would have his change ready.

Winking at Scott as he reached for his change, she trapped his hand in hers and said, "Tsk! tsk! Too bad. I seen you looking for her—that sick puppy look on your face. Still all hot and bothered for her, are you? A pity. Maybe you should go for something more available like."

Scott forced a smile and said, "Don't go giving me ideas, darling. But . . . has she been in?"

The woman let go his hand. "No, she hasn't been back. Not yet, anyway. P'raps you didn't make that much of an impression on her, but maybe if you was to wait around awhile . . . ? I'm on me own this morning, you see, and now the rush is over I could maybe, well, lock up the shop for an hour and make us a coffee or something—er, in the back room—you know?"

Oh, yes, Scott knew, and answered, "Of course I'd love to, but I've an appointment—er, with the doctor—you know?"

For a moment she looked shocked and leaned back from him, then said, "Garn! You're puttin' me on! Ah well, that's me: no luck at all. But I must say I don't know what you sees in that one. A tarty-looking piece if you ask me."

Scott fished for a card in his inside pocket, gave it to her, and said, "Look, do me a favour—and who knows, maybe one day I'll repay it? But if she comes in again give her my card, will you? I really would appreciate it."

"Really?" She was almost panting.

Returning her wink from earlier, Scott said, "Now then—you will be a love, won't you?"

Outside the shop he shuddered, lit his first cigarette of the day, got in the car, and headed for home . . .

Scott wasn't his usual, or more properly his recent, self. Not by any means. He realized this on the way home, knew that what he had felt after the mystery woman had touched him had stayed with him; that he had been . . . been what, changed? Definitely. And maybe uplifted? Well, a little of

both, actually; which had to be a good thing, because he
sensed that he knew where he was going now. No more arriving at this, that, or some other destination without knowing how he'd got there. He didn't *quite* have it all together,
not yet, but at least there was a direction, a desire for—

—For what? For revenge? Absolutely, if Kelly's death
had been anything other than natural. And thinking of it like
that, why, it had been anything *but* natural! A wasting disease? Oh, it had been that alright! But one they couldn't put
a name to? How often does that happen? All he'd known at
the time was that she was sick. He'd simply accepted what
they told him, what his own five senses had told him: that
the love of his life was shrinking away and dying.

Yes, he had asked the usual questions initially: could it be
cancer? Leukemia? Even AIDS? (For there were more ways
than one of catching *that* horror!) But . . . were there no references to this thing in the medical books? And if not, why
not? Christ Almighty, we were into the 1990s, the new computer age (that's if you needed and could afford one, which
Kelly had argued they didn't and couldn't: that nationwide
"computer virus" thing in the USA in '88 had turned her
right off the idea), so what had happened to the advance-
ment of medical science in this wonderful enlightened era?

These people who appeared to have given up on her, they
were bloody doctors, so-called specialists, weren't they?
They were supposed to be the best. So why weren't they
bloody *doing* something? But they had been; they'd been
doing all that they possibly could.

And then, as quickly as that, she was dead, and Scott had
died, too. He'd been dead inside. Or at least it had felt like
that . . . until now.

But now—now if there was even a remote possibility
that Kelly hadn't died an entirely natural death—*now* he
wanted to know about it; especially since one of those
spooks who interrogated him had tried to insinuate that
Scott himself might have killed her! And anyway, what did
they have to do with all this, if anything? Them and their
utterly ridiculous questions, their insistence that Scott

was . . . what, psychic? Or could it be that every one of these weird occurrences was totally unconnected to the rest, like a series of almost simultaneous coincidences?

There was a word for it, yes: synchronicity.

Scott laughed harshly, perhaps even a little hysterically; laughed aloud as he drove through the outskirts of North London along green lanes leading to open country. The very idea—that he might in some way be psychic—was a hoot! But on the other hand some very strange things had seemed to be happening to him during that weird little chat session. And following hot on its heels, then there had been that dream that kept coming back to mind, in fact to haunt him. A drugged dream, true, and probably inspired by those . . . those what? Mind-spies? Them and the mystery woman, anyway. But a damnably insistent dream nonetheless. His dream of *One,* himself; *Two,* the woman; and *Three* . . . a dog.

A dog? Ridiculous! Madness! But equally strange, there had also been a golden dart, or a spear of bright light: a sentient something that entered into his mind and . . . and *empowered* him. Oh, he remembered that. But what sort of power?

I'm losing it! Scott thought—and almost missed turning into the cul-de-sac where he lived. Braking heavily, he swerved around the corner and just managed to avoid a police car coming the other way, causing it to swerve, too. Which really focussed his mind! In the lane—as the police car's siren began to sing its demanding *de-dah, de-dah* challenge—Scott pulled over onto the grass verge and stopped.

And sitting there, gripping the steering wheel and cursing his luck, he didn't need to be remotely psychic to know that he was in big trouble . . .

They breathalysed him (he was way over the limit), took his car keys, and conveyed him to the local police station. There he was required to provide a urine sample—and did so, albeit reluctantly—before being put into an almost bare interrogation cell with a small bolted-down table and one bolted-down chair, where he would have to wait until they decided what to do with him.

The room did have a large mirror . . . well, a mirror on *his* side, at least, but Scott couldn't help wondering if in fact it was a view-screen, a means of watching him unobtrusively, without him knowing. It probably wasn't, and he'd been watching too many American crime shows on TV; but he pulled a face at it anyway, then sprawled in the chair and gradually accepted that he was indeed in trouble.

"Drunk in Charge of a Motor Vehicle." So on top of everything else, he was about to acquire a criminal record.

And so he sat on his own and waited . . . and now and then glanced at the mirror. Could he hear people whispering on the other side? Probably not. Why would the police whisper? He was just another Drunk in Charge after all; no big deal. Why would they even want to watch him? But *someone* was talking about him, he felt sure. And anyway, the mirror got on his nerves . . .

And he waited, and waited . . .

Standing up, Scott began prowling four paces one way and four the other, pausing in front of the mirror every so often. The last time he did this he thought: *What was it she told me? If there's something strange, avoid it and only study it from a distance? Something like that, anyway. I can go out on a clear night and stare at the stars a million light-years away, yet I can't see somebody a few inches away on the other side of this mirror, which might just as well be the far side of the moon. And what if someone is studying me from a distance, even this very small distance? And if so, how? And why?*

At which her voice came to him again, but much stronger now: *Scott, don't concern yourself with them. There's no harm in them. The harm lies elsewhere. But still they must be told. I shall try to tell them, through you: that if they must seek after knowledge of you, or of me, or of he who is Three, then they must do so from a distance so as not to compromise us . . .*

The voice tapered off into silence, leaving an echoing, aching void in his head.

"What? Who's there?" Scott whispered the query to himself, then blew his nose to clear his head. And again: "Who's there?" But his whispers went unanswered. There was no one and nothing there.

I'm losing it, he thought then. *I'm definitely losing it!* And he stared at the mirror, then glared at it, before turning away, disgusted with himself and his situation both . . .

Scott sat some more until, after perhaps an hour and a half on his own, he went to the door, tried it, and found it locked. At which he lifted his fist to pound on it, only to back away as a key grated and the door was opened.

A young policeman entered with a telephone that he plugged into a wall socket. And placing the phone on the table he told Scott, "When it rings, it's for you."

Bemused and frowning, Scott waited for the phone to ring, then picked it up and said, "Scott St. John."

"Ah, Mr. St. John!" came a high-pitched voice that Scott at once recognized. "What it is to have friends in high places, eh?"

"Xavier!" Scott exclaimed, knowing he was right.

"The same," said the other. "Or you can call me Mr. Immaterial, if you're so inclined. Anyway, we're still hoping that sooner or later you'll begin to see things our way and give us a little cooperation. And so—since no one wins if you've got problems with the law and your life only gets more complicated—we're going to bail you out. There won't be any charges and we hope you'll think about that and appreciate what we've done for you. So now, if you'll just give the telephone back to the gentleman in blue, I shall speak to him again and in a little while you'll be driven home."

"Now wait a minute," Scott began. "Listen, I—" But:

"No," said the other, patiently but firmly. "*You* listen. If you want to get home anytime in the not too distant future, *please* give the telephone back to the officer!"

Scott said, "God *damn!*" but did as he was told. The young policeman pressed a button for the operator, had the call transferred to the reports room, took the phone with him, and left Scott on his own again. This time, though, after only a minute or two, he returned to tell him: "We're sorry for the mistake, sir, and we hope it hasn't inconvenienced you too much. Still, better safe than sorry, eh?"

Scott couldn't believe his own ears. They had him dead to rights but considered that *he,* Scott himself, had been somehow inconvenienced? There had been a mistake but "better safe than sorry"? As for having friends in high places: "friends"? those Secret Service types? And utterly baffled, Scott wondered: *Now what the hell is going on?* But in any case he was relieved.

He was still wondering, and still baffled, when they dropped him off at his house and drove away. It wasn't until later that he began to ask himself what the police had been doing so close to home in this leafy, out-of-the-way sort of lane where he lived in the first place?

To which, just like everything else, there didn't seem to be an answer . . .

Scott's hangover was fast fading. Now it was merely a headache; but little wonder, with everything that was going on in there.

At noon he nuked himself a pizza and drank a beer to wash it down. Just one beer, a so-called hair of the dog, but not really. It would have to be brandy to be the dog that bit him, and right now he couldn't bear the thought of brandy. He remembered a joke someone had once told him:

"Sex? Before you have it you could eat it, and afterward you wish you had!" Well, maybe it didn't *quite* fit the current brandy situation, but what the hell—he knew what he meant . . .

He took two more aspirins, then settled into an easy chair with his newspaper. Not that he was particularly interested in the news, but at least it might help in diverting his

thoughts from all this . . . this other rubbish! If it was rubbish. *Damn!*

And what was wrong with the house? Scott sensed that
something was different here, but what? Well, to hell with
it! And determined to shrug it off—whatever "it" might
be—he again tried to read his newspaper. But it wouldn't go
away, and anxious now he went to the window and looked
out over his overgrown garden. Was there something out
there? Something watching him? Something listening? Or
was he still being paranoid, like with that police station mirror? Anyway and whatever, there'd be no more brandy
binges for Scott St. John!

He made himself a pot of coffee—black, one sugar—and
finally got started on the paper.

Some trouble in Central Africa: the tyrant Wilson Gundawei found butchered in his palace HQ. Gundawei's son,
too, though he had already been as good as dead: a victim
of AIDS, apparently. And "General" Gundawei's tiny Zuganda Province invaded, annexed overnight by two thousand troops of neighbouring Kasabi in what appeared to
have been a walkover, an almost bloodless coup. No big
deal on the international front; Zuganda had once been part
of Kasabi, annexed by Gundawei! As to how that had come
about:

Several years ago, when the then Colonel Gundawei had
been strong in gold from a supposedly rich mine in his
tribal heartland, he'd deposed the weak king, taken over the
country in the role of Military Commander, rearranged his
borders, and advanced into a narrow strip of land previously
belonging to Kasabi. And the two countries had been cold-
war enemies from then on.

In recent years, however, the stream of gold had gradually become a trickle, the mine had collapsed and flooded,
and with his large army to maintain General Gundawei had
been living on borrowed time—until now it seemed time
had run out . . .

Scott turned pages to a story about this odd faith-healer
chap, the reclusive Simon Salcombe. Whenever Scott had

seen him surprised by some TV cameraman, or on this occasion his picture in the tabloids—rare events both, because the man generally avoided publicity like the plague—he had always, and perhaps unkindly, likened him to a stick insect or praying mantis: tall and thin, jerky in his movements, gaunt-faced and oddly repellent. Yet Kelly, herself an investigative freelance journalist, had found him fascinating, despite that (or maybe because) she considered him a fraud. She had even collected a file of newspaper articles on Salcombe and would definitely have kept this one, which read:

LORD ZITTERMENSCH SERIOUSLY ILL:
SEES PSYCHIC HEALER

Recently diagnosed with inoperable stomach cancer, self-proclaimed "Lord" Ernst (Ernie) Zittermensch, the UK's eighth richest man, has undergone treatment from faith-healer Simon Salcombe. The seldom-seen anchorite Salcombe—who has described himself as a religious person and "a seeker after God"—has in fact been seen on several occasions in the last fortnight entering or leaving Lord Ernie's Mayfair apartments.

High finance wizard Ernst Zittermensch came to England in 1948, a German orphan with a 50-deutschmark mini-bar of gold on a chain around his neck—the only legacy of his war-dead parents. Such small bars may be bought over the counter in most German banks. Currently worth a half-billion pounds sterling, he made his fortune as a property tycoon. His large collection of solid gold statuettes and other precious artifacts make up the bulk of his wealth.

Simon Salcombe, believed to be a Swiss "mystic" or "layer-on-of-hands"—a mysterious figure of no fixed address—is said to offer his services only in cases where there is no known cure, and only to the very rich.

His alleged cures are, however, very expensive. Seven years ago Gina Giapardo, aging screen goddess of the forties, is rumoured to have paid Salcombe four million dollars for "an unspecified treatment." Contemporary reports state the money was paid in gold.

"Miss" Giapardo is still alive . . .

Kelly's cuttings: Scott remembered something about Kelly's cuttings. Once when she tried to take a picture of Salcombe, a BBC newshound she worked with had got a shot of her attempting to talk to him. It had been just before her decline, when she'd looked especially beautiful. He must look at it again sometime, fix her memory in his mind, because he daren't let himself forget how she'd looked. He panicked every time he couldn't bring her face back into focus! It could be that he'd mend emotionally—well, eventually—from having known and loved his wife, but he must never let himself forget her . . .

Scott frowned, laid the paper aside, and stood up. What was wrong with the house? It felt *wrong* somehow . . . or was it simply the emptiness of her not being here? And what about his study? Something different in there? Something gone missing? His eyes were drawn to the telephone. Did he want to call someone?

He called directory inquiries, asked for Xavier's number, waited impatiently until he was put through. At first he got a woman's voice and was asked to hold the line. Then—

"Mr. St. John," came a male voice, deep and resonant. "Is there something?"

Just like that: so very casual. *He,* the owner of this new voice, was casual, but not Scott. Scott felt like he was losing it again. "You're not Xavier," he said. "Xavier is tall, gaunt, slope-shouldered, and looks like he spends a lot of time around coffins. He's not as mantis-like as Simon Salcombe, and he has this squeaky—no, not squeaky, just high-pitched—voice. I don't want to speak to you. I need to speak to Xavier."

"Mr. St. John, we're *all* Xavier," said the other, sounding slightly concerned. "It's a code, that's all. Are you alright?"

"Yes, I'm fine," Scott lied. And: "So then, you'd know

all about your people drugging me because they think I'm psychic?"

"Yes, I know all about that. I've read the notes."

Scott thought: *Notes? They have a file—on me! What did I ever do that people would want a file on me?*

And the voice said, "Mr. St. John? Are you there? What was it you wanted?"

Scott pulled himself together, cleared his dry throat, and said: "Maybe you can tell me what kind of ESP you people think I have?"

And after a short pause: "Well, no, not really. Actually, we were hoping you would tell us."

Scott considered that for a moment—two moments—then lost what little patience he had left, let frustration come to the fore, snarled, "Fuck you, too!" and put the phone down . . .

8

An hour later in Ben Trask's office at E-Branch HQ, the precog Ian Goodly looked uneasy as he reported a failure of sorts.

"What do you mean, 'of sorts'?" Trask asked him. And looking at him, the Head of E-Branch wondered, *So then, what is it that's bothering me about you now, my fortune-telling beanpole of a friend? What are you still keeping back from me, eh?*

"I mean I don't think close-quarter surveillance is going to work," said the other. "I've learned . . . *something,* and I'm sure it's important, but it's very vague. Extracting information from someone who doesn't know he has it is no easy thing."

Or from someone who doesn't want to talk about it, like a certain precog! Trask thought. "But he does have something?"

"I believe St. John could be telepathic," said Goodly. "At least partly. Or perhaps he's an empath . . . in fact, he could be any one or even several of an entire range of things! But whatever he has it's either dormant or not yet fully developed, or it might have atrophied through disuse; which means he'll lose it without knowing he ever had it . . . but I don't think so."

"But which we know could happen," said Trask. "After all, we've seen it before."

"Yes." The precog nodded. "Some years ago we had Jim Weir. We picked him up in a London casino. He believed he was just a very lucky player, but in fact it was telekinesis. That little ball on the roulette wheel? Three times out of seven Jim could put it right where he wanted it. We got hold of him, and after a week of training he was levitating small items. Then, suddenly, nothing . . . he burned out. It's analogous to more physical things. If we put our muscles to tasks which are too heavy for them they'll sometimes tear. On the other hand, if we don't use them at all they'll shrivel and become useless. Weir overtaxed himself, that's all. Since then, well, we've looked at him from time to time—to see if maybe he would get it back—but no, he's broke and a loser now. Our fault? Perhaps, perhaps not. He could have been due to lose it anyway."

Trask put aside his most recent batch of paperwork, sighed, and said, "Have you eaten yet today?"

Goodly shrugged. "No, but it's not—"

"And Anna Marie? Has she been with you on this since first thing this morning?" Trask stood up, came from behind his desk.

"We were working together, yes," said Goodly.

"As for myself," said Trask, shrugging into his jacket, "I somehow forgot to have breakfast . . . too much on my mind. And I still haven't eaten. So go and find Anna Marie, and the pair of you can put me fully in the picture over a late lunch."

"Well, if you think—"

"I do," said Trask. "You're skinny enough already, and

she rarely looks much better than three-quarters dead! Okay, I know her condition has little or nothing to do with her diet, but it does no one any good to walk around empty! Go get her, and I'll meet you downstairs in the restaurant. Lunch is on me."

"As you wish." The precog nodded.

Downstairs was the hotel. The elevator used by E-Branch personnel stopped on three floors only: the ground, the hotel restaurant, and E-Branch itself on the top floor. Other than E-Branch operatives no one else was able to even use the elevator, which was situated at the rear of the building. The hotel's common or garden residents and diners had their own elevators in front.

Trask's guests arrived at the restaurant as he was apologising to the head waiter for ordering out-of-hours lunches, but since most E-Branch agents were regular diners he knew it would be okay. Where the hotel's staff was concerned, "those upstairs people" had to be respected as highly successful "international entrepreneurs"—whatever that was supposed to mean—and the restaurant's cupboards would have to be bare indeed on the day they got turned away unfed.

"We have salmon in a piquant sauce," said the head waiter, "and the asparagus is excellent! As for a pudding—"

"No pudding." Trask shook his head. "But a bottle of wine, perhaps? Not too expensive."

"A nice liebfraumilch?"

"That'll do fine, thank you," said Trask.

"Salmon for three then?" And they all three nodded, though Anna Marie English looked a little pained.

"Is there something?" Trask asked her as the waiter went off to the kitchen.

"Only the usual," the ecopath replied, massaging the junction of her neck and shoulder where a nerve was visibly jumping. "Mother Earth is a pain in the neck—but *literally*, where I'm concerned—and ecologically speaking, things are in a mess all over the place."

The wine arrived, and filling their glasses Trask glanced at Anna Marie. He couldn't help feeling sorry for her—yet at the same time felt uncomfortable in her presence. It wasn't her fault but that of her singular talent or curse. It was what her condition signalled, the statement her ailments confirmed about the ecology of the planet he lived on.

"And are you saying this St. John fellow is a part of it?" he inquired. "Part of the mess? Or was that simply a generalization?"

Sipping her wine, Anna Marie peered at Trask myopically—through her thick-lensed spectacles and the curving rim of her wineglass both—and hunched her shoulders in a shrug signifying nothing in particular, or perhaps apathy at best. But it wasn't that, Trask knew. Rather it was that she wasn't feeling very well. She rarely if ever felt well, and usually required time to put her unique physical problems aside before responding to everyday events; on this occasion Trask's questions.

Trying not to show any discomfort, he looked back at her, waited, and inwardly considered what he saw. Not who but what, but that wasn't to belittle her. For despite that Trask's ESPers were his colleagues, he considered most of them in exactly the same way. Yes, they were his friends, certainly—but they were also his subordinates, the tools of his esoteric trade.

Anna Marie English, he thought. *English by name but never a typically English rose.* It was her talent, yes. Or her curse. Of all the ESP skills of all his agents, hers was the one most likely to be considered a curse. For whatever disturbed or damaged planet Earth's well-being, it also disturbed and depleted Anna Marie's. And in recent weeks she'd been withdrawn, dowdy, and down in the mouth generally.

She was twenty-four and looked ... what, fifty? The brown liver spots on her trembling wrists and hands; her hearing aid, and the thick-lensed spectacles that magnified her owlish eyes; her stringy, lustreless hair and anemic appearance in general: and all such *stigmata* betokening planetary diseases and disasters. That was why Anna Marie's physical presence disagreed with Trask, because the ecopath mirrored the decline of the world.

But at last she spoke. "Right now it's not the work, it's the salmon." Their meal had arrived while they were talking.

"The salmon?" Trask was surprised. "You don't like it?"

"I *do* like it," she answered, "but I know I shouldn't."

"What?" said Trask. "You're going all vegetarian on us?"

"Eventually, perhaps," said Anna Marie. "But not until I become so ashamed that I have to. I mean, look at it this way: it's only in the last two decades that salmon have returned to the Thames. The pollution level is at its lowest since Viking times. Salmon, back in the Thames! That's amazing! And here we sit enjoying -. . well, what else but wild salmon? While in the Far East it's shark's-fin soup and—by far the most monstrous—dolphins! Right now they're killing off entire pods of dolphins! That really hurts; it hurts *me!* And it's all connected up and getting worse, while very few of us seem to care. Listen:

"In March I visited my parents down in the wilds of Devon. My father has a few acres and he was cutting down some trees—for firewood!—these old, beautiful trees! He's going to dig out their roots and put a pool in, heat the water with gas and put chlorine in to kill off the algae; and when it rains he'll run the overflow into the local brook. And he's *my father!*"

She paused to take a ragged breath, then asked, "Should I go on?"

Trask nodded and said, "Yes. Get it out of your system."

"Then listen," she said again. "Just eighteen months ago we had that Armenian earthquake. It killed one hundred thousand people, and I can still feel the tremors! And a year ago it was that nightmarish Exxon Valdez disaster; I could hear the crying of the seabirds, and feel the monstrous agony of all those poor sea creatures drowning in oil. As for the year in between: well, it's hardly been any better! Hurricane Hugo, the San Francisco quake, and all the pollution worldwide. The Thames is cleaner, true, but rivers in other places are in desperate trouble. PCB levels are on the rise in almost every lake, and Pennsylvanian spruce trees are dying from acid rain. Then there are all the radiation leaks, and the defoliation—in fact, the *massacre*—of the great rain forests! And what of the animals? The pandas and gorillas, deprived of their forests, the green things they live on: a pitiful handful of survivors, gradually succumbing, disappearing. It's like a row of standing dominoes, apparently unconnected, but once they start to topple . . ."

The ecopath paused, stared hard at Trask, and again asked him, "Do you *still* want me to go on?"

"No." Trask shook his head. "It isn't necessary. I think I understand you well enough. We've asked you to ignore everything that you're constantly suffering—to look right through it—and try to discover what affect this Scott St. John, just one man in six billion, will have on an entire world's future." He paused to glance almost accusingly at Ian Goodly. "A needle in a haystack sort of task, right? Almost impossible."

"A tall order, yes"—she nodded, appearing to agree—"but not quite impossible. So with Ian's help . . . I looked anyway."

Surprised again, Trask leaned forward a little. "And?"

"Wait!" said Ian Goodly, mainly to the ecopath. "It might be best if we started at the beginning. And anyway you haven't eaten anything yet, so give yourself a break. You eat and I'll talk."

Anna Marie nodded, however reluctantly, and began to eat. And the precog took over where she had left off:

"Yesterday," he began, "while St. John was here for questioning, I had his place bugged. Just a bit of foresight on my part, because 'foresight' is my field, if you see what I mean. Anyway, the techs did their usual superb job; they put bugs in his telephones and a listening device in his living area.

"In the afternoon he used his telephone just once—checking us out, as it happens—but later last night the Duty Tech reported a lot of clinking of glasses and some stumbling around coming from the audio link. At a guess he was drinking, mixing himself a few stiff ones. But then, who could blame him?

"Anyway, that gave me an idea. You may remember I said we should put a few obstacles in St. John's way to see if he would use his unknown talent to overcome them? Well, with the cooperation of his local police I did exactly that. This morning they arrested him—ostensibly for drunk driving, which he probably was anyway—and I picked up Anna Marie at home on my way out to the police station. This was our chance to observe St. John close up without his knowing about it . . . or so we thought."

The ecopath touched Goodly's elbow, patted her lips clean with a napkin, and said, "Ian, let me take it from here." Then, after a sip of wine to clear her throat:

"We watched him through a two-way mirror—is that what you call them? Anyway, we could see him but he couldn't see us. We talked in whispers, even though it wasn't necessary because the room was soundproofed. And from here on it gets confusing." She thought about it for a moment, then said: "Do you know the Heisenberg Principle?"

Trask nodded. "I *know* it, even if I don't fully understand it. Whatever we study we change, right?"

"Exactly, and that's why it's confusing. We were studying St. John's behaviour. Did we therefore change it? After a while he seemed to know we were there; he became agitated, frustrated, and anxious; he 'performed' in front of the mirror. But if—as Ian believes, and as I'm inclined to agree—if he *knew* he was possessed of some kind of extrasensory power, some wild talent, surely he would have known who we were and would have tried to conceal it. Well, that's if he also knew that we were pursuing it." She shrugged. "As I said, it's confusing. Perhaps if we'd had Paul Garvey with us . . ."

Trask finished eating. "So far this is all very theoretical," he said. "All ifs and buts and nothing solid. You ask what if we'd had Paul Garvey on the case? But Paul's already had his shot. And David Chung, maybe? And myself? And everybody else? I have to limit this thing some time or other. I wouldn't be much bothered about St. John at all if Ian hadn't brought him to my attention in the first place. There are more immediate, perhaps more important, things to attend to—plenty of them." Again he looked at the precog, and again Goodly felt accused; but before he could begin to defend himself Trask continued:

"However, Ian did bring it to my attention, and because I know it worries him I'm bound to want to know all about it . . . which I don't, not yet, and not by a long shot. So, Anna Marie, please continue. Before you were interrupted you were about to tell me how with Ian's help you tried to gauge St. John's ecological impact, or its lack, on the future. I imagine you went about it in the usual way?"

" 'Usual'?" she answered. "Well usual to E-Branch, anyway. But yes, we joined forces, holding hands like . . . like what? A pair of shy young lovers? *Ugh!*" She smiled wryly at the precog. "What a repulsive thought, eh? No, actually it was quite emotionless. We simply clasped hands, concentrated on the subject, and did what comes unnaturally, our own special things. I let Mother Earth wash over me, while Ian—"

"I looked to the future," said the precog. "I got what I call a 'flash'—just a momentary thing, a few brief seconds, a string of mental images and/or perceptions—but I prefer to keep it to myself, until Anna Marie has finished. There's only one thing I'll mention now: whatever it is that Scott St. John has, I think it's possible that for those few short seconds it *may* have enhanced our talents, too. Even dormant, embryonic, or atrophied, it was that dynamic!"

Trask thought, *So finally we're getting to it*, and turned back to the ecopath. "Please go on. So what does Old Ma Earth, or her future incarnation, think of Scott St. John?"

"As Ian has said," Anna Marie answered, "it lasted only a moment, a second or so, but it was the strangest thing! Everything felt, I don't know, *twisted* somehow, as if I was experiencing a breakdown—even a total reversal—of the rules of science, the laws of physics. I sensed a planetary devolution, a massive collapse, perhaps a mass extinction . . ."

"What!?" Trask's jaw dropped. "You sensed a mass extinction? But of what? You can't be talking about mankind!"

"I'm talking about everything," said the ecopath. "And if I didn't actually feel it—because it hasn't happened yet—I certainly sensed it coming and felt it looming . . ."

The way she said it, so quiet and thoughtful, had Trask's blood running cold. He opened his mouth to say something, and nothing came out. But by then Ian Goodly was speaking:

"Of course," the precog was quick to put in, "you have to take into account the fact that she did her reading through me. And you'd also do well to recall that the truth of the Heisenberg Principle is nowhere more evident than in precognition."

"Come again?" said Trask, blinking.

"It's like the past," said Goodly. "If we could go back in time and change the past, we'd also change the present, perhaps drastically. And when I try to look at the future—what then? The things I see frequently come to pass, that's true, but they rarely come to pass the way we expected them to. It's almost as if by looking at the future we change it. A new spin on Heisenberg's Principle, possibly explaining Goodly's Principle, which in turn reminds us that the future is a devious thing."

Trask frowned at him and said, "Yes, and which also tells *me* something: that while what you just said was definitely the truth, it's also some kind of anaesthetic designed to take the sting out of something you *haven't* told me—not yet! So come on, my friend, what did *you* get out of it? What's your impression of Scott St. John's future? Is he or isn't he the enormous danger that Anna Marie registered and which so far you've only hinted at? And if he is, what can we do about it?"

The precog shook his head and smiled a thin smile. "Scott St. John isn't the danger. It's through him that we've learned of it. That much is now obvious, to me at least. And it's also fairly obvious that you're beginning to think I'm as

devious as the future, which to me is rather like the coal
scuttle calling the kettle black!"

Sitting up straighter, for a moment Trask looked confused. Then, narrowing his eyes, he said, "What? Explain
what you just said. In fact, tell it all, everything you *haven't*
said."

"As you wish," said Goodly evenly. "In connection with
St. John—concentrating on him—I tried looking at the future in a chronological sequence. So imagine my surprise
when the first thing I saw was my good friend and colleague, the locator David Chung! Chung, who was watching me looking at St. John! But not for much longer . . ."

After several seconds of total silence, Trask reddened
and said, "Ah, that. Well you see—"

"But I wasn't offended," the precog cut him off, "because
I knew you thought it was for our own good. That way you
could quickly find us, Anna Marie and myself, and pull us
out if you believed things were getting too problematic."

Trask sighed and said, "Well, yes. And there goes the
wind flying right out of my sails! But I think I'll save any
apology for later. Have you spoken to Chung about this?"

"Just before I came to see you." The precog nodded.
"Yes, I mentioned it to David, but it's not a problem. Not as
long as he returns the Continental Airlines ballpoint that he
took from my desk. I like the way it writes, and I thought
I'd lost it. I might have known better because I don't usually
lose things. Of course, he was using it as his divining rod to
locate me. Makes me wonder what other odds and ends he
has in that locker of his . . . something of Anna Marie's,
too, I'll wager. But there's at least one thing I now *know*
he's got."

"Oh?" said Trask. "And what's that?"

"It's a paperweight," the precog replied, "from St. John's
study. I asked the techs to get something for me when they
were bugging his house. And I've given it to David."

"I see," said Trask. "And now I know what's been bothering me, what you've been keeping back from me. For it's
obvious now that you intend to play this your way, that

you've come to some sort of decision on your own about this case without consulting me. Why else would you, er, *borrow* one of St. John's belongings if not for future use? Am I right?"

"Yes," said Goodly. "But of course, in any final analysis, your decision will be the only one that counts."

"Oh, really?" There was a touch of sarcasm in Trask's voice now. "So I can continue to play at being boss? You're giving me a choice, then?"

"I would never try to usurp you, Ben," said the precog. "I really wouldn't want to. But the choice we're talking about now is a very big one, very likely a life and death choice."

"And you didn't think I'd get it right?" Trask's voice was wry now. "Now tell me, Ian: how is it I'm supposed to trust you in almost everything you do, when it's obvious that on certain occasions—times like this—you don't trust me?"

"Ben," said Goodly, "there may never have been a time like this. As for trust: one good reason why you trust us is because it comes naturally to you; you'd know it immediately if we ever lied to you! But this isn't so much about trusting us as trusting our talents. So before I tell you what I saw in St. John's future, I'm asking for even more of your trust. Promise me that this time you'll play it my way."

Trask looked at Goodly—looked *into* him and saw the truth of him—then nodded and said, "Okay, I'm listening."

Plainly relieved and grateful, the precog sighed and said, "Very well. This is how it was . . ."

9

"Looking at Scott St. John through the mirror, I tried to scan the future," the precog began. "His future, to all intents and purposes, but also ours, our world's. And yes, I saw the chaos that Anna Marie described. But the impressions I got were very fleeting, kaleidoscopic, and obscure; they were *made* obscure by the darkness of the vast evil that Scott St. John was fighting! He was fighting it, and he was aware—even as I am now aware—that he and his small group are the only ones who *can* fight it. St. John, the female figure I've spoken of previously, and one other who . . . who remains vague and shadowy in my mind. But there's one thing I am certain of: none of the three is one of us. Not me or Anna Marie—not anyone from E-Branch. But there *will* be three of them, yes.

"That was something that impressed itself deeply upon me, the number three. It sounds strange, I know, but it's there in his future, in the future of the entire world, and it's there with a capital 'T.' Three. In a single instant that number was emblazoned on my mind: 'Three!' But *only* Three. And while none of it makes much sense, I'll tell you what else I saw in those flickering, chaotic seconds:

"A mountaintop, all snow and ice, in places hollow, with manmade tunnels and caverns . . . a huge machine, like the barrel of a gun, all metal and plastic . . . with heavy, golden bullets racked as high as the ice-cold ceiling . . . electronic circuits, computer screens . . . white-smocked workers, afraid and toiling without knowing what they toiled at . . . and Death himself, the old man with a scythe, coming and going as at the beck and call of—

"But of who, or what, I couldn't see. Finally, it all went up in flames, everything, a colossal explosion that shook me to my roots and took it all away from me. And if Anna Marie hadn't been there, clasping my hand, I believe I might have fallen. It felt very real, Ben. Felt like . . . like Anna Marie's 'planetary devolution,' and I know that it *will be* very real!

"But again, the one thing I sensed above everything else was that the Branch won't be a part of it, not in the thick of it. We may be there on the periphery, but this is his business, St. John's. Our future may well depend on its outcome, but it's his fight, him and his group, just the 'Three' of them, yes . . ."

After several long seconds, Trask said, "On the periphery? You're saying we can only wait and watch?"

"That's the essence of it, yes," the precog answered. "As I concentrated on St. John, that was made very clear to me; it dawned on me as bright as day. I mean, I'm not a telepath, Ben, yet I would swear I *heard* these words:

" 'If you should sense anything strange, keep your distance but try to explore it.' Those were the words I heard and I know—or believe—that they apply to us. We can explore St. John, his background, life, whatever it is that makes him what he is, but we can only do it from a safe distance. We can neither help nor interfere; we *can't* be a part of what he's doing. But don't ask me why, for I don't know. We are . . . peripheral, yes. We're not needed. Not yet, anyway."

Trask shook his head as if to clear it. Despite what he'd promised he now seemed undecided. "You've told me, both of you, that there's a threat to our world," he said, glancing first at Goodly, then at Anna Marie. "Yet we can't interfere? We're here, in E-Branch, to handle precisely this kind of work, and yet all we can do is sit and watch? And if I'm to deal with this as you suggest—which is to say *not* deal with it—it will be on your say-so, your word alone?"

"No, not quite ours alone," said Goodly. "For when we got back from this business with St. John I found a note from Paul Garvey on my desk." He fished out a crumpled slip of paper and passed it across the table for Trask to read.

Ian—
What's all this? Are you messing with my kind of stuff now, or have I been working too hard? This morning, some time after 10:00, I had a thought that wasn't one of mine. It was a "voice" in my head, but it had your fingerprints, your aura, all over it. It said, "If you should sense anything strange, explore it from a distance." Something like that, anyway. Of course it could have come to me from anywhere—I am after all telepathic—but it felt so much like you! Could it have anything to do with the Scott St. John case? I wonder. Any ideas?
Paul G.

Trask looked at the precog, who again said: "So then. Not quite our say-so alone, eh?"

And Trask said, "So what do we do? We can't do nothing!"

"We can check him out top to bottom," said Goodly. "All of us. We check St. John's entire history, his where and his when, his then and his now . . . because we already know something about his future. We find out what makes him tick, what's happened or *will* happen that's going to make him fight. And maybe that way we'll learn what he's fighting against, and who is siding with him. But we must do it from a distance, going nowhere near him. We can't afford to compromise him."

"Compromise?" Trask was quick to pick up on the word.

"Just something else that got lodged in my head," said the precog with a frustrated shrug. "But don't ask me where it came from. It seems logical, though. For if St. John is about to go to war against dangerous unknown enemies, we don't want to let our presence alert them to his activities."

Trask shook his head, rubbed his chin, and said, "I don't know. It still seems very vague and somehow unreal to me."

"I know," Goodly answered, nodding. "Oh, I know."

"So how long do we have?" Trask asked then. "Couldn't you at least gauge that much?"

"No." Goodly shrugged again. "But for all that these were fleeting images, still they were very insistent. So whatever it is, it can't be too far off."

And finally the Head of Branch was convinced, which transformed him into his usual assertive self. "Very well, let's get to it," he said. "And right now! Ian, I want you to call in all our people, everybody who's available. We'll hold an O-Group in the Ops Room, in"—he glanced at his watch—"an hour's time? Is that enough? Can you do that?"

The precog nodded. "Consider it done," he said . . .

Scott St. John cried out and started awake in an easy chair in the little upstairs room that had been his wife's study. For a moment or two, uncertain of where he was, he imagined it to be the hospital in central London where Kelly had died.

He had been dreaming—no, actually he'd been night-maring, and monstrously! Then, as an involuntary shiver shook his body, convinced that the time would be 3:33 A.M., Scott looked at his watch. But no, it was 6:25 in the evening.

The evening of a totally weird day at that! he thought, as he gradually stopped trembling and came more surely awake.

Scott didn't remember coming up here to be close to Kelly again, something he used to do all the time in the first couple of months. He supposed that he'd been worn out, physically and emotionally exhausted by the inexplicable things that were happening to him, and that he had wandered up here "instinctively" to see if he could find her again. Dumb really, because he knew where she was, the precise location of her plot in the Highgate Cemetery. But he couldn't go there anymore because when he did he didn't want to leave.

In his dream Scott had been with Kelly, sitting in a chair on the right-hand side of her hospital bed in her private room, holding her shrivelled little-girl's hand. Now, fully awake, he knew there was something he should remember about that hand . . . Kelly's fragile left hand.

She had been conscious but too weak to speak to him, or to do much of anything else for that matter. But her eyes had been huge and unblinking in her parchment face. He had seen her like that on many occasions in the last few days of her life; except this time, in his dream, Scott had felt some kind of urgency in Kelly's mute gazing, as if she had been trying to tell him something.

Her huge eyes had kept straying from his face to the hand Scott held in his hand. This had never happened in life he was sure—in fact, he'd only ever sat on the *left* side of her bed, holding her *right* hand—but in the dream Kelly had seemed to be trying to redirect his gaze from her face . . . to her hand?

Scott forced himself to remember—

—No, not to her hand, to her wrist! Until, answering her silent directions, finally he'd looked where Kelly required him to look.

Her pure white smock had partly concealed . . . what? A mark or blemish on her wrist? Yes, Scott remembered now. Like a very faint bar code a shade paler than her flesh, the mark or brand had consisted of four white near-parallel bars that crossed her wrist at ninety degrees. Maybe it was some kind of identification for the doctors and nurses, like a tag on your toe but less conspicuous and far less emotive and gruesome. A fanciful idea, which he didn't for a moment believe. Kelly had been in a private room; her details had been there on a clipboard at the foot of her bed; how could anyone not know or mistake her identity?

But those marks, they rang a bell. Where had he seen them before? And suddenly Scott remembered something else: how Kelly had scratched that wrist repeatedly while he was driving her to the hospital. That was on the morning of her collapse, when she had tried to get out of their bed and just crumpled up. She had thought the itch must be an allergic rash or something . . .

Remembering Kelly's collapse brought Scott's dream back to mind, giving him the shudders again. She had also "crumpled up" in his dream, though not in the same way. No, for the dream had been . . . oh, something else. Something else entirely!

In his dream she had nodded at Scott, an almost imperceptible up and down movement of her head, her way of saying "yes," when she knew he'd seen those marks on her wrist. She had even managed a faint little smile—following which she'd collapsed, but literally! And Scott had seen her *fold up on herself* like a little-girl-shaped crepe paper bag with all of the air suddenly sucked out! Which was when he'd come starting awake and crying out in his horror. *God!*

Scott went downstairs, made a pot of coffee, took it into his study. It was gloomy in there, even with the sunlight slanting in across the garden; but then again it was gloomy almost everywhere now. More than three months worth of fine dust, disturbed by his movements, glowed faintly in the filtering beams like so many miniature galaxies. It was his study and familiar, of course, and yet there was something strange here. Something missing? He gave an irritated shrug of his shoulders. Whatever the problem was, he would probably solve it sooner or later . . .

Slumped in an armchair sipping his coffee, Scott wondered about those marks that he had dreamed of on Kelly's wrist: *had* they perhaps been real, something he'd experienced in real life other than Kelly scratching herself during that hospital drive? They rang a bell, those marks, and every time it rang it got a little bit louder.

What was it that his mystery woman had said he should do? He should "think about his loss coldly, without anger, pain, or passion"? Maybe she'd simply meant that he should try to think more clearly. Well, that's if there had been any meaning to it at all and she wasn't just a crazy woman!

Now Scott snorted in disbelief, and laughed aloud in self-derision. What in the . . . ? Had he actually started to take what she'd told him seriously? But then he quickly stopped laughing, because what with his dreams and all—and everything else that had been happening to him—yes, he'd been taking it seriously, and for some time now! Why else would he have tried to find her this morning?

But whoever she was, and crazy or not, she'd advised Scott to empty his mind and think clearly about his loss—even about investigating his loss—which had to mean there was something about it that *required* investigation . . .

Except he *couldn't* think clearly, not even here in his own study! He felt too far removed from Kelly here. Her study would be the place to, well, study! Perhaps that was why he'd gone up there in the first place: to try and think things through, only to fall asleep and have that oh-so-real nightmare.

Taking his coffee back upstairs, Scott left one dusty room for another. Dusty, but well ordered. Unlike her husband, Kelly had always been the tidy one and wholly organized, particularly where her work was concerned. She had kept records, memos, notebooks, and diaries, a filing cabinet full of newspaper clippings and photographs . . .

Photographs? That set the bell ringing again. Had he seen something in a photograph that Kelly had shown him? In connection with ... with ... with Simon Salcombe? Some job she'd been working on? Possibly. And in some of her previous journalistic columns she'd as good as called Salcombe a charlatan, which he probably was but still wouldn't have been too pleased about.

But had there been something more recently?

Yes, Scott remembered it now: it was back in January when he had been preparing for a trip to Berlin to work as an interpreter at a conference on Germany's possible future reunification. And by the time he'd returned from that Kelly was already terminally ill.

Opening the lower drawer of the filing cabinet and checking under "S," Scott soon found what he was looking for: two manila envelopes labelled with Salcombe's name, one fairly bulky—old work from 1988, 1989—while the other was dated January 1990. That would be the one he was interested in, the work Kelly had been doing right up to her decline. Now he recalled something of what she had told him about it:

She had been freelancing, or "paparazzing" as she'd called it, trying to get photographs of camera-shy Simon Salcombe. She had wanted to get some good shots of her own, but had agreed to distract Salcombe, make him turn toward her and expose himself to the cameras of a team from the BBC. Kelly had an arrangement with her BBC friends that if they should fail to get any worthwhile footage they might make her a decent offer for her stuff, *if* she managed to obtain some good still shots. It was unlikely that they would try to cheat her, for Kelly was very well known among the newshound pack and admired for her work, but if they did she could always sell her pictures to the daily newspapers.

On this occasion, however, it appeared she may have killed two birds with one stone—or one camera. For when Scott tipped out the envelope's contents onto her desk, not only was there a set of five six-by-four photographs but also a newspaper clipping and an eight-inch strip of coloured BBC film. Perhaps there had been some mutually advantageous horse-trading here.

Choosing at random, he picked up the strip first, slotted it into a viewer from Kelly's desk, and held it up to the light from the window. And scanning it frame by frame, he could see at once why this section had been edited out: it showed a much better picture of Kelly than of Salcombe! There she stood with her camera at eye level and one hand on Salcombe's arm. He was looking the other way, keeping his face averted as he made his way through a small crowd of reporters and passersby. His minders, a pair of broad-shouldered heavyset types, were clearing a path just a few feet ahead of him. Kelly must have held back to let the heavies pass her by before moving in closer.

That was the first frame, but then things speeded up. The sequence of Salcombe's movements became very jerky, indicating his rapid reaction to Kelly's sudden close presence, her unforeseen intrusion. Which is to say that while the frame-by-frame motion of Salcombe *himself* appeared spasmodic, everyone else's seemed far more fluid and natural. Now, following the sequence, Scott saw how the man shook Kelly off, how he caught her wrist to free himself and thrust her away. But not before she'd managed to snap at least one picture as he turned angrily toward her.

It had all happened in less than a dozen hazy frames, but it had set Scott's eyes flickering even as the still scenes had seemed to flicker; as if he'd been viewing them in some seaside peep show, through the viewer of one of those ancient "What the Butler Saw" machines. Also, it left him feeling anxious that he was missing something. But he could check that out later. As to why this sequence had been edited out of the BBC's coverage: in Scott's opinion it was unusable, a poor piece of blurred, badly jostled film, that was all.

Setting the footage aside, Scott picked up the photographs from Kelly's desk. Undated, the first showed three sick-looking children in a hospital ward. Scott hadn't seen it before but it did bring something back to mind, something that Kelly had told him. He had been busy, preparing for Berlin at the time, and so hadn't paid too much attention. Now, however, sensing that this was important, he forced himself to remember.

"Those poor sick kids," she had said, shaking her head. "As if anyone could do anything for them at this late stage, or any stage for that matter. Not with what they're suffering from and as sick as they are. But of course, their poor parents would do anything. They had tried everything else, so why not this faker Simon Salcombe? They must have felt they were drowning—grasping at straws—but how could it do any actual harm? He'd told them he wouldn't expect payment for his 'services.' *Huh!* It was like he was doing some kind of benefit or something! The damned faker! That bloody awful creep!"

Scott knew this wasn't exactly what she'd said; his memory of the conversation wasn't perfect, but it was close enough.

Laying the photograph to one side, he took up and looked at three more. These were of the same kids but taken individually, perhaps some time *before* the group shot, because despite what Kelly had said about their illness they weren't nearly as sick-looking as before. But that could be the lighting; so far all of the pictures had been dark, of very poor quality.

The last photograph was of Salcombe himself: Kelly's snapshot, taken just before he pushed her away. And Scott knew what she had meant when she called the man a creep. He looked almost reptilian! With sallow, sunken cheeks, snarling lips drawn back from little fish teeth, eyes of black marble sunk in that waxy, skull-like mask of a face under the bony, bald-shining dome of his head . . . not so much Scott's praying mantis as some kind of leprous cobra! As for his reaction at being touched, surprised like that: it was hardly a natural one. He wasn't just shocked but furious, as mad as hell! He looked hateful—yes, *full* of hatred—for Kelly!

And now, glaring back at the picture, agreeing absolutely with his wife's assessment, Scott thought, *You fucking creep!*

But on the other hand, maybe Salcombe's expression wasn't that significant after all. Maybe it was a trick of the camera; there had been something wrong with the light, or Kelly's flash had failed. Whatever it was, something had certainly gone awry. Badly focussed, distorted, and grainy, the picture wasn't nearly as good as her usual work . . .

And finally there was the newspaper cutting, where again Kelly had been less exacting than usual. For while she had cut out the picture and its accompanying column, there was nothing to indicate which daily it had appeared in. It was very definitely her work, though, because it carried her byline.

Scott recognized the picture—it had been printed from a photograph that Kelly had shown him probably on his last night home before flying to Germany, and it was the picture that had sparked this search.

Now, narrowing his eyes, he studied it more closely.

Despite that it was on newsprint, the picture was clearer than any of the others he'd seen. It showed seven people on the steps of the impressive, marble-columned frontage of St. Jude's Children's Hospital: three male figures flanked by two couples, and the gangling central figure was that of Salcombe sandwiched between his minders. Kelly had caught him looking back over his shoulder, apparently *hissing* directly into her camera! And this time there could be no mistaking, no misunderstanding the look on his face—which was murderous!

This wasn't a close-up shot; Kelly had wanted to get the entire group and had snapped them from maybe twenty feet away, possibly from the curbside. But as Scott looked at Salcombe's expression again—and for all that it made no difference now—still he felt glad that on this occasion at least his wife had been at a relatively safe distance . . .

10

With the light from the window beginning to fail, Scott seated himself in Kelly's work chair and switched on her desk lamp to read the newspaper cutting. Maybe something in her words would focus his memories, give them clearer definition.

The trouble with his and Kelly's lifestyle had been their work, which was forever intruding; with Scott frequently away—"speaking in tongues somewhere," as Kelly had used to describe it—while often as not when he was home she would be out and about chasing down some story or other. But on the other hand, maybe that had been of benefit. They never felt they were tripping over each other; indeed, they'd never seen *enough* of each other, and so their time together had always been special.

On the downside, and as far as Scott's current quest was concerned, he had never been fully *au fait* with what Kelly was working on; only that once she had made her mind up about something, her convictions—pro and con, right or wrong—were always of the very strongest. She had stuck to her guns. Which was more than ever apparent as Scott scanned the column's heading, then carried on reading, nodding to himself and murmuring: "Yep, that's my girl!"

SIMON SALCOMBE: HEALER OR HEEL?
by
Kelly St. John

The wonder workers. We've known them since time began, and by a great many names—so many that we may even say they're legion. Fakirs climbing their Indian ropes, and vanishing into thin air before they can be investigated; stage magicians who will readily admit to their ingenuity without explaining their tricks; blindfolded mentalists with their fast-talking assistants—not to mention the occasional plant in the audience.

Then we've had great escape artists such as Harry Houdini, who amazed the entire world with his fantastic feats, yet was himself a lifelong sceptic and debunker-in-chief of the spiritualists. And let's not forget all the spoon-benders, the illusionists, the fire-walkers (and eaters), the telepaths and telekinetics, and all the tele-these, tele-those, and tele-the others.

Et cetera, et cetera, *und so weiter.*

Yes, they've been conning us forever, but we don't mind because right from the start we knew it was just a scam. It's entertainment—show business, of course—and we don't believe everything we see, because as a certain song has it, it ain't necessarily so. It's smoke and mirrors, that's all, and all done for fun—

—Right?

Ah, but then along comes Simon Salcombe—the so-called psychic healer—and bang goes all the fun.

Simon Salcombe is something of a mystery man: rarely seen in public, his comings and goings are cloaked in such secrecy that no one can say where he'll put in his next appearance or to which hideout he'll then depart. But recently his activities in the highly lucrative "psychic healing" business (where he claims to heal by touch: the "laying-on-of-hands") have been somewhat curtailed by various adverse reports . . . several of which, I'm delighted to admit, were mine.

Frankly, it must be fairly obvious to anyone who gives it even a moment's thought that this man is a complete quack who preys on rich and gullible hypochondriacs. Certainly his affluent clients "get well"—but of course they do, because they weren't physically sick in the first place. And as for Salcombe's healing touch: well, I don't know if all the people he has touched feel healed, but most of them were *well heeled* for sure! What's more, it seems to me they've been the very softest of touches!

   And now we hit a new low. Sinister Simon—and the accompanying picture will perhaps explain why I call him that . . . he really *hates* having his picture taken—is attempting to recruit new donors to his private personal pension fund by offering his "services," free of charge, to the distraught parents of very sick children. He can get away with advertising his rotten business in this heartless fashion simply by virtue of the fact that no one will ever dare to mention the possibility of him failing, which would be to predetermine the outcome for these kids. And if or when—no, God help me, but I must say it—*when* Salcombe's psychic "treatments" are seen to be utterly worthless, why then this unscrupulous faker will explain that his patients (in fact the victims of his scam) were simply too far gone.
   But what a cruel, cruel game this vile creature is playing, and . . .

   . . . And so on.
But halfway through, Scott stopped reading. He knew the column would continue in more or less the same vein to the end, for Kelly always stuck to her guns. And what he had read so far had already helped to determine a better chronology of events:
   Kelly had somehow received advance notice of Salcombe's visit to St. Jude's. She had been on hand to get a shot of him, his minders, and two sets of parents as they entered the hospital. Then, scrambling to Kelly's grapevine alert, other reporters—including her friends from the BBC—had gathered outside hoping to catch Salcombe when he came out. And meanwhile *inside* St. Jude's, someone had taken a picture of the sick kids.
   Eventually Salcombe had emerged; Kelly had confronted him and taken her second close-up picture as he turned toward her. End of story. She'd written up *her* story in the next day or so, at which time Scott had been in Berlin. And by the time he got home . . . but no, he must try to avoid going there yet again.

So then, was all of this connected to her death? And if so how? And if Salcombe was so secretive, how had Kelly known that he'd be visiting St. Jude's to "lay hands" on those sick kids? And why the hell was he, Scott St. John, doing all this probably meaningless research in the first place? Because he had been *advised* to, that was why . . . by a woman he didn't know who he'd met in a newsagent's shop, for Christ's sake!

At which he almost stopped, but not quite. Because despite feeling utterly confused Scott knew he was on to something, that there *had* to be something here! And shaking his head sharply to clear it, he thought: *Right, so then . . . what was I doing?*

Ah yes! Working on a chronology of events.

Chronology: another word that got the wheels turning. And right there, in a corner of Kelly's desk, her diary that she'd always kept up-to-date. "It's far better than relying on memory alone," she used to say. "If something is written in detail it can't be forgotten. Events can't get confused."

Scott's hands weren't quite steady as he took up the journal—a six-by-eight ring binder with a full page for each day of the year—because he knew it had to contain Kelly's final thoughts, or at least the last words she had considered worthy of recording. And still uncertain of what he was searching for, but nevertheless hopeful that he would recognize it if or when he saw it, he turned the leaves to the last few days in January, found the very last pages she'd written on, and quickly turned back a week or two in time until he found mention of himself:

Scott all signed up and preparing for Berlin. I suppose I could go with him, make a holiday of it, but money's too hard to come by, and the mortgage won't pay itself off— more's the pity! Scott: no sooner back from Berlin, he'll be getting in shape for that OPEC thing in Venezuela end of Feb. But I really shouldn't complain. We have our lovely home and it will be great having him all to myself here for the next few days . . . (but more especially for the nights).

From which point on the entry got even more personal (and saw Scott getting more choked up), causing him to move forward a page or two.

Tues. 23rd Jan. 1990:
Fantastic news! The USSR has agreed to pull its troops out of Hungary. Gorbachev looks all set on peace . . . it seems he'd like to kill off the last remnants of the Cold War for good. Scott's Berlin conference just three days off . . . they're perhaps jumping the gun a bit, but it could be that German reunification isn't too far away now. Anyway, they certainly intend to be ready for it. So hoorah for perestroika! (If that's the right spelling.)
   Scott out buying smokes—I must try to get him to stop smoking! Anonymous telephone call . . . someone with a German accent and an alleged "tip." Probably a hoax but I can't ignore it. What, Simon Salcombe visiting St. Jude's to work his quackery on sick kids? I'll be there for sure . . .

There was more, but Scott had picked out something of what he wanted to know. An anonymous tip-off? So that was how Kelly had known about Salcombe's "benefit" at St. Jude's. As for the reason she hadn't mentioned it to Scott—or if she had why he hadn't remembered—it was because he'd been busy with his own stuff preparatory to flying to Berlin.
   Skipping the next page he moved on to:

Thurs. 25th Jan. 1990:
Must let the boys from the Beeb know about this creep's alleged visit. But I'll call them after I know it's for real and when I've got a good shot or two of his arrival, *if* he arrives. I owe them a few favours after all, and it will help keep me in their good books . . .

This was followed by half a page of day-by-day stuff, and then a sad note on Ava Gardner—

Oh, dear me! "The world's most beautiful animal" was what they once called her. Sixty-eight years old, and died today in the city . . . pneumonia, of all things, and I can't even picture her having a cold! It just goes to show that we're all mortal, even the "goddesses."

Followed by:

Well, he showed! Got one shot as he was going in with his gorillas—then my camera had some kind of weird flare-up. *Damn!* But this fellow has certainly read my stuff. If looks could kill his would have definitely done for me when we, er, "met" on his way out! And not only his looks but his touch, as cold and slithery as ice! A loathsome character, and I wouldn't want to get that close to him again.

Scott off to Germany tomorrow. I'm not feeling too well, but I won't say anything—I know he'll only get all concerned. So if something is coming on I'll just stay home, work on my articles. Bill Comber says he might have some damaged footage of my clash with Salcombe that he can give me . . .

There was other stuff at the bottom of the page: about an Avianca Boeing 707 crashing on its approach to Kennedy airport, killing seventy-three people; and Benazir Bhutto, the Pakistani premier, giving birth while "in office." But Scott wasn't much interested in those things. Instead his eyes returned again to those ominous, those all-important words, the first indicators of what had been about to happen to Kelly:

"I'm not feeling too well . . ."

And with numb, unfeeling fingers he turned the page.

Friday the twenty-sixth of January, the morning Scott had flown to Germany. He remembered it well: a Black Friday for some, but he had been lucky; his plane was airborne before a ferocious storm caused a good many cancellations. And as the winds picked up to gale force some forty-six people had died across the south and southwest of England.

While Kelly had noted this briefly in her journal—showing her usual, natural concern for Scott—by then she'd also been displaying not a little concern for herself:

Fri. 26th Jan. 1990:
Scott caught early morning plane. Glad he got off before the winds hit. Something has hit me, too! I feel really, *really* down. Don't even feel like working; feel I could just sleep for a month. But no, I shan't let it beat me . . . I'll work on my Salcombe article, maybe finish it and send it off.
    Bill C. called: says he's arranging for some pics of the St. Jude's kids to be taken *inside* the hospital. I find it a bit ghoulish, but that's why I'm "Kelly, Kid Reporter" while Bill and the other guys are pros. What me, Paparazzo? Forget it!

Reading these paragraphs again, Scott felt a genuine pain, a wrenching in his guts, as he scanned Kelly's words, the evidence of her continuing decline. God, he should have been here! But why blame himself? He hadn't had the slightest inkling . . . she hadn't mentioned it; why would she when she herself hadn't known how sick she was? For all she knew it could have been a dose of the flu, for Christ's sake!

But it hadn't been flu . . .

Turning the page to the twenty-seventh of January, Scott saw just a few lines of Kelly's minuscules looking not quite so neat now, which read:

Worked at home. Gave my Salcombe article to the postie when he delivered the afternoon mail . . .
    I was sick this morning. I'm tempted to call Scott, but he'll be home again in just a few days. If I'm still down, maybe we'll do something about it then . . .

On the twenty-eighth a blank page, and then on the 29th:

Scott home day after tomorrow. So glad. Now I'll crawl back to bed. But I do feel a little better, probably because I know he'll soon be here . . .

Got a call from the Hatfield Evening Standard. They'll use my Salcombe thing tonight and I'll get a copy (and my check) by courier tomorrow.

Still tempted to call Scott. But no, he'll be busy. And anyway he'll be home noon on the 1st Feb.

Jesus, God! And he'd spent the evening of the thirtieth with a German friend, Herr Karl Meister, Dolmetscher, in a pub on the Kurfurstendamm, when he could have been on a late flight home! If he'd known, if only he'd known!

And there were no more entries in Kelly's journal . . .

Scott squeezed his eyes shut, clasped his forehead, and slumped down in the chair. He had arrived home at noon on Thursday, the first of February; and wouldn't you know it, Kelly had met him at the door! She'd got out of bed so as to be up and about when he got in. And as tottery as she was, still she'd refused to see a doctor that afternoon or evening. It was as if she'd known that this was the last time they'd be together in their own home.

Friday morning after a sleepless night worrying about her, Scott had been up early. When Kelly collapsed as she'd tried to get out of bed, then he'd carried her to the car and driven her into the city. He had been very glad then that they had private health insurance, and by 8:30 A.M. Kelly had been in a hospital bed . . . from which time on she never got out of it.

Since when, for close on four months, she had rarely been out of Scott's mind; never for more than three or four minutes at a time. And *all* that time, even knowing he wasn't to blame, wasn't responsible, still deep inside he had felt that Kelly's not being here was somehow down to him. Until now—

—Until now it appeared he was looking for a way to

blame someone else. It could be coincidence, of course, but whatever the explanation and whichever way Scott turned he kept bumping into a certain name. And that name was Salcombe.

Simon Salcombe: the man with the healing touch. But Kelly hadn't thought so. To her Salcombe's touch had seemed slippery, cold as ice. Not at all like the touch Scott had received from his mystery woman.

A touch, or touches . . .

One strange and warm, and even a little uplifting . . .

And one cold, slimy . . . and debilitating? One giving, and one taking.

Just suppose, *suppose* that Salcombe really did possess an incredible skill: hands with healing powers, the gift of life. Might not they also contain the seeds of death? Might not this "healer" have the power to extract life as well as to save and prolong it? Scott knew there were poisons that could be administered with a touch or a blow. In what had been known as "the silent assassin" case, not too long ago, Russia's KGB had been suspected of using Bulgarian poisons—tiny capsules of lethal chemicals in the syringe-like tips of umbrellas—as an almost undetectable means of murdering enemy agents.

And what about Kelly's anonymous tip-off? Someone with a German accent? But wasn't Simon Salcombe Swiss or Swiss-based, and didn't the Swiss speak German? Of course they did. So was it possible that someone acting for Salcombe had deliberately leaked the timing of his imminent St. Jude's visit in order to lure Kelly into his presence?

But why? Revenge, for what Kelly had written about him in earlier hard-hitting articles? If so the man must be mad, or a monster, or both. And it might be a good idea to look into the health statistics—the current well-being, *or otherwise*—of Simon Salcombe's several other detractors among the media pack, to see if any of them had also been the victims of unknown illnesses!

Or was all this sheer fantasy—Scott's own wild fantasy—as he searched for reasons for his great loss? But damn it all, he had been as good as *told* to investigate! And if he was going to be suspicious of his own reasoning and introspective in respect to possible fantasies or obsessions, then what about those Secret Service types who had kidnapped and questioned him about *his* suspected parapsychological powers? Now surely that entire episode would *have* to be classified as fantasy—

—Surely?

But no, nothing was sure, over the top, too unbelievable, not anymore. Certainly not in Scott St. John's life . . .

Dusk was settling outside as Scott replaced the strip of film, Kelly's *Hatfield Evening Standard* article, and the four grainy photographs back in their manila envelope. It was then that he saw and recognized a name scribbled on the envelope's flap: B. Comber, along with a telephone number.

Scott remembered having met Comber.

Some three years ago, before Comber had begun working for the BBC, at a time when he and Kelly were doing some lucrative work together, Kelly had invited him and his wife Joanne around for drinks one night. Just a month or so later Joanne had run off with a tax adviser from Liverpool and her husband had sued for divorce. After that Scott had lost track of him but Kelly had stayed in touch through their work.

Aware now that the film strip had come from Comber—and some of the photographs, too—Scott wondered if the man could perhaps tell him anything else about the day that Salcombe had visited those poor sick kids in St. Jude's Hospital. There was an easy way to find out.

Switching off the desk lamp, he left the now gloomy study and took Kelly's diary and the manila envelope with him, downstairs to his own study. And putting on the lights, he poured the last of the cold coffee, took a sip, and called the number on the envelope. After two or three rings:

"Comber," came a slightly slurred male voice.

"Bill?" said Scott. "It's Scott St. John."

"Eh, who? Oh, St. John! Kelly's husband." And then, after a pause: "Lord, but I'd intended calling you! You know, commiserations, and all that? It must've slipped my mind."

The man had obviously had a few and it had left him a bit careless how he phrased things. "Don't worry about it, I understand," said Scott.

"Shoulda called about Kelly, I mean," Comber mumbled on.

"I understand," said Scott again, trying not to get angry. "In fact, it's about Kelly that I'm calling you. I'd very much like to talk to you."

"A good kid," said Comber. "Big heart. Sad loss. Deserved better. Really liked her."

"Right," said Scott, and before Comber could say anything else, he followed up quickly with: "So would you mind if I came to see you—tonight maybe?"

"Tonight?" Comber considered it for a moment or two, then said, "Not at all, old chap—in fact, it would be my pleasure. You see, I could maybe use some company. Me and the bottle, we don't do too well on our own. Or rather I should say we do *too* well on our own, if you know what I mean. But you want to come and see me? Well, that's fine. Do you know the way? I remember we live pretty close, actually."

And he gave directions . . .

11

Bill Comber's house was something less than a mile away, in the direction of Wood Green. A detached, high-gabled two-story, it stood central in a large garden that had been left to run wild. Arriving there at around 8:30, Scott parked his car just inside the leaning iron gate and made his way along an overgrown crazy paving path to a porch with wet and rotting woodwork and a door that was flaking paint. To say that Comber's place showed signs of neglect would be a serious understatement. Lights were burning in two of the downstairs rooms, however, and another glowed dimly under sagging ceiling beams in the porch.

Having heard Scott arrive, Comber was there to meet him at the door. They shook hands and uttered the usual greetings, and Scott entered and shrugged out of his coat. Comber took it from him, then led the way down a corridor to his study: a room much like Scott's and just as untidy.

Comber was probably in his late forties. He was short and burly, overweight, starting to run to seed, and getting pretty thin on top. Tonight he was also flushed with liquor—it was on his breath and there could be no mistaking it—but he was steady on his feet and coherent, and Scott thought he probably handled his booze quite well; it could be that he'd had plenty of practice since his wife left. And anyway, who was Scott St. John, drunk driver, to sit in any sort of judgment on anyone?

Comber poured him a liberal glass of whisky—not Scott's preferred tipple; he could take it or leave it—before seating himself at a desk and waving his guest into an easy chair. And then he said: "Really, I had meant to call. Don't know why I didn't. But . . . we put things off, and suddenly it's too late. How long's it been? Six weeks, seven?"

"Going on four months," said Scott.

"Christ!" Comber seemed genuinely astonished. "Like, where does the time go?"

In answer to which Scott shrugged and said, "It just goes, but it takes a lot of stuff with it. And before everything goes completely there are some things I've been trying to work out."

"About Kelly? Know what you mean. I've been working things out myself, but on a different level. Well, how can I help? And what's that you've got there?" He nodded, indicating the envelope in Scott's hand.

Scott got up and tipped the contents of the envelope onto Comber's desk. "It's some stuff you sent to Kelly, about a job she helped you with."

Spreading the photographs, the strip of excerpted film, and Kelly's article across his desk, Comber glanced at each item in turn, frowned, and finally looked at Scott. "Simon Salcombe?" he said. "You want to know about that time Kelly saw him arrive at St. Jude's, called us, and let us in on it? Yes, I remember. She really didn't care too much for that bloke, and for that matter neither do I. That wasn't the first occasion when I've tried to pin him down, but nothing works right when he's around. Lights, cameras, microphones, and watches: everything goes on the fritz, completely out of whack!"

Scott sat down again and said, "Really? Well, it looks like things were on the blink that day, too. These photographs aren't very much good, are they?"

"Only this one." Comber grinned and tapped the picture in the cutting from the *Hatfield Evening Standard*. "Yes, she was a clever kid, your Kelly. Never said a word about this one! Let's see now . . . *hmmm!*"

While Scott sat waiting, trying not to show his impatience, Comber speed-read Kelly's article. And in a little while:

"Yes," he said, "that was Kelly all right. Do you know why she had problems selling to the nationals, the broadsheets, the big-timers? It was because she was too outspoken. Other fellows might *hint* at this, that, and the other: in this case that Simon Salcombe was a fraud. But not Kelly. She always—"

"—Shouted it out loud," said Scott. "Yes, I know."

"Right! Not that Salcombe could sue or anything. He's some kind of recluse, rich but retiring. To sue, say for defamation, he has to prove he's not a fraud and Kelly's telling lies about him. Which means a court case, which also means he'd be appearing in public. But the big papers couldn't take the chance that he wouldn't sue, and so couldn't use Kelly's stuff. Too fucking conservative by far! Chicken-shit bastards! They're not slow to run down the little people, but they back off quick enough when they're up against money."

"So you think Kelly was taking chances?"

"I don't, but the media probably did."

"But do you think Salcombe was capable of making it, well, a more personal thing?"

Comber frowned. "How do you mean?"

"Forget it." Scott shook his head. "It's nothing."

"Nothing? But you didn't come here to talk about nothing!" Comber got up, took Scott's glass, and poured more whisky. Scott found that odd, because he barely remembered drinking the first lot! It was all about how hard he was concentrating, how determined he was to track this thing down, how badly he needed some form of closure. But was it really closure he wanted? Or was he in fact seeking revenge?

"Well," said Comber, "what else can I tell you?"

"About these pictures." Scott went to the desk and picked up the group shot of the three sick children in their hospital beds. "How did you ever get permission to go inside St. Jude's and photograph these poor kids?"

"We didn't." Comber shrugged. "It was an intern. A junior doctor who had about as much faith in Salcombe as Kelly and the rest of us. He took this shot secretly, just after Salcombe and the people who were with him cleared the ward."

Now it was Scott's turn to frown. "Three kids in this picture," he said. "Also in those other shots . . . but only two sets of parents?"

Comber nodded. "That third kid, the youngest, he was there out of an orphanage. How's *that* for a hell of a note? No Ma, no Da . . . just pernicious anemia. Doesn't it get you right there?"

"Yes, it certainly does," said Scott, thinking, *So that's what they were sick with.* "It makes you question a whole lot of things." Then, picking up the rest of the photographs he asked, "What about these other pictures of the children? Did that same intern take them?"

Again Comber's nod. "He was trying to make a little money on the side. He was going to get some 'before and after' shots, sell them to us and do some debunking of his own. But he wasn't much of a photographer. Either that or his camera was some kind of cheap foreign model. I mean, just look at these photographs. They have to be some of the worst shots you ever saw! Or there again, maybe it was the Salcombe influence."

"Come again?" Scott thought he was missing something here.

"Like I told you," said Comber. "Whenever Simon Salcombe's around nothing seems to work. For example: Kelly's picture when she got up close and personal with him outside St. Jude's. Just take a look at it."

"I've looked at it," said Scott. "Your strip of film, too."

"That, too," Comber agreed. "We couldn't use it so I binned it. I kept the bit with Kelly on it; dropped it in your letter box on my way home one night, along with copies of the intern's crappy pictures."

But Scott was again looking at the group photograph of the three children, the shot that had been taken after Salcombe and the others had left the hospital. It was something he'd noticed—or half noticed—before, but he'd taken it to be an effect of either poor lighting, a faulty camera, or the quality of the photography in general.

Comber saw Scott's deepening frown and said, "What now? Is there something?"

"Do you have a magnifier?"

"Eh? Yes, sure. Hey, I'm a photographer!" And rummaging in a drawer in his desk, Comber produced a magnifying glass with a light. "It's also good for reading road maps at night," he said. "Can't promise the battery is any good though. I don't drive at night anymore and haven't used it in a long time."

Scott took the magnifier, switched it on, gave it a shake until he saw the small bulb glimmer into reluctant life. Still frowning, he took extra care in studying the picture: a row of three children in their hospital beds, one too weak to look at the camera, another with a thin little grin on his face, actually waving, the third with his bald, baby-bird head tilted on one side, lolling there, looking for all the world like it was about to snap off at the neck. They were all bald in fact, all hollow-eyed boys, and all in deep, terminal trouble. But—

"Are these kids wearing bandages?" Scott's voice was very quiet, musing, almost as if he spoke to himself. "Some kind of cotton wool bandages on their wrists? What do you make of this, Bill?"

Comber took the magnifier, squinted through it, said, "No, that has to be fuzz on the camera lens. Didn't I say this bloke was a lousy photographer? Couldn't even clean the lens off!"

"Fuzz?" Scott wasn't convinced. "Three lots of fuzz on the one picture, and all of it obscuring those kids' wrists? That's some kind of coincidence, isn't it?" He took back the magnifier to use on the individual photographs this time, and said, "More fuzz here, too. And again it's on their wrists . . ."

"So maybe I'm wrong and it isn't fuzz?" Comber was looking baffled. "Maybe they'd been given shots for their illness, some kind of chemo or mild radioactive treatment. Hey, I'm a photographer not a doctor!"

Even less convinced, Scott shook his head. "No, and you're no scientist either. Mild radiation couldn't have done this. If it was radioactivity it would have to be hard. But *hard* radiation? In a children's ward? And if that were so the whole photograph would be ruined, not just these small areas. So this has to be—I don't know"—he shook his head again—"something else? Yes, and something very strange . . . very different."

Scott returned to studying the group photograph and for a while was silent. But then—once again in that quiet, musing voice, almost a whisper—he queried, "What *is* this? Is there something . . . something wrong with their wrists?" And giving a sudden, massive involuntary start, jerking as if galvanized as memories and images conjured by his own words flooded his mind with ice water, he husked, "Yes . . . it's on their left wrists!" Then:

Comber snapped back in his chair and almost toppled it as suddenly Scott leaned right over the desk, grabbed up the

strip of discarded footage, and in anything but a quiet mode
snarled, "God Almighty! *Damn it to hell!*"

"Whoah!" Comber rocked forward again, sat up very
straight and stiff-backed, and said, "What the . . . ? I mean,
what's *wrong,* St. John? What is it?"

Shooting Comber a fierce glance, Scott growled, "Eh?
What is it?" But a moment later he blinked, shook his head,
and said, "I . . . I don't know what it is." And as quickly as
that he was in his musing mode again—quiet but not quite
calm, his hands trembling a little—as he stared at the film
strip under the lens of the faintly glowing magnifier: those
badly blurred and jerky frames that showed Salcombe as he
grabbed at Kelly, holding her for a moment before thrusting
her away.

And repeating himself, but hoarse-voiced now, Scott
said, "I'm not sure . . . I don't know what it is." And then,
his tone of voice hardening, "But one way or the other, I'm
definitely going to find out!"

For there it was again, the blur that he'd seen before in
Kelly's study when he'd suspected that he was missing
something—and indeed he had been. That selfsame fuzzy
area that showed up on the wrists of those kids in the photographs.

As for that look on Salcombe's face: Scott saw now that
it expressed a lot more than mere shock or surprise. In fact,
Kelly was looking more surprised than Salcombe! Probably
at the speed of his reaction: a rapid reaction indeed . . . perhaps because he wasn't surprised at all, because he'd been
expecting her to put in an appearance! Oh, the man's hatred
was there as before, but it was masking emotions other than
hate. One more at least.

And Scott saw it now.

Salcombe's was the look of a killer as he drives the knife
in; his was the lightning strike of the cobra, sinking deep its
fangs to inject its venom. And where Salcombe's fingers
gripped Kelly's wrist—her *left* wrist—there was that same
blurred area, Bill Comber's "fuzz."

Scott began stuffing the photographs, film strip, and

newspaper article back into the envelope . . . then paused. There was one last thing he needed to know, at least for the time being.

"Bill," he said to the now completely sober, wide-eyed man sitting behind the desk. "There's something else you might be able to tell me . . . about these pictures of the kids. In their individual shots they all look a little bit better than in the group photograph. But if they were in the final stage of their disease, getting sicker day by day, how can that be? Some kind of brief remission, or what?"

"Or what," said the other, emerging cautiously from behind his desk. "I mean, it's the damnedest thing! Remission? You can say that again! But we didn't run the story; in fact, no one has run it—not even the more sensation-seeking rags! Why? Because One: nobody gives a damn for sodding Salcombe, and won't do his advertising for him. Two: because it's just too weird, a one in a billion freak that can't ever happen again. And why should we put every parent with a sick child through all that, eh? They'd all want what isn't possible, and all they'd get is hurt."

"They'd get hurt?" Scott repeated him. "A one in a billion freak? What do you mean? What kind of freak?"

"The freakish kind, of course!" Comber replied. "St. John, listen. I don't know how they work their miracles at St. Jude's Children's Hospital and I can't say how it happened. But as for Salcombe's involvement, well, that was a coincidence, of course. But I can tell you this: inside three weeks those kids were out of their beds, running riot in that place. What's more, I have it on good authority that they've all made a full recovery . . ."

Comber saw him out of the house. In the porch Scott offered his hand and his thanks. "This has been a real help," he said. "I'm seeing things a lot clearer now. I only hope I haven't been too much trouble." He was being cool, calm, deliberately playing it down.

"No trouble," said Comber, still mystified as to what this was all about. "But, St. John—you take it easy, right?"

"Yes, of course." Scott nodded, knowing full well that he wasn't going to take it easy. And breathing deeply of the night air he went back to his car.

A full moon sat low over distant roofs and it was a beautiful night. Scott hardly noticed. He sat in the car, wound down his window, and lit a cigarette. Sitting there smoking, he tried to put his thoughts in order. But it wasn't easy. Even here, in a stranger's garden on a quiet night in early June, still there were distractions. One distraction at least: a distant, insistent barking. A dog's voice—as sharp as a well-honed knife—slicing through the still night air.

The animal itself might be more than a mile away, but its barking, punctuated with brief bursts of howling, sounded crisp and clear in Scott's ears. It seemed odd, though, that he heard no answering cries from other dogs . . . But that aside, the more he listened the more he felt able to interpret this one's barking; well, its meaning in general: an acceptable notion because obviously it must mean something. Dogs are intelligent and this one might be protecting its master's property from prowlers, or it had treed a cat, or it was simply tracking a bitch's spoor.

But somehow Scott didn't think so. It wasn't like any kind of barking he'd ever heard before. Neither warning, threat, nor challenge, it was more as if this animal was asking a question. The same vexed question over and over again.

Well, it wasn't the only one. Scott St. John had troubling questions of his own, too many of them. And stubbing his cigarette, he wound up his window, started the car, and backed out of Comber's garden into the road . . .

As Scott headed for home a now familiar thought—more properly a phrase or phrases—returned to haunt him:

"If you sense anything strange, keep your distance but try to explore it. Think about what has happened to you—your loss—but think coldly, without anger, pain, or passion."

Well, he *had* sensed something strange, and while he wasn't sure how well he'd kept his distance, he had certainly tried to explore it. But on the other hand, back there at Comber's, he'd totally ignored his mystery woman's words of warning until just before leaving. Passion? Oh, he had displayed plenty of that—though more out of sheer frustration than anger—while as for keeping his cool, well obviously that wasn't his forte.

But the girl, woman, mystery person had also said: "Don't search for me. When it's time I shall find you." All very well, but when it was time for what? As far as Scott was concerned it was time right now—for whatever! And it was certainly time to have a closer look at Simon Salcombe. Or then again, maybe not. Maybe Salcombe was the one she'd warned him to stay away from.

She, she, *she!* Scott would find her if he could, despite that she'd told him not to. For she had also admitted that she didn't understand all of this herself, which surely meant that she understood some of it. Frustrating? The whole bloody thing just went around and around!

When an oncoming car's headlights momentarily blinded him, Scott wrenched his mind free of this fatiguing, endless enigma, this maze without an exit, and concentrated on his driving. He certainly wouldn't want to get picked up again, not with whisky on his breath. But the thought of being picked up only reminded him of his . . . well, what could he call them? Kidnappers? Those Secret Service types? No, hardly that, not any longer. In fact, the more Scott thought about them the more he was reminded of a certain voice he *thought* he'd heard when he was standing before that two-way mirror in the police station.

It had been *her* voice, of course, even though she herself wasn't there. And when she'd said, "Don't concern yourself with them," he'd known she meant his Secret Service types. Moreover, Scott had even believed he could sense their presence somewhere close by. In which circumstances it was hardly surprising that he'd also believed he was losing it!

But no longer. Scott knew he was somehow different from the man he'd once been—even radically different—but he wasn't crazy. And he remembered how his mystery woman had assured him that there was no harm in those Secret Service types, that the harm lay elsewhere. But if only she'd said where . . .

Scott was glad that he was almost home, for even above the sound of his car's motor he could *still* hear that dog's insistent barking! Now, pulling into his driveway, he brought the car to a halt and went to wind up his window—

—Only to discover that it was already up! He'd wound it up before leaving Comber's place. Then, as he turned the key in the ignition and the silence fell, Scott wondered, *What the . . . ?* Which in fact was him answering one question with another question . . . which in turn was what someone had wanted. And a very strange someone at that.

For the barking had become something else entirely. It was still a dog's voice, yes, except that now it made sense and was inside Scott's head!

When are you coming for me? said Three. *Each day they hunt for me, and this place has become too dangerous. If you are The One you must come for me soon . . .*

Sitting motionless in the car—listening so intently that the silence pressed on him like a physical weight and his heart thudded with a pile-driver's force—Scott shook like a leaf in a gale. He wasn't afraid; he felt shock and astonishment, definitely, but it wasn't fear. And it was no longer disbelief. This time he accepted what was happening. He accepted that while his *ears* heard the tick, tick, tick of his vehicle's cooling motor, his *mind* heard something else entirely:

Why are you silent? If you were The One you would hear and answer me!

"I *do* hear you," Scott finally whispered. "I *can* hear you! But . . . but I don't know where you are!" He really didn't know what else to say.

Scott "heard" a vexed whining, a low growl, and sensed a single sniff at herb- and resin-laden air. Until finally: *Then I must find a way to show you,* said Three. *But promise me that when next I call you will hear me.* And:

"Yes," said Scott, nodding if only to himself, and however pointlessly. "Absolutely. Whatever you say."

With which Three sprang away and was gone—vanished from his mind, fled into the high, the wild, and to Scott the as yet unknown places—leaving him sitting in the car, alone with his whirling thoughts and tingling scalp . . .

12

Scott hadn't been down into his compact cellar gymnasium since the day Kelly died. But needing the exercise, and badly in need of a good night's sleep, he had decided on a thorough workout. He would work hard at it for as long as it took to wear himself out *physically* . . . as for mentally: no problem, for in that area he already felt exhausted! And after his workout he would take a cold shower before turning in.

Stripped down to shorts and rubber-soled shoes, he worked on the weights, on the wall and parallel bars, and especially on the overhead beam, chinning himself until the muscles in his arms, shoulders, and neck felt like jelly, then easing off for a minute or two for fear of hurting himself. Then he went to work on the punch bag, which he also used as a kick bag, trying his best to kick and punch all of his pent-up frustrations (his "passions"?) right out of his system. At least for tonight.

And while he worked at it for well over an hour—trying and testing his body, and using it in ways that he hadn't possessed the will to use it in for some sixteen weeks—so Scott's thoughts turned to what he had learned tonight. Not to his bizarre contact with an apparently telepathic dog, though he could hardly ignore it; neither to that nor to those other incredible events in which it appeared he had somehow become involved, but to something that for now he must continue to consider mundane by comparison and therefore accessible.

And over and over again as he sweated it out, Scott found himself focusing on that single question that had now become one of the most important things in his world, his entire life:

If a man—not one of faith and integrity but one who was vile and evil—if such a man's hands were gifted with healing powers that enabled him to cure the sick, extending and improving life . . . might he not also be empowered to shorten and even destroy it? That was the question that Scott continually asked himself, even knowing that he could never ask it of any member of any orthodox medical profession.

There were, however, other questions—allied but safer and more reasonably sane questions—that tomorrow he could put to the staff at St. Jude's, and not least to the doctors at Kelly's private hospital. He would, he simply *must* ask them, even if by involving himself, failing to remain "distant," he went against the advice of his mystery woman.

It was as simple as that: Scott couldn't any longer remain distant (whatever that meant, and if it was what he'd been trying to do) for there were things he had to know.

All of these thoughts and resolutions hurrying through his head as he began to climax his workout with a series of karate disciplines: whirling, falling flat and sweeping with his feet, rolling, leaping high and striking; then back to the punch bag, working on it until the leather was red and wet and his aching body dripped sweat and his torn knuckles dripped blood . . .

But then, seeing the blood, Scott knew he had to stop. And dragging himself upstairs, it was time for his shower.

Scott dreamed of his father, Jeremy St. John, a true blue blood if ever there was one, and from a long line of the same. Jeremy had frequently declared that he'd married "beneath himself—to a girl with a pretty face and the morals of an alley cat." This after discovering one of his wife's affairs and divorcing her. The scandal had developed while Jeremy was serving at an embassy in the Far East. More complicated than a majority of marital breakdowns, his wife's refusal to leave her lover and return to England had sealed her fate and destroyed her utterly. Not only had Jeremy washed his hands of her, he had marooned her, literally penniless, in Hong Kong. Following which he had done whatever was necessary to "live it down" and forget that she'd ever existed.

At three years of age and with no say in the matter, Scott St. John had been obliged to do likewise and forget his mother. But it hadn't been easy because he'd loved her. And four years later she had died a diseased alcoholic drug addict's death in a Singapore opium den.

As for Jeremy St. John: he had outlived her for more than two decades . . .

And now, for the first time in his life, Scott walked with his father in a dream; at least one facet of which was the same as in his last awful nightmare of Kelly in the hospital: namely that Scott's father didn't seem capable of speech! It was as if he'd been struck dumb! Moreover, Scott somehow knew that he too was without voice, just as he'd been when he sat beside Kelly's bed holding her hand. The urge to converse was there, but something prevented it: an invisible barrier standing between Scott and his father, just as it had between him and Kelly. And so he knew that this wasn't simply familial disassociation.

And despite that he preferred not to be reminded yet again of that revelatory dream, Scott felt obliged to reexamine it:

Before her horrific *collapse*, Kelly, too, had been incapable of speech. She'd attracted Scott's attention with her eyes, and with them directed him to the source of her problem, her wrist. Then she'd corroborated his understanding, not with words but a nod of her head. Similarly, Scott had made no sound—well, not until he'd started awake . . .

And so now, knowing he was once again without voice, Scott contained his natural desire to speak (though weird as it felt, he sensed that he would be able to converse . . . *just as soon as he learned how!*). As if there were some medium in certain dreams that only permitted of conversation between those who knew its secret wavelength. And for now, since Scott was unfamiliar with this medium, his dream must remain devoid of sound . . . which in turn and for some reason reminded him of an old expression:

"The silence of the tomb—"

—And certainly of this graveyard, where he and his father walked. His father: a stiff, sombre man, in an expensive Savile Row pinstripe; but a man with blurred and unrecognizable features, mainly because Scott couldn't remember, or didn't want to remember, how he had looked. Yet now they walked together among the tombstones.

Coincidentally, Scott's Kelly was buried in this selfsame cemetery, but her plot lay to the south while Jeremy St. John's lay to the north. That was where they were walking now, Jeremy and his son, toward his marker. Scott had visited him here on one occasion only; that had been enough; he hadn't seen why he should spend time at the grave of a man who had never had much time for him. Indeed, the only thing Scott would ever have any reason to thank his father for was the pittance of a legacy he had bequeathed to him, which had let him complete the language studies that now furnished him with a living. That and nothing more. But there again, Scott's father hadn't by any means been rich when he died—his second wife had seen to that. For history repeats, and he had married "beneath himself" again—but this time to a spendthrift.

And Scott just might have thought, *Well good luck to her!* Except even his thoughts were muted now; he couldn't hear them in his head; it was as if his brain fired blanks . . .

Anyway, so much for his father. Scott didn't hate or even dislike him, he simply didn't know him. Yet here in this misty evening graveyard he walked with him, without even knowing why. It was the way of dreams. They were ever mysterious, and Scott St. John's dreams even more so.

They had reached Jeremy St. John's marker; Scott's father stood with bowed head before it, while Scott seated himself on the raised pedestal and read the name, the dates, and the legend: "A Man of Manners, a Man of Breeding." That was all. This would have been his father's chosen epitaph, of course. But he probably wouldn't have wished the same for Scott, whose mother had been "a woman with the morals of an alley cat."

And once again wondering why he was here, Scott looked at his father and saw something he'd never thought to see: tears, running down that mainly blank face! And even as he stared, so that face began to assume the angular features he had known as a child: the features of a proud, not unhandsome man—and one who had once loved him.

So then, perhaps there had been that about Scott's father which was worth remembering after all. Those oh-so-brief years of his love. While as for pride . . . of what use that to a dead man? And now:

Jeremy St. John got down beside his son, pointed to those words on his stone, and traced them with his finger. He mouthed something; Scott heard nothing, but he saw what his father had traced—"A Man of Manners, a Man of Breeding"—and he also saw where he was now pointing: directly at Scott himself! And still crying, his father touched his own heart, shook his head, and denied his own epitaph. His meaning was obvious: Scott was the more mannered of the two, and while breeding was of little or no consequence without compassion, whatever Jeremy St. John had possessed of it, the best of it had carried down to Scott.

Not all of this had been "said," no, but Scott understood it anyway.

And now, suddenly, his father embraced him, and Scott was surprised at himself that he allowed it!

He allowed it, while suppressing the thought: *Better late than never!*—another old saw—which in any case the unknown medium smothered before it could take form in his head. And to complete Scott's astonishment, he now found himself comforting his father and patting his shuddering back. And he *felt* rather than heard an oh-so-faint tremor coming right through the dead man's chest . . . not only the sobbing, but *words* he would never have thought to hear (or even to feel) from Jeremy St. John:

Son, I'm sorry! In turning my back on you because of your mother I did you wrong. It was my pride. Guilty of many things—but especially of my coldness toward you—I have lain here a long time, but without my pride. Guilty and knowing it, yes, but unable to ask for your forgiveness until now.

Until now, when Scott couldn't answer?

Clutching his father more tightly yet and trying to force words from a throat with no vocal chords, Scott felt desperate in his need to console this poor man. But there was nothing he could do. He didn't know the nature of the esoteric medium . . .

There came an interruption; something called Scott, tugging at him. A cold wind blew and he fell against the headstone, which at once dissolved beneath him even as his father had dissolved! And where it had been evening, now in the east a silver thread heralded dawn in the sky over pale, amethyst-rimmed hills.

The graveyard was gone; Scott smelled flowers rather than mould, and his sense of smell had never been more acute! There were many scents, several that he couldn't put a name to along with others that he could. Aniseed, wild thyme, and pine resin, together with a salt tang off the sea. But what sea?

And why was he viewing an unknown horizon from down among these coarse, spiky grasses?

Because that is where I am lying on my belly, said Three. *I called you and you came. It appears that you must be my One!*

Scott's mind whirled. A wolf's thoughts were in his head, and he saw and sensed this foreign place with a wolf's senses! "I . . . I was dreaming," he said, not knowing what else to say.

You still are, said Three, *but it is more than a dream, I know about dreams, for wolves dream, too. You are far easier to reach when you are dreaming. There are no barriers.*

"Barriers?"

Like dense woods and brambles—or steep cliffs and broad rivers—but all in your mind! Awake, you put up your barriers, which makes it far more difficult to reach you. Don't you remember? How not so long ago I called out to you? I tried and tried to reach you but you failed to answer me. I had almost given up before you heard me.

Scott nodded. "Yes, of course I remember. And I'm sorry if I have been difficult." And then he looked around—but through a wolf's eyes. The crack of silver light on the eastern horizon was brighter now and the dawn chorus was well under way.

Scott (or his host) was lying on gritty soil on a hillside burgeoning with herbs and flowers. Below, cut into the hill and following its contours through wind-warped Mediterranean pines, a road ribboned away to a village some two or three miles distant. Almost every house and building in the village was painted blue and white, and was roofed with either fish-scale slates or terracotta pantiles. Set back from the village and climbing the slopes, olive groves were plentiful.

The village nestled in a bay in the lee of the brightening hills, where the sea was dark blue against dark yellow beaches. This could be one of many places: Spain, Italy, Greece, Turkey, the French Riviera. When the sun came up, Scott would be better able to decide.

When the sun comes up, said Three, *I shall be on my way to a cave in the high hills where the hunters can't find me.*

"Hunters? In this day and age?"

I'm a wolf of the wild, Three growled, *as my father before me . . . before he found his Zek. I eat meat, and sometimes I grow weary of rabbits. But in the farms around they keep chickens. I like chickens, but the farmers do not like me. I carry metal in my tail where it is raw.* (A wolf shrug.) *It will heal in time.*

"You understand the principle of time?"

The sun comes up, the sun goes down. That is time. I don't know about principles.

"Do you know where we are?" Scott was curious now. He

knew this was a dream, or more than a dream, but it was also fascinating.

We are on a hill, said Three impatiently, *in a place where there are trees, flowers, wild things, machines on roads carrying men, and houses where men live and keep their weapons. That is where we are.* It was Three's understanding of things, a wild wolf's point of view.

"You're real, aren't you," said Scott, more a statement of fact than a question.

Real? As real as you, I think! I know things; sometimes I am glad, often sad, especially so now that my mother and brothers are gone. Sometimes I hurt, when I cut a paw. And sometimes I am afraid, when I hear the hunters and their weapons.

And wryly, Scott said, "You think, therefore you are!" But not wanting to explain, he went on: "You mentioned your father, a wolf of the wild before he met Zek. But who is Zek?"

She is his One. They live there, with a man. Three turned his head, redirecting Scott's gaze to a place in the trees set back from the winding road down toward cliffs with the deep sea beyond. A pantiled roof showed red in the dawning light, where blue wood smoke rose from a chimney. *Zek's man is not a hunter. He is called Jazz. So my father tells me.*

"And no one hunts your father?"

No, of course not! Three growled. *Have you not understood? He has his Zek; he is no longer a wolf of the wild! But he was, once in a far different place. You ask too many questions. And there is something I want you to see before full daylight—by which time I must be gone from here.*

"Show me, then," Scott told him. "And the reason I ask my questions is to understand better. For if I don't know where to find you, then how may I come for you?"

That is what I want to show you, Three replied, getting up and loping low through dry, spiky shrubs.

He headed for the pines, moved under them in the direction of the road, stepped carefully where the pine needles lay thick underfoot on the stony ground. And soon he (or they?) came to a scarp some twelve feet high where the road had been cut through the rock of the hillside.

Pausing there, tongue lolling, flat on his belly again and looking down from this vantage point, Scott's host said, *There! Do you see?*

Scott looked—where Three looked, obviously—and for a while saw nothing of any special significance. Some twenty-five yards to the right, where the main road led away from the village, there was a junction of potholed tracks, one leading down to the sea, apparently, while another cut inland. And directly across the main road from where Scott (or his host) was perched above the defile, there a pebble path wound through the twisted pines to the barely glimpsed villa that Three had said was his father's home, along with "Zek" and a man called "Jazz."

Scott looked again at the road and secondary tracks, none of which might truly be called "main roads" by the standards of British highways, and saw that they were signposted . . . at which he at once understood what he was seeing and knew why Three had brought him here.

Yes, said Three. *Men come in their noisy rolling machines. They are strangers, not local. Like you, they do not know where they are. They stop, look at the signs, then go their different ways. These signs are the spoor used by men!*

Signposts! Of course they were Man's "spoor"!

Men use their eyes to find their way, said Three. *I use my nose. A wolf's way is better. But since I was struck by my dart even my nose is inferior. Now I could find my way . . . anywhere! I don't know how, but I do know that there are places out there beyond the sea that are . . . BIG!*

"There are indeed," said Scott. "As for your dart: I find that very interesting, and you must tell me about it when there is time. Also about Zek and Jazz. But right now—can we move a little closer to that signpost?"

As you wish. But then I must be gone. Three got up, shook himself, made his way along the steeply sloping rim of the cutting to a point as close to the junction of road and tracks as he could get without emerging from the cover of the pines. And now Scott could read the signpost. It was in Greek, large white lettering on a blue background; and beneath the Greek in smaller characters, their English equivalent. The signpost arm that pointed in the direction of the village said, "Porto Zoro. 5 Km.," a second arm said simply "Beach," and a third, pointing inland along the track, said "Dafni" and "Ano Vassilikos."

"Greece," said Scott, both to himself and to Three. But as for where in Greece: that was something he would want to check later—*if* he remembered!

You will remember, said Three. *If not call me, and I will show you again. But One—if you are my One, which I believe—don't leave me here too long. Now I must go, for she will speak to you. I sense her close to you.*

With which he turned and sprang away from Scott, or rather from his mind.

Feeling himself drifting, Scott called out, "Wait!" But in a single instant a vast darkness had crashed down on him like a shroud. Yet still he cried out, "Three, wait! There are so many things to talk about. What of this 'she'? Who she? Which she?"

The Two she. Three's wolf voice was only a sigh now, gradually fading. *You are One, she is Two, and I am Three.*

"Listen," Scott called into the darkness. "I accept that I am your One, but I have another name. I'm called Scott. You can call me Scott. And, Three, we have to talk!"

But not now, came a far faint echo. *For the sun comes up, and there are goats in the hills and the men who guard them. I can avoid them in the dim dawn light but not in full daylight. And the climb is long and the way is hard. I go . . .*

And he was indeed gone—

—But still Scott wasn't alone. He sensed a presence and heard a quiet voice urgently speaking his name. "Scott! Scott, wake up!" It wasn't in his head this time but in his ears, and it was real. It was a woman's voice . . . in his room . . . and he believed he knew which woman.

Fighting his tired, aching body he stirred, forced himself

back to consciousness as again that earnest voice said, "Scott, please wake up now!"

With a strangled cry he came awake, and in the darkness of his room, for a single moment, he thought it was Kelly standing there beside his bed! He cried out, fumbled with the light cord, and finally gave it a yank, then snatched himself into a seated position and shielded his eyes against the sudden glare. And as his eyes grew accustomed to the brightness—as Scott realized the error of his troubled mind, the yawning hole that was there where a very special someone had been—he knew that the figure standing beside his bed was not and couldn't possibly have been his Kelly.

But at least he had been correct in his recognition of the voice. For it was his mystery woman. It was Two . . .

13

It was 3:33, Scott knew it without even glancing at his bedside alarm clock. But right now the time wasn't of the least importance. And as for his dream of Three, it was already fading from his mind.

Or maybe it wasn't. Maybe he was still dreaming and it had simply changed to this! But the woman shook her head. "No," she said, "you're awake now—to certain things anyway. May I sit?"

Scott's bedclothes covered him to his waist; beneath them he was naked. "Sit?" he vacantly repeated her, and with a small start, still not fully in command of his senses: "Oh, *sit!* Yes, of course!" He indicated a corner of the bed. "But facing away from me, if you don't mind. I'm going to get up."

And fumbling with his trousers—as the initial shock wore off and the true nature of the situation dawned on him—Scott gasped, "*What?* What in the . . . !? You? Here? I've been wanting to find you, talk to you, but—"

"Can I face you now?" she said, sounding closer, her soft voice no longer urgent.

Tucking in his shirt, Scott turned and saw that she hadn't sat down; she was already "facing," or rather watching him, and probably had been when he got out of bed! She was also approaching him, her eyes widening, staring at his skinned knuckles and bruised left cheek where the punch bag had punched back; and at his upper rib cage, grazed and bruised from multiple collisions with the bar when he'd chinned it more forcefully than necessary. Her expression mirrored genuine concern.

He sensed her questions coming and read them: *Why are you damaged?* (Not hurt but damaged.) *How did it happen?*

He read these questions in her mind, and knowing she could read *his* mind at once erected his shields (Three's "barriers"?) against any further invasion of his privacy. And again—as at least once before—he wondered: *How in hell do I do that!?*

"Are you afraid to tell me?" she said. "Were you attacked, or was it an accident? Oh, and didn't I tell you to be careful? You don't know how important you are!" And before he could move to avoid her she reached out a slender hand to touch his cheek, then his chest. But from the first contact—her fingers on his face—Scott didn't want to move. It wasn't a sexual or even a sensual thing; it was simply very calming, very soothing. And:

"I . . . I was exercising," he said. "Probably a little too roughly." And blinking sleep from his eyes: "Maybe I was trying to burn off some excess 'passion'?" He stared at her, searched for a response. "You know? So that I could think 'coldly, without anger, pain, or—' "

"—Passion." She nodded. "Yes, I understand." Her fingertips were light, cool as they traced the rough, grazed skin of Scott's chest. And for all that her touch wasn't what he might have expected, still when she withdrew her hand his flesh continued to tingle.

The ceiling light had been flickering—even buzzing and sputtering a little, from the moment she touched him—but now it burned steadily again. A minor problem at the power station, Scott supposed. That happened now and then.

Buttoning his shirt, he asked, "How did you find me?" And then, checking his alarm clock—even though he knew what time it was going to be—"And what do you think you're doing here at this time of night . . . or anytime for that matter! And how did you get in?"

"Ah!" she said, and for the first time since approaching him she blinked, lowered her eyes, looked away. "How I arrived here, and my getting in here: I think these are questions best left until later. We have plenty of other things to talk about. I'm sure there are many things that we both want to know."

Putting on slippers, Scott said, "That woman in the newsagent's. She gave you my card, right?"

She shook her head. "No, I haven't been back there. But I *always* know where you are. I've known that ever since . . . well, almost four months now. And like Three I can reach out to you. Most of the time."

Scott shook his head in bewilderment. He felt like pinching himself but was sure it wouldn't work; it hadn't thus far, anyway. "I need a coffee," he said. "We should go downstairs."

On their way they passed Kelly's study. Scott didn't remember leaving the door open, but now it was. His mystery woman paused there, took a deep, slow breath, and said, "Kelly's room. She worked here."

And suddenly Scott was angry. Taking the woman's elbow he said, "Come on, you've got some explaining to do!"

Pulling free, but gently, she said, "That's why I'm here. To explain if I can, and if you'll let me." And then she followed him down the stairs . . .

He made coffee; she accepted a mug; they sat in his study, and Scott actually found himself apologising for the general untidiness of the place!

"But you haven't been yourself," she said. "It's difficult to carry on, to adjust when . . . when things around you

change." And Scott knew that she had almost said *when you
lose something special* (not someone but something), because he'd heard it like an echo in his head! And knowing
he'd heard it, she said, "Yes, that, too: when almost *everything* changes. You know, of course, that you are not the
same, that you have changed?"

Scott didn't answer at once. After all, he was the one who
should be asking the questions! Instead he just sat there
looking at her, getting her fixed in his mind, so that in the
future he would remember and be able to describe her, if
only to himself. By which time he might even have found
out who or what she was!

Right now, though, he didn't even know her name.

"My name is Shania Two, or simply Shania," she said
then, because he had let his shields down. He went to
reerect, reinforce them—and didn't. Why should he when
he had nothing to hide? In another time and place, in the
company of a woman with the looks of this one, Scott or almost any other man might wish to keep his innermost
thoughts concealed. But that was the last thing on his mind.

And so he sat there, silent for now and rapt in the weirdness of it all, looking at her and wondering what she would
say next. And over and above everything else, Scott was
fully aware that Shania Two, or "simply Shania," was completely and utterly different. But:

"No, not utterly." She shook her head, then sat still, as if
to allow Scott's inspection. Except now *her* shields were up,
making this a purely visual and entirely physical thing as
opposed to metaphysical.

She was five-seven or -eight and her smoky hair framed
her face like dusk, yet somehow managed to be as deep as
space. But Scott needn't look any farther . . . he knew full
well where he'd seen her like this before, and it wasn't in a
newsagent's shop.

He looked anyway: at those slightly tilted eyes, as green
as fine jade, yet by no means wholly oriental—perhaps
Eurasian?—which were suddenly and completely familiar
to him. Yes, definitely, he had looked into them before. And

her skin, with its smoky saffron or olive tints, or something between the two, natural-seeming but yet so smooth and perfect it might well be the product of rare, expensive cosmetics, though Scott was sure that it wasn't. Her perfect neck, delicate ears, straight nose, and ample mouth; but especially those stars, shining luminously in the depths of her emerald eyes.

Oh, Scott had seen her before and knew where: in what he'd half considered a drugged dream as he lay on the backseat of a car while those Secret Service types drove him home! But remembering that, a sudden niggling doubt caused him to ask: "You're not one of them, are you?" His shields were down, which allowed Shania to know who and what he meant.

"No," she said. "But in any case they are not our concern. They're watchers, protectors, guardians. And as long as that is *all* they are, and so long as we are not compromised, we needn't worry about them."

"Then we do have something to worry about?"

"I do, certainly," she answered. "And if you wish to right a great wrong—indeed a great many wrongs—so do you. So does Three, and not only because of his situation. He, too, has been empowered, and why else if not to assist us? We are three."

"You know that Three is a dog," said Scott. "Well, in fact he's a wolf—or so he says. But you *do* know that, right? That he's only a wolf?"

"Only?" she replied. "But Three *is* empowered, changed just as you were changed—made cogent and caused to be different—and at the same time. It's important that you believe that."

Scott took a sip of coffee. "Me?" he said then. "I'm different, 'changed'? Well, I know that *you* are different for sure! But why should I believe that *I* have somehow been changed?"

"Because until you believe I can't explain further. Scott, you were not extraordinary but now you are. And I know you know that to be true. If you *didn't* you would have

called the police and had me arrested for this invasion of
your home. Yet here we sit and talk." She paused for a moment, then went on:

"And you, you *were* arrested—taken into custody of
sorts—by men who tried to prove you are possessed of
powers. And I know you have considered your own sanity,
and I understand why. It was because of your dreams, your
nightmares, the connections you've made . . . with a wolf,
yes, and with me. As for telepathy: you *know* it to be real!
You've seen it in use and used it yourself . . . with me, here,
tonight. If that isn't sufficient proof of your elevation, then
tell me what is."

"My 'elevation'?"

She nodded. "Your senses are six, and there are powers in
you, burgeoning even now. I don't know what they are, but I
do know they're growing stronger."

Scott stood up, paced to and fro. "And you understand all
of this, right? Everything that's going on?"

"What? Oh, how I *wish!*" she answered fervently. "I understand *my* side of it, my involvement, yes. I know why I
am here, what I must try to do, but as for what has activated
you: that is a mystery to me. And Three is an even greater
mystery!"

"Funny thing, that," said Scott. "You see, I thought *you*
were the mystery! But okay, you're right, I have been
changed, yes. And I think I know when that change occurred. It happened in the small hours of the morning on
the day—"

"—The day that Kelly died," Shania finished it for him,
without reading his mind. "Yes, I know—because that was
what brought you to my attention. From afar I heard you cry
out . . ."

Scott blinked, but he was more able to accept such state-
ments now. And so, nodding, he said, "That's when it happened, yes. So why have you waited so long before
approaching me? And why did you *want* to approach me in
the first place?"

"But I *have* approached you!" Shania answered. "Surely

you know that? I was certain that you had felt my presence."

Again, slowly, he nodded. "On the other side of a crowded street, yes. And on a tube train, your face mirrored in a dark window. In other places, too, and then in the newsagent's shop when you finally spoke to me. But somehow, though I don't *know* how, you've never seemed to look the same twice."

Ignoring that last, Shania said, "Scott, I had to speak to you. I feared you might want to . . . well, end things. Your pain was so great I wanted to ease your mind, if only a little."

Scott stopped pacing, thought back on that first meeting, and frowned. "You thought I might be suicidal?" he said. "Well, perhaps I was! And you did ease my mind. Simply by speaking to me, you—"

"No," Shania stopped him. "It wasn't just because I spoke to you. You see, I have powers, too—other than telepathy—but different from yours. You would consider them powers, anyway. But to me they are very natural."

Sitting down again, Scott stared at her across his desk. *Who are you?* he thought, almost without realizing that he was reaching out to her with his mind. But then, coming up against a blank wall, out loud he said, "Or perhaps I should ask what are you? The things you say and do, you're like no one I ever knew before."

"Thank you," she said, simply.

"What?" Scott was completely thrown. "You're thanking me? But why? For what?"

"I think you admire me." Shania smiled, which he couldn't remember her doing before. "And you find me attractive. That's a great compliment, because I really have tried."

"You mean to say other men don't find you attractive?" He could hardly believe it. "And what do you mean, you've tried?"

"I don't know any other . . . men," she answered. "But yes, I've really tried . . ." She gave a shrug, and as quickly as that brushed it aside. "We can talk about it later."

"You're changing the subject," he said.

Shania shook her head. "No, you are. We were talking about certain skills, or powers. And—"

"—And before that about how I've changed," Scott cut in. "But now that I've acknowledged that, isn't it time you told me about yourself, or at least something of what's going on here?"

"Perhaps it is time," she answered cautiously. "The reason I haven't been too forthcoming is simple: until I was sure that you could accept such things I didn't want to burden your mind. For four years I've studied your science, your religions, read your books, and watched your films. Your prisons hold many criminals, and your asylums—even your streets—are filled with disturbed minds. Physically you are strong, but mentally . . . ?"

Scott's frown deepened. "*Our* science, religions, books, and films? Now listen, I've thought of you as a foreigner since the first time I really saw you . . . please forgive me if that makes me sound xenophobic. But whoever you are, whatever your origin, what gives you the right to question my mental balance? No, I'm not going to commit suicide; I've never once considered it! And whatever this is all about, I'm certainly not going to go crazy over it!"

"Oh, Scott!" she said then. "I'm so sorry if I've somehow wronged you, but please let me explain. You see, even if I were to spend another four years here, or ten if we were that fortunate, still certain concepts—human mores, beliefs, emotions, cruelties—would fall beyond my understanding. Remember, too, that while I have only known you at a distance, for a few short months, almost *all* of that time you've been stretched to the breaking point. I simply didn't dare overburden you."

Shania's shields were still up, and Scott was beginning to understand why. He had suddenly realized that she wasn't speaking as someone from any specific foreign country but as someone who was foreign to humanity. Speaking in fact as an alien!

She read him, hesitated, then nodded, *Yes,* in his mind.

Scott believed in telepathy—he could scarcely do otherwise, not any longer—but aliens? Well maybe, and then again maybe not. And narrowing his eyes, he said, "Can you show me?"

"Show you what?"

"Something, anything." He could only shrug. "These powers that you say you have?"

"You want more proof? Other than what you've already seen and experienced? You don't believe me?"

"Yes—no—I mean, I want to—but I want proof anyway." Shania shook her head, seemed disappointed in him. "You'll have more than enough later."

"When, later?" Scott was eager for proof, knowledge, right now, even though he already more than half believed her.

"Later tonight," she said. "When I've gone."

"You're going?" Scott's voice showed his dismay. He didn't want to know that. He wanted to know everything *but* that!

"I must," Shania insisted. "Two minds like ours, together? We're like a beacon! Those people—the ones who 'rescued' you from the police—they are bound to know. And so might others."

"Others?" He was beginning to feel like a small child, the way he seemed to be always repeating her.

Shania's face now wore a very serious expression. Standing up, she walked around Scott's desk to stand beside him where he remained seated, and said, "Scott, I shall say a name. On hearing it things may begin to fall into place. Now is *not* the time for action, however, and I know you for an impulsive man. Which is why once again I'll ask you to remain calm, to think coldly, without anger—"

"—Pain or passion," Scott nodded. "Go on then, speak this name." But he believed he already knew it. And he was right.

Simon Salcombe, she said, in his head. And then, out loud: "But he is only one, and there are others."

Scott growled low in his throat, came to his feet, and took hold of her shoulders. Shania didn't resist him. And staring at her, holding her close, he wondered how much else she knew and, maddeningly, what it was that she knew about!

At the same time, however, he knew this wasn't the way; he *was* angry—if not with Shania—and he *wasn't* thinking coldly, dispassionately. But whatever she knew and whatever she wanted with him, he couldn't force it from her. She would tell him in her own time. And that was probably for his own good.

He released her, moved past her, began pacing the floor of his study to and fro.

But no use to pretend he hadn't been affected. At the back of his neck the short hairs stood erect; his skin tingled as if from the effect of a mild electrical current, and his heart was pounding. Also, like an image printed on his mind's eye, he was seeing again that blurred picture of Simon Salcombe: his spider hand grasping Kelly's left wrist!

Abruptly he turned to Shania. "He killed her, didn't he?"

"I believe so." She nodded. "In fact, I'm certain. But try to understand: as much as you loved her, Kelly was only one and Salcombe has killed . . . oh, a great many. Why, you couldn't even count them! And, Scott, even if you knew where Salcombe was you couldn't accuse or even approach him. He is that dangerous, and he's not alone."

Scott nodded, tried not to scowl but couldn't help it, and said, "In many ways he's like you, isn't he?"

"In certain ways, yes." Shania wouldn't lie about it. "But in other ways, the ways that count, he and I are poles apart. I detest him! In fact, no one is quite like the creature you call Simon Salcombe, except perhaps—"

"Those others you mentioned?"

"Yes." Shania looked at her watch, made a small adjustment, and hurriedly said, "We'll talk again, and very soon, but right now I have to go."

"Not yet!" Scott snapped, turning his angry face away from her and beginning to pace the floor again. "Tell me about these others, Salcombe's friends. How many are they in total, and him included?"

She made no immediate reply. Instead Scott heard the *pop!* of what sounded like a small implosion, also the sound of loose papers fluttering on his desk, and spun on his heel. Shania was no longer there. But before leaving she had answered his question. And:

Three! Her answer came home to him, out of the telepathic aether. And now he knew how she had got in here—or he didn't. Which worked out at precisely the same thing . . .

So much for a good night's sleep.

Scott cleared off the top of his desk and opened an atlas. Searching the index, he found no mention of a Porto Zoro or Ano Vassilikos, but he did find a Dafni: a village standing central in the Peloponnisos. It was Greek, yes, but miles from the sea, and having no view of the Mediterranean or any other large body of water, it couldn't be Three's location.

Then Scott remembered Kelly's collection of fold-out maps. Well into her twenties she had been a consumate sun-worshipper, a Grecophile and regular visitor to the Mediterranean islands. It might well be that she had visited Three's location.

In Kelly's room, he located some two dozen faded, folding tourist information charts and took them down to his study. And he was right: she *had* been to Three's island, but it was almost dawn before he found it. It was Zante—short for Zakynthos in the Ionian Sea—and not far west of the Peloponnisos at that.

All well and good, but simply knowing where it was wasn't going to get him there, and it definitely wouldn't get him out again—not in the company of a wolf of the wild, muzzled and leashed or not! But as Shania had foreseen, things were definitely starting to come together . . .

Scott was tired now; those long hours spent searching through small print had strained his eyes, and his muscles were aching from last night's exercise, though not as much as he had expected. And that pleased him. Maybe he wasn't as much out of shape as he'd thought. Still, an hour or two of sleep wouldn't hurt, and it should certainly freshen and help focus his mind.

In the bathroom, mindful of his bruises as he patted his face dry after laving his eyes with cold water, Scott checked himself out in the mirror—

—And his jaw fell open. His face wasn't bruised at all, his knuckles were no longer raw, and his rib cage wasn't grazed! Indeed, he looked about as well as he could ever remember looking! But then when he thought about it, why not?

It was Shania's touch, one of her powers. Hadn't she told him he would have his proof after she left? And if this wasn't proof what was?

Dawn, and Scott finally climbed into bed. Before sleeping he wondered how Three was doing high in the mountains of Zakynthos, avoiding the hunters. He also wondered how long it would be before he saw Shania again. And soft as a whisper, from not too far away:

Not long, she said. *Not long . . .*

14

High in the Swiss Alps, Herr Gunter Ganzer drove in third gear and at the lowest, safest possible speed up a steeply zigzagging mountain road toward the hollow crest of Schloss Zonigen. While the crag itself, originally nameless, was no more than a trig point on modern maps, its local designation derived first: from its dramatic appearance, and second: from the name of the dubious founder of the complex it housed. "Schloss"—meaning castle—referred to its blackly glittering, ice-sheathed pinnacles and fantastically terraced outcrops, the illusory turrets and battlements of a troll's keep; "Zonigen," to an unqualified "Doktor" Emile Zonigen, the man who had opened up the facility almost thirty years ago. As to its function: it was (allegedly) a cryogenic repository, sanctuary, and experimental laboratory.

Currently and also allegedly, or more properly ostensibly, Herr Ganzer was Schloss Zonigen's "Direktor"; though for the last five years he would much prefer not to have been . . . in fact to have been almost anything and anywhere else in the world . . .

On one of the road's longer straighter stretches, with the snow chains on his BMW's tires reassuringly biting into the ice-crusted surface, Ganzer took the opportunity to look out of his window at a familiar, once-friendly scene. To his right and far below—some two miles distant as viewed across the metal crash barrier—a picture-postcard village lay snug in its sheltering valley; the sun glinting on the roofs and windows of its mainly wooden, chalet-styled houses and taverns, with bluish-grey wood smoke spiralling up from a dozen chimneys. Then, as Ganzer made a slow, careful turn around a hairpin cut through a rocky spur, a different scene opened: that of a cable car descending toward what was once a ski lodge—but no longer.

In season there were still skiers on the lower slopes, but not up here; not for five years now. Now the cable car conveyed only the facility's trustees, its shift-working supervisors and foremen, or at least those of them who were allowed the freedom of time spent away from their work; in which respect Ganzer was one of the most fortunate. Competent neither as a scientist nor an engineer—nor yet fit enough for hard labour, but accepted by outsiders as the complex's true manager—he could come and go more or less as he pleased . . . more or less.

However, like every other worker at Schloss Zonigen, when Ganzer's presence was required he had to make himself available as quickly as possible; and just *exactly* like the others, whatever work he was given in addition to his duties as "Direktor," it must always be performed to the best of his limited talents, or else incur the awful wrath of his masters. And Ganzer's masters being what they were . . . the very thought of that made him shudder. He had erred in this respect only once, a minor detail at that, and was still paying for it. It was the reason he was incapable of hard labour, the reason he limped . . .

He thought back on *Their* coming:

Five years ago, yes. And Schloss Zonigen had been in a bad way, tottering on the edge of a financial black hole. Inflation was to blame, that and the fact that people had stopped believing in frozen immortality. Twenty years ago when the rich died, some of them came here, bringing *some* of their money with them. Wills had been made, endowments, grants, and donations. But the descendants of those in suspension—their sons and daughters, agents, executors, solicitors, creditors—*their* main concern was only for the now of it; they had no interest in their father's, mother's, client's, or debtor's possible future resurrection, not after he, she, or they had been dead awhile. Their own more immediate futures took precedence. And ever the threat of investigations, sequestrations, insolvency; mounting costs and backed-up bills; *and*—along with inflation and a lack of new, rich, and recently dead clients—always the actual, available funds dwindling away to nothing.

Add to that a succession of unscrupulous governors of the complex (not excluding Ganzer himself) since Herr Doktor Emile Zonigen's disappearance in the mid-1970s when he had absconded with a six-million-franc donation from a future "sleeper," and it was easy to see how the advent of the Three with their apparently inexhaustible funds had seemed like a godsend.

The Three.

They had names on paper, used other names when they spoke to each other, and accepted only "sir" or "mistress" in conversation with their so-called employees, in fact their slaves, when they issued orders, offered threats, or carried them out. Only three of them, yes . . . as cold, hard, and terrifying as an entire army of merciless automatons.

But it hadn't always been this way.

At first they had appeared fascinated by Schloss Zonigen's conceit; they had seemed to accept the feasibility of cryogenic suspension; they wished to carry out studies and experiments of their own in an environment that almost perfectly suited their needs. They would pay off all debts and bills, apply themselves to pressing, legal obligations, install

NECROSCOPE: THE TOUCH 149

machinery and equipment necessary to their endeavors, and continue to employ and even augment staff numbers. As for the monies Herr Ganzer was in the habit of "allowing" himself by way of a salary—by no means a pittance—they would double it; double *every* employee's wages, in fact, in return (they said) for their loyalty. In effect and to put it in a nutshell, they would simply buy Schloss Zonigen outright. And they had.

But right from the beginning there had been something very strange about them. In fact, everything about them had been very strange. Physical descriptions? At every early meeting, as they had worked things out—the nitty-gritty of the purchase of the facility—Ganzer had noticed . . . discrepancies. The female, or *She*, apparently had a "thing" about her appearance: she enjoyed changing it, frequently. Her shape, very hard and angular for a woman, rarely seemed the same from meeting to meeting. Sexually unappealing in general, she would be flat-chested one day, full-bosomed the next. Also, the colour of her hair, lip gloss, even her eyes! Contact lenses, of course. The only thing that hadn't changed (which Ganzer wouldn't have expected to change) was her height; well over six feet tall, she could hardly compress herself . . . now could she? But on the other hand he hadn't thought she would want to. She seemed to enjoy standing aloof and looking down on people. And thin almost to the point of emaciation, still he'd sensed a nameless but overpowering strength in her.

As for the men, Simon Salcombe and Guyler Schweitzer: they were much the same. Tall, awkward in their movements one minute and as flowing as mercury the next; mercurial in general. Ganzer's first opinion had been that they were all three suffering from a rare genetic disorder, perhaps gigantism; especially the men, who were at least six feet seven, and possibly an inch or two taller than that! And there was that about their looks that also hinted of genetic problems; it had seemed likely they were related, from some obscure isolated region where inbreeding had damaged their genes. In which respect their interest in Schloss

Zonigen might lie on an associated plane: they could be searching for some kind of remedy, if not for themselves perhaps for others of their kind, their clan or community.

And at first, despite that Ganzer sometimes felt repelled by their strangeness, still he'd felt genuinely sorry for them *because* of it. He had actually pitied them, yes.

But not for long, for the changes had come fast . . .

. . . And so had Ganzer come fast—to his destination. With his recollections fading as his car rode up onto Schloss Zonigen's plateau, he found his usual parking spot and switched off his motor. He was here once again; he had been *called* here once again, to this now nightmarish place.

Well, it had been nightmarish before—with its many dead, gradually crystallizing time-passengers, whose paid for, prayed for reincarnations weren't ever going to come— but never more so than now. And reluctantly leaving his car, with a nod to the parka-clad attendant valet who was approaching across the high, flat plateau of the walled esplanade, wheeling his trolley containing an insulated car jacket, Ganzer paused for a moment and stared at the ugly black bulk of Schloss Zonigen.

And indeed it looked like a castle, with its ice-sheathed, turret-like spires soaring on high, and above its great doors a facade of fractured rock like tottering merlons and embrasures, and behind the doors and guarded wicket the honeycombed complex itself: a cavern labyrinth that, when the ice withdrew twenty thousand years ago, snared the tail of a glacier, swallowed it, and kept its bones frozen still—and a great many other bones and indeed entire carcasses within it.

As if that thought were an evocation, Ganzer felt a sudden sharp chill, a stabbing pain, a deep-frozen ice pick gouging at his mind: prelude to a voice that said, *Gunter, we are waiting!*

That voice—the telepathic voice of the female member of the Three—spurred him to activity as nothing else ever could. And with his twisted, in fact his reversed, left foot dragging, he limped across the concourse to the wicket door, and was let into the complex by the armed guard on duty.

Inside, in keeping with the mighty cavern that housed it, the former administrative area was vast despite that its space was but a fraction of Schloss Zonigen's total volume. As usual the place was mainly vacant; it echoed like a gothic cathedral, an empty hangar, or disused railway station; but from corridors, chambers, workshops, and various levels buried deep within came the faintly echoing hum and throb that spoke of no small level of industrious activity. And for all Ganzer's familiarity with every nook and cranny of the place, still he remained ignorant of what was being fashioned here. And not only the "Direktor," but each and every one of the one hundred eighty plus persons who worked here . . . with the exception of the Three.

They knew, of course, unless they were insane. As to that, Ganzer couldn't say, but he knew they were evil for a fact—at which he gave a start, wincing in anticipation as again he felt that icy flow of thoughts and heard: *Gunter, do not loiter!*

From behind the long marble reception and information desk (as it had once been and still was ostensibly, though it served now as a work and quota distribution center) a clerk was beckoning him. Hobbling over, Ganzer asked, "Where are they?"

"In there," the hollow-eyed man husked, indicating a glass-fronted room or recess in the solid rock wall at the far end of the desk. "The VIP Room. They've got some new people with them. A family, the poor bastards!"

Ganzer nodded his acknowledgment and hurried as best as possible in that direction, only pausing at the glass door to throw off his overcoat, adjust his tie, and wipe his sweating hands on a pocket handkerchief. It was strange, but even in Schloss Zonigen's colder places he was wont to perspire. Or perhaps not so strange, for even his sweat was cold.

Behind the VIP Room's frosted glass frontage, he saw four seated figures and two standing. The images of the latter were blurred, but from their height and stick-thin outlines he knew who they were: two of the Three; the terrible female and one of the males. Ganzer found it easier to think of them that way: as creatures, not as men and women but as male and female. Indeed, he was by no means certain that they *weren't* creatures! But he knew it was the female who had called him.

He knocked, and without waiting for a response entered. He was, after all, the Herr Direktor . . . the role in which *She* now greeted him:

"Direktor Ganzer!" She smiled at him. "We are so very glad you could make it." (This entirely in keeping with the scenario and without a touch of sarcasm.) "For as you can see, we've had unexpected guests: the Steins." Very politely, the seated persons stood up; the husband in his early forties, small and slim, wearing thick-lensed spectacles on a thin nose; his wife, seven or eight years younger, pretty, blonde, smiling a little uncertainly; their children, a boy and girl, perhaps seven and nine years old respectively.

"Ah, the Steins!" said Ganzer, extending his now dry right hand toward Herr Stein, who took and firmly shook it. And trying his hardest not to gabble, Ganzer quickly went on, "I am so very sorry I wasn't here to greet you when you arrived! But . . . am I not correct in believing that your interview was scheduled for tomorrow?" (He took a deep breath . . . he allowed himself to relax a very little . . . he was off the hook, he wasn't to blame! Thank God! Oh, *thank God!*) "Indeed," Ganzer continued, controlling himself more surely now, "I'm quite certain that such was the arrangement."

"Well, you see—" a slightly concerned Herr Stein commenced to say, only to be interrupted by *She,* the female member of the Three, who called herself (at least on paper) Frau Lessing:

"It appears there have been complications, Gunter. You are of course correct about the arrangements: we were due to interview Herr Stein—Herr Roberto Stein—tomorrow. And the family have been staying in the village for a few days in anticipation of their visit."

(Oh, yes, as usual, the entire family! Ganzer knew exactly what that meant. And he wanted to scream, "Run! Get out of here—keep your children safe! Don't let her—don't let *any* of these monsters—so much as touch them!" But he said nothing, and was probably too late even if he'd dared.)

Smiling still and continuing to address Ganzer, Frau Lessing, or "Gerda" when it was deemed necessary, went on: "Gunter, as you are aware from Herr Stein's excellent references, he was recently employed on experimental high-intensity laser technology in Zurich's Schröeder Institute. And on that basis, and one of trust—his word that he will make no disclosure on anything he may see here—we've already escorted him around certain of the laboratories. But—"

But now it was Herr Stein's turn to cut in, and to Ganzer he said, "Even though I am not yet familiar with the nature of the work being done here, which is understandably secret, still I find myself amazed at the size of your workshops and laboratories, your excellent equipment, and the advanced technologies which you appear to be developing and employing! But I am also very interested to know how the experiments you are conducting apply to Schloss Zonigen's original, er, concept. For frankly, the consensus among the most respected scientists of our times is that the cryogenic suspension of bodies, with the intention of eventual revitalization, is, well, how best to put it—?"

"Far-fetched?" Now the male member of the Three—the one who called himself Guyler Schweitzer—spoke up, his voice deep, resonant, but deceptively quiet. And allowing himself a condescending smile, he continued. "Perhaps it was, when this facility first opened. And of course we know the history of Schloss Zonigen and that of the alleged fraud who ran it. But the truth of the matter is that he did succeed, at least in the *preservation* of his clients. Most certainly he succeeded, for they are still here, still frozen! And the more the future extends itself, the more feasible their resurrection becomes."

And so back to Gerda Lessing. "Herr Stein," she addressed the visitor. "One of Schloss Zonigen's principals—a one-third owner of this facility, along with myself and

Herr Schweitzer—is presently engaged upon a routine inspection of the cryogenic units with members of our technical staff. The principal's name is Simon Salcombe. Perhaps we can take advantage of this coincidence. If you desire to see for yourself what can be achieved, I believe we might arrange it."

"You mean right now, today?" Stein was eager to accept.

Frau Lessing nodded. "This very minute."

"But how could I refuse?"

"Except," she quickly went on, "your family . . . your wife and children . . . certain things are not at all pleasant to look upon. I am sure you will understand . . . ?"

"Oh, indeed!" said Stein at once. "My wife and the children will wait here, certainly." He turned to his wife, who had once more seated herself upon an upholstered couch. "Mira, you wouldn't mind, would you, dear? And I shall be as quick as possible." Mira made no answer.

"You do realize," said Guyler Schweitzer in that quiet and totally deceptive way of his, "that the same restrictions apply as before? We're not quite ready to excite the curiosity of the entire scientific community with regard to our successes here."

Herr Stein, yet more eager, nodded his understanding. "But of course. I would never dream of breaking a trust. I mean—"

"Yes, of course," said Guyler Schweitzer. And he turned to Ganzer. "In that case we shall persuade Direktor Ganzer here to conduct you to the cryogenic facility. Gunter?"

To which Ganzer could only reply: "Delighted! My pleasure, I assure you." (His *pleasure?* A ghastly joke! In truth it could only be an extension of the nightmare. For Simon Salcombe—the absent member of the Three—was already down there in the ice tunnels, down among the frozen dead, doing the monstrous things he did; the things that all three of them could do, whether the flesh they did it to was living *or* dead!)

Frau Lessing moved to a desk with an intercom, pressed one of two dozen buttons, and spoke into a microphone.

"Erik Hauser, attend the VIP Room for escort duty, if you please." The if-you-please was completely redundant, of course, a small part of the overall subterfuge. As for Erik Hauser: he was a trustee and, from Ganzer's viewpoint, a collaborator. But then, weren't they all? Wasn't anyone who knew what was happening here and yet did nothing about it? No, not really. Because, like Ganzer himself, not one of Schloss Zonigen's slaves *dared* do anything about it. The penalties he would have to pay were simply too high. And if not him, then his loved ones. And Ganzer knew all about that.

But so-called trustees, like Hauser . . . well, he *enjoyed* the imagined position of power that came from his obedience (or his obeisance?) to those who were more powerful yet. And Ganzer knew why *She* had called him: to watch over himself and Stein on their tour of the frozen tombs. To make absolutely sure nothing untoward was said. For it wasn't unlikely that Frau Lessing had read something of Ganzer's thoughts, or she may have seen something in his face when he met the Steins: that pretty wife, and those innocent children.

"The poor bastards," as the clerk on duty at the reception desk had phrased it . . .

15

The trustee called Erik Hauser was a slab-faced, five-foot-six, arrogant, overweight blimp of a man with narrow eyes, a sloping forehead, and the supercilious attitude of someone who was sure he was something in a world full of nothings. He was trusted by the Three, who treated Hauser and a handful of others just like him as their personal pet sniffer dogs; not to hunt for explosives or drugs, but to seek out would-be troublemakers, rebels, insurgents. It served their purpose to trust such men, because while the Three could be anywhere, they couldn't be everywhere, and the implementation of mind-taps—mental contact—with all of their workers all of the time just wasn't feasible; it would be too exhausting, too time-consuming.

And of course there were rewards that men of Erik Hauser's "caliber" simply couldn't resist. For example: utterly unappealing to the opposite sex, he had never known a woman in that way except for the ones he'd paid for, and even then he'd sometimes been refused. But in Schloss Zonigen, where there were certain "emoluments" to be earned, this wasn't a problem. Sex, like an allowance of fish to trained, well-behaved dolphins, was regularly doled out to trustees as a premium, commensurate with the adequate performance of their duties; this on the understanding that anyone who availed himself of this "privilege" wasn't too fussy about the physical and sometimes mental condition of the imprisoned woman he was effectively raping—which Hauser and a good many others just like him weren't.

And Gunter Ganzer hated, indeed loathed and could happily kill Erik Hauser, who was wont on occasion to ask him in quiet, private asides: "How's your missus, Gunter—you old 'Direktor' you? Still visit her now and then, do you? I was thinking, perhaps I'll drop in and see how she's doing—have a nice little, er, chat, with her—you know? So if you've got anything you'd like me to tell her, any little message I could pass on during our, er, conversation . . . ?" And with a suggestive chuckle, whistling a merry little tune, he'd then go waddling off about his dirty duties.

Ganzer had dared approach Guyler Schweitzer with the problem one time. And Schweitzer had told him, "Pay no attention to him. We don't allow such. He is provoking you, who was once his superior. He would perhaps like you to attack him—would then report you—and we must needs punish you for causing an incident, an unsettling disturbance. I am sure you don't want that, do you, Gunter?"

"No, sir, of course not. But I—"

"As for your wife: you should see her more frequently; see for yourself that she remains safe. And I shall ensure that she is more . . . *lucid,* if or when you desire to visit her. Only try to remember, Gunter, that when our work is done here everything shall be as it was, returned to its former condition. If things should go awry, however—if we find our work obstructed in any way—then nothing is guaranteed. Currently your wife is alive and one day she may even be well again, her infirmities mended; everything depends upon your own conduct, Gunter. So do nothing to change the status quo but believe me when I say that however unsatisfactory things may appear, still where you are concerned they are far superior to what they *might* so easily become."

"But, sir—"

"And now you are beginning to annoy me, which is a dangerous thing to do!"

A warning that had been followed by a rare and terrifying event, something Ganzer had witnessed only once or twice before in all the five years of the Three's occupancy of Schloss Zonigen. For as he mumbled his apologies and tried to back off from Schweitzer, so the man—*if* he was a man, which Ganzer had long doubted—leaned forward, reached out a long arm and claw hand, caught him by the shoulder, and lowered his narrow head with its silvery comb and black eyes seated in crater darkness to stare deep into Ganzer's eyes. Then:

Schweitzer's head had jerked in an apparently involuntary spastic movement, and beneath his jaw in the hollow of his long neck something had moved, pulsing and bulging out his skin. His flesh had seemed momentarily to part, splitting open and permitting a sudden eruption—a bubble of greeny-grey matter as big as a child's head—to swell forth. Detaching itself, the thing had flowed around Schweitzer's neck, up onto his narrow sloping left shoulder, where it extended a pseudopod of writhing purple matter into his small round ear.

And then his look, scarcely benevolent in the first place, if ever, immediately changed. No sign of any previous tolerance now, his deep-sunken eyes seemed to smoulder as they glared into Ganzer's. By which time the loathsome thing on Schweitzer's shoulder had developed features; it, too, had staring eyes and small black nostrils that sniffed, but no ears and no mouth—nothing to speak with—and yet Ganzer could hear it speaking to Guyler Schweitzer:

Will you hurt him now, Mordri?

"No!" Schweitzer (or Mordri) had answered out loud. "Causing him pain would serve no purpose but only waste my energies, wherefore I will not. You must not tempt me, Khiff!"

But it would *serve a purpose, Mordri. If only to . . . amuse me? And I have been so bored recently.*

(And Ganzer, wincing from Schweitzer's iron grip and knowing he must be hallucinating, had wondered—"How can an almost featureless, bodiless thing like this contrive such a monstrous look of pure evil on its jelly-blob face?")

"You shall have your amusement later," Schweitzer had meanwhile answered the thing. "If I were to leave you awhile with a prisoner, then you could amuse yourself all you wish."

And as Schweitzer had released Ganzer, thrusting him away, the monster on his shoulder had grown excited, saying: *You will leave me with one of the prisoners? With a female? You promise?*

"I promise."

With this *one's female, perhaps?*

"Perhaps. For it may yet teach him a lesson: not to bother me with trivialities."

With which the thing had fashioned a mouth, laughing maniacally before shrivelling down into itself and entering through Schweitzer's ear into his head!

And Gunter Ganzer had fled gibbering, doubting his sanity, from the tall man's—the tall creature's—apartments, with Schweitzer calling after him, "Yes, run Gunter! Run as fast as you can, before I change my mind!"

So much for complaining to one of the Three . . . to *any* one of them. As he'd fled Gunter Ganzer had wondered: what would be worse? A thing like that with his wife—

doing whatever it did—or an animal like Erik Hauser, doing what he would obviously do? It was difficult to know, and far worse to think about.

But at least Hauser was a *human* animal. Barely, anyway . . .

Fitted out with hooded parkas and overboots, Herr Stein, Ganzer, and Hauser, led by the latter, had made their way down into the maze of natural caves and tunnels once filled with ice. How the labyrinth had been formed, in what geological age: these things were anybody's guess. But now the ice formed an inner sheath on translucent ceilings, walls, and floors, where passages had been carved through the glittering, bluely luminescent, once-glacial deposits. The footsteps of the three made muffled, softly thudding echoes where the only other sounds were the slow, far drip of water and those of their muted conversation.

At least, they had started out talking, but Ganzer's fearful thoughts and memories had been distracting him for the last five minutes or so. Now, vaguely aware that Stein had said something to him, questioned him, he gave a sudden start, came back to earth and said, "Eh?" when the scientist repeated his question:

"I was inquiring about your principals," said Stein, just a little impatiently. "Why do they insist on meeting the families of prospective employees? It seems odd to me."

Hauser, having fallen to the rear, now gave Ganzer a prod in the back by way of saying, "Wake up, Gunter, you old 'Direktor' you!"

"Ah, yes! I'm sorry!" said Ganzer. "I was miles away!" (He wished that he really had been.) "My principals? I believe it's a trend out of America, yes. They like to ensure that the prospective employee's family life is settled, well established. No disrespect intended, you understand, but a happy man is usually a better worker. And in Schloss Zonigen continuity is a necessity. The principals don't much care for . . . well, disruptions."

Nodding, Stein answered, "Yes, I believe I understand

that well enough. But tell me, what am I to make of it if an unknown person tries to advise me—indeed, to warn me— to stay away from here, and under no circumstance to bring my wife and children here? For you see, that is what has happened."

Oh, my God! thought Ganzer. Someone, some would-be hero, had broken one of the rules—and the first rule at that! When the culprit was discovered, which he would be, the Three would make him pay for it . . . horribly! They would make an example of him, and it wouldn't be the first time. Some people never learned.

But as for right now: "What!?" Ganzer replied, in his best "shocked" voice. "But I'm at a complete loss to understand! Are you really saying that such is the case?"

Again Stein's nod. "I got a letter—more a note, a scrawl on a scrap of paper, really—just yesterday. It arrived in an envelope, slipped under my door at the inn. 'Stay away from the Schloss,' it said. 'Go nowhere near but simply take your family and leave. In no event take them up there!' "

"Fantastic!" said Ganzer, hating himself and hating Hauser even more. For if the trustee wasn't here . . . but no, even then he wouldn't dare speak out but must continue to play the coward for his poor wife's sake, not to mention his own. And hurriedly, without thinking, he continued: "So then . . . why did you come?" An utterly *stupid* question, for it tended to suggest that perhaps Herr Stein *shouldn't* have come! Which prompted another sly prod from Erik Hauser that silently but insistently warned:

"Careful now, Herr 'Direktor'! Don't say too much."

But Stein appeared deep in thought himself, and he finally said, "My wife was quite put off by the note. We weren't due to visit until tomorrow, as you know, but she thought we shouldn't come at all. On the other hand my children were keen to see the Schloss, and I thought perhaps I might just drop in—you know?—to see for myself if there was anything—?"

"—That you should be concerned about?" Ganzer finished it for him. "Yes, of course. But as you have seen . . ." He shrugged and left it hanging there.

"The salary your principals have offered me is most tempting," Stein mused; and then continued with some certainty, "but I must admit to finding them . . . strange. It may be that Schloss Zonigen isn't what I'm looking for after all."

Too late! Too late! thought Ganzer.

Erik Hauser had moved to the front and was leading the way again. They had emerged from an ice tunnel into a gallery where the ice was in its original state, with huge icicles descending from the ceiling and others rearing from the floor like so many stalactites and stalagmites, except they gleamed like sapphires where the blue light of looping neons shone through them.

Here a wooden catwalk along one wall made the going a lot easier, so that they soon came to a junction with a side tunnel some twenty-five to thirty feet wide whose mouth opened high in the wall. Climbing steep wooden steps to a landing and entering the tunnel, they found a man-made floor inlaid with metal rails on wooden sleepers; and while neons continued to light the way, they saw some sixty yards ahead a rough disk of true white daylight shining in from the external world.

Now once again Erik Hauser took up a position at the rear of the party. And speaking quietly, with his breath pluming in the bitter air, he muttered, "This is it. The cryogenic units. We're there." Much more alert now, the trustee seemed suddenly nervous. He had thrown back his hood and looked paler—which *might* have been an effect of the lighting.

But Gunter Ganzer knew it wasn't . . .

The tunnel was a natural tube of massively thick ice whose walls had been drilled into so that cores of some thirty inches in diameter could be removed. Skids had then been inserted into the niches, and the freezer units with their contents slid into place. The niches were numbered, and along every six feet or so of wall the handles and frost-rimed ends of these metal cylinders protruded some three inches from the ice. Under each unit's crystalline coating a small green light winked on and off.

Thus Erik Hauser's nervous comment had been quite unnecessary, for the silent mausoleum atmosphere of the place made it perfectly clear that they were indeed "there" in the cryogenics area.

Ganzer, who knew every inch of the entire complex as well and better than Hauser, now led the way. Not that he wanted to, but someone had to. He knew that at the far end of this shaft a ravine fell sheer for almost two thousand feet down to the ski slopes; knew also that they weren't going to make it that far, for someone else was here in the cryogenics shaft. Someone who called himself Simon Salcombe when he went abroad in the world of men, but who was also known to his colleagues as Mordri Two. And Mordri Two was a very terrible someone indeed.

Twenty paces deeper inside the tunnel, with his tall, angular frame silhouetted against the disk of distant white light, Salcombe cast a long, spidery shadow. Hearing them approaching, he turned his head, saw them, slowly straightened up from what he was doing and stood taller still.

"Ah, Herr Stein!" he greeted the scientist. "My colleagues told me you were coming. I am Simon Salcombe. I had intended to send this vehicle to wait for you at the end of the tunnel, but instead I became engrossed with this small problem here. I apologise." The vehicle he spoke of was a four-seater electric car, its motor softly humming, where it waited on the tunnel's central tracks.

"No matter," Stein answered, his mouth half open, looking up at Salcombe, staring in fascination at his smiling face. But such a strange smile on such a strange face; he could well be a brother to those two up above! A moment more of this inspection until, realizing how rude he must seem, Stein gulped and turned his gaze to a cryogenic unit that had been drawn out of the ice on its skids. The seals on its convex metal lid had been broken and the lid itself thrown back. The figure of what was *probably* a young woman lay within . . . it was hard to tell without moving closer. But:

"By all means do," said Salcombe, still staring piercingly at Stein as he answered the scientist's *unspoken* question!

"What?" Stein glanced again at Salcombe—and at once drew back as the tall, apparently leering man leaned toward him. "I mean"—Stein faltered over his words—"did I say something?"

"You *thought* something," Salcombe answered, leaning closer still. "You thought this was probably a young woman. And so she was, upon a time. Now she is an old woman who has lain here for more than twenty years waiting to be revived. Alas, today something seems to have gone wrong. A seal has worn out, or perhaps there's a fault in the electrical circuitry. But anyway, and as you can see for yourself, the unit's green light has failed and a red one is blinking in its place."

Both Ganzer and Hauser had backed away a pace or two from Stein where he was now bent over the unit peering into its dark interior. "One moment," Salcombe told him, "while I try to shed some light on the subject." He shone a torch into the cylinder.

"Good Lord!" Stein gasped at once, his gloved hands gripping the unit's rim.

"Ah, but see!" said Salcombe, actually chuckling. "Perhaps the system has been faulty for quite some time, eh?"

For the flesh on the face of the surgically gowned figure in the unit was as brown as leather, with shrivelled lips drawn back in a rictus grin from brilliantly white teeth. A girl, her hair was luxuriant still, shining curls lying soft on her scant shoulders. But the fingernails on the hands that were folded on her chest were more than two inches long.

"But . . . this is gross negligence!" Stein looked up again into Salcombe's face. "How often are these systems checked? You really don't seem to care!"

The monster held up a hand, stopped smiling, looked stern. "Checked? The systems? No one cares about these systems! Do not concern yourself, Herr Stein. It is a small matter. And anyway, there's life in this young-old girl yet. Now look—and see!"

Handing Stein the torch, he reached into the unit and tore the corpse's shift, exposing the girl's right arm from shoulder to wrist. And taking hold of that wrist where it lay across her chest, he bared his little fish teeth in an expression that was almost a snarl. Then Salcombe's face took on a strained look— or if not that then one of concentration, his black-marble eyes half closing—and Stein took the opportunity to study him more closely: his sallow, sunken cheeks, waxy mask of a face under a shining domed head that was close to acromegalic in its length; looks that were oddly reptilian, despite that his gape would be small. But no, Stein corrected himself, deciding that there was little or nothing of the reptile in Salcombe's looks . . . it was simply that he *repelled* like one. And:

"Look!" the man said again.

Stein looked, he stared. His jaw dropped and his eyes went wide. There was . . . a transformation.

The dead girl's wrist where Salcombe held it had taken on a different hue. A pale pink blush suffused the withered flesh, seeming to flow down into her hand and up her arm to the elbow, and the desiccated meat around the bones was visibly taking on substance. Stein's eyes bugged; his mouth went dry, which made it hard to voice his thoughts even if he'd dared. But he could still think them:

This *had* to be some sort of grotesque trick!

"A trick?" said Salcombe out loud, gutturally. "You think so? But no, I assure you, it is nothing of the sort. Keep looking—look even closer—and see for yourself. It is a *skill*, Herr Stein. You have surely heard of faith-healing, am I right? Then have faith in this, in me, and believe what you see."

Have faith in you? Stein thought—with the merest glance at the other before his fascinated gaze returned to what was or had been in essence a dead girl in a coffin—*No, I think not!* For to his mind faith was a matter of one's religion or belief, a spiritual process, while this was just the opposite, in fact ghoulish!

"Oh, ha!-ha!-*haaaa!*" Salcombe laughed out loud, as alien a sound as Stein could ever have imagined, and yet again answered his unspoken thoughts. "You are right, of course. I am no god—I only seek him out across the universe—but I do have godlike powers. Now see how her flesh quickens."

Stein was almost on his knees now, his legs trembling, his drawn white face peering over the rim of the failed unit. Purple veins were beginning to pulse however sluggishly in the back of the girl's hand, while her bare arm had taken on the texture and pinkish marble colour of living flesh. Moreover, to Stein's utter amazement, her chest had commenced a slow, jerky rise and fall! But the changes were as frightening as they were amazing.

Petrified yet fascinated, Stein had failed to notice the onset of a different, perhaps more mundane sort of change; but in an abrupt sputtering of electrical fixtures, the strobing of suddenly erratic neons, and the faltering beam of his torch, he couldn't any longer help but notice. For even the muted humming of the railcar had increased; the vehicle was actually vibrating on its tracks, as if striving to drive off on its own!

Finally, despite the strangeness of his location and situation, the scientist gulped, moistened his throat, looked again at Salcombe, and found his voice. "What did you do to this girl? I mean, is she . . . but how *can* she be . . . alive?"

For the girl's (or corpse's?) face had filled out a little and her body was now . . . "alive," yes, with twitches and spasms at least. And even as Stein had asked his question, so her eyes had come unglued and cracked open—but behind their lids they were yellow, filled with pus!

"Oh, my good God!" Stein gasped, paralysed with terror and clinging to the rim of the open cylinder for all he was worth.

Salcombe had released the girl's wrist, and laughing again he said: "Without me she cannot last. She will revert. This was merely a demonstration. But for the moment, as you see, she has life. Well, a sort of life. She is at least 'lively,' eh?"

"Lively," Stein repeated faintly. And again, "My God!"

"However," said Salcombe, "I think it's only right to warn you, *mein Herr,* that while common flesh responds readily enough, quickly accepting a partial revival, the brain—or mind—is wont to take longer. And as for the soul, it is lost forever!"

The yellow pus had flowed away from the girl's pupils; her eyes swivelled and stared at Stein; her jaws snapped open, issuing a gut-wrenching stench. Then:

She screamed—a nerve-shattering sound, like chalk on a blackboard, like a shovel in cold ashes—and her long-clawed hands reached out to clasp and rake Stein's face!

The scientist at once collapsed, blood streaming from his gashes, and sat hunched up in an almost fetal position against the wall of ice. Simon Salcombe let the girl draw her suddenly limp hands back inside the cylinder, slammed its lid, and without pause slid it back into its niche.

Then he leaned and touched the shuddering Stein's bleeding face, saying, "That will heal, don't worry." And beckoning Erik Hauser and Gunter Ganzer from where they had spread-eagled themselves against the wall at what they obviously hoped was a safe distance, he called out, "Come now, you two, come! For I believe Herr Stein requires your assistance. Help him into the car, and then let us be gone from here."

As they scrambled to obey him, the buzzing and sputtering lights and other electrics were slowly returning to normal . . .

16

Schloss Zonigen, in its upper and most highly restricted levels, was abuzz with rumour among the guards, trustees, and foremen—the self-styled "upper echelon"—and fraught with dread among the "working classes." Since rumors only rarely agree with the actualities, however, on this occasion it was the upper echelon who by rights should be the more concerned. But in any event in this place the divisions of class—those characteristics that would usually distinguish between lower, medium, and higher IQs, skills, abilities, worthiness in general, at least according to human gradations—were far less apparent than in the world's more orthodox communities.

Here a bearded, myopic nuclear physicist with thick-lensed spectacles, a reasonably white laboratory smock, several honour degrees, and a list of similar qualifications as long as his arm was a "worker" no less than the sweaty, heavily muscled, slack-jawed man in dungarees who fetched and carried, spat and cursed, and wouldn't know *pi* from pie in the sky. Exhausted, they slept in exactly the same hollowed-out "accommodations"—cavelets in essence—each with a mattress and blanket; grubby, they bathed in the same tepid shower stalls; thirsty, they drank drip-filtered water from the same communal basins. They would also have eaten the same food if necessary; which it wasn't because they didn't any longer require to eat—or masturbate, or even defecate—not the more permanent residents of Schloss Zonigen. For they had been "fixed" by the Three, by which means their needs, the so-called basic essentials of life, had been reduced beyond what doctors and nutritionists would consider a minimum. And in that respect their situation could only be compared to that of political prisoners in some gulag in Stalin's USSR; except life in a gulag would be far preferable and its prisoners would not have been "fixed"—although in certain cases they would have been ideologically brainwashed.

As for the current excitement, unease, and terror: there was a traitor in the Schloss, and the Three would investigate.

And they *would* find him . . .

Having dealt with Herr Stein, administered a powerful sedative, and lodged him in a holding cell, Gunter Ganzer and Erik Hauser had only just finished when they heard first the alert klaxons, then the instructions of the Three issuing

loud and clear from the Tannoy system: all trustees, foremen, and other privileged employees—especially those
who had been allowed down to the village yesterday—were
to proceed at once to the great workshop cavern in the heart
of Schloss Zonigen.

"Direktor" Ganzer and trustee Hauser knew well enough
what was going on, but despite that they personally were innocent of any misdemeanour still they hurried to the speci-
fied area. Even at the "best" of times, meaning anything
better than the worst, no one but an idiot would disregard
the "instructions," in fact the orders, of the Three. But at
times such as this—one would have to be suicidal or else a
complete lunatic.

The complex was a vast gorgonzola of hollowed rock, a
maze of natural shafts, chimneys, crevices, caverns; even
crevasses, split almost as deep as the mountain's roots by
the pressure of ancient ice. Central to all of this, the workshop area was like the subsurface chamber of a volcano's
caldera, drained of magma in a forgotten geological era.
More recently it had been filled with ice, but the last twenty
or so centuries had left it windswept, dried out, and empty,
at least until men climbed up here.

As for its contents during the last few decades, up to and
including the present day:

In the olden times, the time of "Doktor" Emile Zonigen,
it had been a warehouse for the Schloss's cryogenic equipment. Now all such machinery had been cannibalized for
certain electrical components, and the rest of it put aside,
heaped up and rusting in a disused bay like so much useless junk.

Now, too, in the north-facing corner of the domed ceiling,
work was in progress where scaffolding had been erected,
enabling engineers to drill into the rock preliminary to cutting an angled shaft through to the clear mountain air of the
exterior heights. Like light through a circle of pinprick per-
forations in a card, narrow lances of dusty daylight now outlined a perimeter where small holes had already been drilled
through to the outside. This perimeter defined the extent of

the project: the volume of ceiling that would be removed en masse in a blast of coordinated, simultaneous explosions; a considerable mass, for when finished the shaft would be about twelve feet in diameter.

Down below, in an area somewhat off-center in the mainly level floor, an as yet incomplete cylindrical machine like the barrel of a huge gun was tilted at precisely the same angle as the projected ceiling shaft. And all around this great gun—if such it was, for no one but the Three knew—were strewn coils of shiny copper wiring, leagues of insulated cable, instruments of apparently alien design and purpose, dynamos and generators, panels of lead shielding, and all manner of experimental equipment. Spreading concentrically from the centre, two dozen huge benches supported the components of elaborate circuitry; while set back in the base of the great cavern's walls, laboratories with strengthened-glass doors, windows, and portholes crackled with man-made energies, issuing rays of purple and blue light, and smells of ozone and sulphur.

Coinciding with Gunter Ganzer's and Erik Hauser's arrival, these laboratories were the last to fall silent, their experiments, lights, and emissions shutting down one by one. All other work had slowed and ceased soon after the Tannoy had issued the Three's orders, when the complex's trustees, gangers, and other persons of privilege—especially those who yesterday had gone down to the village on special licence—had commenced arriving and merging into small groups in an area close to the gun. And as more of them had arrived, swelling the groups into one body, so its members had spread themselves out around a stone dais surmounted by a huge steel cross on a disc-shaped base of some nonreflective, jet-black material some four inches thick.

This was the last place in all Schloss Zonigen, or in the rest of the entire planet, where any of these people would wish to be. Their gaunt expressions reflected that fact; their faces—even those of the completely innocent, which as yet everyone here was—were pale, bloodless, terrified.

The ceiling workers on their high scaffolding looked down on the scene; skilled men at their benches looked across at it; the scientists and their assistants gradually came forward from their laboratories, finding positions of higher elevation where such existed; labourers put down their various burdens, slapped dust and dirt from their denim coveralls, turned inward toward the dais and crucifix on its black disc base. And the scene was set.

No one wanted to watch what was about to happen, but each and every one of them knew he must. Indeed, that was why it was happening: as an example, a warning, a reminder of the price to be paid for breaking Schloss Zonigen's rules—and especially the first rule. Which was also the reason why no one wanted to be caught *not* watching. For who could say? There might even be a penalty for that!

And yet not everyone was here; a dozen of the privileged, the group that Gunter Ganzer had seen descending in the cable car just an hour or so ago, had gone down to the ski lodge and by now would have proceeded into one of the local villages and perhaps even farther afield . . . but never too far afield. Then there were the guards, Schloss Zonigen's armed militia or "security personnel," who were on a par socially with the trustees; which was to say generally loathed by everyone else. But as for their absence—it spoke for itself.

From the moment Herr Roberto Stein, physicist, had entered Schloss Zonigen and talked about his warning letter, guards had been dispatched into every tunnel and cavern in the vicinity of the reception area, the only possible escape route out onto the false plateau and any imagined freedom. By now all of the vehicles on the esplanade would have been immobilized; there would be cold-eyed, parka-clad watchers with binoculars, walkie-talkies, and rifles with telescopic sights in the high turrets and other vantage points; and *anyone* seen on foot, or by any other means, attempting flight from Schloss Zonigen by descending its precipitous access road would be shot dead and his body recovered and disposed of before any outsider could see it.

That was the current scenario, whose anomalies anyone new to the Schloss must surely find as puzzling as they were alarming. A young foreman of electricians who stood close to Gunter Ganzer in the crowd was just such a recent recruit, and he had questions that required answers. The problem was, who could he trust to answer them in a place where it was probably questionable even to ask them? Nearby, a quiet man favouring a twisted left foot seemed a mild sort, not one to complain too vocally; and with his mind made up the young electrician moved closer . . .

Unhappy with Erik Hauser's proximity, Ganzer had gradually edged away from him into the circle of workers around the dais. Hauser had taken up with other trustees and stood whispering to them, no doubt describing the events he'd witnessed down in the cryogenic ice tunnel; while Ganzer stood with a group of people he considered more acceptable, as if it mattered in this place: gangers and the like whose intelligence and—sometimes—human decency stood them head and shoulders above Hauser and his ilk. But despite that these foremen were intelligent, it didn't make them any less vulnerable to terror; on the contrary, their fertile imaginations only increased it.

Knowing what was happening here, however—its cause, and the fact that he was in no way guilty—Ganzer felt much easier in his mind than he might otherwise feel; but still, on sensing someone standing closer than necessary, and feeling a tentative nudge in the ribs, he gave a start and softly said, "Eh? What?"

"Excuse me," said the young man, who might be twenty-eight years old, fresh-faced and red-haired, "but you look like someone who knows a thing or two. Can we talk?"

Ganzer looked all around. Others were whispering together, conversing in low tones, bunching up if only for human companionship. And so he nodded. "But quietly. What is it you want?"

"Ah! I know you now," said the other, drawing back a pace. "The Herr Direktor. I'm sorry if I—"

Ganzer took his elbow and cut him short. "Direktor in name only," he quietly answered. "And who are you?"

"Hans Niewohner," said the other, a little too loudly for Ganzer's liking. "Of the firm Niewohner Electrics—well, as it used to be. But I've been here for almost a month now."

"Hush!" Ganzer cautioned him again. "You must keep it down or we can't talk. And I'll ask you again, what is it you want?"

"I just want to understand!" Niewohner answered, his eyes earnest and anxious. "I've heard some talk and pretty much know what has happened, but why would a traitor— hell no, a bloody hero if you ask me!—why would he want to come back here after committing his alleged 'crime'? Also, why do those three *things* assume he's still here and hasn't already run away to somewhere where he'll be safe?"

Gunter Ganzer knew the answers to both questions. But now he cautioned the young man for a third time, saying, *"Hush!* If you can't keep your voice down we can't talk! And let's move a little farther away from that lot, shall we?" He indicated the now fairly large group of surly-looking trustees.

They moved deeper into the ranks of the gangers, but kept slightly apart even from them. There, speaking almost under his breath, Ganzer answered Niewohner's second question first. "You ask why the Three assume the culprit is still here? They assume nothing but *know* he's here! As to how they know: that's the answer to your first question. Also, you ask why hasn't the alleged 'criminal' run off somewhere safe. *Huh!* My answer: because there is no such place. But tell me . . . you say you've been here for a month now? Haven't you been introduced to a Khiff, one of their familiars?"

"A Khiff? I've heard such mentioned in whispers, what-ever it's supposed to mean, but no one wants to enlarge upon it. Did you say something about a familiar? What, like a witch's familiar?"

"Exactly," said Ganzer. "They each have one. In fact, for a long time I've half believed that they are witches—or one of them at least—while the other two are wizards. Who knows?" He shrugged.

"And the Khiff? Their familiars . . . what do they do?"

"So then, you're *sure* you haven't yet been introduced?"

"No, not that I know of."

"Oh," said Ganzer with an assertive nod of his head, "you would know right enough! These are the stuff of nightmares! As for what they do: they get inside your head—and they can do that literally, if it's warranted—and they find out all about you; they get to know your weaknesses, which we every one of us have, and they know how to prey on them. After that, no matter where you are or what you're doing, they can sniff you out and locate you for their masters. Today, I myself was called back here from my house in the village. *She* spoke to me, her voice in my head, amplified through her Khiff."

The other shook his head, looked dazed. "It sounds fantastic. I'm not sure I can believe it."

"You're a ganger, a foreman," Ganzer told him. "If you're a family man they will have leverage . . . your wife, children?"

"I have none, no one." Niewohner shook his head again.

"Ah!" said Ganzer. "That's why you haven't been introduced to a Khiff. They can't let you leave the Schloss and so have no need to take your mind pattern. As for a majority of the people here—trustees, foremen, scientists, guards, and all the more important workers—they have all been 'recorded' by the Khiff. Some seventy-two of them, from what I can make out."

"But . . . a creature with such mental capacity?"

"Three creatures," Ganzer answered. "Haven't you been listening to me? They each have a Khiff."

Niewohner took Ganzer's elbow. "There are so many things I want to know!"

Ganzer found that he liked the younger man. Here was someone he could at least talk to; a rarity in Schloss Zonigen. And so: "Yes, I fully understand your curiosity, but for now we had best be quiet. I can seek you out, later perhaps."

"Good! But until then, one more question, please?"

"Quickly then."

"What *is* this thing we're building? Is it a weapon of some sort?"

"Perhaps it is," Ganzer replied. "Like anything else here, that seems entirely possible. But I really don't know for sure. No one does."

"But—" Niewohner began again, and came to an abrupt halt as Tannoy speakers in the walls sounded a gonging note of warning. And:

"*Hush!*" Ganzer whispered, gooseflesh creeping on his arms. "Be quiet now. They're coming!"

And moments later the Three began to arrive . . .

17

The Three arrived. Like a trio of stage magicians they came—if the dais could be thought of as a stage; which, constructed of solid blocks of stone, it could not. There were no trapdoors here, no cabinet marked with moons, stars, and comets, no smoke and mirrors. Only the solid stone dais with its great cross set in a disc of some nameless substance as black as space. And the cross, more properly a crucifix, was by no means a holy symbol; sinister, it dangled chains and manacles. As for the manner of the Three's coming, however: that did seem mystical, magical.

The air above the dais shimmered like a mirage, like the air over a blacktop road in the middle of summer: a horizontal blurring effect that heralded the arrival first of the female, Frau Lessing, more properly Mordri One. *She* blurred into being on one side of the dais like a hologram made solid; and just a moment later, on the other side, came Simon Salcombe, or Mordri Two. Finally, a heartbeat later, and Guyler Schweitzer was there, Mordri Three, materializing out of the thin air between the other two.

For one long minute the Three stood absolutely motionless, tall, straight, as thin as reeds, staring out over the heads of their audience; then the female thing stepped forward. Dressed in a white kaftanlike shift in common with her companions, she reminded Gunter Ganzer of nothing so much as one of the candles in a three-pronged candelabra . . . a thought that, knowing how easily she could reach him, he immediately put out of his head! And as Ganzer shrank down into himself—in the total silence commanded by the sheer presence of the Three, with the cavern's acoustics serving to amplify her voice four or five times over—Mordri One spoke out:

"It has come to our attention," she said, "that we harbour a traitor in our midst; a man who, given the shelter of Schloss Zonigen, has conceived and committed an act of betrayal against our first rule, against the security of the Schloss, against we Three. He is on his way here even now, in the custody of two of our guards. He heard the orders and, as we anticipated, made to flee . . . only to be arrested in the act of throwing himself down from a high place. That would have meant a merciful death; alas that we can't allow such. *Ah!*" She pointed a long arm, hand, and finger at one of the access shafts. "And here he is."

Then, speaking to the guards who hauled and buffeted their prisoner into the central area, where those about the dais made way for them, "Bring him up here," she said.

The guards climbed the dais steps, manacled the man to the cross, then quickly backed off, got down, fell in with the rest of the observers. Guyler Schweitzer, or Mordri Three, now stepped forward in his central position in front of the cross. "You see before you a traitor. Now we question him, and we *will* have the truth."

The Three turned inward to face the man on the cross, and as one they took a flowing pace toward him. It was Mordri Two, Simon Salcombe, who spoke this time, his voice shrill, rasping like a blunt file, grating on the nerves of all who heard him; for indeed his message wasn't only for the prisoner. "You will not lie to us; you are not able to lie. But should you attempt to do so, there will be pain. There will in any event be pain, which any attempt at lying can only exacerbate."

Like the jaws of a vise the Three leaned forward, stepped up onto the black disc, lifted spindly arms and hands to grasp their victim's jacket, and effortlessly tore it to shreds. The garment now hung down in strips from the belt at his waist. He was quite small, something less than Ganzer's height at around sixty-six or -seven inches. He was lean; his belly hollow, his ribs prominent, thrust out by his weight where he dangled with his wrists manacled over his head, his naked toes barely touching the disc. His pale face was a mask of despair: his cheeks were sucked in, his eyes hollow, his mouth half open, moaning.

He had been beaten; bruises showed on his arms, his thin ribs, his sides; a trickle of blood smeared his cheek from the corner of his mouth to his chin. His left eye was beginning to bulge; it was bruised and closing.

Until now the man had merely moaned, albeit in a trembly, terrified manner . . . that was about to change.

Without warning Mordris Two and Three reached out again to take hold of his arms; while Mordri One, Ganzer's *"She,"* placed a long-fingered hand flat on his belly close up under his ribs. They didn't so much grasp as simply touch him. And Ganzer found himself panting shallowly, muttering, "The touch! The touch!"

"Eh? Touch?" Niewohner whispered.

"Oh, you have been touched, too," Ganzer told him, between each snatched breath of air. "Not like this, no, but they've at least tasted you. They've tasted everyone. So now watch, learn, and for God's sake *be quiet!*"

Simon Salcombe, Mordri Two, was again speaking to the prisoner:

"You were a trustee—you have a son here, who guaranteed your discretion—and yet you would have betrayed us, betrayed him, betrayed yourself! Which in the end you have done anyway."

"No! No!" the man cried out, his voice shrill and echoing, almost a scream. "I did nothing! It wasn't me!"

"*A lie!*" Mordri Two screamed back at him, bending a little to bring his face closer to his victim's face. "Look!" And with his free hand he produced a scrap of paper, sniffed at it, held it up for the man on the cross to see. "Your treachery, in your words. I can *smell* you on this paper, and I can *read* it in your mind! Now admit it, that you have lied."

The man saw that denial was useless. "I . . . I was *drunk!*" he sobbed. "It was the schnapps, too much schnapps. But I knew my duty and when I woke up sober I came back here. My poor boy is here. I didn't run—I *couldn't* run—for his sake. And I swear I'll never make that mistake again. It wasn't me, not me. It was the schnapps!"

"No, you didn't run," Salcombe snarled. "Because to do so would have given you away. You hoped this letter would never be produced. But it has been produced, and you are its author! Ah, but when you heard the alert, the instructions we issued—our orders to gather here—*then* you ran! And you would have killed yourself to rob us of our revenge. Also, it's possible that you thought your death would somehow lift the burden from your son. But the children of you people, your wives, relatives: they are our surety. Therefore your son will be made to pay—*and in the same measure as you yourself!* So then, now the pain—but only the *least* of the pain!"

"Then do your worst, you bloody *thing!*" The prisoner tried to lift a leg, kick at Salcombe, but only managed to swing with his chains. "If I pay then I pay; at least I tried to save some other, him and his family. And anyway what is death after four years in the hell you've made of this place?"

"*Ahhhhh!*" howled the Mordris in unison.

The Three leaned inward more yet; their hands on the prisoner's body appeared to blur with rapid vibrations. Then, as he commenced to jerk and writhe, crying out in some nameless agony, so the neon lights over the workbenches, and other lighting in the walls and domed rock ceiling, began to sputter. The speakers of the Tannoy system were also affected; they squealed and made other raucous sounds, interspersed with a crackling and buzzing synchronous with the wild flickering and strobing of the lights.

It lasted for several long moments. Then:

On the cross, the victim no longer cried out; writhing and jerking as before, he now seemed struck dumb, making only humming noises with his nose, which gushed blood. But in fact these sounds *were* his screams; his mouth was sealed over . . . his lips had grown together in a patch of pink flesh!

"And now tell them." Mordri Two's high-pitched shriek—of joy? Of pleasure? Of purest evil—rose over the clamour of the electrical sputterings and the outcry from the Tannoy speakers. "Tell these men—these *ex*-colleagues who knew you, who worked with you—how it hurts and how you'll gladly welcome the death which will shortly follow. Explain to them if you will what you would say to your son; how you would attempt to acquit yourself if you could be there when we send him also to his death, which we surely will. Why don't you cry out for forgiveness? Not that you'll receive it."

Then Salcombe paused in his ranting; leaning closer yet to the agonized figure on the cross, he angled his long head in an attitude of listening and screeched, "What? What are you trying to say? You may not oblige me, for your flesh is no longer your own and your lips are sealed? A pity you haven't kept them that way! Oh, ha-ha-*haaa!* But of course your flesh isn't your own . . . for it's ours, to do with as we will!"

And turning his face to the stunned, slack-jawed onlookers where they stood around the dais he said, "Now see what befalls them that break Schloss Zonigen's laws: agony! Pain such as you cannot imagine, but which you yet may witness. Pain, when flesh and blood and bone become as one element, dead as time past and black as space!"

He turned his face back to the twisted, flailing, *changing* man on the cross, and along with Mordris One and Three used the touch to send mutative energies blasting through their victim's racked body.

His arms seemed to be melting; like softening candles they lengthened, dangling long hands with globular tips on foot-long fingers. His legs, too, until his naked feet stood on the black disc; except the word "stood" gives a false impression. For the flesh was folding out from inside the legs of his trousers like puddings of soft dough, forming elephantine pads with flattened toes. His face was now freakishly elongated, with his lower jaw slumping onto his chest on a neck that was collapsing into itself like a concertina stood on end.

He was now a travesty of a man. His eyes stood out an inch from their sockets; his ears, pulled by gravity, were beginning to slide out of place; the place where his mouth had been throbbed, pulsing like a bellows as he tried in vain to suck through a hole that was no longer there. And even though the Three had withdrawn their hands, still he continued to melt, the flesh of his body, and even the bones, pooling and folding over his belt and the tatters of his jacket; while his head slumped onto what remained of his shoulders, his shoulders into his ribs, and his ribs into his lower body. Thinned down to little more than skin over bones, his fleshless arms slid from their manacles, flowed into the rest of him; and *all* of him began to sink down through his clothing onto the disc.

And as he sloughed away, so the *totality* of him, his complete self, was turning black, merging into and becoming part of the black disc. And now too the nature of that disc became apparent. It was what remained of men, their elemental *ingredient,* when nothing any longer remained of their humanity, their form, their minds and personalities, their very being. And now in the briefest of moments the man on the cross—who had *been* the man on the cross—was part of the disc, which was just a fraction of an inch thicker!

In silence absolute *She* and her leering companions

turned again to the crowd. "It is done," she said. "Now you go back to work, and remember: in mere weeks, a month at most, our work is done here. Then all shall be as it was, all put back to rights, all set free. All you have to do is live until then—and work, of course. Guards, trustees, foremen, gangers—see to it."

She made an adjustment to what might be a bracelet on her wrist, as did her colleagues on the dais. And in another moment the dais was empty . . .

Ganzer was as good as his word. Later that day, when something like normality—at least a semblance of calm—had returned to Schloss Zonigen, he sought out Hans Niewohner at the benches in the great cavern where he supervised a handful of electricians, took him aside and mainly out of sight, and spoke to him.

"As for why I'm doing this," he said, "it is because I can sense desperation in you. You are a pleasant young man, Niewohner, and I wouldn't want you to come to harm."

"About my desperation: you're right," said the other. "And yes I would run—but after I think about it for a while, then I begin to see the problems."

"Have you considered them all?" said Ganzer. "I doubt it. For after all you spoke to me, and without first assuring yourself of my loyalties."

Niewohner nodded his shock of red hair. "Well, you looked honest enough to me. As for the problems: I'm fairly sure that by now I have considered most of them. But yes, the difficulties would seem to be a great many."

"To say the least," Ganzer agreed. "I would have said too many. This place is a towering crag. There are three ways down: by road, by cable car, and by a leap into space."

"Yes," said Niewohner, glumly. "Or maybe four—if I had a thousand feet of good rope!"

"You won't find much climbing rope here," Ganzer told him. "Plenty of cable, but it's heavy. And how to move it unnoticed, from here to one of the ice shafts?" He shook his head. "Forget it. Even if you got that far you'd be seen. They have a watcher stationed at every vantage point; you would be hauled up, which would leave you with a choice: either to let go the cable or to be dragged before the Three. Me, I would let go the cable first—but it will never come to that, for I'm no climber; nor am I in any fit state to climb." He waggled his twisted foot. "And anyway, why do you even consider it? You haven't been here very long, and if they speak the truth there's an end to all this in just a few weeks' time."

"You take their word for that?" said Niewohner, lifting an eyebrow. "They have a weapon that they've spent years designing and building, and in a month's time . . . what then? Surely their intention must be to test it. But to what purpose? Shouldn't we be trying to warn the outside world of what's going on here?"

"But we don't know what's going on here," Ganzer replied. "And we don't even know if it's a weapon. Indeed, all we do know is that everything here is illegal and that we are slaves, literally."

Niewohner shook his head, chewed his lip. "None of which eases my feeling of desperation one jot. I just want to be out of here!"

Ganzer said, "So does everyone—so did I—and look what it got me." Again he waggled his foot. "This was when I determined to test their precepts by staying in the village beyond my personal curfew; I was one hour late returning. That was in the first year of the Three's occupancy, since when there have been plenty of others who just wanted to be out of here, who pursued their desire to its end. And its end is over there." He pointed across the cavern to the central dais. "You see that black disc there? There was nothing there when first they came here—not even a dais. That disc is made of men who, much like you and I, 'just wanted to be out of here.' "

Niewohner stood straighter, pulled back his shoulders, and said, "Why don't we rise up? They are Three and we are many. We could be all over them in moments!"

"And the trustees?" Ganzer had learned practicality. "What of the guards?"

"Couldn't they be swayed to our cause?"

"Now hold!" said Ganzer, suddenly alarmed and looking all about. "*Your* cause, Niewohner, not mine! In fact, I'm only here to talk you out of it! And as for the guards and trustees being swayed to *your* cause: impossible! They have crimes of their own to answer for. My wife, my poor wife . . . ! And she is only one of the many poor creatures—women, children, and some men—who are daily abused in this place."

"But I have no one here," Niewohner answered. "Only myself. And I feel like . . . like a damned *coward* for not doing anything! If I could only hot-wire a car and get down to the village—"

"The plateau is under constant surveillance," said Ganzer, "and there are watchers in the village."

"Watchers?"

"The Three have been here for five years. One of the first things they did was to secure the village; also, certain of the villages around, unless I miss my guess. Face it, Hans, Schloss Zonigen is locked down!"

"The cable car—"

"But you don't have a pass; the guards and trustees would question you, find you out in a moment. And even if you somehow succeeded where would you go? Across the mountains on foot? No, you would go to the village, the only route out . . . and then be brought back up here."

"But—"

"Now listen—" Ganzer paused; but then, after a moment's thought, "Oh, to hell with it! What matter the niceties of polite conversation now? Do you use the toilet? Do you . . . relieve yourself of your body's natural desires: which is to say, masturbate? Do you even eat?"

Niewohner shook his head. "No. None of that. They've done something to me, some chemical in the water . . . I really don't know. That's another of the things I wanted to ask you."

Ganzer nodded. "Yes, yes. You have been touched! There is no chemical in the water. They have *touched* you when

first you came here. They have this power; they control
flesh, interfere with natural functions. Why haul edibles up
here when they can stop you eating? Why install toilet facil-
ities to clog Schloss Zonigen up and slow the work? And
why permit small, well, 'comforts' to weaken us and similarly slow us down?"

Standing straighter yet, Niewohner glared and clenched
his fists. He looked about to burst out with some loud im-
precation, and Ganzer immediately cautioned him: "*Quietly* now!"

Niewohner deflated. "Damn!" he said, between his teeth.
"I still think we could take them."

"Then you think wrong," said Ganzer. "Three years ago
one of the guards went mad. He turned his gun on the female. We saw her cut down, there on that dais, where she
delivered some kind of inspirational oratory. Her Khiff *detached* itself, and like a bubble of blue-grey snot it sped to
the madman and entered into his head. His brains came out
through his ears and he fell like he'd been axed! In a matter
of moments his entire body . . . God! It turned inside out!"

Niewohner stepped back from Ganzer, as if he, too, were
mad. He looked about to laugh, however shakily, but
Ganzer went on: "The Khiff sped back to the female; she
got up; she was entire, whole again! She went and stood in
his entrails, and they were *alive*—at least until she'd separated them out!"

Niewohner blinked, and said, "And that's the truth?"

Ganzer shrugged. "There are others you can ask."

"I don't think I would dare."

"Rightly so. Nor should you 'dare' consider escaping.
But you are not alone. I, too, am a coward; or maybe not.
Think on this: if the Three were done away with—*if* that
were possible—who would there be to put right the mon-
strousness which even now lives a life, of sorts, in Schloss
Zonigen's cells?"

"I've heard something of that," said Niewohner.

"Oh, I expect you have," said Ganzer, with an uncontrollable shudder. "But you haven't *seen* it!"

Then, suddenly aware of a prickling sensation at the back of his mind, Schloss Zonigen's "Direktor" excused himself, letting Niewohner get back to his work . . .

Hurrying to return to his own station in a small office close to the reception area, Ganzer was almost at once brought to a halt in a well-lighted access shaft when *She* flowed from a side tunnel into his path. Seeing Ganzer go pale as the blood immediately drained from his face, Mordri One smiled and said:

"Ah, Gunter! That was well done. I commend your response—your sensible arguments—in a most indiscreet conversation."

Oh, God! She knows! thought Ganzer, before he could control his mental processes.

"But of course I know," she said. "On occasion my Khiff is wont to scan those within his sphere of responsibility. In this way unusual circumstances are at once brought to my attention."

"I . . . I . . ." said Ganzer.

"Fortunately your responses to, er, certain rash ideas and proposals do you great credit—fortunate for you, that is! And meanwhile this young person of our mutual acquaintance performs his duties inadequately because his mind is full of troublesome thoughts. I go to see him now; my Khiff is anxious to meet him, in order to explain things. He is in any case due a visit, and perhaps even overdue."

"Yes, of course!" Ganzer gasped. "Quite right."

"You may carry on."

"Yes, indeed!"

Trembling, Ganzer watched her glide off down the shaft in the direction of the great cavern. As she drifted away a malignant grey-green blob of a face peered avidly at him from behind the collar of her kaftan . . .

18

"Not long," Shania had told him, but already it had been *three* days (well of course it had!) and Scott still hadn't heard from her. Now on the evening of the third day he looked back on what little he'd achieved since her extraordinary visit.

He had contacted St. Jude's to see if he could acquire any leads on the parents of those no-longer-sick kids. His thinking was that if he could track them down they might be able to tell him how to contact Salcombe . . . not that he intended to contact him, not yet, but he would certainly like to know where the man was located. But the receptionist and then the staff at the hospital had given him the runaround and in the end told him nothing. It was all highly confidential, they said; it went against hospital policy that didn't permit them to discuss ex-patients or their relatives, they said. Well, Scott hadn't been too hopeful in the first place, but at least it had been worth a try.

Then he'd tried several of the better known orphanages, to see if he could locate the third once-poorly kid. Here he found himself on firmer footing, even though it went somewhat against his natural instincts to pose as the father of yet another sick child. But:

As "Quentin Mandeville" on the phone to the Geoffrey Bartholomew Sanctuary for Bereaved and Orphaned Children, his sixth such inquiry, Scott explained how he'd been given hope—indeed how he had been inspired—by what he had heard of the works of the faith-healer Simon Salcombe, and desired to seek him out to discuss the case of his own son, whose extremely rare disorder was slowly but surely killing him.

He'd then been put through to the so-called Head Warden, who had answered him: "Er, this is Pastor Patterson speaking—Mr. er . . . ?"

"Quentin Mandeville," Scott had growled in reply. "And by the way, that's 'the' Quentin Mandeville. It's possible you may have heard of me in connection with various charities—?"

"Ah! Er, indeed!" said the other, trying to sound at least as convincing as Scott, and falling just a little short.

"—But none so charitable as that person with whom I now wish to acquaint myself, through your good offices," Scott continued. "Namely Simon Salcombe. Pastor, I have this sick child, my own dear son, and if it is at all possible that Mr. Salcombe can do for my boy what he did for your ward in St. Jude's Hospital—"

"My dear sir," the pastor had cut him off. "Is it that you are seeking a connection?"

"Precisely. I wish to contact Mr. Salcombe at the earliest possible opportunity. My son's life may well depend upon it. No one else can offer any hope to my only son and heir. Perhaps it is beyond the powers even of Mr. Salcombe, and I will be spending a vast sum of money to no avail. But still I must try."

"And so you have answered my next question before I asked it," said Pastor Patterson. "You see, I have been given permission to pass on information with regard to Mr. Salcombe only to persons of proven means. This may sound very *un*charitable, but as it was explained to me, the facility in Switzerland where Mr. Salcombe and his colleagues, er, meditate and aspire to perfect their healing arts has a multitude of overheads; in short, huge expenses. Mr. Salcombe's time being limited and costly, he must perforce charge those who can afford him in order to compensate for those who cannot, such as the children at St. Jude's Hospital. Myself, I understand this well indeed, since the Geoffrey Bartholomew Sanctuary struggles under, ahem, similiar financial burdens. For which reason I know you'll understand if I require you to supply certain, er, documents, credentials, and validations . . . ? All in compliance with Mr. Salcombe's instructions, of course."

At which Scott's tactics had changed up a gear. It

seemed distasteful but he *must* continue with his lies, making promises he couldn't keep; this wasn't at all to his liking but now that he'd started he simply couldn't let it get away from him.

"Sir," he said, "tomorrow I attend a children's charity in Washington, DC; a ball where my dinner will cost four thousand dollars, and each glass of wine two hundred more. Forgive me if I seem vulgar in respect of such sums—if I toss them off as lightly as certain men drop famous names—but money is literally *nothing* to me! What good are millions if one's health, or the health of one's family, is in jeopardy? No good at all. And please rest assured that the finances of the Geoffrey Bartholomew Sanctuary will not suffer as a result of this conversation. Indeed I have a check which I'm prepared to fill in now, this very minute, but since I'm flying tonight I cannot immediately satisfy all of your other requirements."

"My dear Mr. Mandeville, I'm so sorry! I really would like to help you; why, I even see it as my duty! But—"

"If you insist," said Scott, "in my absence my agents will contact you with the various documents you require. But time is of the essence. My poor son is dying . . . surely you can appreciate the life-and-death urgency of the situation? Simply supply me with Mr. Salcombe's address, or a way of contacting him, and all concerned—yourself included, or rather your Sanctuary—will benefit by reason of my gratitude."

"Mr. Mandeville, I see you are a man generous to a fault," said the pastor. "Your offer to assist with our funding is appreciated beyond my ability to convey. Even so, I can only give you the barest of details, for these are all I have! The faith-healer Simon Salcombe may be reached at his research establishment in the Swiss Alps. And the only address I have is Schloss Zonigen: an icy, honeycombed crag, or so I am led to believe. I do have permission to telephone this mountainous retreat, but I may not under *any* circumstances divulge the number. Such are Mr. Salcombe's very strict instructions. However, if you would like me to call on your behalf, in a purely introductory capacity, I find myself once again obliged to require that—"

"Pastor Patterson," said Scott, cutting in and barely concealing a sigh, "my agents, trusted men who are able to contact me at all times, will be in touch with you—with my check, of course—at which time you may make the necessary introductions. Meanwhile I shall look forward to dealing with Mr. Salcombe himself. Now I am afraid I must get on; I fly within the hour. But you'll never know how relieved and grateful I am for your assistance in this matter." (Well at least *that* was the truth!) "And now I leave it up to you and my agents, and bid you good night."

"One last thing!" said the pastor, hurriedly. "While I and the Sanctuary look forward to receiving your check, I think it best to forewarn you that in this respect Mr. Salcombe is, well, oddly specific. It would appear to be one of his—how may one put it?—foibles, to take the bulk of any payment in gold. And this, er, *very* discreetly since his offices are in Switzerland, if you follow my meaning: the international laws with regard to trading in precious metals, et cetera—er, *ahem!*"

"Well then," said Scott. "But surely in his case we should make allowances. Many great men have their eccentricities and I entirely understand. Indeed, I thank you for this item of valuable information, and you may consider my lips sealed."

"Good!" said Pastor Patterson. "Good night then. I wish you a safe journey and look forward to speaking to your agents."

"Again my thanks, and good-bye," said Scott.

And holding the telephone to his ear a moment longer, finally Scott had heard the pastor mumble something unintelligible, and then the *click!* when the handset slipped into its cradle to break the connection—in fact a double click, and very hollow-sounding. Odd, that. There must be a fault on the line: static, probably. Well, that happened occasionally.

So then, Kelly and Bill Comber had been right: the "altruistic" Mr. Salcombe's visit to St. Jude's had been a recruiting exercise. He had definitely, albeit covertly—by reason of his alleged aversion to public appearances and the measures he took to protect his comings, goings, and knowledge of his whereabouts at any given time—he had indeed been seeking to attract rich new clients.

And Scott thought:

Murderers, of necessity, must needs be a cagey lot; especially when they're weird, alien bastards like Simon Salcombe!

And he also thought:

Schloss Zonigen, hmmm!

But he could find no mention of such a place in the index to his Great World Atlas . . .

Now it was the evening of the third day, and it found Scott St. John sitting in his study frowning at a sun-bronzed girl on the glossy cover of a package-holiday folder, lying on his desk. In the folder: some tourist information, one hundred pounds' worth of drachmas, and an airline ticket to Zante. He had heard Three in his dreams but had only contacted him once, and had been met with a barrage of "barked" telepathic queries about when he was going to come for him. And now the date was set: tomorrow.

Well at least he would go *to* him, see what he could do for him, but as for getting him out of there: how does one smuggle a "wolf of the wild" off a Greek island? And yet in the back of his mind Scott felt certain that there was a way . . . if only he could *remember* it. But that—like his recently discovered telepathic abilities—was another mystery that he couldn't as yet fathom: the feeling that he should *know* things, that he'd somehow been enabled, gifted.

But gifted by a golden splinter in a dream? And Three, too?

As best he could, Scott shrugged it off; in his mind, he'd turned these things over so often now that he'd reached a stage where he even avoided thinking about them. They would just have to work themselves out, revealing themselves (or perhaps returning to mind, as the case might be) in their own sweet time.

He had checked the weather, the temperature in the Ionian Islands. Hovering in the mid-twenties centigrade, it was hot by anyone's standards. Scott could very nearly "sense" Three's tongue lolling and wondered how he was coping with it. He would doubtless find out tomorrow. And he also wondered if he could hire a boat to take them to the mainland, the Peloponnisos—and then what? Lay claim to the animal, license him, and put him in quarantine? What, for six months?

Something inside said: work it out when you get there. And something else said: don't worry about it, because it *will* work itself out. But he worried anyway . . .

A velvety dusk had settled in, and a milky ground mist had come drifting from a stream in a nearby copse to lap Scott's garden. Daydreaming, and drowsy, his eyes not quite focussed where they stared moodily, vacantly at the picture of the sun-bronzed girl, suddenly he became aware of mental presences. And moments later Shania and Three got through to him almost at the same time.

Scott, said Three first, and Scott gave a massive start in his chair. *Scott, do you hear me?*

"I hear you loud and clear, yes," he answered. "You startled me. But you also remembered my name."

Listen, Three growled. *If you are coming for me it must be soon. I mean* really *soon! They have started to lay traps for me with poisoned meat. Fortunately my nose is good. Not only can I sense directions, the outside world, yourself and Two—*

"Shania," said Scott.

—Yes, Shania, the joining one—but I also know foul meat when I smell it! I've taken to hiding near Zek's house where my father's scent confuses the trackers.

"Trackers?"

Tame dogs on leashes that the hunters use to sniff me out. But Zek protects my father—who is "legitimate"—and so protects me. I stay in a cave near the shore, where sea spray blows my scent away. But all the local chicken coops are well guarded now, the rabbits are wise to me, and I can't stay here forever. Zek knows I'm here; I believe my father told her. She sometimes puts out meat. And so I survive, but poorly.

"I'm coming for you tomorrow," said Scott. "At noon, or an hour or so past noon, when the sun is still high, I shall be at Zek's place. Sooner if I can manage it. There may be difficulties, but I will be there—"

There came a sudden small disturbance of air and a flutter of loose papers on Scott's desk, and:

"Good!" said Three and Shania together, the latter's voice coming from directly behind Scott, making him jump again before turning around in his swivel chair. And there she stood: Shania Two.

And Three said, *One thing before I go. You are Scott, she is Shania, and I am Wolf as my father before me. We are One and Two and Three, but we are more than numbers. I understand names but have trouble with numbers. Is it well that I am Wolf?*

"Yes, it's well," said Scott and Shania together. At which Wolf's thoughts dwindled to nothing and he was gone.

But Shania was still there.

"You healed well," she said.

"I know, and I still don't believe it."

Her face fell. "You don't?"

"It's just an expression. Of course I believe it. I mean, how can I fail to believe it? Here you are just stepped out of nowhere, and I've been having a telepathic conversation with a dog—or rather a wolf of the wild—and so yes, I believe. In just about anything you want me to believe in!"

And now that smile of hers, so warm he could feel it. But it quickly faded as she said, "Scott, it was important that you believe: in me and in Wolf, but especially in yourself. That is why I said 'good' when you told him you would come for him. The fact that you accept his plight, that you are his One, and that you've taken steps to rescue him—"

"Which may prove difficult and even impossible," Scott cut in, coming to his feet.

"—was the final step that you needed to take," she continued. "I've been waiting for you to take that very important step. As for the problems you foresee, the difficulties: there may be some, but I do not accept that it's impossible."

"Oh, really?" he said. "But you're not going to Zante."

"Zante?"

"Zakynthos, a Greek island in the Ionian Sea. That's where Three—where 'Wolf'—is. You didn't know that?"

"No." She shook her head. "His general direction, yes. His 'voice,' on those occasions when he contacted you: I also heard that. Also his howl of sudden awareness when he was stricken—"

"Stricken?" Scott frowned.

"When he was enabled." She also frowned, looking for a way to best express herself. "When whatever it was that changed you changed him; when he sensed there was a One and began to search for you, however gropingly. That was why I assisted him—why I became the joining one—because I sensed that we were Three."

"Whoah!" said Scott, making a hand signal to tell her that most of what she'd just said had flown right over his head.

"I know," she said, reaching to take his hand, which made him shiver a very little. "It's difficult, isn't it? But, Scott, you may believe it's just as difficult and even more so for me. But getting back to Wolf: you were his magnet no less than you were mine. In fact, you are more a magnet to him, for you're his man, his One."

"And the three of us together?" said Scott. "What the hell are we together?"

"We're a unit," said Shania. "And that's something I understand, for in my world there were many such units of three. All of us were units of three. But none of them had a wolf. No, for in my world there were no wolves. And now there is no world."

Suddenly she was sad, so sad. Scott looked at her and saw a tear forming in the corner of her eye. "You're crying."

"I try too hard," she said as he took her by the shoulders. "Your women cry."

For the moment, as he took a handkerchief from his pocket, her words made no real impact on him. "I'll be careful not to ruin your makeup," he told her, wiping away the small trickle. But then he paused and looked again, as she said:

"There is no makeup."

And finally he noticed the differences. She was the same woman with the same voice; her straight yet shapely posture was the same; her eyes with those pinpoint stars that seemed to expand and then shrink like strange pulsars, they, too, were the same. Yet Scott knew that in some subtle way she was different than the last time he had seen her; like a twin but not quite, not entirely identical. And of course she was right: there was no makeup for him to ruin. Her skin tones were real, natural.

But: "No." Shania shook her head. "They're only as natural as I can make them."

From the moment she had touched him his desk lamp had been playing up, dimming and brightening, almost switching off, only to flare back to life. Scott reached over and hit the button on the lamp's base. The dusk in his garden, as deep and as haunted now as Shania's hair, at once seemed to flow into the room.

"There was no need for that," she told him. "I can control it with a small effort. A very small effort, if you will let go of me. It was the contact."

"Ah!" Scott's jaw fell partly open. "The contact? You mean when we touch? So then, the trouble I've been experiencing with the electrics is down to you?"

"It was the contact, yes," she said, releasing herself and switching the lamp back on. Now that they stood apart it burned fairly steadily again, with just the occasional flicker.

"And my telephone?" he said. "Was that you, too?"

Shania looked at the telephone and again frowned. Stepping forward a pace, she touched the phone. "No, that wasn't me. It was someone else, someone who tampered with the instrument. Can we find anything strange, do you think?"

She unscrewed the cover of the mouthpiece and held out the handset for Scott to look inside. Stuck to the cup's inner wall he saw a dull metal disc about one-quarter of an inch thick and three-quarters of an inch in diameter, like a small battery. It was connected by a wire as thick as a hair to the phone's diaphragm.

Taking the phone from Shania, and glaring at it with angry narrowed eyes, Scott took a deep breath and growled, "Well, I'll be . . . !" And yanking the tiny listening device from its seating, letting it fall to the floor and crushing it underfoot, he went on, "Damn! *I've been bugged!*"

19

Scott stared at the tiny fragments of intricate circuitry and crumpled foil casing on the floorboards at his feet. "Bugged!" he said again. "But by whom?"

"Not by the Three," said Shania, with a quick shake of her head. "They're not aware of you, or perhaps only faintly aware, on the outermost rim of their sensory periphery. As your powers grow, however—and if you fail to keep them shielded—they'll become far more aware, as they would be of any psychically endowed person. One thing is sure: if they knew of your potential, then by now you would be dead."

Staring at her, Scott said, "Well thanks a lot for that!"

"But it's the truth," she said, and shrugged in a matter-of-fact but by no means casual manner. "No, this could only be your people, E-Branch, the ones who picked you up."

"E-Branch? Is that what they're called? You're sure?"

"Yes," she said. "For when they were looking at you I was looking at them. Because their minds were open and receptive to your thoughts, they were also open to me. It is much easier for a telepath to read a telepath than a nontelepath. I even tried to send them a message: a warning to keep away and avoid jeopardizing what we are doing."

Scott gave a derisory little snort, aimed more at himself than at her, and pulled at his ear. "You might want to tell me about that sometime," he said. "I mean, about what we're doing. Because apart from being a member of a unit, one of a very odd team, or rather Three's One, and One of Three—for God's sake!—I don't know if I'm coming or going, on my head or my heels!"

"You are naturally confused," she told him.

He gave another snort, let out his breath in a long sigh, and said, "Only slightly!" And followed it up with: "I'm sorry, Shania; I'm not usually so sarcastic. It's just that I'm finding it very hard to put all this together."

"But I know that you *are* putting it together," she argued. "You've accepted your telepathy, which is maturing in you. You have accepted your position as a member of our Three. You have decided to attempt Wolf's rescue. And—perhaps less sensibly, and despite my warnings—you've begun delving in places where you shouldn't go."

"I've what?" But Scott couldn't help feeling guilty, and he probably looked it, too.

"I can contact you at any time," she reminded him. "I have done so during the last three days, if only to be sure you were keeping safe. I've 'overheard' you thinking about conversations with St. Jude's Hospital. And much worse, I was just a few minutes too late to stop you talking about Simon Salcombe. We *dare not* bring ourselves, or yourself, to his attention! Not yet."

Scott scowled. "That man is a murderer and must be brought to justice!"

"Yes," she answered. "But how to do it? Through the authorities? I'm sure we'll discover that in Switzerland, where he is domiciled, Mordri Two has already bought and otherwise suborned several so-called authorities. The Mordri Three, they pay their way, Scott, and your world is full of avarice."

"Mordri Two? That's Salcombe?"

"That's his name in his Three. The others are Mordri One, female, who calls herself Frau Gerda Lessing; and Mordri Three, who has adopted the name Guyler Schweitzer after the land where they are based."

"Now it comes thick and fast," said Scott, sighing. And as he began to feel the pressure of things: "Let's go into my sitting room, take the weight off our feet, have a drink—a small one—er, you do drink, right?—and be comfortable. I really would like to think I'm absorbing at least some of this!"

"Very well," said Shania. "But first let's check the rest of the house for—what, 'bugs' did you say? That term is new to me."

"Listening devices, yes," said Scott. And on afterthought: "Also, there's something missing, gone from this room. It can't be anything hugely important, for then I'd know what it is; but whatever, it's no longer here. So, do you reckon you can maybe help me with that one, too?"

He could see that his request gave her pause, but after a moment she said, "Possibly . . . but first the bugs. Hold me."

Momentarily startled, he said, "Hold you?" Then: "Ah! You mean the touch, contact, yes?"

She had already moved forward, facing him at close range. "Yes, by which we may sense any intrusive devices."

"We?"

"As two, together," she explained, "if we apply ourselves to the task, our powers may be doubled and possibly redoubled; even trebled, if Wolf were here. Especially with his nose. But even without him we should be able to discover such devices by their failure."

"Come again?"

"Just do it!" She was getting impatient now. "Hold me!"

Scott knew that Shania wasn't a woman, at least not of the human variety. But she was so much like a woman—like essence of woman—that if he *didn't* know he wouldn't give a damn! And as for holding her: he could feel her warmth from twelve inches away; he could smell that tantalizing scent, which was probably as "natural" as her skin tones were "natural," but so what? And she really was trying very hard to be a woman. He'd known girls from time to time who hadn't tried nearly this hard!

"Scott," she told him, moving closer still, "I *am* a woman, and if all works out I may remain a woman until all my time . . . until everything is done. Indeed, almost four million years ago when the Shing't first came here, our blood flowed in the first of your women. My race brought your women about! Therefore hold me as a woman—or not, as you wish—but do hold me."

So he did. His arms went about her and her breasts pressed against him; her thighs were warm against his; she felt so real, so alive, so vital, that her clothes seemed mere wisps, flimsy wrappings around an astonishing gift, so that she might even be naked in his arms. It made Scott feel naked, too; made him wish they were! Shania's breath and the almost hypnotic scent of her incredible body permeated his pores, went straight to his head, and caused his blood to pound. And as for her hair . . .

"So then," her voice was husky now, "you choose to hold me as a woman." Whichever, his desk lamp was acting up again, more so than before. It caused a slow strobing effect where the dark between the light intervals was as sensual as smoky silk.

Choose to hold you as a woman? Scott thought. *Damn right I do!* And he immediately felt guilty again, but this time because of Kelly.

"And now concentrate," she said. "Feel out the intrusions. Search for the strangeness, for anything unusual here."

Scott felt he could do it, even if he didn't know how. And tightening his embrace a little, he did it anyway.

Something fizzed and popped on the wall behind a Beardsley print in its black and gold frame. A shower of sparks flew, and there were electrical crackling sounds from upstairs and in the sitting room.

"What the—?" said Scott.

"Aha!" said Shania as she eased herself away from

him—reluctantly, Scott thought, which pleased him inordinately. But she quickly continued. "You will want to examine things, checking for damage, also to ensure there is no lingering electrical danger. Meanwhile, as you suggested, I will wait for you in the sitting room. What would you like to drink?"

"Pour me a brandy," Scott muttered, still dizzy from their contact, almost staggering as he headed for the stairs . . .

The telephone in Kelly's study had been bugged; the phone was now useless, its diaphragm exploded, melted, and congealed out of shape. An acrid stench and a thin spiral of smoke from under an oak coffee table in the living room led Scott to the discovery of a burned-out listening device; the living-room telephone still worked but its bug had fallen to bits. And as for the bug behind the Beardsley: that had scorched the wallpaper a little, but was now dead.

"What a job they did on me!" said Scott, still furious as he sipped at a half inch of cognac in his sitting room. "And I still don't know what they took from my study, or why."

"It's not unlikely I can tell you why, if not what," Shania told him. "Perhaps we can look into that later?"

"Later? You're not thinking of skipping out on me again?"

"No," she answered. "Previously I've been worried that the two of us together might make too much of a disturbance, but in the last day or two the Mordri Three have been concentrating on their murderous business—a terrible machine they're building in an icy crag in Switzerland—and as far as I can tell they haven't been scanning abroad to any great extent. Which is why I believe their fearful project is moving into its final phase, and that in their excitement they may have let their guard down if only a little; they are after all quite mad. Also, I've been engaging my mental shields as best I'm able, to ensure psychic invisibility. And, Scott, you should try to do the same."

Scott blinked, sighed, and said, "You see, there's the rub. For in a single minute, or maybe two at most, you've mentioned some kind of disturbance we might make, a fearful machine, mental shields, and psychic invisibility. And I'm not even halfway there yet!"

"But you are!" Shania got up from her easy chair, came and perched on the sofa where he sprawled with his drink, trying to relax. "I *know* you can shield yourself; you even shielded yourself from me! Also from E-Branch when they questioned you."

Nodding, he answered, "Yes, I remember. But I still don't know how I did it."

Suddenly she looked angry, her face clouding over and her eyes flashing dangerously. She leaned over him, took his shoulders, stared deep into his eyes. "Now I shall probe your innermost thoughts, to discover what you really think of me!"

With that scent of hers, and Shania's cleavage just a few inches in front of Scott's eyes, the very last thing he wanted was that she should "probe his innermost thoughts!" And:

"No!" he said, shutting her out.

The wrath vanished from her face at once; it hadn't in any case been real. And having made her point she smiled in genuine triumph. "You see?" she said. "I couldn't read you!"

Still shielding himself, Scott thought, *An alien creature you may be, but you're similar to our females in more ways than one! And I can easily see how your blood, your essence, runs in the women of Earth.* While out loud and still a little wonderingly, he said: "Well, what do you know? It seems I did it, and it wasn't too hard at that!" As for just *how* he had done it: that no longer mattered. The fact that he could was sufficient.

"Bravo!" said Shania.

Scott looked at her where she now kicked off her shoes and seated herself on his sofa, legs crossed, elbows on knees, chin in hands. Her skirt was quite short; she seemed naive, unaware, or unconcerned. But Scott remembered: she didn't know any other men, not as intimately as she knew him. She would perhaps know something of the mores of the day, but as for sexual attitudes and practices . . .

Like his jaw, his mind had fallen open. Too late, he once again closed it.

"Oh!" she said, straightening herself and moving closer to him. "Do I seem forward? Perhaps I am trying too hard."

And right out of nowhere Scott said, "Show me how you look . . . I mean the real you. Because—" He paused and chewed his lip.

"Because you want to kiss me," she said. "But I can't show you, because then you might not want to."

"Are you so . . . so very strange, then?"

"Not at all, but it would remind you that I am not of your race. And, Scott, my sexuality runs deep; it knows of many cultures, many odd practices, many of the diverse ways of universal nature. And I know I would enjoy your kisses, caresses, and all that goes with them." Her voice was such a low seductive growl that Scott felt himself slipping toward her.

He sat back—jerked back, into the corner of the sofa—and husked, "Too fast! And this is all too crazy!"

"Yes," Shania breathed, moving away. "And I think that now would be a good time for us to start at the beginning. You have earned the right to know everything. So now let's sit apart and I'll tell you all that I know, all that you'll believe, and perhaps certain things that you won't . . ."

Scott drew the drapes across bay windows to shut out the dark, and satisfied now that they couldn't be "overheard"—but still with their mental shields in place in case strange metaphysical talents were at work in the night—they sat facing each other, Shania back in her chair and Scott on the sofa.

And finally, folding her feet up under her again, but more decorously now, she began to talk.

"The Shing't is—or at least it was—my race. Our planet, Shing, orbited a white star so old that only a few billion years of fuel, of life and light, remained to it. Because Shing hung close, however, the star's warmth sufficed. Now, thanks to the Mordri, only a handful of the Shing't remain, and the world Shing and its star are gone, destroyed in a great rent in space-time. It will be something of a miracle if any of the race survive, for when the far travellers return to Shing they'll find only a vortex, a dark region where all is chaos.

"We thought of ourselves as one of the oldest, perhaps *the* oldest, race in the universe, and like many other races held to our beliefs, legends, and religions. Many of the Shing't—most of the Threes, our Units of Learning and Endeavour—believed in a God much like yours. Others didn't. But no one Three Unit claimed to understand all the riddles of creation. Much like your scientists, philosophers, and religious men, we sought for enlightenment through the laws of Physics, Nature, Mathematics, and pure Thought. Oh, yes, we, too, 'thought and therefore were,' except we thought it some four million years before your ancestors came down out of the trees; which is not to belittle you, for your evolutionary development has been most remarkable!

"As to our development:

"We had the same savage origins as most other races across the universe. Our wars, at first tribal, became planetwide; our weapons evolved through clubs, spears, and energy guns, finally to devices of mass destruction. We might easily have destroyed our world, as others have destroyed theirs. Scott, I have seen, even walked through, the most magnificent ruins on a number of dead cinder planets . . .

"Our world Shing had three major continents—"

(Scott thought: *I just knew you were going to say that!*)

"—whose races were only very slightly different by reason of evolution. Realizing the looming threat, their leaders developed a system of planetwide cooperation: the Three Units, where persons from each continent became members of millions of teams working together for a better understanding of . . . well, everything! The Threes carried out their studies, their works, based on a rotational system, moving from continent to continent in a constant round and never staying in any one place for more than three of our years. And all knowledge, discoveries, and revelations were shared by all Shing's scientific establishments, made public for all our world's citizens.

"There could nevermore be a case for hostilities, for only a lunatic nation would deliberately attack one-third of its own people, and at the same time invite retaliation from *two*-thirds of the planet's populace! Thus our dreadful weapons were either done away with or put to benevolent use, for in their development many new scientific principles had been discovered. Understand, however, that all I have told you so far is as much myth as historical fact, for in millions of years even a world such as Shing will pass through troubled times. Invaders from other star systems struck twice, faced defeat, and went away. A comet hurled our oceans all about and created a darkness that almost doomed us to extinction. But always we recovered, buoyed up by our Three Units' scientific advances.

"During the space wars, for example, our astrophysics Three Units had finally fathomed gravity, and—"

"Wait!" Scott cut in. "Look, I'm no scientist, but I'm not a dimwit either. Surely gravity is gravity; it's why it's a lot easier to walk down a hill than up one. What I'm trying to say: what is there to fathom?"

Shania smiled. "I'm not a scientist either—well, I'm not a physicist—but I do have the benefit of experience. Gravity was always believed to be one of the universe's weak forces, but it isn't. Even light, when it strays too close to a black hole, cannot escape the gravity. And beyond the black hole: what laws of physics apply there? I shall put it as simply as possible:

"Gravity was the first of things, coming even before light and time. In the Very Beginning gravity was created and broken, and created again. For without it there was nothing to hold the universe in place."

"This was after the Big Bang?" said Scott.

"After creation, yes." She nodded. "But gravity is—how best to put it?—layered, yes. There are levels of gravity not only *in* our four-dimensioned universe but also above and below it; beyond the black holes, for example. There are levels that exist in subspace, and some that exist without time, omnipresent. Oceans of gravity wash all unseen all about us, but by no means languid or lacking in shoals, storms, and whirlpools.

"During the space wars certain physicist Threes developed a gravity weapon to deter these ferocious alien attackers. The undertow of the weapon's powerful gravity wave caught up their vessels, sucked them into subspace, and hurled them to the very rim of the universe itself. Thus the space-faring technologies of the Shing't took a huge leap forward. No longer confined to the planets of our own star system: a swamp world, a gas giant, and Shing itself—three of them, yes—we headed out across our galaxy and beyond. When I say 'we,' I mean our most remote forebears, of course.

"So the Shing't voyaged into deep space. Hostile planets were avoided; nascent worlds were often cultivated and brought on, especially if they had features in common with Shing, such as Earth. On planets like Earth the work of our exobiologists was . . . it was . . ." But here she paused, then said: "Scott, why do you frown at me like that?"

And Scott said, "Because I can't help wondering why anyone would find it necessary to fiddle with the natural evolution of entire planets. What exactly did your biologists do to Earth?"

"Who can say, 'exactly'?" she replied. "Not I . . . I wasn't there four million years ago! But I am assuming it was the same for primal Earth as for a small handful of worlds whose records still do exist—or existed until recently—on Shing."

"You're assuming it was the same . . . as what?" said Scott.

"Our biologists would have sought out the life-forms with the greatest potential—early primates—and performed some sculpturing." Shania offered a small shrug. "Is it important?"

"Sculpturing?" Scott frowned more yet. "You mean interfering with their genes and such?"

She nodded. "Most likely. And with their DNA. I don't know—perhaps they were presumptuous, those ancient scientists, in introducing something of the Shing't into other races."

"You're saying we might have sprung from you?"

"I would say definitely. But haven't I already said so, in connection with your females?"

Remembering, but frowning still, Scott slowly nodded.

And seeing what troubled him, Shania said, "Then think of it like this: if those Shing't biologists had not 'interfered,' you might not even be here. Would you prefer not to be here, Scott? Perhaps you would prefer to be an ape in a tree?"

How to answer that one? And Scott said, "You've given me a great deal to think about. Maybe we should take a break now."

"I agree," said Shania Two. "I'm weary. I have worried for long and long. About you, and Wolf; about myself and the Mordri Three. It can wear on one, worrying like that. Now I'm tired."

"You're going to do your disappearing act?"

"No." She shook her head. "I've left my hotel. Now I shall stay here—if that is fitting?"

"You're welcome to take my bed," said Scott. "And I'll be in the spare room." But:

"No need for that," said Shania. "I find your smell quite pleasing, and our hearts beat at a similar speed."

Well, right now they do! Scott thought. And "hearing" him, Shania laughed . . .

20

Scott tried to dissuade her, but not very hard.

For the first time in a long time he wore pajamas—after first going into something of a panic trying to find them while she was in the bathroom. The trouser bottoms were old but still serviceable—still decent?

Shania came to the bedroom not quite naked, in panties and a bra that she really didn't need. Already in bed, Scott looked at her, looked away, then thought: *What? Have I gone crazy?* and looked again; he would have defied any red-blooded heterosexual man not to. But Shania was already slipping into bed on Kelly's side. *God! What would Kelly have thought of this?* He had deliberately left his mind wide open, at least at close range. Maybe Shania would see how he was torn two ways. He hoped so, anyway.

And Shania murmured, "Scott, we're both tired, and you are loyal to your memories, loyal to a fault." Reaching across from her side, she touched him. And all the tension went out of him; he felt himself melting into the bed, and the sigh going out of him was audible at first, then silent, because by the time he'd sighed it Scott was asleep . . .

Scott dreamed of many strange and wonderful things. He dreamed of Kelly. She appeared to know everything yet wasn't angry with him. Indeed, she seemed to want only to comfort him.

They sat on the grassy bank of a Thames backwater outside London, a place that they had used to visit in their courting days, and it was summer. They fed ducks with the dry crusts of picnic sandwiches until Scott, living half in memories and half in mourning, tried to pour his heart out to her. But as in that other dream—that nightmare in which Kelly had crumpled into nothing in her hospital bed—he had no voice! And in any case she couldn't answer. But still he knew that everything was okay with her, and that he had nothing to explain. Odd, though, that he could talk to a wolf in his dreams yet was unable to talk to Kelly. Now why was that?

Because Kelly was dead, perhaps? But in dreams most things are possible, and this was only a dream, surely?

And Scott was amazed that he *knew* this was a dream, when previously he wouldn't have known until he was awake. So then, was it that he could only speak to *living* persons and creatures in his dreams? That seemed reason-

able, for he definitely couldn't speak to the dead ones in his
waking hours!

In seeming confirmation of this theory, Scott suddenly
remembered how he hadn't been able to speak to his father
either. He remembered, too, that there had been a barrier
between himself and the dead, some secret medium to
which he wasn't privy. Not yet, anyway.

Toward the end of this phase of the dream, the ducks
swam away, the sun went behind a cloud, and Kelly took on
a far more serious expression. Then, as once before, she
drew his attention to those now sinister marks on her left
wrist, nodding to confirm his suspicions about Simon Salcombe. When Scott nodded gravely in return, clenching a
hard-knuckled fist by way of an answer, then Kelly, the
river, and everything else slowly faded away . . .

Scott dreamed of a world where "meat forests" were cultivated, insensate vegetable crops with the texture and pro-
tein content of flesh without the wholesale slaughter
attendant to the preparation of livestock for consumption.
The beings of this world were tall, willowy, very elegant
and beautiful in an alien way. Their cities were soaring
spires fashioned to the same sparing design as they themselves, where they lived in a harmony utterly unheard of on
Earth.

He found himself in a room in one of the cities, a laboratory of sorts, and experienced a very strange thing. Scientists or perhaps doctors of the tall graceful race spoke
reassuringly to a couple who appeared to be the parents of a
small, glowing infant in its crib. Scott was unable to understand the complex musical language they very sparingly engaged in, but he seemed to find something of meaning in
their motions, their gestures, and perhaps even their
thoughts. And it soon dawned on him that their means of
communication was as much telepathic as vocal.

They were a very advanced race, yes. And a thought
came to him that perhaps in some far future human beings
might evolve into just such creatures. But as for now:

In their magnificent robes of office, the doctors, scientists, or priests, whatever they were, appeared to be engaging the parent beings in a sort of ritual, during which the basket with the child was placed in a transparent receptacle attached to the side of a huge and highly complex machine. Then they all blessed the child and the machine was switched on. Gases flowed through a conduit that joined the transparent receptacle to the machine, and after a while a creature (there was no easy way to describe it, except perhaps as a "thing") emerged from the conduit into the crib. A shapeless blob of protoplasm as big as a large fist, it hovered over the infant and gradually developed features, becoming a bodiless jelly-like head with a beatific, even angelic face! And gazing on the glowing child with a joyful, adoring expression, it let itself be *inhaled,* breathed in like air, to become one with its host. And somehow Scott understood that from now on the insubstantial jelly-thing was to be the infant's lifelong companion, a beneficial familiar.

Beneficial, yes; even as the creature which now descended upon him in his bed, entering him through his breathing. Scott experienced it—felt the thing permeating his being, his mind—in its oh-so-gentle search . . . for what? For his memories!

He was downstairs in his study, five or six months ago. He stood there in the centre of the floor, looking at the room and knowing it as an old friend. He turned in a slow circle, taking everything in. The pictures and photographs on the walls, books and bric-a-brac on their shelves, varnished wooden trays, word processor and memo pad on his desk . . . and a unique paperweight that Kelly had given him as a Christmas present: a tight spiral of polished, pre-decimal British coins encased in a clear plastic hemisphere two and a half inches in diameter!

His old-money paperweight, yes: there one minute, gone the next! *That* was what was missing! And something in his head made him promise to remember it when he was awake.

Then the creature in Scott's mind detached itself; it made

a silent, painless exit, leaving him to drift back to the present—

—Where as so often before in his dreams, Kelly was in bed with him. He felt her warmth, turned on his side, draped an arm across her lower back, fingers extended across her left buttock. She was very still; still as a marble statue. Then she stirred, turned on her back, and his hand slid across her belly. Her arm slipped gently under his head until she cradled him against her breast. Her shape, the way she fitted against him . . . this could only be Kelly, definitely. And warm, pliant, soft to his touch, she smelled wonderful—

—Too wonderful . . . ?

And she didn't smell like Kelly!

Scott jerked awake, quickly drew apart from Shania who was also awake—wide awake!—looked across the weft of her dusky hair at the alarm clock's luminous figures, and saw that it was 3:33.

But of course it was . . .

Downstairs in their dressing gowns (Shania wore one of Kelly's), they sipped coffee, and after a while she tentatively inquired, "Do you feel refreshed?"

Scott had said nothing so far. But while preparing their drinks the fog of sleep had cleared from his mind, allowing him to come more properly awake and aware, and he'd thought through his peculiar dreams. Now he said, "Yes. I've had something over four hours sleep, which is about as good as I've been averaging lately. But let's not worry about that; instead I want to know what happened up there." He lifted his chin to indicate the upstairs rooms, and more especially his bedroom.

"Something happened?" Trying to sound innocent, she failed miserably.

"You know very well it did," he answered. "In fact, several things happened and another thing might have. It's possible I'm sorry it didn't, but if it had . . . well, I'm sure that would have confused things even further. But I'm not talking about that. I want to know about my dreams, because I don't think one of them *was* a dream! I'm talking about something that got into me, something that knew my thoughts and unlocked my memories. Something you sent to me. But was it just you, your telepathy—or was it something else?"

Shania sighed, looked away for a moment, and said, "Scott, do you remember I told you there would be things you'd believe, and others that you might not, which perhaps you wouldn't want to believe?"

"You said something like that, yes," he said.

"Well, you are right: I did send you a dream. Or rather, I thought it and you dreamed it. A dream about—"

"About Shing and its people," Scott cut in. "Your people?"

"Yes," she said. "It was easier, and quicker, to show than to tell."

"And their shapes—those shapes I saw—are your shape?"

"Their shapes are many shapes, almost *any* shape, as determined by the circumstances, the situation." Suddenly she looked anxious. "Did you find them unpleasant?"

"No." He shook his head. "I found them . . . very appealing, in their way. Their eyes and their graceful movements: somehow they reminded me of dolphins. A certain warmth, a friendliness, and an incredible intelligence. But it's very obvious that when you travelled to other worlds you disguised yourselves in imitation of the actual inhabitants. In short, the Shing't are shape-shifters who daren't show themselves in their true form. Either that or they are spies manipulating worlds to their own design; perhaps sleepers, preparing alien worlds for conquest."

Shania shook her head in denial. "Unthinkable!" she said. "Well, except to someone who lives on a world where such a monstrous scenario is all *too* thinkable!"

Scott ignored the implications of that one and said, "But it is one possible scenario: an acceptable conclusion from the point of view of someone who surely has a right to feel uncertain about Shing't motives—such as myself."

"A very narrow-minded conclusion," she replied, "from

the point of view of someone who is only here to help you, such as *my*self! But let me put you straight and explain that as well as one of the highest life-forms we were also one of the basest—biologically speaking, that is. To 'disguise' ourselves, as you put it, is one of our simplest skills. In the earliest of times we were like your chameleons; no, not as lizards, but having the same camouflaging abilities. In the threatening silence of primitive, predatory forests, we conversed by gestures, by sympathetic motions and empathic feelings, often over great distances; all of which evolved into the telepathic abilities I use today. All of my kind had these skills . . . when I had all of my kind."

Scott nodded thoughtfully. "The first time you came here, came into my bedroom and woke me up, I thought you were Kelly. Because you looked like Kelly. And the same last night while I was sleeping. But *you* were wide awake."

Again Shania sighed, then bit her lip as any woman might. "In Kelly's study," she said, "there sits a glass with Kelly's lipstick on its rim. Hairs from Kelly's head are trapped in the curtains. A piece of broken fingernail rests in a groove in the casing of her typewriter. Only stir the clothes in her closet, Kelly's breath floats in the air. Her DNA is everywhere. I can *be* Kelly—but I would not go so far. Only far enough that you would accept me. As for last night . . . well, we are both lonely creatures."

Scott softened, drew her down onto his sofa, sat with his arm around her while she snuggled close. But then he frowned and said, "Yes, but there is something else. There was some kind of ceremony—a weird sort of, I don't know, baptism?—where a Shing't child was given what seemed to be a blessing before being introduced to a semisolid parasite thing."

Shania stiffened, narrowed her eyes. "A parasite? Are you talking about the Khiff? The Khiff is no parasite but an entity from a primitive gravity layer. There they are as nothing: mere plankton in the gravitic oceans, moving with the currents, with nowhere to settle. There they have no sentience—no intelligent substance at all in that unthinkable environment—only the most basic instinct for survival. In your world a tuft of grass knows more of being than the Khiff in theirs."

Scott's frown deepened. "Oh, really? But the thing that was in my head knew things. It knew how to dig into my past, how to show me things I might otherwise have forgotten; things such as the paperweight that's missing from my study. Also, I'm willing to bet that it was real and that it was yours: your Khiff. Tell me, do all of your people get these creatures as young ones?"

"They used to, yes," Shania answered, and her eyes were as sad as can be, beginning to film over with welling tears. "When my people were, then they had the Khiff."

But Scott was relentless. "And last night, that thing that entered me was yours?"

"Of course. Didn't I tell you we could solve the riddle of what was missing from your study later?"

"By using your Khiff?"

"Yes," she answered, dabbing away a tear. "At least let me explain—"

But Scott was already asking, "So why didn't you just show me?"

Shania sat up straighter, tossed her head, and flashed her eyes. "Because you had made it perfectly clear that you already thought of me as . . . as an *alien!* Well then, should I exacerbate your xenophobia by showing you that which would seem to make me more alien yet? Tell me, Scott: have I harmed you in any way? I have not. Nor would I, ever. I only came to save you—*to save your entire human race*—and I deserve better treatment! As for my Khiff: she is not some kind of freak I would put on display. She has been my lifelong companion, adviser, friend, the keeper of my thoughts, my memories. You will *never* see her, for she is also my guide, my conscience and innermost self."

Through all of this Shania's mind was open—she had laid it bare, as if it were her soul—and everything she'd said was the solid truth. Scott took her in his arms, which for a moment she resisted, until he thought: *God, you are so very beautiful! And I'm sorry I'm being such an awkward bastard to deal with.*

And still you don't know everything, she answered him. "In fact you know so little. And there are many things that I don't know—and that *you* don't know—not even about you!"

It was almost 4:30 and Scott said, "Too late to go back to bed. I have to be at the airport by 8:30. I'll take a taxi. But meanwhile we have a couple of hours spare. So if you're willing to talk, or think, I'm willing to listen. Why not tell me about the Mordri Three? For I think I should know as much as there is to know about someone I hope to kill!"

She nodded. "That is my duty, too—to terminate three ultimately deviant Shing't lives—but it's the only way." She gave a small shudder. "The Mordri Three must die, yes. Too late to save four other worlds, but at least I must try to save this one."

This one, meaning Scott's world: Earth.

And the way she said it—so matter-of-factly, so coldly, and yet so earnestly—he felt an involuntary shiver run up and down his spine. And:

"Well then," he said, more urgently now, "let's get to it. I'm listening . . ."

"Understand," said Shania, "that each Shing't Three had its own area of endeavour; from the study of microorganisms and insects to astrophysics and gravity wells. Some went out to alien planets in the search for strange life-forms; others were satisfied to remain on the home world, piecing together our broken histories; even the Meaning of Colours and the Evolution of Time were subjects for intensive study. Only let a person so much as allude to an unknown or esoteric area of learning and a Three Unit would emerge into being prepared to give its all in striving to understand it. There were in existence so many Three Units that every facet of all known and accepted—and one or two imagined—sciences came under scrutiny. So with the Khiff to assist us, is it any wonder that our technologies advanced at such a rate; our scientific achievements following one upon the other, until we truly believed that almost all was known? Except, of course, that just as the universe is as infinite as the ebb and flow of its gravity waves, so is it impossible to know everything.

"As for the Khiff: it is reckoned that the first of their kind came to us from the gravitic flux at the time of the first space war. As I've mentioned, several physicist Three Units got together to devise a gravity weapon. Upon penetrating a certain unstable sublevel or layer, they freed a large number of Khiff onto Shing.

"They were vacant, empty envelopes, but as Nature abhors a vacuum so these creatures from gravitic chaos appeared to abhor their own dullness, emptiness, and ignorance. Like iron filings they were drawn to the magnet minds of the Shing't. They inhabited my people! At first the Shing't were horrified, but eventually they saw the astonishing benefits of the Khiff, who took their name from the principal scientist of the Three Unit which discovered them—rather, who uncovered them—its One, whose given name was Khiff.

"Incidentally, I was the second member of my Shania Unit, which is what made me Shania Two. My born name doesn't matter; in your tongue it is barely pronounceable. What is more, I now accept that I'm St. John Two, but I know you prefer Shania . . .

"Where was I? Ah, yes:

"You are thinking, what has all this to do with the Mordri Three? Well, now we get to it.

"The Mordris, after Gelka Mordri, or Mordri One—now Frau Gerda Lessing—were a specialized Three Unit studying twinned subjects. Physicists on the one hand, they also explored religions. And they had noted an obvious fact: that right across the Shing't galaxy, and on every world that swore to a god or gods, in every case these gods were different! No two were alike. And they concluded that the only real 'god' was science itself. And, Scott, I know there are similar groups on your world who follow the same precept; also naturalists, who believe that Nature is the god, or goddess; and so on.

"Now, I know I said 'twinned' subjects . . . but surely the physical universe could not be farther removed from the notion of some metaphysical Supreme Being? Oh, really? But couldn't we also argue that with all of its diverse dimensions, its marvels and monstrosities, the utter impossibility of The All bursting into existence, from nothing, *without* that divine all-powerful hand, or tentacle, or mind? Thus, in the same way as a bar magnet's poles are opposed yet joined, so the Mordri Three Unit's studies encompassed both concepts, finally eschewing the one in favour of the other.

"And of course their proposed Science-as-God doctrine was disavowed by every other Three Unit engaged in similar studies. What is more, the Mordri Three were challenged to prove their religious—or possibly irreligious?—theory.

"They set about to do so—to search for a god—first by extracting from previously unplumbed gravity wells, such as the one which had produced the Khiff. They could not venture there, no one can; as well attempt to enter and survive the event horizon of a great black hole! But with their machines they could dip into such places and extract matter, antimatter, and other essences that your science has not as yet recognized. And they had conjectured that if indeed there was a God, then surely He must be one such essence. For He was nowhere discovered in all the worlds and dimensions they knew.

"Believing they were safe from such extractions, that they could contain and study them at their will in their laboratory, the Mordri experimentations ventured into the very deepest gravitic levels, and eventually conjured into being that which was uncontrollable, which defied the restraints of their machinery. They were poisoned by nightmarish concepts, maddened by confusing thoughts, infected with delusions. In short, they were made to lose their minds, driven insane. And not only them but also their familiar creatures, who dwelled with and within them!

"Placed in care, they escaped. But even mad they clung to their theories and were determined to prove that the notion of God was a fallacy, and only science was the True Supremacy. And how would they do that? In the most terrifying way imaginable. For if God was good, then evil was surely His enemy. Wherefore they would create universal evil, challenging God to oppose it, and by His failure proving His nonexistence!

"And what could be more evil than the destruction of God's worlds and entire races of sentient beings? Scott, my world was the first; Shing is no more. And three more planets since then, gone into atoms or shrivelled to dust. And Earth? Your Earth is next, unless you and I, and Wolf—our Three Unit, yes—can do something about it, something to stop it!

"That is why I'm here. And that is our mission . . ."

21

In a cramped seat, on a package-holiday flight to Zante in the Ionian, Scott St. John found himself wondering what the hell he was doing here. In the midst of a cabin full of excited holiday-makers already decked out in brightly coloured garb—aware of their chatter, and grimacing at the occasional nerve-shattering shrieks of a discomforted babe-in-arms with his young, worn-out parents in nearby seats—Scott had suddenly been confronted by the "real world" and made to consider yet again the possibility that this weird, daunting *new* reality in which he'd somehow got himself involved was in fact some kind of interminable dream.

But then, as if to corroborate this extraordinary reality, during a comparatively quiet period when Scott actually managed to nod off for a few minutes, there was Wolf yet again, asking: *Are you coming? Are you at last on your way? I hope so—and I believe so—for I think I sense you that much closer to me.*

Startled awake, Scott unthinkingly answered out loud, "Yes, I'm coming. Just hang on in there!"

"Wazzat, mate?" said a man seated next to him, whose great fat belly was partly overflowing the narrow arm and margin that separated them.

"Nothing," Scott answered. "Talking to myself, that's all. I do it all the time."

"Really?" said the fat man. "Well I should watch it, mate. That's what they call the first sign! Har har har!"

Fuck you, too! Scott thought, then returned to considering his reality. But no, for in fact he knew it was real. It had to be; it was why he was here. But why him? He had asked a similar question of Shania in the early hours of the morning:

"Why me? Why can't *you* go and rescue Wolf? I mean, the way you come and go . . . surely you're better equipped?"

"First," she had answered, "you are his One. Next: only so much power remains in this device I use, which was damaged when first I arrived in your world." She showed him her right wrist, and a metal strap holding what looked like a watch that was anything but. "That is one more reason why I have visited you less frequently than I might otherwise have done. I need to conserve its energy, make sure it doesn't burn out, expire. And last: as I believe I've already explained, I don't know where Wolf is. I don't have his spacial coordinates."

"But I can tell you, show you where he is."

She had given her head a frustrated shake. "If I had *been* there, or anywhere close, then I could *go* there. My device records coordinates at a touch."

"So how is it you were able to come here, to my house, on your first visit?"

At which Shania had sighed impatiently. "Scott, I thought you understood that. I had been *watching* you, and so knew this place." And seeing his frown she'd quickly added: "I had to be sure of you! There were so many things I had to know about you before I dared to approach you! But this I will say: I can now find *you*, if not Wolf, anywhere! It's your aura; it is that we are two of a Unit. And if there are major difficulties in this place, this, er, Zak—?"

"Zakynthos, or simply Zante."

"If there are major problems in Zante, then I may be able to help you. But not until you're there. Once you're there you will be like a beacon. But please remember, I can only help *if* there are problems!"

"And how will you know there's a problem? I mean, won't it be a case of radio silence?"

"Radio silence?" She looked puzzled. "Your pardon?"

"Keeping low, shielding ourselves from the Mordri Three."

"Yes, they are a real danger. But you're now aware of that danger. Together and unshielded, the Mordri Three might pick us out, it's true. But we will not be together, except in an emergency, and from now on we'll keep ourselves at least minimally shielded at all times. Wolf isn't such a worry; his skills are rather more specialized, and his thoughts are not . . . they are not what the Mordris have become accustomed to."

"Not human?"

She sighed and shrugged. "I didn't want to say it, because I myself—"

"You're very human," Scott had told her. "And I'm sorry if I'm asking a lot of questions, but they're all things I need to know if I'm ever to fully understand. For example: if the Mordris can't read Wolf because he's a wolf, how come we can?"

"I don't know. Because he's one of our Three Unit? Perhaps that's the answer. Because he has been enabled? That would seem more likely. But as to how, why, or by whom he was enabled—or how and why *you* were, for that matter—who can say?"

Then, during a few moments' silence, and while he searched for other questions, Shania had asked him, "Do you really think that I'm . . . that I'm very human?"

"You are a very desirable, very lovely, very human woman," he'd told her. And before he could stop himself: "But I wish I could be sure that you would be permanently so . . . er, I mean—"

"I know what you mean, and the time is coming when I

will, when I *must* be permanently so. For Earth is my world now. I can journey no farther and I no longer wish to. I'll stay here with you and Wolf, if you'll have me and if we see this through . . ."

Which had pleased him inordinately.

And lost now in his memories of last night, lulled by the dull drone of the plane's engines, Scott relaxed a little and relived something of the rest of that strange conversation . . .

"Fill me in on some basic stuff," he said. "Tell me how you got here. You said that your world was—or had been—billions of light-years away. Well I'm no scientist, as agreed, but still I know that nothing can travel faster than light."

"On this three-dimensional level, that is correct," Shania told him. "But on certain timeless sublevels that law of physics doesn't apply. Only drop to such levels in a grav-ship, and there ride a gravity wave that has lasted forever and which *has already gone on forever,* and the light-year—even the billions of light-years—become as nothing. In fact, from my last location, it took me less than a month to get here; which is to say in local measurements of time. But I know of certain far places which would cost a year of journeying even on a massive wave. My Shania Three Unit spent ten months out on one trip, and another ten back again to Shing."

Scott shook his head. "I'd probably go out of my mind with sheer boredom!"

Shania smiled and said, "No, for you wouldn't have time to be bored. Even at light-speed time stands still for the traveller. On those far journeys my heart didn't beat once, the last breath I breathed stayed fresh in my lungs, my eyes never blinked, and I did not age by a single second of time; well, not until the grav-ship returned to 'normal' space-time—if there ever was such a place. The entire trip was easier than taking a single step, and took no time at all. Not *my* time, anyway."

Again Scott shook his head. Such concepts! "Where is your vessel—your, er, grav-ship—now?"

"I was low on fuel. I had hoped to refuel on a moon of the last world I visited. But that moon no longer existed, and the world itself was a shell. Of its cities and myriad inhabitants, nothing. The Mordri Three, yes . . . Almost empty, I came on here, emerging from subspace over the Atlantic Ocean where my ship's antigravs lowered it to the wild surface. By then, seeing that land was in sight however low on the horizon, I had exited. In something of a frenzy I miscalculated the coordinates and got wet for my pains; but finally I stood on solid ground. It was Scotland."

"And after that?"

"By trial and error I survived. Having followed the Mordri Three to this star system, as soon as I was established I commenced covertly to discover their works, always searching for a means to dispose of them; which never sat well with me, for the Shing't of latter years were the most peaceful of people. There were lunatics, of course, deviants as in any society, but these were cared for in secure places—at least they had always been thought of as secure. As for the ordinary folk of Shing: we had trained no troops, waged no wars since time immemorial. Scholarly academic argument and scientific discussion in halls of highest learning: these were as close as the Shing't ever came even to quarreling!

"Also, and if I would try to kill them, how to accomplish it on my own? They were a mad, evil Three Unit, while I was all alone. Years passed while I watched them and pondered the problem, while I practiced to become more properly a female of your world. Physically that was nothing; I *am* female, and humans and the Shing't have a great many similarities. But mentally it was hard. While I am no longer totally, er, 'alien,' I find a great many human female traits totally alien—to me, anyway. Not in every case, you understand, but in many. And to be truthful, it seems a majority of your men are even worse."

"Trouble with our women? With their traits?" Scott raised an eyebrow.

"They are frequently full of deceit, often with too high a regard for themselves and too low for others of their sex." She was very open about it.

"And the men? You've had problems? You told me you knew no other men."

"Nor have I known men . . . but be sure I could have! For on several occasions 'the touch,' as you call it—my transmutative talents with organic plasms, flesh—has delivered me from severe embarrassment! But I prefer not to go there . . ."

"But I *do* want to go there!" said Scott. "The Mordri Three also have this talent or so-called skill, 'the touch,' right? And they use it to kill?"

"All Shing't have it," Shania answered. "It is their birthright! Why, for long and long the Shing't saw themselves as the universe's single formative species, from which all other sentient Mammalia were destined to spring. But they were not unique in this and similar precepts; what of speciesism, the human conceit or assumption that man is superior to all other creatures, and that they only exist to serve man? Anyway, it helps explain why the Shing't 'interfered' with the fauna—and sometimes the flora—of other worlds."

Scott was relentless. "Okay, I've got that," he said. "But the Mordri Three: they use it to kill, right?"

Shania hung her head. "I am ashamed of them—of anyone of my race—who would use their skills in this manner. You have a voice: do you use it only to curse? You have eyes: do they look only on evil things? You have hands: do they only defile, torture, murder? No, for these things were gifted to you by who- or whatever governs life! And so were the Mordris gifted, but they are mad! Yes, they use them to maim, to change, disrupt, deform, and . . . and kill! Mordri Two, now called Simon Salcombe, killed your Kelly. He murdered her, Scott. *But it could have been much worse!*"

"What?"

"He used 'the touch' in a way that killed her slowly, with only so much pain, and in a way that could never be traced back to him."

"I traced it back to him," said Scott, grimly.

"Yes." Shania nodded. "Aided by some unseen power, enabled by it, you did. And I know you're capable of much more, if only we knew what that power was. But I can feel it growing in you, and given time I'm sure it will burst out. Let us hope that it happens sooner rather than later."

"Tell me what you meant about Salcombe and this murderous skill, 'the touch,'" said Scott. "How else can the Mordris use it? How could it have been worse, for Kelly?"

"Disruption, deformation, mutation. He didn't have to kill her. He could have made her an abomination, something which you couldn't even bear to look at!"

For long moments Scott was silent, then said, "Those kids at St. Jude's: they were just a cunning advertisement, to draw others to his list of clients. But Kelly . . . why did the morbid Mordri bastard have to kill Kelly?"

"She opposed him," said Shania, "called him a fraud and a charlatan. The mad Mordris will not suffer scathing comments or criticism of any sort. Once the deed was done, he would feel no remorse; he would not even deem it worth remembering. They have destroyed worlds . . . what matter a single 'alien' individual?"

"You hinted at mutilation, said he could make her an abomination," said Scott. "What, with a touch?"

Again Shania's nod. "There are touches and touches. Delivered with hatred—and there are various degrees of hatred just as there are degrees of love—a touch can determine the amount and speed of the . . . the *alteration*. The Mordri Three can turn people inside out, Scott, while yet they live! They can shrivel skin to nothing, dissolve organs or cause them to move, disrupt brains and bring about madness, or reduce their fluids to basic plasms without any sentience at all. He, Simon Salcombe, could have done that to Kelly, but that would have been to risk giving himself away. Mad he is . . . they are all insane, all three of them, but not *that* mad! When they are enraged, however—if someone or thing crosses them—then they might make mistakes, might be driven to murder, and in the most monstrous of ways. And indeed they have."

"When someone crosses them?" Scott persisted. "Like how?"

"By failing to meet their demands in the matter of payment for services rendered, for example."

"You mean money?"

"No," said Shania. "Not your money as such, but gold! Gold is the heavy metal we use as fuel!"

"Aha!" said Scott as another piece of the puzzle fell into place. And then: "But there are heavier metals, surely?"

"Heavier, and more dangerous, and harder to come by. Shing was rich in gold, which was common there. However, in the planets the Mordris have destroyed, gold was far more rare. I fancy that when they arrived here their reserves were low, as were my own. By use of my device"—she showed her "watch" again—"I detected radiations from their grav-ship in the Swiss Alps, and so knew that this was where they had fallen, probably crashed."

"But," said Scott, "wouldn't they also have detected you—your grav-ship?"

"At the bottom of an ocean? Doubtful . . ."

And after a long pause, as dawn's light began to show as a crack on the far horizon: "Tell me more about these Khiff creatures," said Scott.

"Ah, no!" Shania answered. "Please don't think of them as 'creatures' or 'aliens,' but only as Khiff. As for the Mordris' Khiff: they are gone beyond redemption. They are one with their hosts, and so are lost."

"Okay," said Scott, "so you're happy with your parasite—I'm sorry, I mean your Khiff! But . . . what are they for? How do they serve you? What do you get out of it—both of you?"

Shania fully understood the question, and answered, "Khiff have become like organs of the Shing't body and adjuncts of the Shing't mind and personality. I will accept that they are symbiotic, but more as a cat to a human than a wasp to a fruit."

"Wasps? Fruit?" Scott frowned. Now it was like she was asking him to be a botanist or biologist! Certainly she was admitting to more than a casual interest in Earth's biology!

"Oh, yes, but of course!" She had "heard" the thought. "For in four years I have had time to study all such. Let me go on:

"Certainly a house cat, a pet, is a symbiont: you feed him and he gives you pleasure—you both derive. So does the olive derive from the fertilization of the groves. But the *individual* olive, the fruit on the tree which the wasp hollows out for the purpose of reproduction, it can be said to 'suffer' inasmuch as any mindless plant may know suffering. Do you see?"

Scott nodded. "I think so. But a pet cat lives in a man's house, not inside the man!"

"True, and a pet cat can't do what the Khiff does for its host. Scott, we acquire them as children, as I've explained and as you have experienced for yourself—or did you consider the visit an invasion? No, don't answer, but let me continue:

"My Khiff is . . . she is like a personal diary or an aide-memoire, a storehouse for old memories. Scott, please tell me: can you remember when you were three, four, five years old?"

"No, my real memories start around six or seven."

"But I can—my Khiff can! And my memories reach a great deal farther back in time than yours . . . but do *not* ask me how old I am!"

"You're old?" Scott's face had fallen, if only a little.

"I'm not *that* old!" Shania protested. "Not in terms of the longevity of the Shing't. Why, I'm a mere girl by Shing't reckoning. And anyway, I said not to ask."

"So you do have something in common with Earth women after all." Feeling that he had scored at least a point, Scott let it go and made nothing further of it. And anyway Shania was moving on:

"In fact, I remember everything, through my Khiff. And she is—how may I explain it?—yes, like a gleaner-fish. As great fishes in your seas have gleaners, so I have my Khiff. Everyone has disappointments in life, certain things they wish had never happened, occurrences that have gone awry and strayed from what was desired. It is natural to make mistakes, to suffer failures and follies, and in your world—in your mind—you live with these dismal memories, regretting them. Am I correct?"

"We call it learning by our mistakes," Scott replied. "And in other instances such memories could be a case of conscience: errors which were deliberate and backfired, or which didn't but left a bad taste. We do wrong and we think we got away with it; but it comes back to niggle at us, at the back of our minds."

"As I have learned." Shania nodded. "But I am *not* troubled in this manner. My gleaner-fish Khiff is the storehouse of such negative thoughts or memories, who only calls them to my attention if or when it appears I might make the same error a second time. Also, as humans derive pleasure from their cats and other pets, so I am aware of my Khiff's constant attention. Not aware of a presence so much as a friend; but a silent one, unless she is required. As I've said: she is like an organ, a second brain. And as the placenta sees us through our prenatal stages, so the Khiff sees us through life."

"An organ that can leave you at will . . ." Scott mused.

"But at *my* will, knowing that she will always return."

"Put it this way," said Scott. "My organs don't have minds of their own, and I don't have any that I can simply eschew!"

"I could argue that point," she answered at once. "What of your tonsils, your appendix?"

"My appendix?" Scott laughed out loud. "My appendix is unnecessary, a relic of some former epoch of human evolution that dates back millions of years!" It sounded good. But:

"Aha!" Shania also laughed, and clapped her healer's hands. "And the Khiff could be your *future* evolution, when your men of science finally plumb the gravity layers and so discover them!"

Again Scott was momentarily silent, then said, "But things sometimes go wrong, eh? As in the case of the Mordri Three?"

"A unique case," she answered in lowered, suddenly subdued tones. "And a terrible one. By their delvings, the Mordri Three were driven insane. And in the evil that ensued it must be that their Khiff have followed suit. Now their Khiff store memories of uttermost horror, and their counsel can only be corrupt!"

Scott had fallen asleep again. A fat elbow dug in his ribs when the man in the seat beside him struggled erect. And:

"'Ere, mate." That one loomed over him, touched his shoulder. "Wakey-wakey. We'll be landing in a couple of minutes. Me, I'm off to the loo. Time for a quick pee and then we're there."

We're there, thought Scott, giving himself a shake. *Zante, where a wolf of the wild is in hiding, waiting for me to rescue him. Now we get to see what's what.*

Now it really begins . . .

22

As Scott St. John's plane touched down on the airstrip in Zakynthos, and as Scott himself stepped out into blazing sunlight and Mediterranean heat, at E-Branch HQ, in the heart of London, Ben Trask had called an O-Group, a meeting of his ESPers. 3:00 P.M. in Zante, but the day was two hours younger in the Operations Room in London where Trask's people convened following an early lunch.

Once his agents were settled in their seats, Trask wasted no time in getting down to business. Speaking from the podium, he said, "I think you all know why we're here. In the last few days we've been concentrating our efforts on the Scott St. John case, which isn't proving to be an easy task because we've been doing it under our own internal security umbrella; so covertly, in fact, that it's quite outside previous Branch experience. We *are* gradually learning more about what's going on here, but all we definitely know right now is that St. John—who apparently has or is developing parapsychological skills as good and maybe better than any of ours—has somehow got himself involved in some kind of threat to our entire planet.

"Now I'm well aware that what I just said sounds like the introduction to a work of fantasy—like a load of sensationalist hocus-pocus, and all very if-and-butty—and I admit that even as the Head of E-Branch, an organization of rare talents which came into being to discover, investigate, and deal with precisely this sort of event and/or situation, still I myself had doubts when first this case came to my attention.

"Initial investigations, however, by some of our most respected agents—Ian Goodly, Anna Marie English—would seem to have identified just such a threat. You all know what I'm talking about, I know that; I simply take this opportunity to state once again that we must continue to step lightly, that we can't compromise St. John in what appears to have become something of his personal vendetta against the unknown organization, faction, or group of persons from which this threat springs. For we feel fairly sure that St. John and his allies—two persons of whom we also know very little—are the only ones capable of putting down or defusing this mysterious threat. So as I said, it's all very if-and-butty.

"And that's enough from me." Trask picked out a well-known face in his small audience. "Ian, do you want to carry on?"

The gaunt-looking precog stood up and loomed tall over the other agents in their seats. "I can't really expand on what has already been said," he began. "All I can say is that when I was tasked to examine St. John I found evidence of rare skills, and that when I tried looking to his future I discovered the threat as outlined by the Head of Branch. We think we may have learned *something* of that threat—we do now have at least one name in connection with it—but that's about all. However, my initial concerns have been substantiated in several ways and by some of our finest talents."

Goodly paused and glanced at the almost crumpled figure of the girl seated next to him, and said, "Anna Marie?"

The ecopath, looking frail and weary as ever, perhaps even more so, struggled to her feet as Goodly sat down. Clearing her throat, and then in a voice that was scarcely more than a painful croak, she said, "As usual, the futures Ian Goodly sees are devious and hard to explain. But he gets them right more often than not, and more often than not by unexpected turns of event. When I joined with him—figuratively speaking, that is—in an attempt to discover the 'condition' of Earth in one such future, at first I felt only chaos . . . and then felt nothing at all! As if there was nothing to feel. It's possible, of course, that because of my so-called talent—which not only inflicts all the ills of the world upon me but also on occasion warns me in advance of declining situations—it is *possible* that I had gone beyond Ian's vision. In which case I have to conclude that the current situation *is* in decline, and seriously." She paused for a moment to catch her breath, then continued:

"However, and as the Head of Branch has pointed out, Ian's future vision—while grim and full of danger—is not so dire as the possible future I experienced. Ian at least finds a hero or heroes in Scott St. John and his as yet unidentified colleagues. One last thing: just like Ian Goodly, when I stood in the presence of St. John I sensed the dawning of incredible skills, talents as wild as any assembled here. And I am glad that whatever is coming St. John and his friends will be standing on our side and not on the other side, wherever that may prove to be."

As Anna Marie eased carefully down into her seat, so Trask took it up again:

"Okay, so we've heard from Anna Marie and Ian, but they're not alone in their perceptions and experiences. Paul

Garvey has received definite telepathic warnings with regard to any, well, 'interference' by E-Branch, however well intended. And in addition to our 'ghosts,' our 'gadgets' are telling us something of a story, too." Here Trask referred to a venerable E-Branch maxim, that the Branch was served by "gadgets and ghosts;" the psychic skills of his ESPers being the ghosts, while the Branch's high-tech surveillance machineries were the gadgets. And now he continued:

"Our techs did a top-notch job on St. John's house, bugged it to the rafters. But last night the bugs blew up. They didn't just fail—though one of them was probably discovered—but as far as the techs can tell the rest literally blew themselves to pieces! However, not everything was lost . . . But best if I were to let Joe Scathers and then John Grieve supply the details."

Scathers, a short, burly, crew-cut man dressed in a laboratory smock, stood up. "Those bugs were sited as best as possible in the time allowed," he began, "but as the boss has explained, it could be that one of them—in a telephone, probably—was discovered. After that, and I mean shortly after that, the rest of them went out with two or three small bangs! We can't figure it out; it's sort of hard to explain; couldn't be a power surge because there was no connection to the mains. In any case, we'd been having plenty of trouble with reception . . . static, maybe? The Duty Officer should be able to go into that in more detail, but since me and my techs weren't on the receiving end it isn't our province." Frowning, he sat down heavily in his seat.

"But it is mine," said John Grieve as he in his turn stood up. Grieve was a man in his late thirties who had been with the Branch for almost half of those years. Despite being extraordinarily, indeed uniquely talented—a far-seeing telepath who was able to read minds even over the telephone—he had never been a field operative; Trask and previous Heads of Branch had found him too useful in the HQ, as the Duty Officer or on standby, to send Grieve into the far more dangerous world outside. Also, he wasn't an especially physical sort of person. A lifetime smoker and slightly overweight, thin on top and looking older than his years, he might easily be mistaken as a typical clerk—except of course that with his talents Grieve was anything but typical. Proud, upright, smart in his dress, he was also polite and very British. He had the bearing of an ex-army officer or possibly a once-successful businessman; but however he might appear to the man in the street, John Grieve was E-Branch through and through and Ben Trask relied on him, often heavily.

"I have been in large part responsible for monitoring the tech stuff and listening in on St. John's bugs," he began. "Not that there was very much to listen to, not initially. But right from the start a certain name kept cropping up. I was our anonymous 'Xavier' when St. John put through a call on our special number, which was then patched to the Duty Officer's telephone. On that occasion he sounded a bit hysterical, and he was trying to connect with Ian Goodly who he compared—er, favourably, I hasten to add—with someone called Simon Salcombe, a somewhat dubious 'faith-healer' or 'layer-on-of-hands.' Our conversation was very short; it didn't add up to much, which gave me no real opportunity to read his mind.

"Another call, this time on one of his bugged phones, was to one Bill Comber, a journalist—or rather a photographer, or both—who lives not too far from St. John. St. John wanted to talk to Comber about his unfortunately deceased wife, Kelly, to which end he paid Comber a visit that same evening. We, too, have talked to Comber and we delivered strongly worded, er, 'advice' that he should forget ever having spoken to St. John and especially to us. As for what he told us: it was all rather garbled and quite odd; but he did mention that when he'd seen St. John that night, the man had acted very oddly—and again the name of Simon Salcombe was mentioned.

"I had gone on Duty Watch that night at 8:00, and I freely admit to feeling a bit drowsy sometime after 3:30 when suddenly St. John's tech gear started to act up. He was obviously up and about, but what could he be up to in the wee small hours of the morning? Well, I'm no tech, but still I tuned in as best I could and of course recorded whatever there was to record.

"The sound on the tape is very distorted and lengthy passages of conversation are either missing or so patchy as to make them useless, but I did get something: namely that St. John had a visitor, a woman! The name 'Shania' occurs—which I believe is the name of St. John's visitor—and also 'Kelly,' the name of his dead wife. Also, it appears that for the purpose of some undefined security system, numbers are in use in place of or in addition to names: where St. John is 'One' and Shania is 'Two,' and someone else has been designated 'Three.' Whoever this last person may be, however, he wasn't present and doesn't appear to be greatly appreciated; they can be heard to call him variously a 'dog' and/or a 'wolf'!

"As for my telepathy on that occasion: don't ask! As hard as I tried I was—I don't know—blocked? No, it wasn't mind-smog, but it came pretty close and was just as strong. Anyway, this man Salcombe's name surfaced yet again when he was called 'very dangerous' and 'unapproachable,' if not in those precise words . . .

"A day or so later and a different Duty Officer on watch, and finally St. John's bugs seem to be working to good effect. Trying to discover Salcombe's whereabouts, he makes an exploratory but unproductive call to a hospital. Then, hiding behind an assumed and fictional identity, one 'Quentin Mandeville'—a supposedly filthy rich philanthropist—he contacts an orphanage with similar queries and spurious promises and discovers that Salcombe is situated at Schloss Zonigen, a 'facility' in Switzerland where Simon Salcombe and others of his group 'meditate' and 'aspire to perfect their healing arts.'

"Now as I have pointed out, I was not the officer on duty during these last-mentioned conversations and recordings; thus I had no opportunity to read Scott St. John's mind. Last night, however, when I *was* on duty, 'Shania' was once more present at St. John's house and I was finally able to, er, 'eavesdrop' on them and record at least a little of their conversation. As for her being there: that's quite odd because an observer in situ, our stakeout, failed to see and report her arrival.

"Anyway, I have a transcript right here." And putting on his spectacles, Grieve commenced reading from notes clipped to a millboard:

"Shania's voice: St. John is told of the importance of his belief in both Shania and 'Wolf.' St. John's voice: 'Zante,' or 'Zakynthos,' a Greek island in the Ionian, is mentioned. Shania talks of herself, St. John, and this Wolf person as a unit. But by now the electrical interference—which has been there from the moment Shania's presence was noted—has become a veritable storm of static! Still, I persevere.

"St. John asks Shania a question—which I think is about the telephone in his study. Her answer is quite unintelligible, lost in the hum and hiss of the 'static' or whatever is causing the interference. But then, a few seconds later, I clearly hear St. John say, 'Damn! I've been bugged!'

"Some five or six minutes later, when the intensity of the noises coming out of the tech recorders and equipment is giving me a headache, I decide to take an asprin and a glass of water, and I very fortuitously remove my headphones in order to do so. Why fortuitously? Because that was when St. John's bugs decided to self-destruct! And what Joe Scathers didn't think to mention is the fact that quite a bit of his expensive tech equipment—including the headphones—suffered something of a meltdown at the same time! I consider myself fortunate that I wasn't burned or deafened.

"Now let me be plain: I believe the, er, damage caused was a deliberate act on the part of Scott St. John and Shania, whoever she may be. But I don't think they intended any harm; they were merely protecting themselves. And the mind-smog I've mentioned: that was simply another protective device, which goes to substantiate the emergent powers that Ian Goodly and Anna Marie have mentioned, and which David Chung is ready to corroborate."

He nodded at locator Chung in a seat nearby, and sat

down. A third-generation Cockney, David Chung stood up, and held up a bauble in plain view. Without pause he said, "You're looking at a spiral of pre-decimal coins—old money—encased in a dome of glassy plastic or clear resin. It's a paperweight from Scott St. John's desk, purloined for my use in order that we may know where he is from day to day. And the reason I'm not too worried about having it in my possession is that it's got no electrical or mechanical bits that might explode at any time now!" Chung's audience moved in their seats. One or two of them grinned, however uneasily, and some even managed wry chuckles. But suddenly Chung was serious.

"That's about the limit of anything we might find humorous about this item," he continued drily, "for it's pretty much the weirdest thing I've come across since . . . well, since Harry was with us. *You* see a glass bauble, a desk ornament, a paperweight. And you feel nothing. *I* hold it in my hand and my arm vibrates, albeit minutely. I look at it and beyond the coins I see a man, Scott St. John. Well, no, I can't actually see him—but I feel him there, and I know where he is. And that's how I am with the possessions of most people; it's how I am with your possessions—those of them which you've let me possess. But with Scott St. John I feel a whole lot more than that.

"Yes, I know where he is: right now he's in Zakynthos, not long since arrived. But if I try to look, or feel, or sense too hard . . . then it all clouds over and all I feel is the enormous energy of a human dynamo! Three or four days ago when the techs gave me this thing, the power was there but it was weak. I knew St. John was alive and well, and I was able to pinpoint his location at any given time, but his—what should I call it?—his 'aura' made little or no impression on me. Since then, however, this feeling of latent power has grown by leaps and bounds. And I can only reiterate what Anna Marie has said: that I'm glad St. John is on our side. Or on the side of planet Earth, anyway . . ."

Chung was finished; putting the paperweight in his pocket, he sat down. And from the podium Ben Trask said:

"So that's where it's at. St. John is in Zante, but why we don't know. Ironically enough there's someone—two someones—on that selfsame island who might have helped us out here. Yes, I mean Zek Föener and Jazz Simmons; that's where they live now, on the island she was named after. But since Perchorsk Jazz has sworn off this sort of work; likewise Zek. Also, I know she and Harry Keogh were very close; so close that if she had never met Jazz . . . but that would have only complicated matters more yet. Still, I know Zek gave the Necroscope what help she could while he was preparing for Starside. It's even possible she blames us that we were chasing him out of this world. And I know how she must feel for I'm on the same wavelength. We both know what we owed that man."

As Trask grew silent Ian Goodly stood up. "Just a point," he said.

"What is it, Ian?"

"We couldn't ask Zek or Jazz for their help anyway. Not if it would compromise what St. John is doing. And that's the same reason we can't send anyone out there. So all we can do is wait and watch."

Trask nodded. "Yes, you're right, of course. Meanwhile . . . well we can try to check out this Schloss Zonigen place; that's if we can find it! And we might try doing some research on this Simon Salcombe fellow—his history and such—keeping it all very softly-softly. But I'm sure that each one of you will have your own ideas on where to go from here, so let's go." Then, as he got down from the podium, Trask finished with:

"People, remember, 'ordinary' E-Branch work goes on, and my desk is piled high with it. But I'm there and I'll be available at all times. All I ask is that when you've got something solid you keep me in the picture, right up-to-date. And that's it . . ."

Following the O-Group, having paused in the Ops Room in order to speak briefly to his 2IC, Ian Goodly, Trask was the last man out into the long corridor. By then most of his agents had gone back to their places of work. But as Trask made for his office, and as he drew level with the elevator, so the doors opened and the Duty Officer, Paul Garvey, stepped into view accompanied by the last person on Earth that Trask wanted to see at this time: the Minister Responsible.

"Ah, Ben!" said that one, catching at his elbow, while to his rear Paul Garvey pulled one of his faces. "Just the man!"

"Yes, of course I am," said Trask wryly. "Always." And as Paul Garvey went back to his place of duty, Trask and his visitor proceeded to Trask's office at the end of the corridor.

The Minister Responsible for E-Branch was in his early to mid-forties, small and dapper, with his dark hair brushed back and plastered down. His brow had some few wrinkles; other than these his face was unlined, even young-looking, with eyes that were bright, clear, and blue over a long straight nose, a thin-lipped mouth, and a narrow chin. He had no nerves to speak of, or none that were on display. He wore patent-leather black shoes, a dark-blue suit, and a light-blue tie. He also wore a smile, and seeing right through it Trask knew he wished a favour.

Inside his office and when they were seated, Trask said, "So then, Minister, what can I do for you?"

"Aha!" said the other, smiling again but falsely. "But it might just be what I can do for you!" (Another falsehood—or at best a half-truth as opposed to a barefaced lie—which the human lie detector Ben Trask at once recognized, of course.)

And replying to the Minister Responsible's smile with another that was just as false, he replied, "Very well then, say on. For I'm all ears . . ."

23

The Minister Responsible got down to business. "Ben," he said, "you know of course that I see copies of almost every document and request that crosses over your desk into your very capable hands? Frequently before you yourself see them?"

Trask nodded. "Yes. It's got to be so because you are the man allegedly responsible for our little setup here." *But you don't see everything.*

"Oh? Did you say 'allegedly'? I'll have you know I take my responsibilities very seriously."

"Well, that's good," said Trask. "Because I was wanting to speak to you about our funding, which right now—"

"I know," the Minister cut him short. "You're working on a shoestring budget. You've mentioned it previously, as have your predecessors before you—often. And I promise you I'll bring it up at my very next meeting with the, er, the Lady Herself."

"The Lady?" Trask couldn't help but grin. "You mean you're not on first-name terms with Maggie Thatcher?"

"Er, I prefer to call her the Prime Minister," the Minister Responsible answered tersely. "Anyway, the funding of your organization isn't what I'm here to talk about. So please don't change the subject, Mr. Trask."

That's better, Trask thought. *No more Maggie, and no more Ben. First-name terms are out right across the board. Well, at least until he gets what he wants!*

But out loud he said, "How can I change the subject when I don't know what the subject is?"

"Sophistry!" the Minister snapped. "And time-wasting, too. So now can we get on with it?"

Trask shrugged. "Sure, by all means. But let me guess: you want me to do you a favour, right?"

"A-*hmmm!*" said the Minister, turning his head and casting a sharp glance over his shoulder, as if he thought to find one of Trask's agents there, perhaps a telepath. "Well then, let's say a favour for a favour. You scratch my back, and et cetera. Your funding gets looked into—I guarantee it—and you do a little something for me. A *very* little something."

Trask sighed, leaned forward across his desk, and propped his chin on a cupped hand. "Very well, so what's your problem? But wait—let's have one thing straight—I won't be breaking the law for you!"

"What? You won't break . . . ?" The Minister puffed his cheeks out, grew red in the face, and snapped, "*Mr. Trask!* I—"

"Just kidding!" Trask held up his hands. "My way of taking some of the agony out of it, that's all."

"'Agony'?" The Minister blinked, shook his head in a puzzled fashion.

"Diplomacy isn't my forte," said Trask. "I haven't got the time for it. Political correctness and ministerial double-talk: who needs it? Me, I'm down-to-earth; and you and I, we'd get on a whole lot better if you were, too."

The Minister cooled down; his eyes narrowed to blue slits, but after a while he nodded and said, "All right, I'll tell you what I want. Not too long ago you received a report on a particularly gruesome murder—well, we assume it was murder—of one of the Government's opposition ministers, a lesser-known Labour minister called Gregory Stamper. But as well as a member of the opposition, Stamper was—"

"A very rich man," Trask cut in. "He had shares in various precious-metals mining concerns; and as you point out, he died a bloody terrible death . . . with the emphasis firmly on bloody! Yes, I've read up on it and we're investigating it, making what inquiries we can; but it's only one of a great many tasks we're involved with, including some that as yet you *don't* know about. So what's your special interest in this one?"

For a moment the Minister Responsible looked uncomfortable, then said, "Actually, I'm not all that interested—except, of course, in my official capacity as the man appointed to oversee E-Branch's activities—but on this occasion I'm here on behalf of someone else."

"So," said Trask, "in fact I'll be doing this favour, whatever it is, to make you look good in the eyes of someone else?"

"Please let me explain," said the Minister. "But this time without the customary interruptions. George Samuels, a Metropolitan Police Officer and the son of an influential acquaintance, was the first man on the scene of Stamper's murder when, during a routine mobile patrol, he undertook to investigate it.

"Unusually young for his rank, a so-called whizz kid—but to be perfectly honest, a rather inexperienced Inspector of Police—Samuels's reaction did not stand him in good stead with his superiors. In short, he fainted on sighting the corpse, corrupted and otherwise messed up the scene-of-crime, and in short order had a nervous breakdown. Already the butt of jokes, jibes, and other undignified comments from his peers, he found himself more or less ostracised. And in a fit of pique he quit."

Trask sighed. "I see. And his influential father wants him to reconsider, and probably wants him reinstated, which in some way involves E-Branch . . . but I don't see how."

"Then I'll tell you," said the Minister. "Since recovering from his breakdown, George Samuels has seemed bent upon investigating this case in his own right—one might say as a private investigator, though he is not registered or qualified as such. Nevertheless he has come up with several interesting clues, and he's aware that E-Branch is working toward the same end."

"He is?" said Trask. "And so much for our anonymity! Might I hazard a guess as to how Samuels knows about E-Branch? Can it be possible that our Minister Responsible—"

But the Minister held up a hand to cut him off. "Ben, your branch and its work must always remain invisible to all unauthorized eyes. To George Samuels and his father you are simply an extension of our Security Services, whose works have overflowed into subsidiary branches. But when I was told of young Samuels's interest, indeed his consuming interest in this case, it seemed only natural that I—"

"That you offer to assist him by putting him on to us. And I can't help noticing that I'm 'Ben' again! Okay, so how are we supposed to help him?"

"Well," said the Minister, "young Samuels is of the belief that he has useful information to impart, and he wants to share it with you in order to bring the murderer or murderers to justice. Also, he hopes to be there at the, er, 'kill,' if and when you arrest the perpetrators. Then, having helped in closing the case which caused his, er, downfall, he'll feel fully justified in regaining his rank; he'll be able to return to duty with his head held high."

Uttering a snort of annoyance, Trask said, "We always work alone; you know that. Also, as yet we have nothing to go on. We were waiting to see if the police could come up with some leads that we might then follow up. As you're aware, when they dig up clues my agents can often verify them using their own less than orthodox methods. That's what we're here for, not to play nursemaid to some snot-nosed rich-kid policeman who's lost his way!"

"But you will help me out here? And in return rest assured that I will help you—at least with your budget?"

"When am I supposed to speak to this Samuels?" said Trask, resignedly. "And remember, it can't possibly be here. Our location in this hotel is top secret; it's one part of our security that we simply can't afford to compromise." Then, narrowing his eyes to frown suspiciously at the other: "You haven't actually *told* this Samuels or his father where we are, have you?"

"No, only that you're situated in central London, and that your branch has a special interest in cases such as the Stamper murder. As for meeting with George Samuels: that's at your own discretion. I have his telephone number right here." He fished in his pocket for a card.

Trask nodded, accepted the card with Samuels's number, and said, "Very well, I'll see what I can do. But no promises. Anyway and however this works out, you'll be able to tell Samuels's daddy that we hope to benefit from his errant son's assistance, and—who can say?—it might even prove to be the truth. But that's about the size of it."

"Ben," said the Minister, getting to his feet, "you are, as usual, most accommodating. And I thank you in advance."

"And in advance of sorting out our funding, I hope," Trask growled. Then he buzzed for the Duty Officer, to see the Minister off the premises . . .

At 7:00 that evening, Trask met ex-Inspector George Samuels in the hotel restaurant where they ordered an early evening meal. Also in attendance was Paul Garvey, specifically there to pick Samuel's mind, while Trask of course would immediately know it if the ex-Inspector strayed an inch from the truth.

But from the start—from the moment Trask shook Samuels's hand—he knew he wasn't going to like the man, which premonition was borne out during the meeting. It wasn't so much that Samuels lied; rather that he was pompous and misrepresented or overemphasised his own authority, while simultaneously playing down his break-down as represented by the Minister Responsible. But still Trask heard him out.

"I had been suffering from a very unpleasant stomach bug, which had left me rather vulnerable," Samuels stated again. "It caught up with me at the scene of the crime. I passed out, yes,—but not from fear, I assure you, nor from the horror of the sight that greeted me in that room. And as for the two al-leged paramedics who attended the scene with me, and the hotel's so-called security officer: all three of them proved worse than useless and completely undisciplined. I've been told that following my collapse they treated me with unwar-ranted discourtesy, and I've heard it rumoured that they even hinted at my supposed 'inefficiency'!"

Trask nodded, glanced at his watch, and said, "Yes, I can see how that must have, er, hurt your feelings. But I'm a very busy man, Mr. Samuels, and I really must insist that we get to the point. Now that you've put us in the picture and we're able to appreciate the opening sequence of events, maybe you'd like to tell us about your subsequent investigations. I've been told you have important information relevant to this case."

Samuels put down a forkful of fish, moved uneasily in his chair, and said, "I believe there's been mention of my requirements in this matter, and that we should have an understanding, you and I."

Trask studied the man carefully. Samuels's large ears were turning pink where he tried not to squirm, and a faint film of sweat gleamed on his brow. His grey eyes were nervous and given to fitful blinking, and his small cynical mouth twitched in one corner. He was obviously not yet completely recovered from his nervous breakdown.

Finally Trask answered him. "An understanding? Someone has given you to understand . . . what, exactly?"

"That if I'm h-helpful to you," Samuels stammeringly answered, "you'll be no less helpful to me. I need to be in on this case, Mr. . . . er . . . Xavier, was it? Forgive me, but it's an unusual n-n-name."

"Xavier, yes," Trask answered. "But 'in on it'? How do you mean, in on it? Surely you understand that I have my own investigators?"

"Of course. But I want to work with them; and in the light of my information I believe I deserve a measure of control over them. You see, er, Xavier, in order to prove my capabilities to my superiors—in order to reestablish, reassert myself, with no loss of personal esteem—I really *need* this case, and I—"

"No way!" Trask snapped, cutting the other off with a negative wave of his hand. "Out of the question! You expect me to give you command over a team of my agents? That's unheard of!"

Samuels's grey eyes began blinking again, more erratically than ever. "But I was assured that—"

"Then whoever 'assured' you was mistaken. However, I will guarantee you this: if your information leads us to a successful conclusion, then you'll get the credit. I would personally see to it. But as for actually working with you— letting you run a squad—that's simply not on."

Samuels stopped blinking, dabbed at his forehead with his napkin, and stuttered, "Is that your l-l-last word on the subject?"

"Absolutely!"

"Then we have nothing more to say!" Samuels jerked to his feet, and Paul Garvey rose with him. But:

"Sit down!" Trask snapped.

"What?" Samuels glared. "Don't you know who you're talking to? I'm an Inspector of Police, Mr. Xavier, and I don't take my orders from you. You don't have the power to—"

"You're an *ex*-Inspector," Trask grated, cutting him short yet again. "You're a bloody civilian, Samuels, and I have more power than you could possibly imagine! Now *sit down,* or I shall have Mr. Xavier here sit you down!"

"Xavier?" Samuels gaped, his cynical mouth twitching and a thin trickle of sweat running down his forehead. "But I thought you were Xavier!"

"We're *both* Xavier," Trask snapped, glancing at Garvey and giving him a sharp nod.

Moving quickly around the table, the athletic Garvey made one of his grimaces, laid a hand on Samuels's shoulder, and for the first time spoke. "Now don't go making a fuss, George. Only raise your voice once and you'll be speaking in a croak for the rest of the evening."

"Y-you dare threaten me?" Samuels gasped; but in any case, assisted by Garvey's hand, he thumped heavily down again in his chair.

"Threaten you? I'll do more than that!" Trask snapped. "If you try to withhold valuable information in a murder case, I'll *arrest* you! It's tantamount to being an accomplice! What's more, if you persist in wasting my time there'll be no kudos for you, if or when we bring the perpetrators to book. So let's have it, everything you know, and I want it now, at once."

* * *

"When I was back on my feet," said Samuels, slumped in his seat and looking anything but back on his feet, "I determined to get away from the Met and work the case on my own. I didn't want it bungled, but I did want it solved—if only for my own peace of mind. My God, if you'd seen the mess in that room . . . I mean, no one should get away with murdering a man in that fashion, whatever their reasons! God, but I have dreamed—not only dreamed but *nightmared* about that hotel—and about the terrible *thing* I saw in the corner of the room, that travesty of a man!

"But at work: the sniggers, snide comments behind my back, sneering looks on the faces of my so-called superiors. Maybe I went back too soon, without giving myself time to recover from things—my previous illness, I mean—made worse by working myself too hard, and complicated by the shock of . . . of . . .

"Anyway, I quit the Force and commenced my own investigations. I did still have one or two friends in New Scotland Yard, however, and one of them sent me a set of pictures taken by the security cameras at the airport hotel. Unfortunately these photographs aren't much good, a lot of detail being lost due to the malfunctioning of the hotel's electrical systems. But two hours earlier that night, prior to Stamper being found in that monstrous condition, he did have a visitor!

"A visitor, yes: an extremely tall, very thin man—which was about as much as I could say about him, the pictures being so bad—but now I believe I know who he was, who he is! I'll get to that in a moment . . .

"Next, I had to find out if Stamper had enemies; here I'm talking about real enemies as opposed to people in the Conservative Party, currently in power. I tried to interview Stamper's wife but she didn't want to know. She's a rather cold woman and had already given a statement to . . . well, to the police.

"Obliged to rethink my strategy, I finally managed to come by Stamper's diary, and—"

But here Trask cut in, saying, "You what? Just like that, you 'came by' Gregory Stamper's diary?"

"Er, well yes," Samuels replied after a moment's thought. But his ears had reddened up again and his mouth was twitching furiously. "Please try to remember, I am, or was, an Inspector of Police. I have connections."

Trask glanced at the telepath, Paul Garvey, who nodded and said, "Yes, he certainly does have connections—with the criminal fraternity at that!"

Samuels's jaw dropped. "I b-b-beg your pardon!?"

Garvey looked at Trask and said, "He hired a burglar. And you know, I can't help wondering what George's former employers would make of that! There'd be more than just a few sniggering noises behind his back, I'll be bound!"

Samuels's jaw had dropped more yet. "How could you p-possibly know that?"

"It's our job to know such things," said Trask, beginning to enjoy himself and feeling a little embarrassed by the fact.

But by now there were several diners at their tables, and the Head of Branch cautioned Samuels: "Quietly now, but do get on with it. Your, er, indiscretions are safe with us—so far."

Very much subdued, Samuels continued:

"You may or may not know it, but despite that Stamper was well-to-do he was also a very heavy gambler; indeed, one might even say a degenerate gambler. That was one of the reasons his wife was leaving him. They hadn't lived together for weeks and Stamper had moved into a hotel—but not the hotel in question. That was simply the venue for his meetings with . . . well, with the person I suspect. That person's name was in his diary. And now it all gets a bit weird . . ." Here Samuels paused, as if he didn't quite know how to continue.

Trask raised an eyebrow and prompted him: "In our line of work we're pretty much used to weird, George. Weird is what we do, so please go on."

"The other reason that Stamper and his wife were parting," Samuels continued, "was that their infant son was sick. Indeed, he was more than sick; he'd been born with inoperable heart and lung problems. Some of the best doctors Stamper couldn't afford had said it might be best to let nature take its course, and—"

"Couldn't afford?" Again Trask's raised eyebrow.

"His gambling," Samuels explained. "Oh, Stamper had money in all kinds of ventures, shares, property, but precious little he could lay his hands on in short order. And his wife—a cold woman, as I've said—was demanding half of everything. Anyway, the child's health or lack of it had caused tensions; these and Stamper's gambling, dwindling resources, et cetera, had brought things to the boil. His wife—who Stamper seemingly loved very much—wanted out while she could still get her hands on half of whatever was left."

"All this was in his diary?" Trask didn't think so.

"No, not at all." Samuels shook his head. "But as I think I've already explained, the police were carrying out an investigation—well, at least of the wife, the possibility that she might have hired someone to kill him—and I could still rely on my, er, friend—"

"Your accomplice," Garvey grunted.

"—In the Metropolitan Police," said Samuels. And again he paused. "Should I continue? H-h-hopefully without further interruptions and accusations?"

"Just get on with it!" Trask scowled.

"As for his diary," Samuels went on, "it mentioned a certain sum of money—an enormous amount, and in gold—which was to be paid to someone who Stamper seemed to see as his one last hope in (a) helping his infant son, which would perhaps assist in (b) sorting out his marital problems. As for this someone's name—"

But here Paul Garvey gasped, starting up rigid in his seat as his face performed one of its convulsions.

Alarmed, Trask said, "Paul? Are you all right?"

"Oh, yes," said the other, relaxing a little. "Wind, that's all. Something I must have heard . . . er, I mean eaten."

Having received Garvey's disguised message loud and clear, Trask turned back to Samuels. "Yes? You were saying? This someone's name was—?"

"It was Simon Salcombe," said Samuels. "That faith-healer fellow. As for what Stamper saw in him . . . if you ask me he was grasping at straws! But here's the weird part: in the course of further investigations I've discovered that Stamper's baby son is now fit and well! That child who was crawling around in his father's blood and his own excrement—that allegedly incurable infant—is back with his mother and enjoying sound health!"

Fortunately Samuels had gone on at some length, allowing Trask time to recover a little of his assumed insouciance following the shock of once more hearing Salcombe's name mentioned. And now he said: "So, what do you make of all this? Do you see a connection between this Salcombe and Greg Stamper's death?"

"I've seen pictures of Salcombe in the papers," the other answered, low-voiced. "And I've also seen those security photographs. Now, while it's impossible to say they're pictures of one and the same man, it's also impossible to say that they're not . . ." He fell silent.

"And that's it?" said Trask. "You've told us everything?"

"Everything," Samuels replied.

Trask looked at Garvey, who pursed his lips and shrugged. So then, maybe not everything, but if there was anything else the telepath would probably know all about it. And so:

"Right," said Trask, "you can go. And since you've been straight with us I'll be straight with you. I won't be reporting your little transgressions, but that's on one condition: that as of now you'll terminate your investigations. The fact is you could easily compromise *our* work, and that's something I can't allow. However, and as promised, if and when we bring someone to justice for Gregory Stamper's murder—and if your information has helped us to do so—you'll get full credit."

"Well," the other sniffed, "I suppose that's something."

"Oh?" said Trask. "You suppose that's something, do you? And is that all? Well, one thing's for sure: it's a damn sight better than a lockup in one of Her Majesty's prisons!"

After Samuels left, Trask turned to Garvey and said: "Well?"

"He told most of it," the other answered. "But he didn't mention that he knows where Salcombe is; not his actual location, no, but the name of this Schloss Zonigen place in Switzerland, definitely. He didn't mention it, but there again you didn't ask him."

"And that's it? He wasn't holding anything else back?"

Garvey frowned, with half of his face at least, and said, "I'm pretty sure you got most of it, but I don't think he was taking your warnings any too seriously."

"You think he'll disregard them?"

"I think he'll certainly give it some thought," the telepath answered. "But as for his interest in this case: actually, it's more an obsession. While I don't think Samuels had a very nice mind to begin with, now that it's been knocked out of skew it's that much worse. It's a very complicated, almost a twisted mind, yes. And there are pictures in there that I really didn't care to look at."

And that was that. But Trask was left with a great deal to think about, an awful lot on *his* mind . . .

24

Earlier, in Zakynthos:

Along with many of his fellow travellers, Scott St. John had caught the Sunways Holidays coach heading east for Argasi, where most of them were staying. On the crowded coach, a droning Sunways Holidays rep in a faded uniform had seated himself beside the driver—the only one allowed to smoke, apparently—and gone on about the "natural beauty" of the island: its safe, crystal-clear waters for swimming, its myriad bays and beaches, especially its turtle beach; its industry: honey, wines, fishing, and, most importantly, tourism. Except for Scott, almost everyone on the coach had heard it all before and seemed uninterested. Undaunted, the rep had tried for a laugh with an old joke about mosquitos: "You won't find a single mosquito on the entire island!" he'd said. Followed by the punch line: "That's 'cos they're all married with kids!" Until eventually, realizing no one was listening, he'd given in and fallen silent.

In Argasi, at the Mimoza Beach Hotel, Scott had debussed with a handful of others, then tried to show at least a little interest in his accommodation: a small, sparsely furnished but clean ceramic-tiled room with a small balcony under a blue-and-white-striped awning; but his mind was on other things, namely a dog—or rather "a wolf of the wild"—called unconfusingly Wolf, or perhaps St. John Three. And having dumped his luggage, one small sausage bag containing two T-shirts, socks, an extra pair of trousers, and several other necessaries he'd thought to pack, finally Scott had called for a taxi and asked to be taken to Porto Zoro.

A little less than five kilometres later on a road heading south, Scott's driver—a man with shining jet-black hair, lots of stubble, a cheroot in a gap in his teeth, and wearing an oil- and sweat-stained yellow T-shirt—pointed ahead to indicate a sharp left turn. "Here is thee Porto Zoro," he said. "You going thee beach? You know Porto Zoro is thee beach?"

Scott could see a horizon of ocean and little else. But he also saw a signpost reading: "Vassilikos: 3 Km." And:

"Hold it!" he said. "No, not the beach. Carry straight on, toward Vassilikos."

The driver turned to look at Scott, and said, "You knowing where you go?"

"I think so," Scott answered.

"Okay." And shrugging his shoulders, the driver turned his vehicle back onto the main road.

They swept on; in a little while the road rose up to follow the contours of the rising ground through a region of dense Mediterranean pines; the car was dappled in constantly changing patterns of brilliant sunlight, dark leafy shade. And suddenly Scott knew where he was. The sea on his left, glimpsed through the trees; the embankment on his right, where the road was cut through rock and flinty earth; that pantiled villa down there, almost hidden in the foliage, with blue smoke coiling from its chimney.

"Stop!" said Scott, and the driver applied his brakes and stopped.

Scott got out onto the potholed road, and because he had left his drachmas at the hotel paid the fare in British pounds: three small, heavy coins. Accepting the money, the driver also got out of his car. Looking all around, and obviously baffled, he scratched his head, shrugged, got back in his taxi, and made a jerky three-point turn. Standing in a cloud of dust and blue exhaust fumes, Scott watched him drive back the way they had come, until the taxi rounded a bend and passed from sight.

Then the silence settled in, broken only by the cooing of doves from somewhere close at hand and the soft *hush, hush* of wavelets breaking on a rocky shore down below. But that didn't last for long. From the direction of Vassilikos came a distance-muted babble of voices and the yelping of dogs. Trackers? Possibly. And:

How many chickens vanished last night? Scott wondered.

None! came the answer, startling him. And Wolf explained: *Last night, many men were out with their dogs; they were hunting me! I, too, was out, on the prowl, but I dared not kill and so couldn't eat. Now I'm down in a cave at the water's rim. I didn't speak before for fear of distracting you. But I sensed you drawing near . . . Scott?*

"Yes, it's me, and I'm coming." Scott nodded, mouthing the words in a whisper as if talking to himself; and, if anyone had been there to see him, indeed seeming to talk to himself. "Now tell me," he went on. "Where exactly are you?"

Follow the pebble pathway down to the house, Wolf

replied, with some urgency now. *Then come down to the ledges at the edge of the water. I will meet you there. But hurry, for I can hear the dogs.*

"Okay," said Scott. "I'm coming."

How will you save me, take me away?

"I have no idea . . . but I'll think of something."

He hurried back along the road to where a path snaked down through the trees. If not for the blue wood smoke spiralling up from its chimney, the villa would look temporarily deserted; on the other hand, and if its occupants followed the Greek custom, they would probably be asleep: the afternoon siesta.

Scott went quietly. He passed the house by, found a steep, well-worn track down through the pines, began to descend—and stopped. Suddenly there was a presence. Scott *sensed* a presence and knew there was someone there, behind him.

He turned, looked back. The door to the villa stood open. A woman stood not ten paces away, dappled by beams of sunlight and shaded under the tortured branches of a sprawling Mediterranean pine. Moving hesitantly forward, she came more properly into view. Scott saw that she was beautiful, also that she was holding a hand to her mouth. He didn't know why.

She was five-nine or -ten, slim, blonde, blue-eyed, and perfectly proportioned. She wore a blue blouse tucked into a dark-blue skirt belted with a tasselled scarf, a gold bangle on her left wrist, leather sandals on her feet. Her hair was loose; it framed her oval face and fell forward on her shoulders.

"Oh!" said Scott, not knowing what else to say. "I'm sorry if I scared you. I mean, it's kind of lonely here and I'm probably trespassing." His words sounded stupid to him; probably to her, too.

Momentarily wide-eyed, now she relaxed. Her hand fell from her mouth and her breast moved visibly in a deep sigh of . . . of what? Relief? Or regret? Scott couldn't make up his mind. Whichever, she said, "I think we startled each other! But just for a moment there I was confused. I thought . . . I thought that maybe you were someone else."

"I'm Scott St. John," Scott replied. "And you must be Zek, the owner of a wolf—his One?"

She blinked, and then in a hurry said, "Now I know you—I think. You're *his* One! But time is short and we shouldn't waste it talking out here. You must go and get him, and quickly. He's down by the sea."

"I know," said Scott, accepting the strangeness of it all.

"Listen," she said, cocking her head to the not-so-distant barking. "The tracker dogs. They'll be here soon. You'd best go for him, try to bring him inside the house. Maybe if you enter, he'll come in, too. He doesn't trust people very much—not even me, and I've been feeding him and trying to keep him safe—and he's none too keen on houses, either!"

"I didn't suppose he would be," said Scott. "After all, he is a wolf of the wild." Then, as he turned away downhill, "I'll go and get him . . ."

Down below, jutting ledges of white, sea-carved rock ran horizontal to the ocean. Clambering down over sharply scalloped rims that scarred his shoes and would have cut bare feet to ribbons, Scott called out loud, "Wolf! I'm here!"

And I! that one replied, emerging from his hiding place, a deep cave under a wave-washed ledge. Wolf looked miserable, the soul of unhappiness. Bathed, and with the salt removed from his matted hair, and fed until his ribs weren't quite so prominent, he might even look handsome. But even in his current condition his lineage showed: the fact that he wasn't just a dog.

I itch, he said, *and my paws are bleeding. But if you are my One—no, I know you are—you'll look after me. And I shall look after you.* His tail, at first hanging low, lifted a little and commenced to wag, albeit tentatively. And: *Well,* he continued, limping slowly forward, *so you are Scott, my One. And I am Wolf, and here we are together.*

I also am here, said one other, in a low, growling "voice" that was new to this weird conversation. Over the wash of wavelets Scott heard the scrape of pebbles, turned, and saw—

—A second Wolf, and a *bigger* wolf, crouched with muscles bunched, flat-eared, as if poised to spring from a position two ledges higher!

"Wolf!" came a cry from on high. The man and both canines turned their heads, looked up toward the villa. Zek was barely visible through the trees. The older animal's ears came erect; his brown eyes were fixed on the woman, and hers on him; Scott sensed something pass between them. Then Wolf Sr.—for such he must surely be—turned his head to look along the undulating rim of the ocean.

To the south along the shoreline, figures moved. Men, and dogs, down by the sea.

I came back here along that route this morning, said Wolf Jr. *These poor tame creatures are a surly lot, but their noses are keen!*

I go, said his father, *to lead them astray. They'll chase me instead of you. You*—he jerked his nose at Wolf Jr.—*you go to Zek.* And then to Scott: *I know you hear me. Men who talk to wolves are rare; I knew some on Sunside, a few. And there's Zek, of course. But tell me: you mean no harm? And you'll help this wild cub of mine?*

"That's why I'm here." Scott nodded. "I'm his One."

Then take him to Zek. I go!

And he went—belly low to the earth, loping up the rock terraces—to the tree line where, like a grey shadow, he disappeared into the pines. An ululating, long-drawn-out howl came echoing back. And along the rocky shore the tracker dogs yelped and yipped, and their masters urged them on.

"Let's go," said Scott. "Zek's waiting."

We're to go indoors? (This hesitantly.)

"I live indoors," Scott replied, watching the animal limp. "And if you're going to live with me, you will, too."

Indoors smells strange. There's nothing of the wild.

"Right now indoors is safer than out here," Scott replied, seeing blood splash on the rocks where Wolf stepped, and noticing how he almost fell when a hind leg buckled under him. They climbed the ledges, but here close to the trees the ground was littered with pine needles. From now on the going would be far slower and a lot more painful for Wolf, and meanwhile the barking and snarling of the trackers had come that much closer.

Scott didn't think twice but stooped, grabbed hold, lifted the animal up and across his shoulders. *Huh!* Wolf growled, paws dangling. *Already I am a burden to you!*

You're not heavy, Scott answered telepathically, remembering a song he liked. *You're my number Three—for God's sake!*

In a little while the going was easier, so that Scott completed the final stretch at a jouncing trot.

Such strength! said Wolf, admiringly. *I think I may enjoy us being One, Two, and Three with Shania; though there will be much that is strange.*

And Scott said, *You can say that again!*

Zek was at the door; she let them in, took them to a cool room where she lifted a trapdoor to reveal steps descending to a cellar. Scott lowered Wolf to the tiled floor, and Zek said, "He'll be safe down there for a while."

Wolf cringed back. *You wish me to go down into a hole?*

"It's more comfortable than a damp cave," Scott reassured him. "And as soon as those dogs have gone we'll have you out of there."

Wolf uttered a low whine, limping as he started down into darkness.

"Amazing!" said Zek. "He trusts you completely. And yet he had to be close to starving before he'd even take food from me! And that reminds me—" She went into the kitchen, returned with a half-pound slab of lamb wrapped in clean white paper. "If you give it to him he'll eat it," she said.

Scott took the meat down the whitewashed steps, found the light switch, and put it on. Down there on an old carpet in one corner, Wolf blinked at him and then lay back again, exhausted. Unwrapping the meat, Scott went to him. "This is good food," he said. "What, did you think that maybe Zek was one of your poisoners? No, she's good people, I can promise you that."

My thanks, said Wolf, already beginning to salivate as he pawed the meat down onto the carpet. *And to Zek. Perhaps I was beings too careful. I haven't seen too many good people.*

At which Zek called down, "Scott, come up—quickly now. I think those men are coming here!"

Scott hurried back up the steps; they lowered the trap-door and Zek threw a carpet over it; there was something of a tumult outside: men shouting, the snapping and snarling of dogs. There came a hammering at the door and a man's voice, hoarse and panting, shouted, "In there—you, Englishwoman—please opening thee door!"

Looking through a small circular window beside the door, Zek nodded and said, "I thought I recognized this one's voice." Her own voice was more than a little sour. "In Argasi one evening, Jazz and I were eating in a favourite taverna with a handful of friends. A bunch of local men, usually very nice people, had consumed too much ouzo; they were looking for trouble. This one insulted me and Jazz knocked him down. That was all; it was over and done with. But I think he's been looking for a way to get back at us ever since."

Scott said, "Open the door."

Zek looked at him and raised a golden eyebrow. "This could turn nasty. Are you—?"

"It's okay," Scott told her. "Just open the door."

She nodded and did as he asked, then stepped outside onto whitewashed flags. Scott followed her, closing the door behind him. Three hot, sweaty men, two of them cradling shotguns, and all three with dogs on leashes, had moved aside to let the door open outward. Their spokesman—a bearded, jowly, big-bellied man in sandals, shorts, a wide-brimmed hat, and a safari jacket in which he looked totally ridiculous—now pushed to the fore. Flabby lips quivering, piggy eyes glaring, he pointed a stubby finger at Zek and grunted, "You, Englishwoman—"

"No, I'm Greek," she immediately and haughtily replied. "I was born here on Zakynthos. And I'm also German, on my father's side. But did you say English? I'm married to an Englishman, if that's what you mean. So then, what can I do for you?"

"Huh?" he answered. "Greek, German, English—so what? Do you have thee dog? Do not telling thee lie—I know you do. We track him here. Many times we track him here."

"I never lie!" Zek stood up straighter. "Also, if you know I have a dog, why do you ask? Can it be you're as stupid as you look?"

"What?" His lips quivered again. "You say I stupid? You say why I ask? Because your dog, he killing things. He killing my chickens, and he doing thee shits in my hen-house! Maybe my dog doing thee shits in your house, eh? Maybe *I* do thee shits, eh?"

"Such language!" Zek replied coolly, narrowing her eyes.

Moving her gently aside, Scott calmly and quietly told the man, "Fat boy, you *are* very stupid. Also, you have a big flabby gut and a big flabby mouth. So now take your little friends and these noisy dogs, and go away. Or else you'll make me angry."

The man looked at Scott and puffed himself up. "I wanting shoot thee dog!" he roared. And turning to his weaponed companions, in Greek he said, "Yanni, Stamatis—go into the house—find that bastard rogue and shoot the fucking thing!"

"I can speak Greek, too!" Zek snapped in their own tongue. "You dirty, foul-mouthed animal!"

By now the tracker dogs—bewildered by the raised voices, unsure of themselves without definite orders from their masters—were cowering, whining, no longer straining at their leashes. But looking embarrassed and undecided, Yanni and Stamatis, both of them younger men who were obviously influenced if not dominated by their bullying friend, nevertheless edged forward. Then the youngest one, Yanni, a teenager, halted, shook his head, and muttered, "Kostas, listen. Maybe we shouldn't be doing—"

"Then give *me* the gun!" Kostas cut him short, snatching at the weapon in question. "I might have known you'd back down!"

Scott had understood most of what was said; his knowledge of languages had helped, assisted by his burgeoning telepathy. Kostas had taken a loose, one-handed grip on Yanni's shotgun's stock and was turning back toward Zek as Scott stepped forward. Using his right hand to enclose the weapon's trigger guard, so that it couldn't be fired, and grabbing the double barrel with his left hand, Scott yanked the gun toward himself—then immediately shoved it in the other direction, into Kostas's face!

The butt of the weapon flattened the Greek's nose, splitting his upper lip. He released the gun, reeled backward, then folded forward and crumpled as Scott rammed the butt deep into his fat stomach. Stamatis, the second young man, gasped aloud, began to level his weapon—

—At which a black and grey shape came hurtling as if out of nowhere, snarling and nipping at Kostas's dog, which was about to launch itself at Scott.

It was of course Wolf Sr., all fangs and wet black muzzle, tearing a chunk out of Kostas's mongrel's ear, and then turning on the other dogs who skittered left and right with their tails down, fouling their masters' feet with their leashes.

Stamatis, muttering a low curse, tried to level his gun at Wolf. Scott, stepping forward, rammed the double barrels of his commandeered shotgun up under Stamatis's ribs, growling, "That's enough! Now give it up!" Since there was very little Stamatis could do but obey, he handed his weapon to Zek who said:

"Now call your dogs to heel, and tell me what this was all about." With Wolf on her left flank and Scott on the other, she stood facing the two young men. As for the bully Kostas: he had crawled away and was being sick into a patch of shrubbery. "And then," Zek continued, "once we've settled things. I'll want you to clean up that pig's mess and get his blood off my doorstep!"

And Scott thought: *This is one cool lady!*

Yes, Wolf growled, his fangs still gleaming white, and his ruff still bristling, *she is. And you, too, are "cool." I think you are indeed the One. As Zek is mine, loved above all others, you will be my wild cub's One. One of Three, or so he tells me; even as I am one of three . . . and yet different.*

The heat had now gone out of the situation, and Zek—knowing full well what had been going on—nevertheless asked, "Well then, who is going to tell me what the problem is? Or perhaps I should simply call the police and let you explain it all to them?"

Kostas, crawling away on hands and knees, with his whimpering dog close behind, looked back and mumbled, "Yes, and you can also tell them about my broken nose, about my broken mouth and teeth!"

"No," Zek called out to him. "Instead I'll report how you threatened to break into my house with a loaded shotgun—also how you said you would . . . you would make a *toilet* of my house—you filthy beast!"

He made no reply but crawled away, up toward the road.

Then the younger men told Zek about a wild dog (no, they didn't believe it was Wolf), and about its thievery, its savaging of chickens and such. They had tracked this wild dog along the shore, where the trackers must have picked up the scent of Wolf, which in turn had led them here. It was strange, but the scent had brought them here before, and on several occasions.

"Then blame your silly tracker dogs!" said Zek. "For it's obvious they're not worth their keep. There are *rabbits* in the woods, and that's what they've been tracking! But wait: my dog has a collar with an address; he has a name, and a licence. He is a legitimate house dog, and sleeps in the house every night keeping guard. Now tell me: do your dogs have licences? I know Sergeant Dendrinos in Argasi; he is a personal friend of mine. He tells me there are many unlicenced local dogs. Why don't we go to Sergeant Dendrinos and tell him of your suspicions about my Wolf? And what if I then ask him to check *your* dog licences, eh?"

Suddenly the young men were most apologetic. Backing away, they would have left it at that. Zek stopped them with a single word and called them back. Scott unloaded their weapons, handed them over, and said, "Maybe you'll give your fat friend a helping hand on your way home. Or then again you might think to ask yourselves: is Kostas really the kind of friend you want?"

And Zek added, "You can tell Kostas that from now on he'd do well to keep out of my husband's way. You know Jazz Simmons, I'm sure. When I tell Jazz what happened here there'll be a lot more blood, I can promise you that! Make sure it's not yours!"

A moment later, when they had gone: "Damn them!" said Zek, stamping her foot. "Now I'm the one who'll be cleaning up this blood!" But after she fetched a mop and a pail of water, Scott did it for her . . .

25

Inside the villa . . . Scott sat on the floor in one of the back rooms and bathed Wolf Jr.'s paws with warm water and a spoonful of dilute antiseptic supplied by Zek. While this was happening the animal studied him with warm feral eyes, whined and jerked just a little, licked his chops nervously but in the main kept still.

Zek was plainly astonished. "He's accepted you!" she said, keeping her mind closed to Wolf Jr. himself. "Just like that!"

Scott followed suit: no longer wondering how he did it but just doing it, he shielded his thoughts as he answered her. "In fact, he accepted me long before I accepted him. The first time we, er, spoke I thought I was losing it. And sometimes even now I think I'm losing it! What's happened to me . . . well, I really can't explain it, except to say that it's been like—and even now feels like—some kind of crazy dream!"

"I know exactly what you mean," she said. "In my time I've seen things that could only be described as dream-like, and all too often nightmare-like! But I can't help feeling you already know that, and that I have known you—something of you, anyway—for a long time. Scott, on the one hand you're very much like Jazz. You don't look the same but still, I feel you could have been brothers. It's just too hard to explain!"

Scott looked up from where he now bandaged Wolf Jr.'s rear left leg where it was cut, nodded, and said, "It is *very* hard to explain, I know, but it's like we're old friends from way back. It's like—what? Déjà vu? Reincarnation? Memories from another world, another time—"

"—Another person?" she finished it off. "But never Jazz, I can see that now."

"Someone else then?"

"I thought you were!" she said. "When I saw you going down to the sea—and even before that, when I sensed you out there—I thought you were someone else. I mean, don't read anything of significance into this, though it probably is significant in its way, but I thought you were someone . . . someone I once knew. In this world, yes, and in a very different world."

Zek had relaxed her shields, and now Wolf Sr. "said," *It was my world, and I know who you mean: the one who fought with us against the Wamphyri in the Dweller's garden. But he is not that one. He only thinks like him. A little like him, anyway.*

Scott looked at the mature, older, even old animal curled on a typically Greek-patterned black and brown rug. And:

Old? said Wolf Sr. *Well, I suppose I am. But my teeth are still sharp and strong, and the wolves of Sunside/Starside are long-lived; there are plenty of sunups in me yet.*

"It wasn't meant as an insult," said Scott.

Nor taken that way, said the other. And: *Are you finished pampering this pup of mine?*

Seated in an armchair beside Wolf Sr., Zek reached down

a hand, scratched his ear, and said, "Do you mind if we talk, my friend and I, in private?"

You want me to go out?

"No, but just ignore us and be quiet."

I can do that. And he lay down flat, with his nose on his paws.

Meanwhile, Scott was indeed done with doctoring Wolf Jr., who now asked, *When can we go and see Shania?*

"That . . . *might* be something of a problem," Scott answered him. "I haven't worked it out yet."

"We can ask Jazz about that," said Zek, "when he gets in."

"Where is Jazz, anyway?" said Scott. And oddly enough, the question, or rather its delivery, didn't seem at all strange to him; for it was as if he'd known Jazz before, too.

"He works," said Zek. "He's the security adviser for three of the holiday hotels in Argasi, two in Zakynthos town, another two in Vassilikos. Four days a week he works, and I keep house. The other three days I work; I do research on Greek island history at the museum in Zakynthos town, or sometimes I go over to Cephalonia on the ferry. Most of the islands have ruins, archeological sites. It's very relaxing . . . well, compared to certain of the things I've done. But you asked about Jazz." She glanced at her watch. "Another hour or two and he'll be home. But don't worry; if you have to go before then, I'll be fine. This is our home: mine, Jazz's, Wolf's. And as for that little episode with Kostas and his young friends: it was nothing, just one of those things. But still I'm glad you were here."

Scott nodded, stood up, looked thoughtful. "What can you tell me about this other world? It rings bells . . . Sunside/Starside? It isn't the first time I've heard of this place. I mean, I don't know it . . . yet I *seem* to know it! Tall mountains; sunless, barren boulder plains going on forever on one side of the mountains, and woodlands on the other." Scott didn't know where that memory or vision had come from, but: "Did I get it right?"

Zek nodded. "Yes, but you might have seen it in my mind."

"No, I somehow don't think so." Scott shook his head. "Not yours or Wolf's mind . . . but some other's? Well, maybe. And now it's found a way into mine. Anyway, can you tell me about it?"

Wolf Sr. sat up. *Well,* he began—until Zek cut him short with a single look, and said: "Scott, I can't tell you anything about Sunside/Starside. For one thing it's a best-kept secret—even a top secret in British and Russian governmental circles—and it's a very dangerous subject. I'm sorry. But anyway, what about you? I mean, what's your story? I know that you're a telepath, and that you have a strange affinity with this one." She glanced toward Wolf Jr. "Apart from which—"

"Apart from which you know almost as much as I do!" Scott told her. "And what you don't know I can't tell you. It's possible that lives depend on my silence, lots of them."

"Then tell me what else you can do," said Zek, and it was obvious that she was fascinated. "I mean, you personally. Telepathy is one thing, but does it go further than that? Who else can you speak to that way? Is it only the living, or—"

There came a knock at the door, and a now familiar "voice" in Scott's head said, *Scott, it's Shania.*

Zek tilted her head a little, said, "Not simply Kostas and his boys back for more, then?"

"No," said Scott. "She's a friend, a colleague of mine."

Shania! said Wolf Jr., struggling to his feet. *My Two!*

And as Zek went to the door, opened it, and welcomed Shania in, Wolf Sr. growled: *Huh! More pampering!*

Inside the villa and looking more than a little concerned, Shania wasted no time but said, "Four of us together, all of us talented . . . we place ourselves in jeopardy! Do you know how to shield yourself?" She looked at Zek. "I see you do. Then please apply your best shields right now, and keep them that way until we're gone. You, too, Scott." Then she turned to Wolf Jr.

Wagging his bedraggled tail however spasmodically, uncertainly, he had limped a little closer to her. *Do you under-*

stand? she asked him. *How to still your thoughts and keep them to yourself?*

I know how to be quiet in my head, he answered. *That comes from hiding from men and their tame dogs. Certain of their dogs are sensitive that way.*

Shania nodded her satisfaction and breathed easier. "Very well," she said, and held out her hand to Zek. "I'm Shania, and I'm pleased to meet you."

Looking at Shania with her mouth half open, Zek said, "I'm Zek, short for Zekintha. And you . . . you're very lovely."

Shania blushed. "Thank you," she said.

"An unearthly beauty, yes," said Scott.

Shania frowned at him and said, "But now we must be going. I'm sorry, but it's far too dangerous. Four of us together like this."

Five, said Wolf Sr.

"I understand," said Zek, then shrugged helplessly. "Well, I *think* I understand! But should I call you a taxi?"

Shania shook her head. "Thanks, but we'll walk."

Scott looked at her, glanced at Wolf Jr. "He won't be able to walk very—"

"We'll walk!" Shania cut him off. And now he got the message.

Zek slowly nodded, and without further ado saw them to the door. On the freshly washed steps they said reluctant good-byes; then Scott hoisted Wolf to his shoulders, and with Shania alongside him climbed the path to the road . . .

They had walked just a short distance, some dozen or so paces, along the road toward Argasi, when Shania said, "Scott, I have to go back."

"Back?"

"To Zek's place. There's something I must know. I won't be more than a moment or two." Making some small adjustment to the device on her wrist, she shimmered and disappeared. Scented air swirled into the space where she had been, raising a small dust devil that quickly collapsed.

But she was more than a moment or two; more like three or four minutes. Waiting for her, Scott put Wolf down and sat on a ruined wall by the roadside.

When finally she blinked back into existence, Scott wanted to know: "What was that all about?"

"I'll tell you when we're home."

"Home?" He still wasn't quite with it.

"Your home," she answered. "Can you take Wolf up again and put your arm around my waist?"

Doing as she asked, Scott said, "I guessed that eventually this had to happen, but I'm not sure I'm going to like it."

"Don't worry," she told him. "It's like switching a light on and off. Darkness and then light. You'll feel a little dizzy but nothing worse." And again she touched her wrist device.

The sun went out; there was total darkness, and Scott felt himself falling. Then the light came back, but feebly in comparison with Zante light—for it was the early afternoon light of Scott's study! Loose papers fluttered on his desk.

Shania sighed her relief as Scott let go of her, stumbled, and almost fell. Finally, steadying himself, he lowered Wolf to the floor. Wolf staggered, too, and sat down with a thump. *What was that?* he yelped.

"Well, it was better than riding a cramped, package-holiday jet!" said Scott shakily.

"But not very much safer," said Shania, worriedly studying the thing on her wrist. "I'm talking about this, what my people call a 'localizer.' I could almost feel the energy draining out of it. It moved the three of us, a heavy load. Now I'll have to wait for it to stabilize, recover some of its energy . . . that's *if* it recovers! So from now on—at least for the time being—it looks like you're stuck with me."

"I'm stuck with you anyway," said Scott, collapsing into a chair with Wolf at his feet. "You're my Two, remember?"

And mine, said Wolf.

"For the time being we're a Three Unit, yes," she answered. "But when this is over, and however it works out— what then?"

"What do you mean?" Scott wasn't at all sure why he should feel this sudden pang of anxiety.

"If we get through what's coming," she answered, "I may be here on Earth permanently. In fact, I can't see any alternative. But with women like Zek in your world, in your life—"

"There are no women like Zek in my life," said Scott, with a shake of his head. "There's just you. But speaking of Zek—"

"You want to know why I went back to her?"

"In a moment," said Scott, standing up again. "But first I need a coffee, and two aspirins. And then I want to bathe Wolf. He stinks of sea and salt, and he probably has fleas."

I definitely have them, said that one. *But bathing? When I bathe I do it in a mountain stream.*

"I don't have a mountain stream," Scott told him. "Just a bath—or better still a shower. Me, I'm hot and dusty. If you like we can take a shower together."

With "soap"? Having seen it pictured in Scott's mind, Wolf sounded dubious.

"With shampoo, and you'll like it," Scott tried to reassure him. "Well, you'll like it afterward . . . probably. Anyway, we can give it a try. Meanwhile there'll be a bowl of water for you in the kitchen, and something good to eat."

That sounds better! said Wolf.

"And while you're eating, Shania and I can talk. Then you and me, we'll shower. It'll do us both good."

If you say so, said Wolf . . .

And while Wolf quenched his thirst and sated his hunger in the kitchen, alone with Shania in the living room, Scott said: "So then, why did you go back to Zek?"

"It was something that I 'overheard' just before I knocked at her door," Shania answered. "She had asked you what else you could do, and I wondered how much you had told her. You see, we can't let anyone know what's going on or what our strengths and weaknesses are; I thought you understood that."

"But I do understand," said Scott. "And in fact I told her nothing."

"Still, I had to be sure." Shania chewed her lip. "And now I'm glad I went back—I think."

"So then," Scott nodded, urging her on, "what happened between you and Zek?"

"I . . . I deemed it better that she shouldn't remember that you had been there, so I sent my Khiff to erase her memories of your visit."

Scott's jaw fell open. "You did *what?*"

"Scott, please don't be angry! If she remembered—if Zek was interrogated, perhaps by the Mordri Three—we would all be in trouble, Zek included. But if she knew nothing . . ."

"Her memories? Erased?" Scott was horrified. "But how many of her memories; I mean, how much?"

"Only of your visit."

"But there were others there! Greeks with dogs!"

"Yes, my Khiff saw that," Shania replied. "But Zek and her Wolf, they saw them off. That's all she will remember of that."

Scott calmed down—then narrowed his eyes and asked, "She suffered no harm?"

"It isn't in my Khiff to do harm! Haven't I explained that to you?"

Scott took a deep breath. "Okay. But listen, before you do anything like that again—"

"If it becomes necessary, I'll check with you first."

Scott was silent for a moment, then frowned and said, "Now explain to me how it works . . . I mean the Khiff; erasing memories; things like that."

Shania came to sit beside him on the sofa. "You know how I told you my Khiff stores my memories? Well, she can also remove ones that are offensive. But they are always available to me if ever I need them. You see, I can't keep all my memories; no one can. Do you remember everything? For instance, did you remember what was missing from your desk? It was there in your mind, but it took my Khiff to find it. With Zek . . . it has to be slightly different. She won't, *can't* remember you because my Khiff won't be there to remind her. You are gone from her forever. But more importantly, so is her knowledge of a man with strange talents, who came to her Greek island on a secret mission. And so Zek is no longer in danger. Moreover, she cannot any longer compromise us . . ."

Shania paused, and Scott saw in her lovely eyes that there was something else. And: "Well?" he said.

"My Khiff saw other things," said Shania. "Things close to the surface of Zek's mind. Things that are always there. Memories that were best forgotten—monstrous memories— which she can't ever forget."

"She mentioned nightmares." Scott nodded. "But they're *her* nightmares! Don't tell me your Khiff—"

Shania shook her head. "No. Only your visit, or our visit, that's all that was erased. But as for what my Khiff saw: these were amazing things! Zek has knowledge of a different world—a parallel world—and she has even been there! Her experiences there were very terrible."

Scott's frown was back. "A parallel world? I mean, parallel to what? Have I perhaps read of such in a handful of science fiction books?"

Shania shrugged. "Except for some things I've seen on your television screens, I know nothing of science fiction. But I do understand some things about science. The theory is that parallel worlds exist in time-cones that commenced with the creation of the universe . . . in fact, the multiverse; because there may be many parallels, just as there are many gravity levels."

Scott nodded. "Yes. Science fiction."

"Fiction no longer!" said Shania. "For Zek has visited and lived in just such a world. Also her man—"

"Jazz." Scott nodded again. "Michael J. Simmons." And this time he didn't even wonder how he knew that without having been told it.

"—And Wolf. I mean the older wolf. And . . . and others."

"Other men?" Scott queried, knowing it was so.

"Men, yes," said Shania, snuggling closer. "And one man

in particular; one very, *very* special man. But there were monsters there, too! It was a world of incredible monsters!"

"Sunside/Starside," Scott murmured, as vague, alien scenes jerked and flickered like faded silent movies across the screen of his mind. "And did this very special man have a name?"

"It was Harry," Shania at once replied. "Harry Keogh—but in Zek's mind you and Harry had somehow become confused. I find that very strange because . . . because she also knew that he was dead!"

Harry Keogh.

Hearing Shania speak that name it was as if a cool, gentle breeze had blown on the back of Scott's neck—or the whorls of his brain—or *in* his mind. Harry Keogh, yes.

He remembered lying on his back on a trolley half in, half out of consciousness. He was being pushed along a corridor in a strange building: E-Branch HQ, somewhere in London. Through his three-quarters shuttered eyes he saw that gaunt, mortician-like man, Xavier? Also his two companions. Another moment and he was being wheeled past a certain door. The sign on the door read:

> HARRY'S ROOM

And Scott somehow knew it was the selfsame Harry. The one who Zek had known in a fearful parallel world. The one who had died there!

"Scott?" (Shania's cool fingers were on his arm.) "Scott, is something wrong?" Her concerned query startled him, drawing him out of the flow of previously unremembered things, lifting him up from the depths of extraordinary reverie.

He looked at her, put an arm around her, and shivered. "A ghost just walked right through me!" he said.

"What!?" She stared at him.

"It's just an expression." He held her closer. "A déjà vu thing. You said that name and I . . . I felt a bit weird, that's all."

"Weird?" She put her head in the crook of his neck. "Yes, I understand that. There are many weird things here. Like that question she almost asked you."

"She?" Scott breathed her hair, inhaled its perfume. "You mean Zek? What question?"

"Just before I knocked on her door," Shania replied. "Zek was talking to you about your telepathy. She asked you, 'Is it only the living you can speak to like that, or—' And that was when I knocked."

Scott shivered again. But Shania was so warm, so close, and so . . . so *right*. Almost without realizing what he was doing, his hand was fondling her left breast through the silky material of her blouse, feeling her nipple hardening under its influence. "I know," he said huskily. "It's something I've been trying not to think about."

Shania took his hand away, sat up, turned to face him more fully. "But I *have* thought about it. I heard Zek thinking about it. And I know what she meant."

"So do I," said Scott, reaching for her, feeling her drawn toward him as if magnetically. "But right now I don't especially want to talk about it. Instead I want to—"

Where shall I sleep? said Wolf in the doorway. *My belly is full, and I feel I can sleep in safety here knowing that I have my One and my Two.*

"There'll be a warm blanket outside my bedroom door," said Scott.

"Our bedroom door," said Shania, as the two drew apart.

"But not before we shower," said Scott. And then, looking knowingly at Shania. "And anyway, it's too early for bed."

Smiling, flushed, she shook her head. "I think not."

Wolf sighed. *Then let's get this showering done with. You can mate later.*

So they bathed; all three, in Scott's walk-in shower. And Wolf actually did like it . . . eventually, when he was clean and dry and warm on his blanket.

While in the room he guarded:

Shania was quite right and it wasn't at all too early for bed, but it was very late before Scott and Shania—Wolf's One and Two—finished mating, slipped from each other's arms, and slept. When finally they did it was the so-called sleep of the dead—

—When at last the dead dared make their presence known . . .

26

Earlier, in the late afternoon of that same day:

Alerted to the advent of something new, a strange or even stranger element having entered the "usual" scheme of things—which was rarely less than bizarre at E-Branch HQ—Ben Trask had called several of his agents to a meeting in the Ops Room. It was the locator David Chung who had brought this most recent of various developments and findings to Trask's attention, and it was Chung who was now speaking; his opening statement was at once simple and utterly baffling:

"This morning Scott St. John boarded a flight to Zakynthos in the Ionian. It seemed he was taking a package holiday, maybe to enjoy a little Mediterranean sunshine, though we thought not. Rather, we expected St. John to make contact with someone called 'Wolf.' He reached his destination and was there on Zante until midafternoon; I can guarantee that—not his exact location, because the island is small, has many small towns and villages, and its arc is narrow in my probe. But I can definitely guarantee that he was there." Chung paused to glance uncertainly at Trask.

Trask nodded. "Go on."

Chung took a deep breath and continued. "Well, two hours ago he was back home, just a half hour's drive from where we're sitting. So, what had happened? Had he cut his 'holiday' short? I'll say he had! I'd checked his location around 4:00 P.M. Mediterranean time and he was there, on Zante. But fifteen minutes later when I checked again, then he was home!"

Trask looked at the faces of his assembled crew. "Explanation?"

Ian Goodly shuffled uncomfortably in his chair, and said, "There can be only one: that David is wrong. Something has gone awry with his scanning technique. Er, my apologies if I offend, David, but there's no way a man can get from Zakynthos—some, what, twelve hundred miles away?—to London, England, in just fifteen minutes."

"No offence taken," said Chung as Goodly fell silent. "And I fully understand your reservations. But I assure you, there's little or nothing wrong with my scanning technique, which is to say my locating talent. As for the time interval: it could even be less than fifteen minutes. For don't forget that while there was a quarter hour between checks, I still don't know just when he commenced his return."

At which point Trask cut in. "You're saying he might even have returned, er—?"

"—Instantaneously," said Chung as Trask faltered. "Yes, I suppose I am."

Paul Garvey spoke up. "Can I get a word in before I leave? I have an appointment with my neurologist."

"More surgery?" said Trask at once. "That's very important to you, I know, Paul. But I'd hate to lose you right now. I can feel things coming to a head, and quickly."

The other shook his head. "No, sir, no surgery. More tests, that's all. They're still looking for a way to get my face back in working order again. But as for what I wanted to say:

"David's right—at least about St. John being home again. Or rather, I *think* he's right. Just let me explain. After David had checked St. John's location that second time, he came to me for corroboration via telepathy. Using a small-scale map, David located St. John's house approximately. Then he used St. John's paperweight, pinning down the location more accurately yet; and after he'd done that, I worked in tandem with him, homing in on the house along David's probe.

"Now, I know how careful we have to be with regard to this fellow, so I took a very quick look, just a peep, along David's line of contact, seeking out St. John's mind, his thoughts; and then I at once withdrew and called in Frank here." He nodded to indicate the spotter Frank Robinson, seated close by. "I wanted to see what he would make of it."

By way of explaining or reminding the others in the group of the sequence of events, Trask said: "Frank was with you when you first brought St. John in, right?"

"Correct," said Garvey. "So it was entirely possible he'd be able to recognize St. John's psychic presence, even through a curtain of—"

"Mind-smog!" the youthful Frank Robinson cut in, and immediately held up a calming hand. "No, not that clinging shit that the Wamphyri used to put out. This was cleaner, even as ours is cleaner, but there's no doubt that it *was* mind-smog. Which means that we were bang on target when we first pulled Scott St. John in. St. John, and who-ever else was in the house with him—all three of them, in fact—are highly skilled people. But as for what their talents are, or how they're intending to use them . . ." He shrugged.

"Three of them," Trask repeated thoughtfully. "A trio of ESP-endowed people, apparently working together, like a kind of mini E-Branch. But about their numbers: can we be absolutely sure? I mean, sure that there are three of them; three psychically skilled people, in that house?"

"That's my bet," said Robinson. "Focussing along David and Paul's established lines of contact, it was relatively easy for me. I discovered three separate sources of mind-smog: all different, but all having the same overall effect, the same purpose: to disguise or camouflage the minds that issued them. They were shielding themselves, that's all. Hiding from us? Possibly. But based on our current knowledge and theories, more likely hiding from someone else."

"Three," said Trask again, nodding as he turned and

spoke to the precog Ian Goodly: "The number you had foreseen as working against this bloody unknown threat, this *completely* unknown threat: yet more evidence that you were right about whatever it is that's happening here. And here we are unable to do any damn thing about it—well, except for what little we're doing. Damn it to hell! But this is so—"

"Frustrating?" said the precog. "Oh, indeed it is, and not least because the future is drawing closer, narrowing down, and . . . and *very* rapidly!"

Starting up straighter in his chair, his arms thrown wide, Goodly had gasped the last few words out. Without warning, suddenly he appeared yet more gaunt, his colour paler still as he began wobbling and jerking where he sat, his spastic movements threatening to spill him from his chair.

Paul Garvey, seated on Goodly's right, and the empath Anna Marie English on his left, had witnessed "attacks" such as this on a number of previous occasions; this one had doubtless originated—or had been precipitated—by the case in hand. In any event the pair held on to the precog, supporting him until the spasms had passed. Then:

"What was it, Ian?" Trask rasped, his expression very anxious now. He got to his feet, crossed quickly to the precog who was taking deep, gulping breaths and looking all about the room as if bewildered. "What was it that you saw?" Trask gripped his shoulder. "Was it whatever's coming? But what else could it be? Just looking at your face I can see it was. So then, how close was it, Ian? And how long do we have?"

"I didn't exactly 'see' anything." Still shaken and trembling, but completely coherent, Goodly was at last able to shake his head and gently free himself from the supporting hands of his colleagues. "But I did feel it. It was like . . . like a tremendous psychic shock wave reaching back to me from the future, but I know that it was indicative of something a lot more physical. As to its source: Ben, it was very close. At a guess I'd say we have maybe a week, ten days at most!"

Trask released him, returned to his chair, and slumped into it. He looked at the semicircle of agents facing him, and said, "Talk about frustrating! Well, it means we'll just have to work at it that much harder, that's all. But we're not finished yet, not by a long shot! And we're not done here yet, either."

He singled out a youngish, earnest, perhaps even haggard-looking face in the group, and said, "Mr. Kellway, maybe you'd like to take it from here? Your findings, if you please."

Alan Kellway, relatively new to the E-Branch fold, was a just-turned-thirty spotter. Intense, nervous in almost everything he said and did, withdrawn and thin as a pole, he hadn't yet earned Ben Trask's full respect; which explained the "Mr." Trask had applied to his name. This could be because with only sixteen months on the job he was still unproven material—or it might partly be because he had been involved in the killing of Trevor Jordan, another E-Branch agent and once close friend of Trask's.

Jordan, along with certain others—not all of them as innocent as he had been—had been suspected of vampirism and had paid the price. Kellway was one of the agents responsible for taking him out; he had helped hose Jordan down with fire, with a flamethrower, reducing him to ashes. The trouble with that was that as the then recently elected Head of Branch, Ben Trask had signed the death warrant; Trask had given the orders, and he'd been nightmaring about it ever since. So despite that he knew the truth of it better than any other man, still Trask was only human; it was possible that he'd transferred some of the blame elsewhere. And now:

He used Kellway only as a backup; which was just as well, because the man had never quite recovered from what he'd seen and done that night. He much preferred indoors now as opposed to work as a field agent. And fortunately he had a knack with gadgets, which meant he was beginning to outshine some of the older techs, the men who looked after E-Branch's array of computers and electrical detection and communication devices.

Now he jerked awkwardly to his feet to explain what he'd been tasked with and how he had gone about it:

"My brief was to connect things up, start putting the bits of the puzzle together. I was to explore several lines of inquiry: St. John's background, his wife, his interest in this so-called psychic healer Simon Salcombe, Salcombe's location or center of operations in Switzerland, and at least one murder in which Salcombe was suspected of being involved. I've been working on all this flat out for a couple of days now, so if I look a bit frayed around the edges, that's the reason.

"Very well, so in that order:

"I found nothing especially weird in St. John's background . . . but I should point out that he's not *just* another man. Something of a linguist, which is how he earns his keep, a patriot, and a martial arts expert: he's not exactly your typical 'regular guy.' But like I said, nothing weird in his life—well, at least until his wife died.

"Kelly St. John passed away here in London of some exotic, unknown wasting disease. Her life went into a sudden steep dive and didn't pull out. Then St. John more or less went to pieces; but then, too, it appears that he acquired something special. I mean on the psychic front. We don't yet know exactly what it is that he's got, but as we've just heard from our experts he does know how to shield himself. And those same experts tell us that whatever it is it's getting stronger.

"In connection with Kelly's death: St. John seems to think Simon Salcombe was somehow responsible; just like us, he's been trying to track the man down. Up until our bugs were discovered we knew that he was making some headway: he at least knows that Salcombe lives or is situated at a place called Schloss Zonigen in the Swiss Alps. In fact, we've used what he had discovered to go one step further and pinpoint the place: it's a hollow crag, an alleged cryogenic suspension 'refuge.' Salcombe is just one of three principals who run the place. But as for finding something—or anything—out about them, forget it! I've managed to break into the Swiss Polizei's main computer; it appears that on three or four occasions they began their own investigations, which always got stalled at the local level. They never seem to progress beyond general police inquiries in the alpine villages around this Schloss Zonigen place. Oh, yes, and by the way: despite our 'Cosmic Security' links with Interpol—not to mention seventy percent of the rest of the world's security services—I was *obliged* to hack into the Swiss computer. That was because this Schloss Zonigen place has 'restricted' pasted all over it!

"As for what the Swiss investigations were all about:

"Unsolved abductions/disappearances; accusations of blackmail and alleged ransom demands; financial and banking 'irregularities,' and we know how keen the Swiss are on money matters, and so on. It would seem there's been plenty of charges against Salcombe and Co. but nothing proved: investigations that didn't go anywhere or got stopped dead in their tracks. It's almost as if we're dealing with the Swiss Mafia or something!"

"Or something," said Trask, drily. "But do go on . . . well, if there's anything left to tell."

"Only one thing left to talk about," said Kellway, finally relaxing a little and taking his seat again. "One subject, anyway. And that's these gruesome murders that Salcombe is thought to have been involved in."

Murders? thought Trask. *Plural?* But it could be a slip of the tongue, so for the time being he let it go.

"It's a subject which is of special interest to the boss," Kellway continued. "Er, which is to say Mr. Trask here; because while everything else in this case has proved to be strange and baffling enough, opposition minister Gregory Stamper's death—his, er, 'evagination'?—was right over the top, as weird as hell! But then, so are the other, similar deaths that I've been coming across . . ."

"Deaths?" said Trask, no longer able to let it pass. "Hold on a minute! Other deaths? Like Gregory Stamper's? But didn't I give that Stamper job to—"

"Me," said David Chung, drawing his attention. "You

said I should get someone to look into it, someone who didn't have too much on his plate. So I gave it to—"

"Me," said Kellway, gaunt and nervous again. "I would have reported my findings sooner, this morning perhaps, but you were very busy. And anyway I kept finding these other cases."

Trask's lower jaw had fallen partly open. But now his eyes glinted as he leaned forward and repeated Kellway's words. "You kept finding these other—?" He paused, took a deep breath, and went on: "Okay. Yes, I understand—and you're right: I was up to here in work this morning. So maybe you'll tell us all about it now?"

And suddenly the room was deathly quiet, waiting for Kellway to clear his throat and carry on . . .

27

Taking out an old, battered notebook and opening it, Kellway said, "I have a fair list here, but I'll try to be brief.

"Initially we have Stamper: that happened here in the UK, and if Scott St. John is correct in what he believes, his wife is another UK victim; but as yet we've no proof of that. Kelly St. John wasn't *damaged* or altered to the same incredible, unbelievable degree. But her death certainly seems inexplicable, and she did have a contentious history with Simon Salcombe.

"And now we move abroad.

"Some three or four months before the Berlin Wall came down—which is to say, around the middle of July last year—a leading light in the Stasi, East Germany's Ministry for State Security, a man called Ernst Stenger, disappeared. Stenger, a corrupt, brutal man, with a list of crimes as long as his arm, must have seen what was coming and decided it was time to get out. Since then the Russian, German,

British, and a handful of other security services have been looking for him. It was generally believed he'd vanished into Switzerland where for years he'd been squirrelling away Kremlin gold misappropriated out of payments to Stasi underlings. We didn't find him or the gold, but it appears that someone else did.

"His body was discovered just a week ago in an expensive villa he'd bought in Innsbruck, Austria; his landlord had gone round to ask about unpaid bills, and the smell took him to the outdoor pool where the water was green as soup and Stenger was floating in it like a large piece of raw, badly butchered meat. He was 'evaginated,' yes. He'd been living there under an assumed identity with his twenty years younger wife; she wasn't to be found, hadn't been seen for three months. Erika Stenger is still missing, but Ernst's DNA is what gave him— or his body—away. A funny thing about that DNA, though: it was his, but it was oddly sequenced . . . Don't ask me; I'm no expert in DNA. Various documents in the villa were seen to contain references to someone called Frau Gerda Lessing at—you've guessed it—Schloss Zonigen. Also uncovered at Stenger's villa: a handful, but *just* a handful, of Krugerrands. Strange that, because when his maid returned from a visit to her ailing father in Vienna, she told the police she'd frequently come across Stenger counting these coins, each containing a troy ounce of fine gold, in dozens of stacks of twenty, like a big winner's roulette chips in a casino . . . !

"All this from our friends in German Intelligence via Interpol. And next, we're off to Africa:

"When the UN moved a company of soldiers into Zuganda as a peacekeeping force after General Wilson Gundawei got his, some people from MI6 went with them. The UN didn't have a lot to do; there wasn't much trouble; neighbouring Kasabi was satisfied to see its old enemy General Gundawei dead . . . now all the Kasabis wanted was to reestablish their old borders, get back the territory Zuganda had stolen from them. But the UN picked up one of Gundawei's surviving army officers—one of his bodyguards—a captain who said he'd witnessed the end of it.

"This fellow put the blame for his General's death on someone called Guyler Schweitzer, who had flown into Zuganda in his private jet to claim monies—again in gold—that Gundawei was alleged to owe him: some kind of bad debt, apparently. And I'm sure that by now you'll have noticed how this gold theme keeps cropping up like . . . like I don't know, something from a James Bond novel? Anyway, about Gundawei:

"His palace had been ransacked and set afire, but in the room where his body was found, apparently his bedroom or harem, there hadn't been too much damage; there'd been little enough flammable stuff in there, mainly his bed. The General and his son, Peter, were both there, both dead, both murdered—well, according to the Captain. Murdered by Guyler Schweitzer, or so he alleged. But it was the Captain's bullets that they dug out of the corpses.

"Peter Gundawei: it was possible he had been dead of AIDS before he was shot. As for his father . . . no one has figured out just *why* he'd been shot! UN pathologists agreed that it was the bullets that killed him, but he would have died anyway from his, er—"

"Evagination?" Trask prompted him.

"Exactly. The pathologist's report also says the General's condition must have been due to the intense heat from the burning bed; well, that and his corpulence. Gundawei's innards, his vital organs, must have somehow overheated and boiled right out of him. Even his brain had come out through his ear. And all of his flesh had sort of curled back from his bones.

"As for this Guyler Schweitzer—"

"Schloss Zonigen, right?" This was Trask again.

"It looks that way. The airport at Zuganda isn't much, but at least they keep records. Schweitzer's private jet isn't his; registered in Geneva, it's kept at an airstrip in Berne. That's where its owner/pilot lives, and he hires himself and his plane out to whoever can afford it. But let's move on:

"To another Ernst. This time Ernst Zittermensch, the self-styled 'Lord' Zittermensch."

And again Trask cut in with: "He's still alive?"

Kellway nodded. "I even tried to speak to him on the telephone, in connection with *his* connection to Simon Salcombe, but he wouldn't talk to me. His butler, however, assured me that he was alive and well and entertaining a young lady! Not bad for a man with inoperable stomach cancer, whose doctors gave him only a few weeks to live—and that was three years ago!"

Ian Goodly spoke up. "You tried to speak to Zittermensch? But surely you understand how this is dangerous ground and how carefully we need to be treading here? What did you intend saying to him, anyway?"

Kellway shrugged, but in no way negligently. "I was going to tell him I was seriously ill and thought I might learn something from his experience. Was he satisfied with the treatment he'd received from Simon Salcombe? . . . Something of that nature. I would have used a pseudonym, of course, and if I'd been questioned inordinately would have cut it short. Our secure line is untraceable, and it strikes me that sooner or later we'll probably be wanting to talk to Zittermensch anyway."

"That's right," said Trask. "And likewise to this pilot in Berne and anyone else who's connected. Greg Stamper's wife, for instance. But go on. What else do you have?"

"Well there's quite a bit; I'm still writing up my report, which you'll have as soon as I'm finished. But there's at least one more thing I'd better tell you about right now . . ." Kellway paused, then asked, "The Americans haven't favoured us too much in the past, right?"

Trask nodded. "It's true they can be a bit standoffish, a bit jealous where intelligence is concerned. I'm told they sometimes have problems with their own interagency communications. Why do you ask? What's happened now? They're not playing ball?"

"On the contrary," said Kellway. "In fact, the CIA at Langley have been most accommodating."

"The CIA?" said Trask, drily. "I'm amazed!"

"Oh, they were sort of cool at first," Kellway continued,

"but after we'd matched up 'inexplicable deaths' with 'gold'—then they were onto me like leeches! They had Wilson Gundawei's death in the computer already, also that of some big Texas oil magnate I've never heard of; but when I added Gregory Stamper's name to the equation—just a mention, without compromising anything or anyone—then they really opened up. Would you believe an intruder, a gold bullion thief . . . at Fort Knox?"

Still frowning, Trask held up a hand and said, "Wait! Greg Stamper and Fort Knox? Where's the connection? What's the CIA's interest in a dead English Labour politician?"

"In a word," Kellway answered, "gold!"

"Ah!" Trask nodded. "I see where you're coming from. Stamper's interests in precious-metal mining concerns."

"He was a collector of the stuff!" said Kellway. "Of gold, I mean. And now his wife says she's nearly broke!"

Again Trask's nod. "Okay," he said. "But now tell us about this Fort Knox thing. What, an intruder, a thief, in Fort Knox? How is that possible?"

"That's what the CIA wants to know," said Kellway. "But at least I can tell you what they told me, and what they showed me on my computer screen."

"Wait!" said Trask again. "Did you record it?"

"Oh, yes. I have it on video, in my office."

"Then let's go to your office. Because as the saying goes, one picture is worth a thousand words."

"Well, I've got more than one," Kellway replied, standing up. "In fact, an entire sequence, copied from Fort Knox security cameras. Which also includes pictures of a guard, later discovered dead in the gold vaults. Judging by the single star on the epaulette of his fatigues, he . . . he *was* a lieutenant." Pausing to lick suddenly dry lips, Kellway gulped and quietly added, "I think I should warn you, however, that you probably won't want to see those. Not more than a glance anyway . . ."

Alan Kellway's "office," like most of his E-Branch colleagues' private work areas, was a hotel room—literally.

When E-Branch had moved in here and taken over this top floor some years ago, the rooms had not been altered much; they served their purpose. Kellway had worked on most of his investigations in the big Ops Room, once a conference room; but again, like most of the other agents, he escaped whenever he could to his own place and there kept his files, his reports in various stages of completion, and his personal effects. He'd brought the video cassette here (a) to study it, and (b) to keep it secure until it could be handed in.

Now, with a dozen colleagues crowding the small room, and with Ben Trask directly behind Kellway, watching over his shoulder, he inserted the cassette into the player, fast-forwarding until the blank screen came alive and began to display a short sequence of mainly blurred monochrome stills.

"The shots were taken automatically, at intervals of some fifteen seconds," Kellway explained.

The first picture was of an enormous vaulted area, white-painted walls narrowing in perspective to a far end wall with a circular steel door in an arched-over alcove. The first impression was one of size—of a medium-sized aircraft hangar—but this gave way after just a moment's viewing to an almost claustrophobic sense of subterranean confinement, so that even without prior knowledge the viewer would "know" that he was looking at an underground facility.

Then the viewer's gaze shifted to the layout and precious contents of the place. Elevated catwalks ran the full length of the vault, one at each side, while three wide aisles separated the central area into four ranks of locked, steel-barred cages each containing raised metal pallets loaded with gold bullion. Glowing reflectively in the light of neons in the high ceiling, and glaring blindingly in certain areas, the gold looked as if it were on fire. At the far end of the vault, sufficient space had been left to permit the operation of an unmanned forklift loader, which stood visible in the left-hand aisle. This first picture was starkly clear, its monochrome details standing out in sharp relief except where obscured by the brilliance of the gold.

The screen blinked and showed a second picture, precisely the same as the first.

Then another blink and a third picture appeared, in which the details were blurred and off-centre, as if the camera had commenced to vibrate in reaction to some off-screen activity. And there in the right-hand aisle—having seemingly appeared out of nowhere—stood an abnormally tall, long-necked, stick-thin man in a high-collared kaftan.

Almost everything about him was very pale: his skin like writing paper; his silvery hair worn in a high, stiff coxcomb; his kaftan so white it almost glowed. Only his eyes—black as jet, deep-seated under thin, tapering silver eyebrows—loaned his features any relief whatsoever; so that combined with the blurring effect, and much like the glare from the gold itself, the tall figure was almost painful to look at.

"Only a fifteen-second interval?" murmured Trask under his breath. "Then where did this fellow come from?"

"Good question," said Kellway. "I wish I knew the answer—and so do the FBI, the CIA, and especially the military bigwigs at Fort Knox! But keep watching; the strangest is yet to come." Needless advice, for the attention of everyone in the room was riveted to the screen.

Blink! And the tall man was inside one of the cages, stooping to grasp a bar of gold!

"What!?" said Trask, leaning closer. "But those cages are locked. And their bars are . . . what, maybe six inches apart? I mean, he's not *that* thin, is he? Or is he?"

Blink! There were three bars of gold on the floor of the aisle; they could only have been passed through the bars of the cage and let fall. The tall man was bent over a fourth bar, but his head was cocked in a listening attitude.

"That's when the sensors in the pallets would have picked him up," said Kellway. "If you disturb the weight, the balance, you set off the alarms. And yet—"

Blink! "—Well he doesn't appear all that much concerned, now does he? Except maybe he's working a little faster."

Blink! Another badly blurred picture appeared.

Blink! The man in the kaftan was still busily thieving.

Blink! His spindly, long-fingered hand reached through the bars of the cage, in the act of releasing another heavy ingot.

And indeed the intruder didn't seem too concerned, for now there were fifteen or sixteen bars of gold on the floor outside the cage. But now, too, the circular steel door in the alcove was open and a uniformed male figure had entered the vault. Sidearm drawn, leaning forward in order to keep a low profile, the Lieutenant was mouthing something—an order, or perhaps a warning—but of course there was no audio on these stills.

Blink! Up close to the cage and apparently astonished, the officer held his sidearm pointed loosely at the floor. The tall man in the cage seemed helpless, trapped.

Blink! Despite the blurred nature of the picture, the Lieutenant's face showed his emotion: no longer amazement but fury. Having reached through the bars, he had grabbed the intruder's kaftan—but his sidearm was still pointed at the floor. It was quite obvious that he "knew" he was safe.

Blink! He wasn't safe!

Arms outflung, the Lieutenant was frozen in midair, apparently flying backward with both feet inches off the floor; his sidearm lay where it had fallen close to his feet; the intruder was now *outside* the cage, with one scrawny hand extended toward the lieutenant, having pushed him out of the way.

Blink! The tall man was draping his kaftan over the piled ingots, and at his feet the Lieutenant lay on his side, having coiled himself into an almost fetal ball. But his eyes bulged and his mouth gaped wide open in a silent scream.

Blink! The intruder was gone, likewise the gold. The Lieutenant was no longer fetal but almost perfectly spherical, his fatigues exploding outward from the metamorphosis of his body, his shape! Three other guardsmen had entered the vault through the circular door in the arched alcove.

Kellway hit the pause button and said, "Sir?"

Trask's mouth was dry but he husked, "Yes, what is it?"

"There are some close-up pictures of the Lieutenant taken by the USMPs. They were taken just as they found him, lying on the floor there. Do you want to see them?"

"Not if he was evaginated," Trask answered. "I already know what that looks like."

"He wasn't evaginated." Kellway shook his head. "He was . . . something, but it wasn't that."

Looking down on the wide-eyed man craning his neck to look back up at him, Trask said, "Okay, show them to me. Or at least one of them. I'm sure I've seen worse."

And in fact he had, but not a lot worse.

In the coloured picture that Kellway now flashed onto the screen, at first it seemed that some sculptor had carved a mass of pink-, purple-, and blue-veined marble into an almost perfect sphere some twenty inches in diameter. But as the viewer's eyes finally recognized what they were seeing, the reason the sphere wasn't perfect but somewhat oblate became obvious . . . it was an effect of gravity working on a substance that wasn't nearly as rigid as marble—a substance that was in fact flesh and blood and bone—the former Lieutenant.

Trask managed to still a tic that had begun jerking in the corner of his mouth, and husked, "Show me another."

Kellway's gulping was clearly audible, but he nevertheless obliged. Now Trask and the other agents glimpsed a picture that had been taken from the other side of . . . of this *thing* that had been a man; the side with the Lieutenant's flattened face on it, his eyes staring out in frozen horror, mouth gaping and stilled tongue curled to one side. And alongside this impossibly *fused,* uniform globe of dead flesh, his fatigues and underclothes, all in disarray, torn or split down the seams as his body and limbs had convulsed in the transformation.

Not evagination, no, but Trask would now be willing to bet it had been wrought by the same kind of force. And:

"Turn the fucking thing off!" he rasped, turning away . . .

28

Outside Kellway's room, as Ben Trask's agents went off to their various stations to get on with their work while waiting on his instructions, he called three of his main men aside, taking the precog Ian Goodly, locator David Chung, and telepath Paul Garvey along the corridor with him to his office. Inside with the door closed, Trask seated himself behind his desk; Goodly and Garvey took chairs opposite, and Chung preferred to stand.

After sitting there awhile thinking and stroking his chin, Trask said, "I'm pretty sure that by now you three—hell, and probably all the rest of the crew—must be thinking along much the same lines. Something here, in fact several things here, are just too much of a coincidence. Our man Kellway out there isn't our only capable investigator; in our diverse ways we're all of us detectives, psychic sleuths. Me, I've never relied solely on this lie-detecting thing of mine. While I like to think of that as a God-given talent, I also try to use my God-given brains.

"Gentlemen, I don't believe in coincidences. A single coincidence: you can call it synchronicity. Two coincidences: well, it's just another one of those things—maybe. But in a while, when they start piling one on top of the other, what then? Can you guess what I'm talking about? I mean, do you *know* what I'm talking about?"

Then, before anyone could answer, glancing sharply at Paul Garvey, Trask added, "No, not you, Paul. Because I know you can see right through me! But David, maybe?" He looked at Chung. "I have this feeling that there's more on your mind than you spoke of in the Ops Room. I saw it written in your face. Am I right?"

Chung nodded, and said, "On my mind? Oh, yes, and it's been there for quite a while now, from the moment Scott St. John was brought in here; but *until* now I couldn't really explain it . . . maybe not even now. I remember, I was walking past Harry's Room that day when something stirred in my head. It was just . . . just a feeling, but an incredibly strange one. I mean, if the Necroscope himself had come out through that door into the corridor, I wouldn't have been much surprised. No, of course I *would* have been surprised—I might even have fainted!—but it wouldn't have been unexpected. It was a strong feeling. And then there's what I experienced this afternoon." Chung turned to the precog. "Ian, I can fully understand the concern you expressed earlier: the possibility that my locating skills were out of kilter, but they weren't. And I agree it's impossible for St. John to be in Zakynthos one minute and in a North London suburb the next. But unless he has an identical twin with an identical aura, he was! And Paul here backs me up on that. So . . . ?"

"So," said the precog, acknowledging Chung's sincerity, or at least accepting that Chung himself believed what he had said to be the truth. "But of course you realize that there was only ever one human being who could do that sort of thing: move like that, at will, anywhere he wanted to go, and instantaneously?"

Before Chung could answer, Trask came in with, "But that's now become one hell-of-a-big 'was,' my friend!"

"Very definitely a 'was,' " said Chung, excitedly. "Or more properly a 'no longer.' For all four of us, and almost everyone else in E-Branch, we all saw the coxcomb man—the spiky-haired man in the kaftan, in those Fort Knox security stills—we all saw what he could do: how he moved in and out of that cage, how he came and went, appearing and disappearing like that. I mean, when I saw that, yet again I thought of Harry Keogh."

"Me, too," said Trask, "and probably everybody else who saw it. But on afterthought, it wasn't—couldn't have been—the Möbius Continuum."

"How so?" said Goodly.

"Because Harry had to physically fall, step, dive, or swim through his doors. I mean, he could conjure up *doors,* so-called Möbius doors! Invisible to us, still they were there. The point is that in order to do his fantastic thing Harry had to physically *move* himself through them; whereas that man or creature in Fort Knox, he couldn't *possibly* pick up all those gold bars at one time and just walk through a door! The weight and awkwardness would be just too much for any ordinary man. No, but what he did, he draped his kaftan over that pile of precious metal—and *blink!*—"

"He was no longer there," said Goodly, nodding. "Something *like* the Möbius Continuum, then?"

"It has to be," said Paul Garvey. "And I'm thinking: using the Möbius Continuum, not only was Harry able to traverse four-dimensional space-time, but he could also cut across it. He had been to another world, with Zek Föener and Jazz Simmons, and he had fought the Wamphyri there! But that was only one world, and what if—"

"What if there are others?" This was Trask speaking.

"And not just parallel worlds," said Chung. "I mean, there are billions of worlds out there!" He threw up an arm, indicating everything. "That . . . that *person*, coxcomb man: did he look human to anyone? Well, not to me! He was like some extraordinary version—some otherworldly version— of Fu Manchu. I got an attack of the creeps just looking at him, let alone what he did to that lieutenant!"

"And then there's that," said Goodly. "The way they murder people."

" 'They,' yes," said Trask. "Three of them. Once again that number comes up: Simon Salcombe, Gerda Lessing, and this fellow at Fort Knox, this Guyler, er—?"

"Schweitzer," said Garvey, "who has borrowed his name from Switzerland, apparently. But as for how they kill . . ."

"Almost instantaneous metamorphoses," said Goodly, "making grotesque mutations of men, things that die because they simply can't and wouldn't want to live like that! Worse, they can vary the degree of change, of pain, of punishment, making it last as long as they want or killing in a matter of moments."

Trask nodded. "Kelly St. John," he said, grimly. "She just

wasted away, in a matter of days. That was Salcombe making sure he wouldn't be connected to her death. But what about Stamper?"

Garvey shrugged. "Perhaps he'd stalled on paying the price—in gold—for Salcombe's 'services': the cure for his ailing son. But what I'm wondering now: if these people can change the shapes of others, how about themselves? Are they in fact shape-changers?"

And Goodly reentered with: "They can cure as well as kill. They have this . . . yes, this weird 'talent.' They'll use it for 'good' when it enables them to achieve their own ends, for evil when they're thwarted."

"And then there's this other thing I've been researching," said Chung. "Well actually, all I had to do was check the obituaries and make a phone call, which I'd finished doing just a minute or two before today's O-Group. But . . . do you remember the night we all came in here to watch— well, whatever it was—but let's call it Harry's passing? Yes, of course you do; we all do. For afterward we knew that the Necroscope Harry Keogh was dead, and that he had died on Starside in a vampire world. But it's the *timing* that's important."

"So then," said Trask, nodding and staring intently at the locator. "I was right: you do know more than you've been saying. Not that you've been hiding it but simply haven't found time to tell it. Now let me tell *you* something: it's possible you and I have been working toward the same conclusion, the same end, and that we got there at approximately the same time. Okay, so I'll take a shot at it . . . we're talking about the time of the Necroscope's death, right? Well, and now you know what *I* was talking about when I was going on about coincidences and synchronicity, et cetera. But here's *my* finding: that it was only after Harry Keogh died—in fact immediately after he died—that St. John suddenly began to develop his own parapsychological skills. Is that what you were going to say?"

Chung nodded. "That's part of it, yes. You're right as far as you go, sir, but you don't go far enough."

"Oh?" said Trask. "So what else?"

"Well you see," said Chung, "it wasn't *just* Harry who died at that time, at 3:33 on that miserable Sunday morning. No, for that was when Kelly St. John died, too. *And I do mean precisely to the minute!*"

Trask gaped; Goodly and Garvey, too. And the locator went on, "So unless it *is* a coincidence, pure synchronicity, there's got to be a connection, a link between the dead Harry Keogh and the very much alive Scott St. John!"

Trask found his voice, said, "Despite Harry's final condition, his *affliction* at the end of things, still he was the best thing that ever happened to us. If St. John and the people he's working with have somehow been influenced by Harry—"

"—Then they're okay by us!" said Chung.

"Right," said Trask. "But just who are his friends? Who is this woman, Shania? And what about this Wolf person?"

At which the telepath Paul Garvey gasped, causing all eyes to turn in his direction.

"What is it, Paul?" said Trask, immediately concerned. But a moment later he, too, gasped, then angrily snapped his fingers. "*Damn!* You've missed your appointment with your neurologist!"

"Eh?" said Garvey, looking puzzled. And then: "Why, you're right, I have! I forgot all about it as soon as Kellway started in on the results of his research. But my neurologist? Actually I don't give a damn! Not when we're talking about the world ending in just a week's time! And anyway, that isn't it. It's what you just said that's suddenly hit me."

"What I just said?" Trask repeated him. "How do you mean?"

"Now ask yourself," said Garvey, "who do we know who lives on Zakynthos?"

"Zek Föener and Michael Simmons," Trask answered at once.

But Garvey said, "And . . . ?"

"Eh? And?" Again Trask repeated; and then, barely concealing his impatience, "Why not just say what's on your mind?"

"And Wolf," said Garvey. "I mean a *real* wolf of the wild, out of Sunside/Starside's barrier mountains! And you know something? When I homed in on David's probe to St. John's house, I was one hundred percent certain that even through all that smog I was sensing three minds—but I'll be damned if I could swear that all three of them were human!"

For long moments there was silence, then Trask said, "Are you telling me that the third member of Scott St. John and his mystery woman's team is a wolf?"

"I'm saying I think he could be," said Garvey. "And that I know how to check it out. Do we have Zek's Zante number?"

"But we can't—" Ian Goodly's high-pitched voice came piping in, until Trask stopped him short with:

"But we must! I'm sorry Ian, but we can't wait any longer. Your talent notwithstanding, we have to get a hold on this. And I do mean now! You said yourself that we have only a week left. Until what? Some kind of Big Bang? But that's what you and Anna Marie were hinting at, surely? Well, that's it, that's all, Ian; we can't simply stand aside and let this happen, no matter what the future tells you. I mean, St. John, an unknown woman, and a . . . a *wolf,* for God's sake, against whatever the hell is up that crag in the Alps!? Okay, we definitely don't want to go announcing our presence; I mean, we won't be shouting it aloud, but by God we are going to be there!"

He paused and looked from face to face, then said, "Right, and now I'll tell you what I want done . . ."

In Mordri One's private, rock-hewn quarters in Schloss Zonigen, the Mordri Three sat facing each other around a small circular, marble-topped table with their long-fingered hands linked. They were all three in the Shing't mould, which in the Khiff display that Scott St. John had experienced had shown the Shing't to be a tall, gentle, very graceful, even beautiful race who, despite that they were undeniably alien, weren't so very different from his own people. Finding them acceptable, Scott had even considered the idea that perhaps in some distant future, human beings would evolve into creatures much

like them. Here in the austere Schloss Zonigen quarters of the
pseudonymous Frau Gerda Lessing, however, he would certainly have noticed the difference.

For the Mordris were mad, and madness is ugly. For comparison, they were to those Shing't people that Scott had
seen in his dream as a rabid hyena to an intelligent, well-
bred collie. And as for the flowing grace of Shing't
motion—the choreography of stylized, almost balletic
movement—that was scarcely to be found in the frequently
jerky animation and oddly erratic postures of the Mordri
Three. For not only were their thoughts, their aims and ambitions diseased, debased, and deviant, but the Mordris must
expend great efforts of will simply to retain control over
their bodies. Which was why, unlike Shania Two, they must
on occasion revert to these more familiar physical forms.

All three wore high-collared kaftans: Mordri One, or
Gerda Lessing, in a black material as deep as space; Mordri
Two, also known as Simon Salcombe, in slate-grey; and
Mordri Three, whose Earth name was Guyler Schweitzer, in
white so pure it seemed to glow. Their dark, deep-seated
eyes were closed; their features were void of the warm,
smooth-flowing contours of Shing't forebears, but instead
were sharply angled, severe, and threatening. Clinging to
their steeply sloping right shoulders, their Khiffs coiled ten-
uous tendrils around the narrow necks of their hosts' kaftans, sent others probing in their ears to share and perhaps
enhance their thoughts. Open and staring, the small red eyes
of the Khiffs appeared vacant, as if they gazed into nowhere
or at things otherwise unseen—which indeed was the case.
For along with their hosts they'd been engaged upon one of
their periodic probes of E-Branch, attempting to penetrate
the permanent mind-smog cloaking the mind-spy HQ in
London.

For some hours now they had been sending out their
probes, on this occasion finding the usual mental barriers
more densely packed; but enjoying only a small measure of
success in the one direction, in another they'd discovered
something far more interesting.

And now, as the Mordri Three gradually returned from their mental voyaging—their telepathic, group far-scanning—and opened their eyes, so their Khiffs shrank down and entered into the long heads of their hosts. And shortly, without opening her pale slit of a mouth, nevertheless Mordri One said: *Is it possible, do you suppose, that we have been remiss? Have we perhaps underestimated, been overconfident, taken too much for granted, and even made mistakes? Have there been . . . errors?*

In answer to his Unit Leader's query, Mordri Two's voice—very much like his physical voice, when he deigned to use it—was shrill as he "innocently" inquired, *What? Remiss? How so?*

And as they all loosened their grips to sit up straighter, the one in white said, *She is asking: have our precautions been insufficient? Which I'm sure you understood full well, "Simon." For after all, your catchment area was the inner circle, including London, was it not?*

What are you insinuating? Salcombe, or Mordri Two, replied, turning his head in a snake-like motion to glare at the creature that called itself Guyler Schweitzer.

I imply nothing but merely state a fact! that one snapped. *Only ask yourself, "Simon": where lurks this sudden danger? Who are they, whose thoughts turn to us? And yet more to the point, where are they? Let me answer for you: they are in London!*

But "Frau" Gerda Lessing's thought-tones were clipped when she cut in on both of them to state: *I accused no single member of our Three Unit, but perhaps all of us. We could have adopted their methods but chose to use our own, which we considered far less cumbersome, sublime, and . . . invigorating? As for the touch: perhaps we employed it too often and too vigorously! For in its stead bullets and knives would have sufficed and would scarcely have suggested to lesser intellects evidence of superior powers or "alien" incursions; but they would have been adequate to our purpose.*

Adequate, perhaps, Mordri Three tittered, *but by no means as pleasing! It gives my Khiff pleasure to sense their agonies, to watch their shapes melting as they writhe, bloat, or invert. He* delights *in it! And what are these "people" anyway, that we should feel concerned? They are primitives! Denying our beliefs they espouse a god, even gods! Ah, but where will their gods be when we move on? The Saak'nhi, Yo-mirsh, Masakhrii—hah! Even the Shing't themselves— they, too, gave credence to deity, to an almighty, universal creator. And where are they now? Gone! Gone forever. And we three alone are the last of them, even the last of the Shing't! And for all that we have done to draw* it *or* him *or* her *out, no alleged "deity"—neither a god nor any creature mortal or otherwise—nothing and no one has yet challenged our acceptance of* Science *as the only genuine source and supremacy.*

If only for a moment fazed by Guyler Schweitzer's "logic," Mordri One demurred. Then she said, *Mainly true, but you stray wide of the subject. I am well aware of our superiority; indeed and as a Three Unit we are invincible: our* Science *is certainly invincible! But still it appears that we've shaken these beings from their complacency. And the fact is that we are only three, while they are billions!*

I agree, Mordri Two replied. *Racially they are as a swarm. But as individuals and small groups as opposed to fully cooperative Units, it seems that our real enemies—the only ones we* might *have some small cause to be concerned about—*

Such as the ones you have so clumsily alerted to our presence, our activities, Mordri Three snapped.

—Are very few and merely human! Mordri Two shrilled. And then, showing his pearly teeth in a momentary snarl, he went on to point out: *What is more, "Guyler Schweitzer," you seem oddly confused! No more than a moment ago you yourself argued against their capabilities! So why now these grotesque and unsubstantiated accusations toward me? I agree with you: this planet Earth is peopled by primitives, god-worshippers, religious dupes! And if they really were made in* his *image, where is* he *now in their hour of greatest need? Nowhere to be found.* Bah! *Any threat to us, our*

intentions—to prove beyond all doubt, if only to ourselves, that no such supreme being exists or ever has existed—is minimal. For I repeat: these people, these human beings, are merely *human.*

But before Mordri Three could answer him:

As for their being merely human, said Mordri One, *I cannot any longer believe that to be entirely true. In which case both of you would appear to be in error!* She delivered her statement so coldly, it brought her male colleagues' thoughts to an immediate standstill, causing them to jerk their heads as one in her direction. Then, moving awkwardly, Mordri One stood up, angling herself aloft like some cowled, semihuman phasmid. And jerkily pacing the stone-flagged floor, she continued:

Now tell me: did you not sense—have you not detected—someone? By which I mean a being other *than one of a handful of enhanced humans in London and a smaller handful somewhere in or around the Mediterranean? And if not, am I then mistaken in believing that a Shing't mind is out there, in this world, trying to coordinate opposition to our plans? No, I cannot be mistaken, when of the three of us my senses have always been the keenest; or can it be that I am more in tune with female emanations, and that I know an old foe when I meet up with one? She has opposed us before, this one, and my Khiff recognized her aura. My Khiff knows it well—and* hates *it as much as I do! Moreover, she has formed a Three Unit, this one; she works with one who is human, and another who is . . . well, I cannot make him out! His thoughts seem strange to me; he scarcely seems to think in Shing't terms at all but is closer to the generally inferior human psyche. In any case he is different. But she: yes, I know her well. And so should you.*

Ah! Mordri Three's mental "gasp" was like a small burst of light in the minds of his colleagues. *You must surely mean that female of the Shania Unit: Shania Two? I remember how she stood against us at the hearing, her ludicrous accusations of madness. And yes, now that you mention it, I, too, detected a Shing't mind—a shielded mind—at the edge of consciousness. I thought I must be mistaken and so made nothing of it.*

As to madness, said Mordri One: *each of our minds was examined and found wanting, dangerous to such a degree that we were imprisoned—and our Khiffs were madder still! I for one do not dispute that I am mad and that I am capable of, and indeed have a craving for, monstrousness! But I have heard a saying that is common among these Earth beings: that with some people there is "method" in their madness. Well, likewise in mine; and not only method but a purpose which I must pursue; if only out of spite, in order to exact a small measure of revenge for all the humiliation and degradation, the outrages I've suffered at the hands of misguided religious zealots!*

As she fell silent Mordri Two spoke up. *Much like Three, I, too, sensed a presence and believed myself mistaken. So . . . this Shania survived the destruction on the Shing system. And if she survived, perhaps there are others.*

Obviously there will be others! Mordri Three sneered. *Many Shing't Units would have been exploring and studying off-world.*

But this one, said Mordri One, *this Shania Two, might have been close enough to see what happened . . . in any case she* knows *what happened, and who was responsible. And so she has followed us here. But where we seek enlightenment and justice, she seeks only revenge. Which brings me back to what I said earlier: that she is working with others—humans with advanced mental skills—in an attempt to organize opposition to our plans. In short, in order to thwart us!*

The Mordri who called himself Simon Salcombe jerked to his feet. *She is one and we are three! We shall do away with her!*

No! said Mordri One. *Shania Two will die, of course—with this planet, when it dies. But since I sensed her in two places at more or less the same time, obviously she has a localizer. I do not know what her recruits have—only that they know how to shield themselves, making telepathic scrutiny difficult. But we can't afford to be diverted from the course*

*we're set upon. No, if we must engage in conflict, let it be
that this old enemy of ours brings whatever troops she can
muster to us. This place is a natural fortress. And
meanwhile—*

With all three members of the Unit on their feet now,
Mordri One looked from one to the other of her male companions and inquired—*How does the work progress? How
long before we leave and destroy this terminally diseased
world?*

Nine, maybe eight days . . . minimum, Mordri Three
replied.

Then let us make it seven, even six days—maximum!
Mordri One snapped. *Send out your Khiffs to chivvy up the
workers; let your Khiffs find ways to hasten the slackers and
accelerate the process. Give them free rein . . . well, within
certain limits, of course; for they, too, are frequently
overzealous. And then—if our clever Khiffs can't find the
appropriate, er, incentives with which to increase the pro-
ductivity and speed our departure—then I don't know who
or what can! And now to work . . .*

29

That same night:

Finally exhausted, asleep in the arms of Shania Two,
Scott St. John drifted in troubled dreams; while in and between brief bouts of sleeping, Shania did the best she could
to shield both Scott and herself from outside observation
and interference. As for Wolf: with a full belly, sated, warm,
and dry—and as clean if not cleaner than on the day just
two years ago when his wild mother gave birth to him—he
lay on a soft blanket outside the bedroom door. Even in fitful dreams he followed Shania's example: covered himself
in opaque, intangible thoughts that denied that he was there
at all; while in fact he was well aware there was nowhere

else he would rather be, and only a very few places where he would know *how* to be. For prior to this Wolf had known only the woods and hillsides of southeastern parts of Zante in the Ionian. And in any case his dreams when they showed through the blanketing opacity were of squawking chickens, and rabbits that all too often evaded pursuit.

But Scott St. John's dreams were far stranger—in certain ways terrifying—and Shania listened intently to his heart and dreams both; the first occasionally pounding, and the others as strange as anything in any world that Shania had ever seen. For she knew that they were far more than mere dreams . . .

Scott was a boy again, maybe eleven or twelve years old. As for his location: he didn't recognize it—or perhaps he did, however vaguely—but he sat on a bank in the bight of a river with a friend, their shoes and socks close at hand and their feet in the cool, gently swirling water. It was a summer afternoon, and glancing rays of sunlight sparkled on the ripples and fell warm on the faces of the two boys, Scott and his friend.

"Rather odd, don't you think?" said the latter, in a voice which wasn't at all young and boyish but manly, strong, mature. "I seem to remember that when I was this age I lived elsewhere. I never once came here, not when I was this age."

Scott looked at him. Of medium build, freckle-faced, and sandy-haired, the boy wore plain prescription spectacles balanced on a stub of a nose. Behind the spectacles dreamy blue eyes gazed out of a haunted face in a peculiar, paradoxical sort of expectant bewilderment. Only a little older than Scott himself, the boy wore a crumpled school uniform over a once-white shirt, with a school tie dangling all askew, its end starting to fray. And Scott at once liked him.

"You're a . . . a friend of mine," Scott said. "That much I know. But I don't know—or maybe I've forgotten—your name."

"It's Harry," said the other. "And you're Scott. That much

I know, but not everything. I go places to help out but I'm not given to know everything. You must have taken a dart, right?"

For a moment Scott was puzzled. "I took a . . . ?" But then he remembered. "Oh! A dart! A golden dart, yes!" And then, feeling a little uncertain, even afraid: "But where am I? I wasn't ever here before and I don't know this place. And where's my father? He doesn't like me going places where I'm not supposed to go."

"But this is a place where you *were* supposed to go," Harry answered. "I would hazard a guess we're in my past, or at least in a location from that past. It happens that way sometimes."

"What happens?"

"My meeting people who need my help." Harry shrugged. "But hey! Like I said: I don't know everything. And on this occasion very little. Your name is more or less it! Usually I'm given at least a hint." He shrugged. "That's the way it is."

Scott shook his head, drew his feet from the water and out onto the bank to dry. "That's sort of vague," he said. "And you know something? You don't talk like a boy."

"You neither," said Harry. "And that's because you're not. It's just the way they do things."

"They?" said Scott.

Harry shrugged again. "I don't know who they are; I never did, not really. I had my suspicions, though. Let's just say I work for someone or something who's a lot higher up the ladder. And so do they."

"What ladder? I don't follow you."

"And you wouldn't want to," said Harry, ominously. "Not to some of the places I've been, or will be . . ." And then, changing the subject: "Anyway, you asked about your father."

But Scott was remembering now—remembering what was still to come—and said, "I know: he died a long time ago. And Kelly more recently. I think that's why I got your dart."

"So, you know the dart was part of me?"

"I know that *you* are part of *me*," said Scott. "Only a very small part; but I think that you've been here for some time, in me, trying to tell me things. I mean, I've sometimes remembered things, or half remembered them—people, faces, events—that I never knew, that never happened. Not to me, anyway. I think I got your dart when Kelly died."

"Probably *because* Kelly died," said Harry. "It's usually a great wrong that needs to be righted." Then he frowned. "But on the other hand it's very *un*usual if only one person or thing is involved. Events need to be going very wrong— need to be especially bad—before they'll step in."

All of Scott's future, but in fact his past, had come back to him now. He remembered almost everything. "Why did they make us boys?" he said. "Why couldn't we talk as men?"

"It's a matter of innocence—I think," said Harry. "Boys can talk to each other; it's far easier to believe, when you're young. That's why you're a boy—I think. And if I were a man, then you might have been wary of me. So that's probably why *I'm* a boy. And believe me, there was a certain me you wouldn't have wanted to know at all! That was the last me, before I . . . well, before they took me."

"Harry, you're dead, aren't you?" said Scott then, somehow knowing it for a fact.

"In one sense, yes," said the other. "But in another, hell no! I'm alive all over the place!"

"Like in me?"

"And like in lots of others in lots of other places."

"I'm talking to a dead man!" said Scott, feeling his flesh creep.

"Ah!" said Harry. "That's it! I knew we'd find the reason, if only we talked long enough."

"Reason?" Scott was back to short, even single word questions again.

"The reason for my being here," said Harry. "You're talking to a dead man. And that's because you *can!* That's one part of me that you've definitely got, even if you might not be able to retain it. You see, I was the original Necroscope; I was the man who talked to dead people. I was their only friend, and the dead would do anything for Harry Keogh. *Hah!* It seems my memory is improving . . . a little, anyway."

"Mine, too," said Scott, for the moment ignoring— perhaps deliberately failing to acknowledge—what Harry had said about speaking to the dead. "I'm in a boy's body, but I have a man's memories. And I remember . . ."

He remembered lying on his back on a surgical trolley, being wheeled along a corridor past a door with a name-plate that read "Harry's Room." And so:

"You worked for E-Branch, didn't you?" he said.

"I was part of E-Branch, for a while," said the other, his eyes now misty, as if viewing distant things. "Yes, we did some good work together, me and the Branch . . ." But then, once again, as if certain memories were too powerful, too strong for Harry, he changed the subject. "But I can't stay here too long, Scott, and there are other things you'll need to know; they're difficult things, it's true, but still you should have accepted them by now. They're *in* you even as I am in you; it's just that you haven't discovered them yet."

Scott's head spun; he was confused by what he'd been told, felt threatened by what he didn't yet know. "Other things?" he said. "Difficult things? But I don't yet understand about this dead thing you were talking about! I mean, were you really trying to tell me I can talk to dead people? I remember *trying* to talk to them—once, in another dream, I think—but it didn't work out."

"Because you didn't believe; because you're very hard to convince, Scott, and you hadn't quite let the dart take hold. Which is probably another reason why I'm here: to ensure that it does. So then, no more questions from you for now; but tell me something: what are you like with numbers, with math?"

"Math?" Bewildered by this third abrupt change of subject, Scott could only shake his head. "What do you mean, math? To me numbers are like musical notes or languages . . . they have their own beat, their own pitch and rhythm. Except that *un*like music, math's beat is immutable: it never changes. So yes, I think I'm okay with numbers; I don't often get shortchanged, anyway! But why do you ask?"

"Ah, but you're wrong," said Harry. "Numbers *aren't* immutable. If you know how to 'play' them, how to 'speak' them, you can change them!"

"Play them, speak them?" said Scott.

"Like music, like languages." Harry nodded, and then continued. "Look, close your eyes and let me show you something."

"Close my eyes and . . . ?" said Scott. Something of a contradiction, surely. But since Harry had already closed his, Scott followed suit. And:

There on the darkness behind his eyelids—like symbols on the monitor screen of a vast computer engaged in solving an incredibly complex mathematical problem—a stream of decimals, fractions, algebraic equations, Arabic cyphers, formulae, non-Euclidean and Riemannian configurations, flickered from top to bottom of Scott's "vision" in a constantly evolving, seemingly endless display. And if he had felt dizzy before, now his mind reeled!

He opened his eyes. "What was *that!?*"

"Numbers, that's all!" cried Harry. "It was math! But it's also the answer to everything you'll need to know. So now close your eyes again and keep watching."

Scott did as he was told.

The numbers on the screen of his mind were still in flux, changing at an astonishing rate, becoming ever more complicated. But then, as if frozen for a single moment in the eye of his—or someone else's?—memory, Scott saw *and recognized* a certain fantastic formula. At which a door opened in the darkness where no door had ever before existed!

"Yes, a Möbius door," said Harry. And:

"I know," said Scott. "The part of you that's in me knows. But me, I don't know what I'm supposed to do or how to do it!"

"You just step through it," said Harry. "Like this."

Scott felt his hand taken, clutched in Harry Keogh's cold hand. And before he could open his eyes he was pulled in, drawn into and through the Möbius door—a door that previously existed only in Harry's metaphysical mind, and now in Scott's—to a "place" that was no-where or when, but lay parallel not only to space and time but also to regions adjacent and beyond what men are satisfied to call the universe.

"God!" Scott cried, his cry ringing out across untold ages and infinities.

Well, close enough, said Harry soundlessly, not letting go of Scott's hand; unable to let go, such was Scott's tight grip. *A godlike mind, certainly. But there's no need to speak in this place, Scott, for even thoughts have weight in the Möbius Continuum.*

The Möbius Continuum: Scott felt it all around him, around everything! Here beyond Harry's door lay the ultimate darkness: the Primal Darkness, which existed always, even before the universe began. It was a place of absolute negativity; not even a parallel plane of existence, because nothing *existed* here, not under normal conditions or circumstances. And Scott knew—he understood—that if there was ever a place where darkness lay upon the face of the deep, this was it. And yes, it might well be the region from which God had commanded, *Let There Be Light,* causing the physical universe to split off from this metaphysical abstraction. For indeed the Möbius Continuum was "without form, and void."

Are you okay? Harry's silent voice startled Scott from his contemplation of this surreal "place," caused him to jerk violently; which only served to set him slowly spinning, and Harry with him. But the Necroscope knew how to bring their motion to a halt; and again he asked, *Scott, are you okay?*

"Yes . . . I mean no!" said Scott, each word exploding deafeningly, almost like a thunderclap. Until, accepting what Harry had told him, he very quietly asked, *Can we go now?*

But we only just got here! And there are other things you might want to see. You may never need them, but then again you might, and what good's a tool if you don't know how to use it?

A tool?

This, of course! said Harry. *The Möbius Continuum. That's what I used to call it, anyway. But however spiritual it may or may not be, it's nevertheless a tool no less than deadspeak.*

Deadspeak, said Scott, gradually regaining his confidence, becoming used to the situation. *Is that what you call it? This, er, "talent," this speaking to dead people? I always thought of it as clairvoyancy.*

Clairvoyancy is a fraud, said Harry. *A cheap, lousy trick to cash in on the bereaved. But what I used to do, and what you can do, that's the real thing.*

Hmmm! Scott mused. *The real thing?* And then: *Okay, Harry, you can show me these . . . these other things. But first, do you think I might—*

—First you'd like to try out your deadspeak? Harry knew, or guessed, what was in Scott's mind, because he or part of him was *in* Scott's mind. And so: *Very well,* he agreed, *so let's go there. Show me the coordinates.*

Coordinates? Single word questions again.

Okay, forget it, said Harry. *I can read them in your mind. And I could have guessed the place anyway, because that's probably the only place you would* know *where to go to try out your deadspeak. Myself, I've visited lots of graveyards in my time. And I could have done without some of them.*

Hold on there a minute, Harry, said Scott. *You changed the subject again. Did you say I have coordinates? In my mind?*

Every place you've ever been, said the Necroscope. *If you remember it, it's a coordinate. Now we point ourselves in that direction—and we* think, *we will ourselves there. And—*

There was the very slightest sensation of movement, and a moment later a Möbius door shaped itself out of nowhere. *We're there!* said Harry, drawing Scott through the door and returning him to a gravity-bound environment, the darkness of a well-kept cemetery in northeast London. Flanked by high walls, the place was a quarter acre, where trees and shrubs formed the perimeter. A gentle breeze blew in the shrubbery, making a rustling sound, while a thin ground mist loaned the place a false sensation of desolation and a genuine sense of loss.

Feeling the ground beneath his feet, Scott stumbled a very little; not as much as when Shania had shown him her mechanical version of a similar trick. And the "boy" Harry said, "So then, who will you speak to first?"

Still not quite believing what was happening—or what he was dreaming—Scott said, "My father, I think. He's been suffering for a long time. I think he believes he neglected me; and he did, but he had what he thought were good reasons. I suppose it was all down to his good old British stiff upper lip. Still, I was never left wanting for anything, so I don't have a lot to complain about. I just want to set it straight that's all . . . I want him to be at peace, with himself."

"And you've never wanted that before?" Perhaps Harry's not-so-simple question sounded a disapproving note.

But Scott protested, "What? Hold on there, Harry. I mean, I didn't know that anyone was *there* before! I didn't know that anything was left of them."

"Ah, but they are there!" said Harry. "Some of them for an eternity, or so it seems. The flesh is gone, and even the bones eventually, but *mind* goes on. Just think, Scott: all the learning that's ever been is down in the ground or gone up in smoke, lost to us except where it was written in books for us to read. But did you think that's all there was to it? Not in the least. The creative ones go right on creating: they write their music, the books that they never had time to complete; or they fathom scientific problems, design great architectural works and machines that the living never even imagined! They're very active, Scott, if only in their minds—because mind is all they have left. And the real pity of it is that no one in your corporeal world knows what they've done, for there isn't anyone they can talk to . . . not anymore. Well, not until now."

"You mean me?"

"I mean you." Harry nodded. "But I've a feeling they won't lean too heavily on you, as they sometimes did on me. They will probably understand that you're here for a purpose. No, I think it will be the other way around: you who needs them. And, Scott, once they know you, when they've felt your warmth, you're going to have plenty of friends among the dead."

Scott couldn't find an answer to that, so instead he shuddered a little . . .

While the two had talked, so they'd walked. Now they were close to Jeremy St. John's grave, and Scott found himself walking more slowly. "And do they love?" he said. "Do they remember the loved ones they left behind? Are they maybe jealous of them because they still have their lives? I think maybe I would be."

"I have found," said the Necroscope, "that it's mainly the bad ones—the ones who were bad in life—who go on being bad in death, and usually they're shunned by the others. And as for love: well, mostly the dead feel concerned for the happiness of the loved ones they left behind, not for themselves. Also, it's known and accepted that those who loved the most in their lives are the ones who move along the quickest; their grief—for the living, you understand—doesn't last too long. No, for there's lots of room for love in the other places, Scott."

"The other places?" Scott was baffled again. "They move on to other places? What kind of places, Harry?" But:

"Better places, that's all," said Harry. "So don't go worrying yourself about it. And anyway, here's your father's grave." And sure enough, there was that less than familiar sarcophagus, and the headstone with what Scott had always considered a pompous inscription: "A Man of Manners, a Man of Breeding."

Jeremy St. John wasn't there . . . or he was, but not in the semblance of flesh he'd been wearing when Scott had seen him in a previous, rather more dreamlike dream. For now his father was simply a voice, but one which was faint as a breeze, whispering as if from a million miles away.

"Who is it?" that voice inquired. "Who is it close by, who I sense as warm as life. The dead have spoken of such; a Necroscope who speaks to the dead from life. But what have I done to deserve such a visitor? Are you here to chastise me? If so, too late, for I've been doing that for years . . ."

30

Such was the misery in his father's distant-sounding voice that Scott felt choked. For a moment he couldn't speak—didn't know how to speak, not to his father—until Harry told him: "Scott, it's easy. You hear him, don't you? And you believe, don't you? That's all it takes. So now speak, and he'll hear you, too." And so:

"Father," said Scott, albeit tremulously, "it's me, Scott. I've been given the power to speak to you. It's funny, but I've only just realized that's something I've been wanting to do for a very long time."

"Scott?" said the other, his voice much louder and perhaps a little disbelieving. "Is it really you, son? Or have I needed this so desperately and for so long that I'm only imagining it?"

"No, it's me," said Scott. "I've been shown the way to . . . to do this. And you're the first one I've come to talk to. It's strange but now that I can, and now that I'm here, I don't know what to say!"

"Son! Son!" Jeremy St. John cried, but so close now it was as if he were seated right next to Scott on his tomb. "I dreamed you came to me once before, but we weren't able to talk to each other. Yet now . . . can it be . . . that *you* are the Necroscope?"

"No." Scott shook his head, and knew that his father would sense it. "No, I'm not *the* Necroscope, I'm just Scott. But I've sort of borrowed the Necroscope's powers; how long for, I can't say. I've been given certain of his skills because of some work I have to do, a wrong I must put right. I would try to tell you about it but I don't know how long I'm allowed to stay here and I need to talk to Kelly, too. Kelly was my wife. I got married, Father, but not while you were alive, so you never got to meet her. Kelly was . . . she was *murdered,* by a lunatic!"

"Murdered?" (Horror in that voice from the tomb.)

Scott nodded. "Yes, but it's just one of many wrongs I'll be trying to put right. Just one, but to me the most important, of *millions* of murders—most of them done in distant worlds—and some six billion more that an alien creature and his group are planning to do in *this* world, in the very near future." He explained in brief and waited for a response. And eventually:

"All of this to do," said his father, wonderingly. "And by the sound of it no easy task. And yet you've found time to come and speak to me. Do I deserve it, son? I wasn't the best father in the world, now was I? The best? Hardly that, for I was never there for you." The catch in Jeremy St. John's voice was almost a sob.

"But you stuck to your guns," said Scott. "I got that much from you at least. There are plenty of things I remember about you: how you would never quit or admit defeat; your starch and your pride."

"Pride?" his father replied. "Yes, I was proud, wasn't I? But you know what they say, son: it comes before a fall. And I feel like I've fallen a very long way."

"Then we really are pretty much of a kind." Scott nodded. "When Kelly died I hit rock bottom. I don't think anyone could fall much farther than I fell. It was like a black pit, and to tell the truth I'm still climbing out of it. But at least I've got help."

"But surely that was different," said his father. "I mean, you didn't do anything wrong. There was no guilt on your part."

Scott felt he was losing the argument—or rather that he was losing his father again, losing him to his own misery—

and so said, "There was no guilt *then,* it's true. Or maybe a little guilt, right at the end. But that was then and this is now. You see, Kelly hasn't been dead for very long, and yet . . ."

"Ah!" said his father. "I think I see. But, Scott, son, you can't be unfaithful to a memory . . . can you?"

"I don't know," Scott replied. "But I think maybe you can, especially if what you thought had gone away is still there and you're able to touch it, and you can still talk to it."

"Ah!" said his father again, with a knowing deadspeak nod. "So there's a downside to these powers, is there?"

Scott could only agree. "As I've only now discovered," he answered, feeling the chill of his father's slab creeping into his bones.

"It's funny, isn't it?" said his father, in a tone as soft and gentle as any Scott had ever known him to use. "I think you came here to console me—which you've done and quite admirably—yet suddenly here I am consoling, or perhaps condoning, you. Or trying to, anyway."

Scott shook his head, surprised by his sudden discovery of something new. "It's something I never really knew you had," he said. "Your understanding! But you were an ambassador, a politician; of course you understood things. And you were—and you still are—my father! We should have talked, but we couldn't. I was just a child; what could you have said to me that *I* would have understood?"

"I knew that," his father answered, the catch back in his voice, "and so I never tried. And *still* I'm riddled with guilt, but not only because of the way I neglected you, Scott. For no matter how hard I try to reason things out in order to forgive myself, there can be no escape from the fact that I did what I did to your mother."

"And no escaping that she did what she did to you," Scott answered. "But I know she loved me, and I loved her back; which was where you and I drifted apart. You looked at me and thought of her, and you simply didn't want to look anymore. And though I'm sorry now to say it, the feeling was mutual. But that's all done with now . . ."

Scott fell silent until, remembering something that Harry

had told him, he thought to ask: "Is she . . . is she still there, my mother? Is she still with the dead, or has she already moved on?"

"Oh, she's a long time gone from the Great Majority," Jeremy St. John husked. "But then, she'd suffered more than enough in life; it would have been unfair if she'd suffered here, too. I was never in touch with her, but then no one was. Your mother was beyond that, Scott. And now she's—"

"—Beyond everything, in a better place?" said Scott. "I'm glad for that."

"And I'm glad for you," said his father.

"It's time I went," said Scott then. "But first I want to be sure that things are okay with you—between us, I mean."

Jeremy St. John sighed. "Things are fine with us now, son. And I thank you."

"If I don't get back to you"—Scott got up from the sarcophagus—"well, you know what I mean."

"Yes, I know," the other replied. And then: "Good-bye, son. Thanks for . . . for everything, and good luck with whatever lies ahead . . ."

What lay ahead was Kelly's grave, and Scott had no idea what he was going to say to her—or if he'd be able to say anything at all—or if he did, what her response would be. Indeed, the only thing he knew for sure was that he wouldn't lie to her, because he never had. But in any case Kelly beat him to it, for even as he and Harry approached her plot with its beautiful marble headstone, she said:

"Your thoughts are deadspeak, Scott; and me and the others here, we've been listening to you ever since you got here, from the moment we felt your warmth. We've felt it before, but distantly: like a small, flickering candle burning in a dark cellar room—but so small that we didn't know where or who you were. There are plenty here who remember the Necroscope. They thought maybe he had returned. Myself . . . well, I'm a newcomer here, and I never knew the Necroscope. But that warmth: I seemed to sense something of you in it. Being new, however, I said nothing."

Scott opened his mouth, closed it, then opened it again as finally words came. "Kelly! It's you! You're here!"

"Of course," she said. "Where else would I be? But I'm not destined to stay here for very long; so they've told me, anyway. They put that down to my love for you: so much of it that I can no longer give you. But still it's here, and it has to go somewhere. And I'm told there's plenty of room for it in—"

"—In the other places," Scott burst out as a lump in his throat threatened to shut off his air, and another in his chest squeezed his heart, his soul, and the tears from his eyes. "The better places, I know. Kelly! Kelly!" But:

"No, don't do that, Scott," she chastised him oh-so-gently, "or you might start me doing it, too. And far too many tears are being shed already, on both sides of the divide. In fact, that's the only thing I've been worried about: that you would be hurting. It seemed unfair to me that you should be hurting when I'm past all that."

"You"—Scott tried not to sob—"you don't hurt?"

"Only for you," she answered. "But not physically. There's no lump in a throat that's still, Scott, and no pain in a heart that's stopped beating. I'm beyond all that now. But as for my soul—"

"—There are better places," he choked the words out, "for your soul."

He sensed her deadspeak nod. "And I feel—I don't know—an undertow," she continued dreamily. "Something tugging at me, but pleasantly. It's as if . . . as if I were being called away. Scott, I know I *have* been called! The only reason I've resisted is because you're still out there among the living. I had to be sure you weren't hurting, that you were healing, but there was no way to know . . . until now."

"Kelly," Scott said, "you can let go. I'm okay now . . . not right now and not here, but *now*. You know what I mean. The only thing that hurts me now is the same for me as for you: the fact that I'm here, while you—"

"—While I'm gone? But you're too young to go on hurting, Scott. We found each other, didn't we? So surely you can—"

"Don't!" Scott broke in, stopped her. "No, don't go there, Kelly! I'm not the man you think I am. I'm weak."

"No," she denied it, and he sensed the shake of her head, the warmth of her smile, "you're strong. And if she'll love you as much as I have, then you won't be able to refuse her. That's the kind of love the world is short of, Scott."

"If I'd known—" he cried, "if there was any way I could have known, even suspected that you were still here, there's no way I would ever have—"

"Shhh!" Kelly hushed him. "Do you think I don't know that? Of course I do. But, Scott, that's the main *reason* why there can be no real contact between the living and the dead! Because the material world would be full of guilty, innocent people."

"Kelly, I—"

"You loved me, and I loved you," Kelly said. "We loved our best but now I'm gone while you go on. What sort of woman would I be—what sort of love would it have been— if I didn't want you to love again?"

"Kelly!" And now the tears were unstoppable.

"I'm being called," she said, oh-so-distantly. "It's time, Scott, and I'm ready."

"Kelly!"

"Just remember," she said, her voice faint and fast-fading now. "If you're going to love her at all, love her as you loved me, Scott. Love her . . . the very best . . . you can . . ."

And that was all, for Kelly's last word had come as a sigh that joined with the soughing of the night breeze in the bordering trees. And she was gone.

"To a better place," Scott sobbed.

"Oh, yes," said Harry softly. "I can guarantee it . . ."

Back in the Möbius Continuum, Harry said, *My time's running out now, Scott, and I still want to show you the other things. Like I said before, you may not need them, but it's best to be prepared, right?*

Yes, whatever you say, Scott replied in a whisper, feeling completely drained.

You see, said the Necroscope, *there are doors within doors in the Möbius Continuum. Some lead to other places—but I mean* physical *places, not the kind of place where Kelly's gone—and others access past and future times. We can't manifest in those times, or rather the living can't, though I have known one corporeal person who did; but sometimes there are clues to what has been or will be, which makes it worthwhile simply to trace the time-lines. As to how you gain access to a time-line, let's say into the future: you concentrate on what you imagine the future is going to bring. Like this:*

And suddenly a door opened, but an entirely different kind of door: simply a hole in nothing! And as Harry guided Scott to the threshold, he said, *Look!*

Scott looked . . . and was at once stunned by the wonder and awe of it! Beyond the future-time door all was a chaos of millions, even billions of lines of pure blue neon light, etched on a backdrop of black velvet. It was like nothing so much as some incredible meteor shower, where all of the meteors were rushing away from Scott into unimaginable deeps of space—but in fact into the future. Unlike meteors, however, their twisting, twining trails didn't fade but remained brilliantly printed—fixed on the darkness, on time itself! And the most awesome thing was this: that one of these streamers of blue light issued outward from Scott himself, extending or extruding from him and plummeting away into the future. But looking aside at Harry, Scott saw no such streamer, and of course the Necroscope knew what he was thinking.

That's right, said Harry. *These are life-threads, the blue time tracks of humanity. You have one because you're alive. But as for myself*—he offered a shrug—*I no longer need one.* Then he frowned and continued. *As for that silver thread there, running parallel with yours, that's a new one on me! I don't think I've ever seen one of those before. But it has a tinge of blue, so maybe it's just some kind of temporal distortion.*

Scott suspected he could pretty much guess what the sil-

ver thread was, who it belonged to, even why it seemed to
be turning blue; but right now he was just too overwhelmed
by what he was seeing to offer an opinion, and he could
only say:

I can't believe I'm looking at the future. At my future!

Everyone's future, said the Necroscope. *What's more we
can even venture a little way out there—ahead of time, as it
were—to see what's what; maybe something of what's in
store?*

Trying to hold back, Scott said, *What? Do you really
think that's a good—*

But too late, because Harry had already drawn him over
the threshold. And away down the time stream they hurtled,
with the future always ahead of them. Until suddenly—

A tremor . . . a temporal earthquake . . . time itself seeming to warp . . . and, quite improbably, the darkness turning
a blinding white! But that was only for a split second, a
mere moment, while in the next moment everything continued as before. Or not quite everything.

For as Harry brought himself and Scott to a halt—

Where's my life-thread? said Scott.

It was no longer there, not in front of him, unwinding
out of him. Behind him, yes: his life-thread twined away,
dwindling into the past—his past—but in front: nothing of
Scott sped into the future now. And the silver thread was
missing, too.

Then, when Scott looked to Harry for an explanation:

Time we got back, said that one, very quietly.

But what happened just then? said Scott as the Necroscope reeled them back to the time door and across its
threshold into the "basic" Möbius Continuum. *What does
it mean?*

There's no sure way to tell, said Harry, a little subdued.
*But one thing's for sure: the future's a devious thing. I think
we might be okay.*

We might be okay? Scott repeated him. *But don't you
mean I might be okay?*

Yes! Harry snapped, no longer composed. *Yes, that's what*

I mean. I mean you might be okay, okay? Now if you'll let me I'll show you why you might be okay. Concentrate on the past, Scott. Think about what's gone before. And this time we're looking for my thread.

But you don't have one, said Scott, logically.

No, but I did have one until recently. We'll find it.

They opened a past-time door, and again Scott was stricken with the stunning, the utterly surreal beauty of it. The myriad blue life-threads were there as before; but now, instead of expanding into the distance, they contracted and narrowed down as if to target a faraway, nebulous origin. For that distant blue haze *was* the origin: the beginning of human life on Earth.

And in a little while: *There!* said Harry very quietly, as he once more brought them to a halt. You see that? *That was me, Scott. Right at the end of things, that was me.*

It was a bomb-burst of golden darts, just like the one in Scott, which had changed, empowered, and was continuing to make him into what he was becoming. Indeed one of the darts—a part of the Necroscope, Harry Keogh—*was* Scott's dart, which immediately following the bomb-burst had found reason to come to him. For as Harry had suffered his metamorphosis, his "death," so in another world Kelly St. John had suffered hers. Except hers, of course, had been utter and permanent.

Scott saw those myriad darts angling out and away, intelligent, knowing, seeking. Then they were accelerating, vanishing through doors of their own. But beyond Harry's bomb-burst Scott had seen something else: Harry's crimson life-thread, a thread as red as blood!

And Harry said, *Well, didn't I tell you there was a me you wouldn't want to have known?* And before Scott could answer: *But who or whatever I was then, this was the source of your powers. You can't any longer doubt or deny them, for you've seen it for yourself; you know where they came from. What's more important, you now know how to use them. But if you still have your doubts you can always try calling for me. Who knows? I might even hear you.*

With which he reversed course. The time stream
snatched at them, rushing them along; and speeding back to
the present, the pair returned to the Möbius Continuum.

Along the way Scott was silent; he had seen and learned
a lot, but the thing uppermost in his mind—the person and
event uppermost—was Kelly. He'd met her, the incorporeal
Kelly, and had actually spoken to her. She had passed beyond all that now, to where he could never speak to her
again, but he would never forget his Kelly.

He would be without her, must live without her, but Scott
would never forget her. Not his Kelly. Not ever. Never . . .

Scott came awake no longer a small boy but a man, and yet
a man who sobbed like a small boy. Wrapped in Shania's
arms, he clung to her as if she were Kelly and he wasn't going to let go. Then he heard her voice—Shania's voice—
and knew that he had to let go.

"Scott!" she said. "Oh, Scott!"

"Gone," he choked the word out. "She's gone. But she'll
be okay, now."

"Yes," Shania answered him, "and so will you." And she
was crying, too. For of course she had been with him. Shania and her Khiff, as one with Scott St. John in his metaphysical mind. And emotions such as Scott had known were
catching . . .

31

She was warm and comforting, but she wasn't Kelly, and just
for a moment Scott pushed her away. Then, even in the semi-
darkness feeling, indeed knowing, that he had hurt her, he
drew her close again and said, "I'm sorry, so sorry! I didn't
mean to do that. But I thought I was holding . . . I felt like I
was holding—"

"—Kelly, I know," Shania said it for him. "I saw it all, but don't go accusing me of spying on you. I *had* to see it, had to know. But what I know now, what I begin to understand, is so unbelievable, so magical, so very wonderful!"

Wonderful? What was so very wonderful? Kelly was gone from the world, wasn't she? Gone from everything they had ever known together, and Scott had been left on his own. But no, he'd been left with Shania.

Trying to hide his burning eyes as Shania switched on the bedside lamp, Scott stuffed a pillow against the headboard and propped himself up. "What time is it?" he said, his words still choked, his voice still husky.

"I'm sure you must know what time it is," Shania answered. "You know what and why, but you don't know how—or perhaps you do, now. And when you feel okay, when you're ready, that's something we have to talk about. But the sooner the better, because time really is narrowing down." She dried her own eyes, her own amazing yet very human eyes, and sat up beside him.

It was 3:33, of course: the time when Kelly—when she had gone to sleep—and the time when she'd woken up again, but in a better place. And Scott said, "Are you talking about the time again? Three thirty-three? But haven't we already covered that? I mean, what do we have to talk about?"

"We *have* to talk," she told him. "About that and something else. Something very exciting, very important."

Exciting, wonderful, important. Scott got up, began to get dressed, said, "But we've been there. And I don't know any more than I've already told you."

"But I *do* know more," said Shania. "*Now* I know more. Or at least I think, I hope I do. And why are you getting dressed, if you don't want to talk? We can talk about anything you want to, Scott. For instance: there may be things you need to get out of your head . . . ? And now maybe you'll begin to appreciate the true value of my Khiff. Hurtful things can be taken away; not permanently, no, but stored where they can do no harm. Special memories, too, that can always be re-remembered whenever you're feeling down and need—"

But Scott's voice was gruff when he cut her off with: "We have drugs for that, and I don't take them either!" Then, realizing he was being hard on her for something that had nothing to do with her, he said, "God, I keep putting my foot in it, don't I? But you see, I *want* my memories, good and bad. The good ones buoy me up, and the bad ones—one of them especially—oh, I *need* that one, Shania! I need it as a constant reminder of what still has to be done."

"Yes," she said. "And I find that I'm the same; I have the same kind of memories. Mine are of entire worlds, races. My own race, almost extinct now, is uppermost in my mind. It's the one memory that keeps me going and I won't let it be taken from me, not even for a moment, not even by my Khiff. I say this so that you can see I really do understand."

On her feet now, Shania wrapped herself in a dressing gown and came around to Scott's side of the bed. He was seated, putting on his slippers.

"Coffee, that's why I'm getting dressed," he finally answered Shania's question as she came to stand before him. "I need coffee, need to be awake. I've had enough of sleep for now, and I should be considering all I've seen, heard, learned. I feel I need to be learning more; so whatever it is you want to talk to me about, and anything you want . . . you want to show me . . . ?"

He paused, and then, on impulse said: "But first I'd like you to show me . . . you." Because while he had made love to her, he'd never really looked at her, not like this. And he reached for the belt of her loosely fastened robe.

She beat him to it, let her robe hang loose. Scott looked at the incredible loveliness of Shania's body, reached out and stroked her breasts, and said, "Kelly told me I should love you the best I can."

"I know," she answered, responding, shivering to his touch. "But I wish you would love me for myself, not just for Kelly."

And Scott thought, *That may take time.* But though he tried to keep the thought to himself, still she heard it, and said:

"Time is something we may not have a lot of. And we should make the best of what we've got."

Scott's hands traced the perfect curves of her flanks, and he answered, "But lust isn't love. It's an animal thing. Surely we can't be sure of ourselves, not yet?"

"Well, I'm sure of myself," she replied, her voice low and as husky as his own as she leaned forward so that he could kiss her nipples. "And after all, we are animals."

"I can't believe you've given yourself to me." Scott shook his head in wonder.

"And I can't believe you accepted me," she replied, with a sad, wry little smile. "What me, Shania Two, a female 'alien'?"

Groaning, Scott hugged her close and said, "Oh, really? Why the hell not? Because you're alien? But women are from Venus—aren't they?"

"Women are from . . . ?" she breathed, only half aware of what she was saying, feeling him jerking alive between her thighs.

"Just a stupid expression," he told her, his heart hammering and blood coursing as he hugged her buttocks and tasted her breasts. "Don't worry about it."

And then as Shania slipped out of her robe, suddenly Scott found himself undressing again . . .

"I like your coffee," she said, sipping from a mug down in the study. "It's vegetable-based, isn't it?"

"What, you mean you didn't know that?" Scott was surprised. "But you know so much about us."

"Not everything," she replied. "There's much I haven't had time to even consider, let alone study."

"You're a vegetarian, right?"

"Most of my people are"—she paused abruptly—"or were. A mere handful now: the ones who were off-world when Shing was destroyed. But many of us did eat a little seafood—not fish, but clams, giant tube-worms, mindless things like that."

"Well, I enjoy fish myself," said Scott. "And so did Kelly. She was mainly vegetarian, too." But then, realizing that everything was Kelly, Kelly, Kelly, and that he *must* let her go now, keep her memory to himself, he quickly went on: "As for coffee, it's made by crushing small brown beans." Then he shrugged and added, "But I don't suppose they suffer a hell of a lot."

"Your pardon?" Her mouth had fallen open.

"A joke," he said.

"Ah!" Shania sighed her relief. "You see, I've heard of a number of worlds with semi-sentient florae. Usually carnivores, they're not themselves insensitive to pain."

"We have them, too," said Scott. "Like the Venus flytrap. It eats flies—actually it dissolves them and then slurps them up—but it doesn't think."

"Given time," she replied, "and if your flytrap survives the geological ages, evolution will probably see to that, too!"

"Survival," said Scott thoughtfully. "But shouldn't we be talking about our own survival? I mean, what was it you really wanted to talk about? You said it was important, exciting, wonderful. So what is it? Have you found a way to tackle Salcombe and these other monsters? . . . What was it you called them?"

"The Mordris," she answered coldly. "An insane Three Unit. No, I have no actual plan. Since experiencing your dream, however, I do have hope; some small hope at least, now. But, Scott, you must know that it was much more than a mere dream."

"I know it was, yes," he said as Shania came and sat close to him, shivering and snuggling to him as if the room were cold, which it wasn't. "Far too many of my dreams have been more than mere dreams just recently. You say that you were there with me? That you saw, experienced, what I was seeing and doing?"

"Everything," she answered. "And we—my Khiff and I—we felt your pain, too."

Scott's eyes narrowed a little. "You know," he said, "this is getting to be a habit that I don't much care for. And you're not the only one who can sneak into my dreams. That four-legged fellow upstairs, on his blanket: he's also been known to do it! And it's more than likely he would have been with me, too, if he wasn't physically exhausted and stuffed to the gills with food! What I'm trying to say: surely I'm allowed a degree of privacy? Surely there are dreams I should be able to dream alone? Curiosity aside, we have a word for people who—"

"I know, so don't say it!" She stopped him. "I'm no sleazy voyeur, Scott! But being telepathic—having always been telepathic—I view dreams differently and understand that they're not simply subconscious wish fulfillment. I would think that has to be obvious, for if that was all they were there'd be no such thing as a nightmare! No one would wish *that* on himself. As for this latest dream: your sleep was so disturbed, and you were so restless—tossing, turning, and mumbling—that I was afraid for you. I knew it must be something very unusual, perhaps even dangerous, and I wanted to be with you. Just think, Scott. What if it had been the Mordris? I might have needed to wake you up, and Wolf, too, so that all three of us could erect our shields, fight them off."

Scott nodded. "All right, I accept that. So having entered you saw what you saw. But what was it that so excited you?"

"It was Shing't legend, thought by many to be sheer myth," she replied, her lovely eyes staring and her voice full of awe. "Or perhaps it was race memory from a time predating the Khiff. But in any case it was something out of our fragmentary Shing't history: an immemorially revered theology. Let me tell you what I know of it:

"In the beginning, after The All was created, The One who made everything watched His—or perhaps Hers? Or Its? But for the moment, for simplicity's sake, let's say His—watched His planets and peoples, life of every kind, develop. He was every-where, every-when, and for Him there was no distinction between space, time, the many levels and parallels. And He was so taken with what He'd made that He let Himself become absorbed into it, became part of it; call Him 'Nature' if you will. But before He was completely absorbed He became aware of evolution, mutation, and the rise of evil. Where there was intelligence, eventually, invariably, there would be evil. For as races as a whole strive to improve their lot, so individuals within those races work to improve theirs . . . which is how greed is born!

"Greed is born, and growing and thriving it spawns a longing for power; power spawns corruption; corruption spawns more evil . . . and so it goes. Alas, it is the nature of intelligence almost everywhere to spawn evil, so that perfection is impossible!

"And so, because The One was or was becoming 'Nature,' He saw that He must place restrictions on this evolutionary mutation of intelligence into evil; and He was saddened by the fact that He Himself, 'Nature,' was the cause! But at the same time He was fascinated and wanted to see for Himself how the intelligences He had created would prosper. But since He intended to sleep down all the aeons, how then might He remain conscious of occurrences in The All?

"Well of course He couldn't . . . but perhaps others of His design could! And so while He was still able, He sought out in those early phases of The All certain burgeoning intelligences to imbue them with His essence. At the end of their life spans, and determined by the excellence of what they had achieved in life, they would only seem to die but would become *other:* His messengers, contacts, observers in The All. But He saw that as intelligences even these agents of His would be susceptible to change, to evolutionary mutation, to evil. And so while giving them purpose and almost infinite mobility, He restricted their knowledge, clouded their memories of prior existences, allowed only instinct to guide them: the instinct to work for the good of The All.

"As to their forms at the end of days: they would be many, but some of the chosen would become as myriad golden darts! And now you see why I am so excited; the magic that I feel, and the wonder. For you have just such a dart, Scott!"

And so do I, said the third member of their Three Unit as he padded silently into the room. *But why are you up and about? It's still night, still dark outside. My time more than yours.*

"We're talking," Scott told him as Wolf lay down on a rug under his desk. "There are things we had to talk about. You can listen in if you wish."

"And," said Shania, "if you feel you have something to add to what we're talking about, by all means tell us."

Scott glanced at her questioningly.

"He has a dart!" she said. "Haven't you been listening?"

"What?" said Scott. "To myths and legends? Okay, now listen to me. My people—my world's *peoples*—have many of their own theologies. And they're all different! They all have divine visitations, magical resurrections, incredible revelations. And their various 'truths' are all sworn by, and their laws more or less adhered to by their priests and advocates alike, according to whichever religion they espouse. But, Shania, they can't each and every one be right! And logically if most or maybe even all of them are wrong, how am I to put my faith in *your* theology? I don't have that much faith anyway, and you're not even of—"

"Of your world?" Shania shook her head, in seeming disappointment. "Sometimes I feel you argue like the Mordri Three, or perhaps for the sake of it, or because you always demand proof. Scott, I hate to hurt your feelings, but you think on too small a scale. The Mordris have argued: if there was just one supreme being, one creator, *The* One, then how is it that every intelligent, theologically inclined race—be it of an animal, insect, fungus, or whatever other variety or species—how is it that all of them, on all the worlds which they inhabit, insist that they alone were created in His image? That is one of the principal reasons why the Mordri Three cannot accept a Universal One—or any deity, for that matter. But universal? Even that gives a false impression, for He was *multi*versal!"

Scott threw up his hands. "But we're arguing about a dream, for Christ's sake!"

At which, reminding Scott of something that Harry had said in that very dream, "Not at all unlikely," said Shania. "Or for *Someone's* sake, most certainly! That was your theology speaking, Scott, which I'm sure is as good as anyone else's. But the fantastic things your strange visitant told you, and the things he did: why, they were simply inspirational! Surely powers such as that could only be . . . yes, God-given!"

"It was a dream," Scott said again, almost as a last ditch protest. "Well, more than just any ordinary dream—I'll grant you that—but I was here in bed with you. I wasn't in a graveyard, wasn't in this . . . this 'Möbius Continuum' thing, whatever that's supposed to be. And I definitely wasn't shooting forward and backward in time. I was *here,* asleep in bed with you!" But:

Not all of the time, said Wolf, with his head up, his ears erect, his brown eyes going from one to the other of the two. *I felt a strange thing was happening—something in my own dreams told me it was happening—and I listened for you two. You were there, yes, in your den; my nose is good and I could smell you, the scent of your warm bodies. But your thoughts were somewhere else. I was worried; perhaps I even whined a little. But when I listened your hearts were beating and your bed made noises when you moved. I might have tried to follow your thoughts, wherever they had gone; but when I looked I saw only a vast nothingness, and whatever it was I didn't much care to explore it. While I'm not some cowardly, skittering dog with my tail between my legs, neither am I a fool! And so I went back to sleep, which seemed to me a very sensible thing to do. When next I woke up I heard your movements down here, and now—having come down to ensure that all is in order—I'm very happy to inform you that your thoughts are back where they should be . . .*

Shania stared at Wolf in astonishment, then offered Scott a different, more challenging expression.

"Well?" said Scott. "What? Some sort of out-of-body experience? Is that what you're thinking?"

She nodded. "That's how I would explain it, yes. Its purpose was to remove all the mystery—to show you why you are as you are—to fill in the remaining gaps in your knowledge, and to tell you that *your* purpose has been approved and you've been granted the powers to achieve it. And that's why I find it magical and wonderful, and why I now dare to hope. Scott, we have higher powers on our side!"

Scott believed her, sensed that she was right; at least he knew that *she* believed. And yet he still felt weighed down with seemingly unanswerable questions. "Higher powers?" he said. "On our side? Then why haven't they taken care of this themselves?"

That was something Shania couldn't answer, but she must at least try or Scott's partial acceptance might quickly evaporate. "Perhaps they're incapable of intervention. For as I've already tried to explain, The One ordained that his agents—in particular whatever remained of them, their *residua*—would never be capable of performing harmful acts, not even against the direst of evils. But while they themselves may not participate, it now seems obvious that they can enhance, guide, and influence their flesh-and-blood hosts. And as we've seen, for the time being at least you are just such a host. Yes, and Wolf, too!"

Scott shook his head, sighed, chewed his lip; but while he remained undecided about certain things, there were others that he couldn't deny. His, or his Three's telepathy; Shania and her Khiff; Kelly's death, and the fact that Simon Salcombe had murdered her; the sure knowledge that someone or thing had entered into him . . . if not for the reasons that Shania had given, then why? But of course there were other questions, such as:

"You say that in the legend The One gave his agents almost infinite mobility," said Scott. "In what form? The Möbius Continuum? And what of you with your . . . your localizer? What of the Shing't as a whole? Doesn't that make you—your entire race or what's left of it—doesn't it make you The One's agents, too?"

Shania shook her head. "The localizers are tools; they're machines, products of advanced technology, the *physical* science that the Mordri Three avow is the closest thing to Godhead. But the Möbius Continuum—what I saw of it— that is of the mind, Scott. It's *meta*-physical."

Scott nodded. "Metaphysical, yes. Paranormal: beyond logic and science and explanation, something from outside."

"Or from deep within." She nodded.

And finally he said, "If I'm to accept metaphysical—if I can believe in that, which it seems I must—then I must also believe in this other . . . *thing,* this deadspeak, and accept that it's real, too. And thinking back on it, it *was* so utterly real! I did believe—I *do* believe—that I spoke to my father, and to Kelly. And in that case you're absolutely right, Shania, and it is a very wonderful thing. But it's also terrifying!"

"Oh, yes," she answered, hugging closer yet to him, so that her shivering shook him also. "I know. And, Scott, given all the technology of the Shing't—with all of their entirely natural telepathic skills—no member of my race *ever* conceived or devised a means of communication with the dead! They might be able to induce a travesty of mindless, soulless life into dead flesh—though that in itself was an immemorially forbidden, heinous crime—but no one had ever spoken to souls who had passed on. And so I ask myself this: if you can cause the dead to speak to you, if they love you as their sole living contact with a world they've left behind and will do almost anything for you—"

"—Then what else can I ask them to do? But what else can they possibly do?"

In answer to which Shania said nothing at all; while under Scott's desk Wolf whined softly to himself, then curled himself into the tightest possible ball . . .

32

"So then," said Scott, "let's take a little time out and try to summarize all of this. What we believe is that because I have a motive—because I need to avenge my wife's murder—I've been chosen to wreak vengeance on Simon Salcombe and the Mordris?"

"Yes," said Shania. "You, me, and Wolf. But especially you two, who have become instruments of The One's residua."

"Okay," said Scott. "So you have your motive, and I've got mine . . . but Wolf? What's his motive? Why did he get a dart?"

Shania could only offer a helpless shrug; but Wolf himself came out from under Scott's desk, sat at their feet, and said:

Do I need a reason? As far as I know I'm only here to care for and protect you. He cocked his head at Scott. *And you, too, of course.* Now he looked at Shania. *You two, you are my One and my Two. And I am Three. We care for each other. My Two, Shania, connected me with my One, who brought me out of my misery to be with him. Now I'm no longer miserable but happy . . . yet I smell danger afar and I sense it coming closer, and so I'm needed. My only desire: to do what was done for me, to save and protect my One and my Two, my master and mistress. In that respect I shall follow in my wolf father's tracks and be satisfied to do so.*

Seeing Wolf's explanation as being both logical and reasonable, Scott reached out to scratch a lopsided, twitching ear and said, "Did we miss one? A flea, I mean?"

That seems likely. Wolf whined, sat back, and scratched at the same spot with a hind paw. *Several, I think. Perhaps we can get them later?*

"And as for this master and mistress thing," Scott continued, "do we have to do that? I mean, it's not as if you're some kind of ordinary, er, wolf, now is it? So why don't we just say we're friends?"

As you wish, said Wolf. *But still you're my One.*

Meanwhile, not at all satisfied with Wolf's explanation—far from it—Shania had remained thoughtfully silent. But now she said, "No, Wolf's reasoning isn't wholly acceptable. He has a dart! And there has to be a real reason."

Scott shrugged. "To make him a regular member of our Three Unit, maybe?"

"No." She shook her head. "He's already a regular member—as much as any of us—and I repeat: he has a dart. That can't be taken lightly, Scott. And even though we don't yet know what it is there *must* be something more, over and above his enhanced telepathy. That dart has given him real powers, be sure of it!"

Perhaps there is another reason, said Wolf, done with his scratching. *It could be in my blood.*

Shania stared hard at him and said, "Please explain."

My father, said the other, *was a wolf of the wild on Starside. So he told me when we spoke of this and that: of his life with men and wolves in far places, and of evil beings that came raiding in the night and lived on the blood of men and the good brave hearts of wolves. And he said that certain wolves of this far world were reared by men—they grew up and lived with men, and were their . . . their—*

"Watchdogs?" said Scott.

A term I dislike! said Wolf. *Watch-wolves is far more acceptable. Anyway, my father was gifted and could hear both dogs, wolves, and even certain men thinking. Zek—a woman from your world, whom you have met—was especially talented; she became my father's One; she could speak to him on his own terms as you speak to me! And they fought vampires together: Zek, my father, and a man called Harry who was . . . strange! He talked to people who were no more, passed on, and he called them up out of their places in the earth to fight alongside him. All of these things my father told me.*

So then, my father's blood—and his father's, and all of their forefathers' blood—it is in me. And as they fought evil so shall I. It is my lot. Perhaps this is why I got my dart . . .

Wide-eyed, Scott and Shania stared at Wolf, looked at each other, felt the utter weirdness of it all. At Wolf's mention of that name, "Harry," and when he'd spoken of what the Necroscope could do, their own blood had run cold. But if not a motive, at least there was a strong connection, and if the significance of Wolf's dart remained obscure, still it must surely exist.

Shania took Scott's face in her hands, kissed his brow, and said, "Any further doubts? Any more questions?"

"A million," he answered, "of both! But let it go. We have work to do and I'm damned if I know where to begin. Perhaps the only question that really matters right now is how much time we have? Is there any way to know?"

"Oh, yes," she answered. "There's a way to find out. But it could be very dangerous."

"Then tell me about it," he said. "For as long as Salcombe and his friends are alive I'm going to burn inside. Flames like that can consume a man, Shania, and for me there's only one way to douse them . . ."

Two days later in the Swiss Alps, in the high hollow crag known as Schloss Zonigen, the Mordris were once again together in the great workshop cavern where they had assembled their workforce. A certain uneven area of the floor had been cleared of all useful materials, and a protective screen of stanchions and carbon steel mesh had been erected between the huge cannon-like device and the cleared area.

Standing tall, slender as wands on the central stone dais, the Mordri Three faced outward; and more alien than ever, they no longer paid too much attention to their human disguises, nor even to correcting or controlling the occasionally erratic flux of their protean forms. And not a man or more rarely a woman of their human slaves harboured the slightest doubt about the Mordris' exotic origins, for it was now perfectly obvious to every one of them that they were not of this Earth. Well aware of the fact, the Mordris felt no concern; indeed, they now intended to "explain" almost everything to these captive souls, in order to give them renewed hope—however false—and so impel them to greater effort.

And there they stood on the central dais, their eyes scanning left and right, occasionally pausing to admire their hideous handiwork on the face or form of this or that member of the crowd, as armed guards and trustees trooped the last handful of workers into the great cavern.

Finally silence fell, and Mordri One, formerly "Frau Gerda Lessing," turned her eyes upward to that area of the high domed ceiling that was pierced through by shafts of exterior daylight. The scaffolding was empty of workmen now, and electrical cables snaked down from the roof to one side of the floor, where hard-hatted trustees stood by with handheld detonating devices. The scene was set . . . at least for this part of the act. Nodding her satisfaction, Mordri One returned her gaze to her audience, and at last spoke:

"Now listen to me," she commanded, her clipped tones echoing in the cavern's natural acoustics. "Listen, and perhaps you may understand me. You know, of course, that we are not of your primitive race, nor of this primitive planet. For some time now we have made little effort to hide this fact from you. Why not? Because knowing it will make it that much easier for you to believe what I'm now telling you. Also, you will see why you have laboured here, to what end, and will understand that the harder you work the sooner you will be set free and all put to rights. For there can be no doubt but that we have the ability to order all that we have made chaotic."

While she was speaking, "Simon Salcombe" and "Guyler Schweitzer" moved closer, flanking her, until all three Mordris now stood together facing in the same direction. Keeping watch, however, their familiar Khiffs had perched on the narrow shoulders of their kaftans, their little red eyes scanning in all directions, even covering the cleared area to the rear of the cavern, which lay directly beneath the primed, circular section of the ceiling.

"Very well," Mordri One continued. "Bear what I've said in mind—that all shall be put to rights—and I shall tell you how we three came to be here. We are travellers from a far star whose conveyance failed and broke on these mountainous peaks on this alien planet. The more important parts of our vessel which could be salvaged were brought here; they became vital elements in the construction of a new conveyance, as did you yourselves! For we must continue our journey, and there being only three of us even our great energies were insufficient to the task in the time allowed . . . for we must be gone in just four more days!"

Pausing, she glanced at her number Three, "Guyler Schweitzer," indicating that he should take up a tale that so far had been more or less true: for instance, the failure of their gravity vessel. What Mordri One hadn't mentioned, however, was that far from being castaways here, the Earth had been their target.

Now Mordri Three's sickly mother-of-pearl teeth glinted in a salivating smile; he waved a long arm expansively, if erratically, as if to encompass the crowded mass of sometimes freakish faces before him. And his voice when it came was resonate, booming:

"Our vehicle is now in the final stage of reconstruction," he said, with a second flourish of his long-fingered hand, this time indicating the great metal cylinder where it was seated in its cradle, inclined at an angle toward the explosively charged section of the ceiling, "while as yet our exit from this cavern remains sealed. That, however, is very easily remedied. And now we shall test the accuracy of those who placed the charges."

A third wave of Schweitzer's hand was the instruction that the trustees in the hard hats had been waiting for. One of them shot a hand into the air, almost a salute, while others pressed buttons on their remotes to cause a series of sharp, near-simultaneous gunshot detonations in the ceiling.

Dust and other small particles of stony debris jetted from the circle of drilled holes, obscuring what little daylight had gained entry through other holes where charges had been thought unnecessary. And like a titan plug yanked from its hole a great cylinder of rock slid inward at an angle, crumbling as it came, emerging in shards and fragments from the ceiling, and crashing down onto the cleared area. The sound was thunderous, reverberating, and the cavern shuddered as a billowing wall of dust rose up and chunks of rotten rock large and small bounded, clanging and clattering against the carbon steel barrier before tumbling to the floor on the far side of that protective screen.

For several long moments the thunder of the fall continued to echo; then as the rumbling gradually faded, a circular shaft of light all of twelve feet across blazed through the swirling, thinning dust cloud where the ceiling had been cut through. And its clean ray fell directly on the metallic bulk of the cylindrical vehicle on its ramp.

Meanwhile Mordri Two, called Simon Salcombe, had come down from the dais. He loomed tall where he stalked, apparently idly at first, through the fearful ranks of human slaves. For now it was his turn—time for the second act— when he would find a way to urge or "inspire" these workers to greater, and to truer efforts.

"Now see!" he called shrilly, drawing the attention of any who still peered upward through drifting dust into the morning light. And with all eyes turned to him, he continued. "See what can be achieved when your work is unstinting and . . . *unspoiled*." The last word was delivered with an especially threatening emphasis. "But what a shame," he went on, "that in other areas your work has been . . . so much *less* than satisfactory; and, indeed, that it would have failed—or would have been *caused* to fail—so miserably and so drastically!"

Mordri Two moved with more purpose now, nodding to himself, picking or even pecking his way through the workforce like some strange, agitated bird or insect. He was searching for someone, turning left and right, thrusting his angular, phasmid features first into one man's startled, gasping face, then into another. And not all of these faces were as they should be; neither the faces nor the forms of any who had suffered the mutative touch of the Mordris. Instead they wore the nightmarish masks and the warped limbs of deliberate deformity—like the man whose lips had frozen into smiling lumps on his left cheek, and whose nose had been repositioned between his eyes, leaving twin pits wetly gaping where sinus passages were laid bare . . . or the scientist whose eyes stuck out on crimson two-inch stalks, so that he was obliged to protect them behind goggles . . . or the labourer whose right arm was only half the length of his left, and which ended in a hand that was fused into a club.

But now Salcombe went more surely, until at last he

jerked to a halt midway down the row of electrical work-benches. There, thrusting with his face, he cried, "Aha! And what have we here?" For he had found the one he sought, whose location he had known all along.

It was Hans Niewohner, once of Niewohner Electrics, but he was *not* the same would-be escapee whom "Direktor" Gunter Ganzer had spoken to so very recently. For now he was a gaunt, hollow-eyed spectre of that man, whose mouth had been sealed over with living flesh as if it was never there in the first place, whose nose was a flattened ridge lacking nostrils, and who managed to breathe only gaspingly through the puckered, half-inch blowhole in his fluttering right cheek!

Cringing, almost falling to his knees, Niewohner clung to the workbench with a white-knuckled hand as Salcombe pointed a long, quivering finger at him, slowly arched his pipestem frame over him, and thrust his own insect features down into the hideously transformed face of his victim. And:

"You!" hissed Mordri Two, silvery slime dripping from his curling lower lip. "*You,* given your position of some importance here, only to abuse it!" Straightening up, he looked at the other workers close by; they at once backed off, made room. And speaking to them, Salcombe said, "Now let me list this . . . this treacherous *creature's* criminal deficiencies. Since his arrival here—since first we, er, made him welcome—he has spoken to others of his desire to desert us. Such conversations were overheard, of course, and our leader, known to you as Frau Lessing, found it necessary to reprimand him. Her touch was delicate; no great damage was done; nothing that could not be repaired if he repented and gave of his all. But look, see here . . ."

Hooking a crooked finger in Niewohner's blowhole and drawing him upright, Salcombe looked this way and that, making sure that everyone in the vicinity could see. "Frau Lessing's lesson went all unlearned, wasted, to no avail. She left him this hole to suck at the air—she let him live, to complete his work—the ungrateful wretch! Perhaps it were better if she had sealed his entire face, and so put an end to him. *Bah!* For what did he do but seek revenge for what he must have considered an injustice! What? The Mordri Three, unjust? How completely ridiculous! Oh, ha-ha!" Mordri Two "laughed," but briefly, then sobered and went on. "As for the shape, the design of his intended revenge, his treachery: it was sabotage!"

Releasing the gasping, writhing Niewohner, Salcombe thrust him back against the bench, and continued: "With no thought for his fellow workers, and certainly none for myself and my Mordri colleagues, this *animal* deliberately sabotaged these capacitors. And not just one but two dozen of them!" He snatched a complicated instrument from the bench and hurled it down to the floor. "What? Did he think—did any of you think—that it would not be discovered?" Jerking his head this way and that, looking all about as if searching for an answer, Mordri Two was now plainly insane, made more so by the fact that no answer was forthcoming; and the many members of the electrical team backed away farther yet, well out of his range.

"Hah!" Salcombe snapped at them. "But just as he set about to destroy us, so he would have destroyed you! For if these instruments had failed us that failure would have created a great disaster throughout all Schloss Zonigen, and none of you in the hour of your freedom—with your families returned unharmed to you, and the changes we have wrought reversed—*not one of you would have lived through it!* And all that we have achieved here gone for nothing."

He turned back to the cringing Niewohner, clasped his face in both hands, and went on: "Very well, and now I shall tell you how it's going to be, Hans Niewohner. You have three hours, you and your crew at these benches . . . three hours to put right what you have put wrong. Then we test the capacitors again. And only let us find that your work is unsatisfactory, in any way deficient—then it's the black disc for you, *and* for half of your workforce! Yes, and the ones who pay the price shall be chosen at random."

Again Mordri Two thrust Niewohner stumbling away, and without looking back returned to the dais. Behind him nothing stirred; everything remained silent, static, frozen—for perhaps a count of five. And then an eruption of activity, as frantic men collided, caroming off one another in a sudden, desperate rush to the workbenches.

And Hans Niewohner's tears of hatred, loathing, impotence, washed his face where lips might once have tasted them, and he fell to his knees, crying out to a God who seemingly had deserted him and every other human being in this terrible place. But he cried silently, of course, for as well as his visible mutilations Frau Gerda Lessing's touch had welded the tip of Hans's tongue to the roof of his mouth . . .

33

Two days later, about 2:00 P.M., Ben Trask and his team of five ESPers and two techs were somewhere over France on their way to Lugano in Switzerland. Travelling standard class in a Swiss Air jet, they were ostensibly a party of amateur botanists, destination the Lepontine Alps and pre-booked rooms at a small chalet hotel in Idossola, an allegedly picture-postcard village of one hundred seventy-seven souls in a beautiful valley under the mountains. From Lugano their route would be north in two rented cars, then east following the shore of the lake itself, finally north again, along steep, narrow, precipitous zigzag roads into the heights . . . and into whatever else lay ahead. For Idossola, picture-postcard pretty or not, lay in the shadow of that freak of nature, that jutting, permanently frozen spur known locally as Schloss Zonigen.

Looking down from his window through wisps of summer cloud onto sun-dappled countryside all of thirty thousand feet below, Trask's eyes were half-shuttered against the sporadic, dazzling flashes of sunlight reflected from the silvery hairline threads of rivers where they wandered through

patchwork fields and disappeared into a hazy distance. A
perfect summer day, with never the slightest hint of a threat;
to all intents and purposes the world seemed an entirely safe
place . . . or perhaps not *entirely* safe, for Trask had never
much cared for flying.

Turning his head he looked at Ian Goodly seated beside
him. The precog was poring over a large-scale map of the
Lepontines, and Trask inquired, "Aren't the details too
small to be of use? Large in scale, small in detail—you
know what I mean?"

Goodly nodded, folded the map, and put it away in his
briefcase. "I was trying to memorize the names and directions of the villages and towns in the neighbourhood of
Idossola, that's all. If we have to get out of there fast, it
might be—"

"It *would* be a good idea to know where we're going,"
Trask anticipated him. "And you think we may need to get
out of there fast? But in the event of the sort of disaster
you've been talking about, what would be the point? What
I'm asking: what's the good of scrambling for the barn if
someone is dropping nukes on the outhouse?"

"Well," said the other, shifting uncomfortably in his
seat—which might or might not be because with his height
and long legs he *was* uncomfortable—"well, I had a word
with Anna Marie English before we left, and she's no
longer sure about things."

"Things?" said Trask, turning more fully toward Goodly
and taking a lot more interest. "What things specifically?
This Big Bang you've both been forecasting? So what are
you saying, that it isn't going to happen? And if so, why the
hell have you left it till now to tell me?"

The precog looked at Trask and looked away, then offered an odd little grimace and half shook his head. And
Trask didn't need to know the truth of things to be aware
that his friend of so many strange years and even stranger
adventures was suddenly uncertain.

"Well?" he said. "Is it or isn't it? Take your best shot."

And finally: "Oh, it will happen," Goodly answered. "I

can assure you of that. It's just that . . . that I haven't *seen* it!"

Now it was Trask's turn to frown, and he was getting angry. "But didn't you tell me—you and Anna Marie both—didn't you assure me you'd experienced it and that it was something devastating?"

The precog nodded, shrugged apologetically, and said, "But isn't that just it? Hearing a sound in a dark, unfamiliar room, we can experience fear without knowing what made the sound. And that's about the best analogy I can offer. I've never *seen* this—this convulsion, whatever it is—but I have experienced it, sensed it, *felt* it. And so has Anna Marie, through me. But now, well, now she's no longer sure."

"So what made her change her mind?" But a lot of the heat had gone out of Trask's voice now. Getting mad at someone whose talent was as freakish as Ian Goodly's wouldn't benefit anyone. For after all, it was a long accepted fact that the future was a devious thing. On the other hand, however, Trask's own weird talent told him that the precog hadn't told him everything. He wasn't "lying" as such; it was simply the absence of the truth in its entirety. And so:

"Let me guess," Trask growled. "You were playing at young lovers again; Anna Marie held your hand; you tried to scan the future, and she saw . . . what?"

Goodly smiled a wry little smile, and answered, "If I may quote several American action heroes: 'Damn, you're good!' Yes, we gave it one last try, and for me the chaos was still there, unchanged, precisely as before. But as for Anna Marie, she saw . . . a continuation—"

Trask breathed a sigh of relief, until the precog went on: "—of sorts."

"Explain."

"Well, as you know, she's an ecopath—*the* ecopath—and her concerns are for the Earth. She experienced, she felt, *the Earth* going on! Which of course it will. But that doesn't mean that we'll go with it. The reason I haven't mentioned it until now is because it really doesn't change anything."

Trask sat back and for a moment was silent. Then he said, "You know something? You may be an old friend, but sometimes I don't much like talking to you at all . . ."

Trask used the toilet at the front of the plane and on his way back to his seat looked into the faces of his team. He tried to appear cool, calm, collected—while in fact feeling nothing of the sort. If anything he felt confused.

The techs, Alan McGrath and Graham Taylor, however disparate in appearance, were seated together. The former was a redheaded, rough and ready Scotsman from Edinburgh. Only five feet seven in height, but strong and sturdily proportioned, McGrath was in his early forties. An ex-Ordnance Corps weapons instructor turned computer buff, he'd worked in the field on previous occasions and was wholly reliable. His partner, Graham Taylor, was in his late thirties; tall, spare, and wearing spectacles, his appearance didn't at all do his abilities justice. For one thing his glasses were a front: while they loaned him the fragile, intellectual look he desired, their "lenses" were of clear glass with no optical properties whatever. And for all that he was relatively new to E-Branch, he was top of the range in his specialist subjects. Like McGrath he was ex-army. Intelligence Corps trained in strategy, subterfuge (propaganda), demolition, and espionage in general, he had worked for five years with the British Military Mission (BRIXMIS) out of Berlin into East Germany, and so spoke fluent German. Both men were marksmen with the stripped-down, easily assembled crossbows that were stowed away in their suitcases.

Trask nodded at the pair as he passed them down the narrow aisle, and thought, *Crossbows: the only weapons we're carrying this time out. Remarkable how quickly they've become essential items in our armoury since the Necroscope's time.* But actually it wasn't at all remarkable. A crossbow loaded with a hardwood bolt may make an excellent weapon against vampires—and in the not so distant past there'd been plenty of use against such as them—but it will kill a man just as easily, and silently, too.

As for why they weren't carrying guns: Trask thought back on the last briefing he had given, the startled looks he'd seen on the faces of the team when he told them, "Weapons: we're not taking any." And then he'd given the reason. "We'll get guns in Switzerland, if or when the Swiss antiterrorism squad think we need them. So *if* we get them they'll be Swiss weapons—no 9mm Brownings on offer this time, that's for sure—but stoppers I guarantee. The Swiss are a pretty sensitive lot; they won't let us bring lethal automatic weapons into their backyard. I can't say I blame them. So you might want to familiarize yourselves, get up to scratch, on whatever Swiss artillery our techs have managed to lay their hands on . . ."

Later at that same briefing, the telepath Paul Garvey had asked, "Just when will we get to meet these Swiss specials, and how much of a say will they have? Or will we be as self-reliant and independent as usual?"

"We'll be meeting our Swiss counterparts at the Gasthaus Alpenmann," Trask had answered. "They will be 'tourists,' who just happen to be staying there, too. Whatever their plans are we'll agree to them, but if or when it becomes necessary—if our own intelligence, our gadgets and ghosts, tell us otherwise—then we'll go our own sweet way."

Turning these things over in his mind, Trask was even now making his way past Paul Garvey where he sat in an aisle seat. The telepath was "listening," however, and caught at his elbow. Trask paused and bent to hear what the other had to say.

"Couldn't help but, er, 'overhear you,'" said Garvey. "But, boss, you never did tell us how you managed to get the Swiss to cooperate in all this in the first place."

Keeping his voice low, Trask answered, "It was our Minister Responsible. Working to my brief, and without demanding to know too much, he got in touch with an old school chum from his days at Oxford, someone big in Internal Security over there. He made mention of just four things: inexplicable disappearances; grisly murders; nuclear terrorism—because that's not impossible—and very large amounts of gold. Of these the first three were passé, apparently. But as for gold: well, that never goes out of style, and certainly not in Switzerland! To be fair and unbiased, however, the Swiss authorities have been more than a little interested in Schloss Zonigen for quite a while now. So this was all the spur they needed. Anyway that was our in, and for once we have the Minister Responsible to thank for it."

With a nod of acknowledgment to Millicent Cleary, who was seated beside Garvey, Trask straightened and continued down the aisle. He glanced back once at the girl, whose eyes were still following him, and forced a smile. Millie: an intelligent, very attractive young telepath whose talent had matured rapidly over the past six months to a year. While he'd always thought of her and treated her like a kid sister, Trask occasionally suspected she might have a "thing" for him. But while his talent told him this was so, it was also possible that he was projecting a "big brother" or "fatherly" image, and that this was what attracted her.

And moving on down the aisle he thought, *Why, you poor old bastard!* if only to himself. But still it was a fact that whenever Trask got himself involved in fieldwork and needed volunteers, Millie was usually the first to stick her hand up . . .

Two rows in front of Goodly's aisle seat, David Chung was seated beside Frank Robinson, a spotter. Robinson was "psychic sensitive"—his talent instantly identified other psychically endowed people whenever he came into close proximity with them. Only twenty-six years old, still Robinson's jet-black hair was striped with sharply contrasting shocks of pure white, a premature blanching that wasn't entirely natural. Ben Trask had been there when Robinson had got those white shocks; indeed he, too, had had a "shocking" time of it, the night that he and Robinson and other members of E-Branch had tried to kill the Necroscope, Harry Keogh. That had been the spotter's first real experience of work in the field; Schloss Zonigen would be his second, and Trask wondered how Robinson felt about that.

And so, leaning across Chung, he spoke to him. "Frank, any problems? Are you okay?"

"For now? I think so." The other nodded. Then, having seen Trask looking at his hair, he added, "Anyway what have I got to lose? If the rest of it goes white at least it'll match up!"

And Trask moved on, thinking: *At a time like this, humour! It's just as I always suspected: I'm not the only madman in the Branch after all! So this time around it'll be lunatics against lunatics!*

And as Goodly stood up to let him into his window seat, he said, "You know, this has to be the strangest thing we ever got ourselves involved in?"

"I know," said the precog, squeezing himself into his seat again. "Principally because we still don't know what we're dealing with. What we do know is that an alpine ice cavern houses a very real threat to the entire planet in the shape of a trio of ruthless, probably psychotic individuals commanding ESP talents that may rival and even surpass all of our skills put together. And that three similarly talented, er, beings—*not* members of E-Branch, we should be so lucky—look all set to go up against our mutual enemies. Unable to announce our availability and our intentions to these last mentioned, however, and having no official contact with them, we haven't been in a position to offer our advice and assistance. And the most frustrating thing about all this is that they probably know a hell of a lot more about what's going on than we do!"

"In a nutshell, yes," said Trask. "We might have contacted them earlier, but—"

"I know," said Goodly. "And it's possible I was wrong. But let's face it, would you really want to risk my being right? We *have* done the right thing, Ben! And no matter the route we took to get this far—whether we might have done this, that, or the other—our lives are and will be in jeopardy until this thing has resolved itself one way or the other. That's the way I saw it, and that's how it is and will be."

Trask nodded and said, "I'm sure you're right. And anyway, whatever we might have done was way back then, and all of those possible futures are now the past. Am I making sense? . . . Never mind! But if these crazy people *are* going to bring about a vast explosion, eruption, or whatever, it means that our job will be . . . well, let's be totally honest about it: it will be to limit the death and destruction as best possible, or to die trying!"

"*And* to die trying!" said Goodly, logically. "That is, if they do manage to bring it off."

"But there's a chance we can stop them?"

"Ben, how can I answer that?" said the precog. "Anna Marie says the world will go on, and that's as much as I know. But if we *can* stop these people—"

"Then that's all there is to it," said Trask. "And it's as simple as that—the bottom line—them or us."

"Yes," Goodly answered. "Except I have this feeling there isn't going to be anything simple about it. No, not at all . . ."

That same afternoon, at Scott St. John's place in the suburbs of London, he and Shania—and not forgetting Wolf, who was still busy exploring every corner of the house, and marking out territory in the gardens—had finally come downstairs and were now trying to wake up in Scott's study. There they drank coffee and finalized their plan, covering any last points that they hadn't yet found time to discuss.

They had stayed up very late last night, as usual, and had seen little reason to get up early this morning. Still catching up on months of poor sleep, Scott had been badly in need of it; and nestled in Shania's arms, sated with their lovemaking, his dreams for once had been sweet and her presence healing—literally!

This time Shania, more than Scott, had felt anxious to be up and about their business; but there was very little more to be done before making their initial assault on the Mordris, and she had been loath to disturb him . . . or so she excused herself. But to be completely honest, Shania had also loved simply resting there beside him: the warmth of his fine body against hers, and the slow surge if she touched him in a certain place . . .

At the moment the topic of conversation was Shania's localizer; she was plainly worried about it, and Scott wasn't at all happy about the fate of a gold ring with a cat's-eye stone that his mother had left him . . . just about *all* she'd left him, apart from her love. For right now the ring was gold no longer.

They had left the ring on Scott's desk in a drinking mug, Scotch-taped to the localizer overnight. And now, tipped carefully out onto a page torn from a newspaper, the localizer was as before—for all the world a silver bangle, or some kind of fancy, art nouveau wristlet watch—but the ring had been converted into a small heap of blue-grey grit, in which the cat's-eye stone, still intact, lay half buried.

"I had it valued once," said Scott, sipping from another mug, this one half full of fresh, hot coffee. "That was a long time ago when I was broke. The value of the gold in it was one hundred and twenty pounds sterling. Now it's dust!"

"But I know it's not the money," said Shania, regretfully. "Perhaps we should have gone out and bought something in gold?"

"But that *would* have been money," said Scott. "The money I don't have."

"I could have got money," she told him.

He gave her a hug and said, "Don't worry about it." Then, jokingly: "What, you'd have used what little power was left in the localizer to break into a bank or something?"

She looked surprised, shrugged, and answered, "Well yes, or any other place where they keep money. Or better still, a jeweller's shop with golden trinkets!" Then, seeing Scott blink, the sudden change in his expression, she continued. "Scott, how did you think I survived when first I got here? I had only my clothing and the localizer, and even my clothes weren't at all suitable. There were so very many difficulties at first, but after I found out about money most of them went away."

Scott closed his mouth, shook his head, and laughed. "What? You're a thief?"

"I had to be!" She tilted her chin at him.

"You used your localizer like some kind of—I don't know—like the proverbial philosopher's stone, only in reverse, to turn gold into paper? Paper money?"

"I used it like the proverbial what?"

"I'll tell you some other time," he said. And then, picking the cat's-eye stone out of the gritty grey dust: "So that's where you get this instantaneous travel thing, eh? Your devices are powered by gold. It explains quite a lot."

"No," said Shania, shaking her head. "It isn't instantaneous. It's a great many times faster than light, yes, but it has its limits. Nothing is instantaneous, Scott."

At which Scott frowned, for he was sure that something was . . . just a thought that came and went almost "instantaneously."

"Still," he said, "FTL or whatever, this is some fantastic technology your people developed."

"I'm not very good at the science part of it," said Shania. "I just know how to work it, not how it works. It has something to do with the precise weight of gold. The, er, battery?—the device storing gravitic power in the localizer—leeches energy from gold, which is later expended with use. The purest form of gold, found in plenty on the worlds and moons of the Shing system, meant an inexhaustible supply. But here on your world, on Earth—"

"It's expensive stuff," said Scott. "So tell me, how much energy has your localizer, er, 'leeched' from the ring? Do you have any way of knowing?"

"No, but my Khiff does. Born in gravity wells, the Khiffs are . . . they're as 'familiar' with this energy as you are with air or water."

"But I can't live without air and water," said Scott.

"Nor can my Khiff without my localizer. When she needs it, then she draws energy from it, but in such small amounts as to make no difference. Khiff . . . ?" It was as if Shania spoke to no one. But someone, or thing, answered:

Yes, my Shania? Am I required? The "voice" was softer and sweeter in Scott's mind than any he'd ever heard with his ears.

Shania answered without speaking, and Scott heard what she said. But that at least was something he'd grown used to. Then Shania held the localizer to her brow, shuttered her eyes, and stayed perfectly still. And a moment later:

Ahhh! said her Khiff; or, more properly, Scott "sensed" a sigh of pleasure, of relief. *My thanks, Shania. And the answer to your question: the localizer is low on power. One long trip perhaps—for just one person—and one return, and that will be all. Also, and as you know, the localizer is damaged. Even a small additional input might well cause a total malfunction. No more gold, Shania, or you lose it entirely.*

"And after this last return trip, what then? I mean, what about you, Khiff?" Shania's anxiety was very obvious.

While the localizer will be of no use for further travel, it should nevertheless last me your entire lifetime, my Shania.

"Your lifetime?" Scott was puzzled.

Shania took the localizer from her brow and explained, "My lifetime is also my Khiff's lifetime. We're like one in so many ways, grown that way with time. But I was born as one and I can live as one if I have to. She, however, only came into sentient being when she came to me. And without me—"

"She would die?"

"They don't exactly die," said Shania. "They're like . . . I don't know how to express it."

Scott nodded. "I think I know what you mean. Like old soldiers, eh? They never die, they only fade away."

"Your pardon?"

"Never mind," said Scott.

"But I think I know what *you* mean," she said. "And you are right. Like those who have passed beyond—like your father and Kelly—the Khiff find another place and perhaps another One. I really don't know. No one does."

Scott stirred the remains of his ring with a finger. "This is what happened to your world," he said. "The power of a giant leap across the light-years reduced Shing to dust."

But again she said, "No, that's not quite correct. A vast amount of gold was reduced to this residue, but Shing was destroyed by surplus energy. The Mordris didn't have to use so much gold; they did so deliberately, close enough to the Shing system to reduce it to ashes!"

"An entire star system?" Scott could scarcely imagine such a catastrophe.

"Oh, yes." Shania nodded. "I saw it. Returning to Shing, I was still far enough away to survive it."

"It seems unbelievable."

"Oh, you can believe it, Scott," she replied. "And in fact you can see it for yourself, if you so desire."

"See it? How?"

"My Khiff holds the key to my memories. They can be yours, too. Not all of them, but this one is readily available. It is in my mind—I could even show it to you myself—but my Khiff remembers it far better, because I would rather not."

Scott considered it for a moment or two, then said, "Maybe it's time I got to meet your Khiff face-to-face, only this time while I'm awake. Okay, so how do we go about it?"

"Hold me, and kiss me." Shania drew him to the couch. "And my Khiff will do the rest . . ."

34

Drawing Shania closer, Scott held her, kissing her tentatively at first, and then more fully. But even as his senses swirled, in the middle of the embrace, so he glanced this way and that, not so much apprehensive as curious, and perhaps just a little nervous.

Close your eyes, Shania told him, with their mouths still locked. *It's only her appearance that is strange to you. But I*

*promise you'll scarcely feel her or know she's there at all—
at most a vague but pleasant sensation of duality—until she
speaks to you.*

And Scott answered in the same fashion: *But I don't want
to insult her. What, I should close my eyes, like I can't bear
to look at her? I mean, she isn't ugly, is she?*

Something moved to the right of Shania's face, on the
very periphery of Scott's vision. It was pink; it seemed
gaseous but yet was opaque; it had small, piercing green
eyes and the semblance of a mouth that seemed to smile
precociously, even coquettishly. Scott didn't close his eyes,
and he couldn't look away. The Khiff's balloon-like "body"
elongated; continuing to smile, its face passed from view as
its matter formed an almost immaterial bridge or conduit
between Shania's right ear and Scott's left. And he thought:

Damn! The thing came out of her head, her ear!

Yes, said Shania's Khiff. *I am a thing. And so are you. So
is every-thing. But I understand, and I am not insulted.*

That soft, sweet voice; like that of a beautiful child but
knowing, intelligent . . . persuasive and yet pure.

Shania's Khiff knew his thoughts, and as Scott sensed its
presence in his head, it said: *I thank you, Scott! And now
you are three.*

The kiss was over, but Scott and Shania remained clinging together. And because it came more natural to him,
Scott queried the Khiff out loud: "Now I am three? You
mean you, me, and Shania?"

Ah, no. With Shania you are four.

"What, Wolf? You mean Wolf?"

*No, you fail to understand. You as an individual are more
than one. You have been that way for some time. I feel the
essence of another in you. Therefore, with me within your
mind, we—you and I—are now more than two.*

"Another within me?" said Scott, momentarily puzzled.
But then: "Ah! Now I understand. You mean my dart. Well
at least it was *part* of another."

An important part, said the Khiff, *for you have his pow-*

ers. I was with you, and with my Shania, in that dream that was more than a dream when he reminded you of his powers . . . your powers now.

"Yes," said Scott wryly, "one of which I don't understand, and another that I'm not sure I want to understand!"

But still they are there—the nod of an incorporeal, even insubstantial head—*waiting to be called upon.*

"And what of your powers?" said Scott. "Shania has told me you store memories, keeping them fresh, and that you can remember things better than even Shania herself."

Which is why I am here, said the Khiff. *And ahhh! You wish to see a very terrible thing!*

"The death of the Shing system, yes. It's just that I want to know what we're up against."

A necessary part of your preparations, of course. And yes, I can show you. Now you may close your eyes without fear of insulting me. You'll see better when there is nothing to distract you.

Scott closed his eyes—and immediately, without a single moment's pause, it was as if he drifted in deepest space! Star-shot black velvet, with the closest planetary systems drifting by like so much foam along the sides of a slow ship. Except he knew that Shania's vessel had been anything but slow!

Oh, fast! Very fast! said the Khiff. *And yet at this point we were indeed moving "slowly"—because this was when we were approaching Shing. There ahead, that ancient golden star, with its precious worlds: the Shing system, yes . . .*

They were even now "drifting" past the outermost planet—a gas giant with many red-spot whirlpools, a ring like Saturn's, and seven moons in disparate orbits—but Shing the sun was as yet far distant. *We can move in closer,* said the Khiff. *Indeed, we did move in closer, on the farscry. I remember it well.* And Scott found that he was inside a ship of sorts, looking through a porthole. And he saw a hand, or a slender appendage very like a human hand—in fact, Shania's hand as it had been—reaching to adjust a control . . . at which he saw that his porthole was a view-screen, in which the inner Shing system suddenly sprang up that much closer.

Shing was a blue world similar to Earth but ancient beyond words, whose moon stood off far distant, golden and uncratered. The surface of the planet was all of four-fifths water, a single shallow ocean laving the shores of three great green continents, whose mountains had been rounded by the ages and in many places worn down to little more than hills. Away from Shing the star, on Shing the planet's night side, its cities blazed like diamond incrustations: twinkling patches of white fire, webbed together in the darkness of a sleeping world.

I showed you Yamp, the gas giant on the system's rim, the Khiff whispered, so as not to disturb Scott's thoughts, *and now you see Shing . . . as it used to be and as Shania saw it. Inward lies another world: small, steamy Zull; hot and untenable, with acid lakes and swamps. There, see?*

In the far distance, in toward the sun, Zull was a ball of swirling cloud, of small interest to Scott. And beyond Zull the sun itself, Shing: a great silver orb blazing with nuclear heat still, but by no means as hot as Sol.

Shing the star would have died eventually, of her own accord, said the Khiff. *Alas that she wasn't given the chance, and her billions of remaining years all stolen in a single moment's madness.*

The view-screen reverted to Shing the planet, then changed again to show the gas giant Yamp passing to stern. *And this was where we were,* said the Khiff, *when our sensors detected a vast gravitic disturbance and our alarm system warned us to turn and flee! A ship was leeching on Yamp's innermost moon, a satellite heavy in gold—and it was using* the entire mass *for its propulsive purposes!*

Scott saw a beam of white light, thin as a pencil, reaching from deep space past the debris of Yamp's rings to a small moon that was speeding across the gas giant's mottled disc.

Shania saw the same thing, said the Khiff, *for these are her memories. And of course I saw it through Shania. We traced the beam telepathically—and so heard the crazed*

*laughter of the Mordri Three! But that is something I do not
wish to remember for you, and not even for myself!*

The scene in the view-screen spun through one hundred
eighty degrees; Scott felt momentarily dizzy, and Shania's
arms tightened around him. But now the stars were literally
hurtling past her ship; in another moment they blurred into
nothingness and were gone, and there was only an opaque
grey mistiness.

Gravity drive, said the Khiff. *But even at this speed, a
speed beyond imagination, still we were fortunate to escape
the effect of what the Mordris had done. Indeed, it was felt
in all the levels of space and time! Scientists on Earth many
billions of light-years away have yet to feel it. But
eventually—and if your world is still here, and if it still has
scientists all those billions of years from now—they may yet
record it as an immense burst of gamma radiation!*

Such concepts were stupefying in their magnitude;
Scott's mind whirled; but as yet he still hadn't actually witnessed the destruction of the Shing system.

"Hearing" his thoughts, Shania's Khiff sighed and answered him: *Well, if you must, then you must. So be it. This
is what my Shania saw:*

Out there in deep space, perhaps a whole light-year beyond
the Shing system, the Mordri ship issued its FTL converter
beam at Yamp's innermost moonlet. The beam served a dual
purpose; on the one hand reducing that gold-heavy satellite to
stony rubble and blue-grey grit, and on the other drawing energy released in the conversion back to the Mordri ship to
power its flight. But the ship required only a tiny fraction of
the converted energy, while the rest must expend itself elsewhere. Which it did.

Racing away from that vast wrenching, that gigantic
space-time spasm, Shania's ship was caught in its outermost
flux and dragged out of gravity drive. Spun end over end in
the massive shock wave, the ship's automatic stabilizer
came into play and likewise the view-screen—which flickered in fact into replay—letting Shania, and now Scott, witness what had happened to the Shing system.

On the screen:

The region where Yamp's moon had been was the center of an awesome, blinding, expanding sphere of brilliant light; but the moon itself was no longer there! Atomised, it was the fuel of a nuclear fire that was hotter than the ancient sun itself. Yamp, the gas giant, was hit like a bubble in a firestorm, evaporating in a moment. But that was only the beginning . . .

Other than the things Scott had learned in various discussions with Shania, he wasn't at all ignorant of science and its theories of space and time. Now he remembered reading in a popular scientific journal something about the so-called Big Bang, the beginning of the universe, and recalled that there had been a theoretical period of FTL expansion called "inflation," which attempted to explain why the universe appeared to have happened everywhere at once. But he'd never thought he might *see* such an incredible expansion for himself. Yet here it was, in the view-screen:

A vast sphere of purest energy, with what was once Yamp's innermost satellite at its center, its incredible growth was so much *faster* than the energy and even the light it was made of. Shing was immediately enveloped, vaporised along with its many millions of dwellers, the Shing't, who had never known what hit them. Then the swamp world Zull: reduced first to gas and without a single second's pause to its most basic elements, energy itself.

And finally ancient Shing, making it a double catastrophe.

Supernova! said Shania's Khiff. *But it made no difference, for the Shing system was already dead. And my Shania was fortunate that she—and I—had not died with it. Indeed, we still might have! We put on speed but couldn't outpace it, and in the very last moment before being overtaken we locked on to a gravity wave and reengaged the drive . . .*

Later, tracking the gravity wake of the Mordri vessel, we followed behind . . . only to witness more terror, death, and destruction.

Then as the darkness—the *normal* darkness behind Scott's eyelids—returned, the Khiff said, *I have shown you*

what you wanted to see, remembered it for you. Now tell me,
Scott: have you seen enough?

"God, yes!" Scott answered in a hoarse whisper, still disorientated, half-stunned by the experience. "More than
enough, I think."

Then now I shall leave you. For while you bade me wel-
come, I can only be at home with my Shania . . .

Scott felt limp, exhausted. He forced himself to his feet,
went and stood by his desk, took up his mug of coffee that
had gone stone cold some time ago. His blood felt cold, too;
it ran cold in his veins. But still he sipped at the coffee,
tasted the bitterness and pulled a face, and finally said,
"That's what these bastard maniacs have planned for us?"

"Yes," said Shania, still seated on the couch. "Certainly
for your world and your people, if not the entire solar system. I doubt if there's sufficient gold in all your world to do
that much damage. But as for the Earth: its crust will suffer
a meltdown; its mantle will overheat, erupt; the heavy metals in its core may even explode. There will be no chance
for life of any kind . . . all of it gone in nanoseconds."

"But why? Why did they do it? Why *will* they do it
again?"

"Haven't I explained? They deny a Higher Power. They
defy Deity, and seek to confront it, whatever it is. They attempt to confirm their belief—no longer a theory but to
them a fact—that creation was a natural event and not
brought about through the will of any . . . any Superior Intelligence, this Creator, in which they don't believe. They
continue to pursue precisely the same course that drove
them to experiment and caused their madness in the first
place. They have 'reasoned'—if such a word may be applied to them—that beneficial acts cannot produce a result:
'God' won't react to what He *expects* of His creatures; but
surely He will react to evil, the *destruction* of His creatures!
Therefore, if there is a God, He will confront the Mordri
Three and strike them down. But so far their case seems
proven, at least in their 'rationale.' For as yet no such Being

has so much as cried out against their evil, let alone threatened them or challenged it!"

Shania paused to catch her breath, then said, "Scott, you asked why they've done what they've done, and why they continue to do it. And I've done my best to answer you. But now you tell me something: does madness really need a reason?"

After a moment's thoughtful silence, Scott said, "Shania, do you know what all of this means to me? Boiled down, it simply means that these Mordris are godless. And I think maybe I've been that way myself ever since Kelly left me. But it's not God who let that happen, it's because of this . . . this who-gives-a-damn bloody theory of theirs that she died, was murdered by one of them, and that has made me the perfect vessel for vengeance. God in His many forms may or may not exist as a majority of His worshippers think of Him, but if there is *something*—and Harry Keogh hinted that there is—then I'm now the tool that's going to disprove the Mordri Three's theory. And Creator or no Creator, God or no God, I am going to kill Simon fucking Salcombe if it's the last thing I do!"

Shania nodded and said, "And you're ready now, I think."

"There are one or two things I still need to know," Scott replied, grimly, "one or two questions I've yet to ask, if only to help my understanding. But it won't make much difference how you answer my questions, because my course is set."

"Then ask away," she said, "for if we're going to do anything at all, it has to be now or tomorrow at the very latest."

"And that's one of my questions," said Scott. "How can you be sure of that? That it's coming as soon as all that?"

"I'm sure the Mordris must know I'm here now," Shania told him. "They cannot have mistaken all the signs we've been giving off. Why, the very fact that we've been shielding ourselves has to have been an obvious sign in itself! And who would know better how to do that than another Shing't? But they are three and I am—or I was—only one. So why is it they haven't come to kill me?"

Scott nodded his understanding. "Because you don't matter. Because they believe it's too late."

"Exactly. And the day after tomorrow—if there's to be a day after tomorrow—it could well be too late."

Another curt nod, and Scott said, "Second question. Right from the start, since first we met, you've known about the Mordris: their location, what they're doing, and so on. I remember you telling me about this machine they're building. But again I have to ask you: how do you know these things?"

"I've been here a long time, Scott," Shania answered, "and from the moment my vessel crashed here I've had to be very careful. But almost two years ago, finally I made my way to a small Swiss village under Schloss Zonigen and there used my telepathy to discover what I could of the Mordris."

"What?" Scott frowned. "But didn't they know you were spying on them? You were that close, yet they failed to sense your presence?"

Shania sighed and explained, "I didn't *need* to spy on the Mordris themselves, Scott. Knowing that they had been there for two years, in the heights over that village, was sufficient intelligence in itself."

Scott snapped his fingers. "Of course! You read the minds of the people in the village. For after all the time the Mordri Three had spent in Schloss Zonigen, it was a safe bet that they had infiltrated the village and were using its people."

"That's right." Shania nodded. "And when I looked into the minds of those people . . . all I found was terror! And from them I learned all I needed to know about what the Mordri Three were doing in that mountain stronghold of theirs. And as for now . . . well, the silence of the Mordris tells its own story—"

"That their work is almost done?"

"Yes."

"Then there's only one thing left to do," said Scott. "And that's to go over our plan one last time, and make sure there's nothing we've missed . . ."

35

Because of transportation problems, a flat tire on one of their two rented cars, and a spare that was only half inflated, Trask and his people didn't get into Idossola until 6:45 P.M. local.

The village was, or would have been once upon a time, very pretty even in the shade of Schloss Zonigen whose vertical crag towered to the northwest, partly blocking the evening sunlight and bringing an early dusk. They first saw the place when their vehicles climbed a road of hairpin bends to cross a rocky spur, from which almost aerial vantage point they had looked down on the village at a steep angle.

And there it was: Idossola, laid out below in a crease in the mountainous terrain that was more a mile-wide saddle than a valley proper. And beyond the village the deep green fields and sheltered meadows, gradually narrowing and climbing into a hazy mountain background, with pine trees in the foothills and high, bald spurs rising on both sides . . . and Schloss Zonigen, the crag standing opposite, iced like a grotesque cake in its uppermost peaks, and dominating the entire scene.

As for Idossola itself:

It was typical of its sort: picture postcard, yes; but as the cars wound their way down into the main street, past chalet-styled houses, shops with timbered facades, and a high-steepled church, all well spaced out, it became obvious even in the gathering dusk that Idossola had seen better times. There were vehicles on the streets, but very few; house lights were beginning to come on, but again not as many as one might expect; the shop fronts needed a good paint job, and one large, stately Gasthaus bordering the village square was closed, unlit, and bore a FOR SALE sign nailed to one of the beautifully carved timbers that supported a balcony under projecting, decorative eaves.

"High season," Trask mused as his car drove slowly by with Paul Garvey at the wheel, Ian Goodly and Alan Mc-Grath seated in the back. "And yet the place looks empty, three-quarters dead."

"Aye," McGrath agreed with him. "No much chance o' a knees-up aroon here! Ah cannae see too much thigh-slappin' dancin' or beer-guzzlin' frae steins goin' on the nicht!"

Ian Goodly, who had never managed to fathom McGrath's accent, looked sideways at him in something approaching awe . . .

The Gasthaus Alpenmann stood well back from the main road, halfway down one of four side streets and overlooking a lesser village square. Wood smoke curled from its chimneys, and several of its lights were on, mostly in the spacious, low-ceilinged, pine-panelled foyer. And the desk clerk—who as it happened turned out to be the proprietor, Herr Alpenmann himself—was present to greet his guests, smiling however shallowly as Trask and his team trooped in.

Herr Alpenmann was small, dark-haired, sharp-featured, and thin to the point of emaciation. Gaunt and hollow-eyed, with no shoulders to speak of, his evening-dress jacket seemed ready to slide right off him. His English, however, was near-perfect. He had expected the English *herren* to arrive earlier, he said, but it wasn't a problem. Food was available; the evening meal would be served as soon as the *herren* had approved the accommodation, cleaned up, and came downstairs—say, in forty-five minutes?

Trask thanked him, made to sign the register, gave a small start. He glanced at Herr Alpenmann—who seemed to be watching him too closely—and then with a shrug and a flourish finally put his name to paper. The others followed suit.

Paul Garvey had seen Trask's start; last to sign the register, it came as no surprise to the telepath to find the Head of Branch waiting for him on the wide landing after the others had climbed the stairs to their rooms.

"You saw it?" said Trask, grimly.

"Picked it out of your mind before I saw it," said Garvey,

quietly. "Actually, I thought you'd almost given the game away, starting like that."

"Damn, I know!" Trask answered. "But it did come as something of a shock. That signature was the very last thing I was expecting to see!" And then, frowning at what Garvey had said: "Anyway, what are you talking about; to whom did I nearly give the game away? Herr Alpenmann? Why would he be interested?"

"I only know that he was," said Garvey. "He was nervous as a cat, and his mind was locked tight. He was trying desperately hard to think of nothing!"

"What?" said Trask. "He was trying to think . . . ?"

"Of nothing," Garvey said again. "I would guess he's been, er, *advised* to think of nothing, and he's had practice!"

"Not good," Trask growled, shaking his head. "That bloody idiot Samuels! Who'd have thought it? Didn't we give him ample warning? Damn! Okay, forget that I was momentarily taken aback; that probably doesn't matter now, for it's possible that George Samuels has already compromised us. God only knows what kind of stupid questions he's been asking! And according to the date in the book he's been here since yesterday! We need to talk to him—and soon. What about the rest of the team: did they notice my gaffe or see Samuels's signature?"

"I don't think so," said the other. "They're all a little tired . . . me, too, but there's something about this place that's keeping me awake."

"Like what?" said Trask.

"The silence," said Garvey. "By which I mean the telepathic silence. Usually I would have to shut some of it out. It can get to be quite a babble, you know? But not here. Maybe they're all in the same pickle—the village people, I mean—guarding their thoughts, afraid to even think."

Trask nodded, said, "Well, it isn't too difficult to guess what that means. Okay, did you get Samuels's room number?"

"Eighteen of twenty-one." The telepath nodded. "And I note we're one to five, at the other end of the corridor. Then,

next to us, six to nine are also occupied. Our Swiss specials?
Probably."

Again Trask's nod. "Yes, I saw that. Okay, drop your
stuff off and go see if Samuels is in. If so, make damn sure
he *stays* in! I'll have a quick word with the others and I'll
join you in number eighteen."

"Got it," said Garvey as they headed for their respective
rooms . . .

Trask did as he'd said: put his bags in the room he was shar-
ing with Ian Goodly, told the precog about Samuels, was
about to go and speak to the rest of the team when Garvey
walked in without knocking. The telepath's face was pale,
and his expression grotesque even for him.

"Boss," he said, staggering a very little, "Samuels is in
his room. He didn't answer my knock so I used a skeleton
key. I . . . I think you better come and see this for yourself.
He won't be going anywhere soon, or ever, and whatever
he's already done or said he definitely won't be speaking to
anyone else."

Feeling gooseflesh creeping on his arms, Trask said,
"What are you telling me? He's . . . what, dead?"

"More than just dead." Garvey gulped, his colour beginning to turn from grey to green. "I mean, his brains are
hanging out of his ears and his eyes are on his cheeks! Shit,
he's so . . . so *contorted,* twisted! I think it maybe took him
some time to die. He must have been in absolute agony, and
yet the poor dumb bastard didn't even scream."

"Didn't even scream?" said Trask. "How do you—?"

But Garvey was stumbling toward the bathroom. Throwing the door open and fighting the rising bile, he turned and
said, "He . . . he couldn't have cried out because . . . because his mouth is welded shut!"

Then he kicked the door shut behind him, and Trask and
the precog heard the sounds of his throwing up . . .

Millie Cleary was knocking at the door. Trask let her in,
asked if she was okay. Her face was strained, worried, with

that telltale bruised look around the eyes that spoke of an abuse of her talent, the fact that she'd been pushing it.

"I was trying to contact Paul," she said. "I wanted to see if he knew why everything was so—"

"So quiet?" said Trask.

"Yes." She nodded. "But his thoughts . . . they were a mess! Full of horrible things! He's here, isn't he?"

"Yes, I'm here," Garvey answered shakily, still stumbling, wiping his mouth on a towel as he left the bathroom. "And I think that for now I'm going to stay here. This isn't any kind of place where I'd want to be on my own." He found a chair and flopped down into it.

Trask tried to call reception on the telephone, but there was no answer. "Damn!" he said. "I want to contact these Swiss specials. Maybe I can get them on their room numbers."

And Garvey reminded him, "That's six through nine."

Trask tried each of the four numbers. Again, no answer.

The precog Ian Goodly was at the window looking out on the square. "Isn't that Herr Alpenmann?" he said. "It seems he's in a bit of a hurry."

As Trask crossed to the window a knock sounded and Millie let the techs in. Entering ahead of Alan McGrath, Graham Taylor started to say, "I was trying to test the outside lines . . ." But feeling the tension he at once fell silent.

"And?" said Trask, peering out of the window.

"They're down," said Taylor. And looking from face to face he asked, "What's going on?"

Trask barely glanced at him. "Go get Chung and the rest of the team," he said, then looked out of the window again. And to Goodly: "Yes, that's Alpenmann." At which the figure down below turned to look up at the windows, saw Trask, went wide-eyed and almost fell into the driver's seat of a car.

In the time it took Trask to get his team fully assembled Alpenmann's car had left the village and was accelerating away, heading west across the valley. And in that direction—

"There's just the one road out that way," said the precog. "And that's the road to Schloss Zonigen."

"Alan." Trask turned to McGrath. "Get your binoculars. See if you can follow his headlights. I want to know for sure where he's going."

Next he turned to David Chung. "David, get downstairs, see if there's anyone left in this fucking place. No, wait a minute—don't go on your own. Graham, you go with him—*after* you've put your crossbow together!"

And then to Millie Cleary: "I'm sorry, Millie, but you'll probably be hearing a lot more profanity, and not just from me. Under certain circumstances, decent vocabularies tend to go out the window."

Millie shrugged and under her breath, faintly and shakily, said, "Oh, well then—fuck it!"

As Chung and Taylor were leaving, McGrath reentered; going to the window, he looked through dual-purpose binoculars—standard and infrared—to scan the road out of the village toward the pine-clad, scree-littered slopes at the base of Schloss Zonigen. "Aye," he muttered, adjusting the focus on the binoculars. "There he goes—the shrivelled wee shit! Nae doubt in mah mind but he's off tae see his masters."

"Or if not his masters as such," said Garvey, "the ones he fears—the ones he daren't think about—who have ordered him *not* to think about them!"

"Which means," said Trask, "that they know about us. Certainly they know we have telepaths, and it's possible they know we have other talents, too. And they're not on their own, these maniacs, creatures, whatever they are. Maybe the entire village knows about them! If so, they've probably recruited other spies, like Alpenmann; also guards, soldiers, and enforcers. And as for Schloss Zonigen: that place up there looks almost impregnable!"

Then, glancing from face to face, he said, "It's high time we talked to our Swiss special counterparts. They really should have contacted us by now. Let's face it: you don't need to be a member of Mensa to know that this place is all wrong! Paul, and Alan, you are with me. Alan, first we'll get your crossbow from your room. The rest of you stay here;

wait for Chung and Taylor to get back, then come looking for me. I'll be talking to Swiss Special Forces—if I can find them!"

As Trask and his two went into the corridor, Garvey said, "Boss, I'm sorry about what happened in there just now."

"Oh?" said Trask, innocently. "So what happened?"

"You know what I mean," said Garvey. "My throwing up and all. But when I saw what someone had done to Samuels—the way he'd been disfigured—it brought back too many bad memories."

"Of Johnny Found?" said Trask. "What he did to you on the night the Necroscope nailed him? Paul, that's perfectly understandable. If I were in your shoes I know I'd feel the same. So forget it. Anyway, it's not unlikely that you'll be throwing up again before this is over. We all might!"

Trask wasn't a precog, but on this occasion he could well have been . . .

They knocked on the doors of rooms six, seven, eight, and nine, and got no answer. Then outside number nine, on Trask's orders, Garvey produced his skeleton key, fumbled it into the lock, and stood back. Garvey wasn't a coward, far from it; but as strong and athletic as he was, the telepath had had enough of shocks for now.

Trask and McGrath entered the dark room, switching on the light as they went, and Garvey followed on behind. Just inside the door, however, Trask came to such an abrupt, startled halt that his companions almost bumped into him.

"What is it the noo?" said McGrath, his voice husky.

Trask moved slowly forward toward a table with drawers, a television, a telephone, and desk space on the near-side of the TV set for writing, with room underneath for the writer's legs. The chair that would have fitted that space was on its back in the middle of the floor, and what looked like a huge pink pancake was draped over the desk area, its folds hanging loosely down the side and front of the table. Halfway down the height of the table, the hanging portion of the pancake had separated into two flattened extensions with a small mass of scarlet material between them. The scarlet stuff dripped one last droplet of red even as Trask and the others stared in total disbelief. Another long segment of the pink stuff was draped over the top of the TV, and an ugly bulge of the same material looked about ready to sink into the two-inch gap between the table and wall. "God A'mighty!" said McGrath then. And, "Jesus Christ! Is that what ah think it is? But no, it cannae be!"

But it was. The flattened ugly bit against the wall wore a tuft of black hair and a face without a mouth yet with teeth on the outside. The "extensions" were arms and legs. A bit of torn linen dangling from the red, central area was all that remained of a pair of underpants.

Then, as Trask took a stumbling pace to the rear his movement caused this . . . this *monstrosity*—all that was left of a man—to slither like so much wet dough off the table, buckling into neat, boneless folds on the floor. And there where it fell and folded up on itself, its impact splashed sticky red dollops from a great pool of partly congealed blood, unrecognized until now because its colour was a near-perfect match for the carpet.

David Chung, Graham Taylor, and the rest were now gathered in the corridor. Coming to the door, the locator began to speak: "There's a cook in the kitchen—an old lady in a dirndl and a fancy hat—singing away to herself as she works. I don't think she's entirely with it. And there's a waiter laying out cutlery, food, and wine in the dining room . . ." Chung paused for a moment, then came to stand beside Trask and went on: "There didn't seem to be anyone else around. While the cook seems okay, maybe just a bit strange, the waiter's as jumpy as a cricket, and . . . *what the hell!?*" He had finally seen what the others were staring at.

"Hell is the right word for it," Trask agreed then, backing away and taking the others with him.

And hard-man McGrath whispered, "This poor, poor bastard! And all o' his juices bled oot frae his privates. But for God's sake, where's his bones?"

"They're under the bed," Trask choked the words out as

he lifted the corner of a coverlet and something white showed. "It looks like they . . . like they simply slipped out of him!" Then, letting the coverlet fall, he growled, "The other rooms: go and try them, but go in twos. As of now no one is to do anything or go anywhere on his own. Paul, you stay here with me."

The six were only too glad to leave Trask and the telepath alone in that awful room, and as they left Garvey said, "I appreciate this, boss. Thanks for putting your faith in me."

"No problem," said Trask. "Anyway, I reckoned I'd probably be safe since you've already thrown up on me once tonight." For a brief moment he forced a faintly sardonic grin—

—But only for a moment, until something made a soft bumping sound in an old-fashioned wooden wardrobe in the far corner of the room beside the window!

36

Garvey jumped six inches, said, *"Shit!"* and stumbled two paces backward out into the corridor. Quickly recovering, he called out after Tech Taylor. "Graham, bring that crossbow back here!"

Feeling utterly defenceless without a weapon, Trask nevertheless steeled himself to step over the human remains and the darkening pool of blood that lay between the TV table-cum-desk and a pair of single beds, toward the now threatening wardrobe. Taking the loaded crossbow from Taylor, Garvey leaned over the red mess on the floor and passed the weapon to Trask. With his finger on the trigger, the latter moved closer to the wardrobe.

Almost there, he called out, "Okay, whoever's in there— you have just five seconds to—"

At which the wardrobe's twin doors flew open, revealing a wild, babbling man! His hair was a tangle over twitching fea-

tures, and his eyes, rapidly blinking, were almost starting out
of a face white as death. In his hands he held an ugly-looking
submachine gun! But it had been pitch-dark in the wardrobe,
and the relatively bright lighting in the room had temporarily
blinded him. Also, one of the wardrobe's doors partly
blocked Trask from his view. Making inarticulate sounds he
staggered forward, swinging his weapon in a threatening arc.

Trask's reflexes were good, and likewise his talent. He at
once saw "the truth" of the situation: that this man wasn't
his enemy. Bringing the crossbow's tiller up he knocked the
machine gun aside and hurled himself forward, using his
weight to throw the wild-eyed man back into the teetering
wardrobe. And letting go the crossbow to grab the other's
gun barrel, Trask simultaneously head-butted him, which
finished the job.

By then Paul Garvey had joined him. The telepath wres-
tled the machine gun from the stranger's slack grip and
helped Trask climb out of the wardrobe's wreckage. Trask
came, dragging the dazed, bloodied wild man with him.

"He's terrified," said Garvey, "in shock, didn't know
what he was doing. Look, the gun's safety is still on! Total
funk. I failed to read him in there simply because there was
nothing to read! Even before you head-butted him his mind
was a blank, and now he's in denial—of everything!"

Trask heaved the man across the bed, told Taylor, "Hold
on to him. If he looks like he's going to start raving again,
give him a good crack on the jaw. I reckon he's one of our
specials, God damn it!"

The rest of the team had meanwhile regrouped in the corridor, where locator Chung was gurgling and gasping, determined not to be sick, and Ian Goodly was looking more
gaunt and cadaver-like than ever. "The other rooms," said
Goodly, his piping voice at least an octave higher than normal, "are more or less the same as this one . . . with varia-
tions. But you really don't want to know what they are. We
found six dead men."

And coming forward, a big-eyed Millie Cleary said, "But
we also found some of these in two suitcases, and plenty of

ammunition to go with them." She carried a standard 9mm automatic in one hand and an ugly-looking machine gun like the one they'd already seen in the other. Unable to conceal the shudder in her voice she continued. "This one"—hefting the machine gun—"is mine!"

"Okay," said Trask, "we're all together now and we'll stay that way. Grab your stuff and we're downstairs, everybody. This place has just become our HQ. Paul and Alan, bring our newfound friend with you."

"My name," said that one in English with a German accent, as Garvey and McGrath brought him out of the room between them, "is Norbert Hauser. And you . . . you must be Benjamin Trask?"

"Call me Ben," Trask told him. "Are you okay?"

The other shouldered himself erect, tried to free himself, but Garvey and McGrath hung on to him. Hauser managed to lift a hand, fingered his bloodied nose. "I don't think it's broken," he said. "But it feels like you were trying!"

"Don't go looking for an apology from me," said Trask. "If you'd been right in your head I might have been dead! But your weapon was still on safe."

"Huh!" said the other. "And that's not all: it wasn't even loaded! I didn't have time before . . . before I . . . well, before things got on top of me. That was something that never happened before. Shock, like your friend here said."

At which Paul Garvey nodded and said, "His mind's still on the fritz, disordered. But he's gradually coming out of it." It was the second time the telepath had commented on Hauser's mental condition. Swaying a little, Hauser looked at him, frowned, and said:

"My mind is on the . . . ?" And then: "Ah, yes—of course—I understand! Your reputation has preceded you, Ben Trask. You and your people. I didn't believe any of it until now."

Trask nodded, considered the talents surrounding him, also his own, and thought, *Norbert, you ain't seen nothin' yet!*

"Will you let go of me now?" Hauser looked at Garvey, then at McGrath. "I can manage, I think."

Trask gave them the nod, but as they released Hauser he at once staggered and almost fell.

Trask shook his head, said, "Norbert, I don't think you're quite ready." And to the men flanking him, "Help him downstairs. We'll see how he gets on. Bring those weapons and all the ammunition you can find. Now come on, everyone. Let's move it!"

Downstairs, they could smell cooked food. Trask said, "I don't suppose anyone's very hungry right now, but whatever we're in for we really don't want to be facing it on empty stomachs. No alcohol, but we should all have at least a bite to eat. David, where's the dining room? Lead the way . . . no, never mind, I'll follow my nose."

But the locator did lead the way—down a pine-panelled passage with doors leading off—to a large, well-lighted room with a long, pine-topped table in the central floor space. The table was now laden with local specialities: a tureen of steaming bean soup, wild pig on a carving platter, various sausages, nuts and fruit, breads, wine, and an urn of black coffee.

The waiter was there, too, and dressed for the occasion. An older man with slicked-back hair, long sideburns, and a large nose on a long thin face, he was in evening dress, had a napkin over one arm, and wore a long white apron tied at the waist. But instead of waiting on he was seated in one of the chairs at the table. Chung had earlier described him as "jumpy as a cricket," but that no longer applied. Now he simply sat staring at something, with a tic jerking in the corner of his mouth.

Approaching him, Trask and the team saw what he was staring at—which stopped them dead in their tracks.

Regular as clockwork, something was dripping from the high ceiling directly into the big soup tureen, and it was something red. The tureen's fancy doily was splotched where muddy liquids had splashed out of the bowl. The eyes of the entire team, including Norbert Hauser, turned up to stare at the ceiling, where a bright red blotch was slowly spreading outward from its central focus.

And the precog said, "I . . . I think I know this. It's from one of the rooms. His bottom half was lying naked on a bed; the rest of him was slumped off the bed, with his head touching the floor. The slumping half had peeled itself and was very bloody. I was paired up with Millie; I didn't want her to see too much so we didn't stay—but I *swear* I thought he was dead!"

"Then tell yourself that he was," said Trask, nodding. "He probably was, and it's just that it's taken this long for it to find its way down here. It doesn't run like it's fresh."

At which Agent Hauser collapsed heavily into a chair, moaning, "That's one of my men you're talking about! *Gott in Himmel—oh, mein Gott!*"

"What is *wrong* with these fuckin' people!" Alan McGrath's angry shout shattered the silence. He strode to where the immaculately clad waiter was still sitting in his chair, grabbed him by the lapels, and jerked him upright, sending the chair flying. "You," he said, "ye fuckin' zombie! What's a'matter wi' ye?"

"Bitte! Bitte!" the other protested, suddenly animated and flapping his hands.

"Sprechen sie fuckin' Scottish?" the burly McGrath shouted into his face, slamming him against a panelled wall. "It's best ye say aye, 'cos ah cannae speak kraut!"

Trask stepped forward. "Let him go," he said. And turning to Hauser: "Will you translate?"

"Yes, yes," said Hauser. He conversed with the waiter for perhaps five minutes, and all the while Trask's people were becoming more and more nervous, anxious, impatient. Trask himself was feeling the tension; he took the team aside and said:

"Go to reception, see if you can find keys to the ground-floor rooms in the desk area. Then split into two teams. Check all the rooms, then lock the exit doors front and rear. If you can't find the keys, then barricade the doors as best as possible. If you find people—live ones, that is—bring 'em back here. Millie, do you know how to use that machine gun?"

"Yes." She nodded. "It's a Swiss Special Forces issue. We got an hour's practice on it at the range in London. It's meant for close-quarter fighting and street clearance. It's deadly in any enclosed area, but not so hot over twenty-five yards in the open."

"That's okay," said Trask, "because we're not going out in the open—not yet, anyway. You stay with me and Hauser. And as for the rest of you—go!"

"Wait!" said Paul Garvey. "Boss, there's someone close by, I think in there." He pointed at a door bearing the legend *"Die Kuche."*

"That's the kitchen," said Chung. "It'll be the cook."

"Her thoughts are confused all to hell!" the telepath continued. "And they're getting fainter by the second."

"Okay," said Trask, "Millie and I will see what's up. The rest of you, do your thing. Norbert, continue finding out what happened here from his point of view." He indicated the waiter. "But I'll also want to know about it from yours, okay?"

"Yes, of course," Hauser replied, if a little vacantly. "I shall tell you all that I can remember."

"Good," said Trask. "I'll be right back."

Trask and Millie went through into the kitchen, which was now in darkness. They were unable to find a light switch immediately, but a little exterior light was still finding its way in through a tall stained-glass window, and more yet from the dining room. A figure was silhouetted against the window, looking out. It was the homely old cook in her dirndl outfit, no longer singing as Chung had reported but softly crying to herself.

Millie and Trask approached her, and the latter used what little he knew of the German language to inquire: *"Entschuldigen sie, Mutter—aber was ist, denn?"*

"Was ist?" She turned her head and seemed to stare right

through the pair, then went back to looking up and out into the night. She was looking at the gaunt high crag up there; looking at Schloss Zonigen where lights were now flickering as to illuminate a fantasy castle. The stained glass in the window loaned her its faint evening colours; her face was a ruddy red, green, golden—but the puddle at her feet was black. Held limply in her hand, a carving knife glinted dully in the gloom. Then she swayed, and they saw that her wrists dripped blood!

Trask leapt forward as she dropped, to catch and lower her before she could hit the floor, and Millie was by his side in a moment. *"Was ist?"* said the woman again, faintly. *"Das ist. Was schlecht ist. Das Eisscholle Schloss. Schloss Zonigen!"*

"God, she's almost gone!" Trask groaned where he knelt, holding the woman's head, knowing that from the knees down his trousers were soaking up her blood.

"Ah, English!" she whispered. "Yes, I go. To my children, who won't come home again. *Mein Kinder—mein zwei Sohne—die nicht . . . mehr . . . zuruck . . . konnen."*

"Your sons who can't come home?" Trask believed that he'd understood her. "Why can't they come home? Where are your sons, *mutti*?" But even as she spoke it with her last breath, he knew the answer:

"Schloss Zonigen!" she sighed. And her mouth fell open . . .

Later, in the reception area when the *Gasthaus* had been locked down, Trask spoke to Norbert Hauser.

"You were the leader of the team?"

"Yes," Hauser answered tiredly. "They were my boys. I even trained them, but never thinking to come up against anything so *entsezlich* as this. And now all this death, and this hotel full of bodies. Can't we do something about all the bodies, Trask?"

"I've been thinking about it," said Trask. "And yes, we'll do something—later. But for now I just need you to answer my questions. So there were . . . what, eight of you?"

"Yes. Those machine pistols were for our use if necessary. Frankly, I didn't think it would be. The automatics were—"

"For us," Trask finished it for him. "Big guns for the big boys, and little guns for the little boys, right? Forget it."

"And just in case," said Hauser, "the flamethrower."

"What?" Trask sat up straighter. He and his crew knew all about flamethrowers. "You brought a flamethrower? Where is it?"

The other shrugged. "You didn't find it? Dirk Braun was in charge of it. I think Dirk was in *Zimmer nummer acht*—er, room eight—next door to me. The device is a very compact model and fully fuelled: gases under pressure, which mix and ignite when the weapon is triggered. It will be in a metal case."

Trask spoke to David Chung. "Locator, locate it." And then to Alan McGrath: "Go with him."

After the pair had hurried upstairs, Trask turned again to Hauser. "If you didn't think weapons were really necessary, why a flamethrower?"

Again Hauser's shrug. "Eh? Flamethrower?" His eyes looked glazed.

Paul Garvey spoke up. "His mind's wandering again. The man is still in shock. He's fighting hard but he keeps losing it."

Trask and Hauser were in easy chairs by a small table with an ashtray. The Swiss agent's head kept lolling and his eyelids would droop now and then. But Trask didn't have time for any of that. He slammed a fist down on the table, which caused the ashtray to jump, then shouted, "Hauser! Wake the fuck up! I'll ask you again, why did you bring a flamethrower?"

"Eh? What?" Starting massively, the agent snapped upright in his chair. "Oh, yes! I'm sorry. I must . . . must pull myself together, ja? The flamethrower. Swiss intelligence sources had told me that the big ice cavern up there, Schloss Zonigen, was probably full of crevices, bolt-holes, and inaccessible places. Once again I didn't foresee any real problem, but on the other hand—"

"I get it," said Trask with a nod. "Using a flamethrower, it's easy to empty a dark cramped space without going in there and making yourself a target."

"*Ja,* exactly."

"Okay." Trask gripped the other's forearm where it lay on the table, and said, "Now for God's sake stay with it, Norbert, and tell me what happened."

"*Ja, ja.* Well, we were supposed to meet you at about 5:00 P.M. So we got here, oh, around 4:20, 4:30. We were early so I sent my men to settle in and went off on my own to have a look around the village, see if I could gather any intelligence. The police station—actually it's a police post, served from Domodossola on an irregular basis—was locked up, empty. And while it was still full daylight I saw only a few people. But none of them went out of their way to speak to me.

"So I came here, to the *Gasthaus,* where I found my men in . . . in the *condition* that you've seen for yourself. All of them dead in less than half an hour—and I had heard nothing—and I couldn't, I didn't—the terror, and the horror—it all fell on me like—something in my head just snapped. I got a machine gun, couldn't find the ammunition. And the blood. And my men . . . !"

"Take it easy," said Trask quietly.

"Mr. Trask—Ben? I *cannot* take it easy! I don't even know what happened here. I don't believe *how* it happened. Some of my men were—how do you say it?—inverted."

"I haven't seen all of your men," said Trask. "But there's a certain word I've learned. It's evaginated."

"I don't know that word." Hauser shook his head. "But when I saw . . . when I saw my boys . . . well, after that everything is just blank. I don't remember getting into the wardrobe, hiding, but I suppose I must have."

"Did you see Herr Alpenmann?"

"Who?"

"The desk clerk, the proprietor."

"No. My men must have seen him, to check in and get their keys. But no, I didn't see anyone. I simply went upstairs, and . . . and . . ."

"Okay, forget it," said Trask. "Tell me about the waiter. What did he tell you?" He glanced across the room at the man in question. The waiter was on his own, sitting beside the desk on a steel-framed chair from the dining room. And staring at Trask and Hauser, he saw them glance his way.

"Ah! Herr Gruber," said Hauser. "I think he knows something but he didn't say much. I don't think he *dares* to say anything! The only thing I got out of him: he said his wife is in Schloss Zonigen. Also that whatever is happening here will soon be over and she will be returned to him, but if he speaks a single word he'll never see her again. Also, the few families that are left here: most if not all have members of their men- or their women-folk in Schloss Zonigen."

"Hostages," said Trask. "And with what those evil bastards up there can do to people—well, that explains a lot. You know something, Norbert? If we hadn't been delayed en route, if we'd met you as planned, we might have been up there right now, dead as doornails along with your boys! And as for Herr Gruber: I've got a whole lot more than his wife to worry about. So—"

He stood up and made for the waiter—a serious misnomer, for Gruber wasn't waiting. He was up off his chair and running, loping toward the big double doors leading out into the square. The doors were locked now, but that hadn't occurred to him; or so it seemed.

"Grab him!" Trask shouted.

Tech McGrath was back downstairs with a metal case on his knees examining the contents. Closest to the doors, he put the flamethrower aside, jumped to his feet, made a dive for Gruber—only to hit the floor when the man somehow managed to evade him. But Gruber wasn't trying for the doors.

Flanking the entranceway, a pair of circular stained-glass windows some two feet in diameter stood approximately four feet off the ground in the pine-panelled wall. Herr Gruber was desperate, determined to say nothing else. The window on the right was his target, and with a headlong dive to put McGrath's best effort to shame, Gruber made his exit in a shower of shattered wooden latticework, coloured glass, and twisted lead beading.

"Damn!" said Trask, moving to the wrecked window. "I only wanted to know how those bastards up there do what they do."

Coming up behind him, Paul Garvey said, "He's frightened out of his wits, in a panic, doesn't know which way to turn."

The telepath was right, of course; out there in the night, Gruber lurched this way and that, a ghostly scarecrow skidding on the cobbles of the square. But he wasn't alone.

"There's someone else out there," cried Millie. "There are several someones!"

"She's right," said Garvey as she joined them at the broken window and took his hand. And together they peered out into the darkness. "There's at least three others. They're furtive, intent, concentrating on their business—hunters!"

Trask nodded. "And we're their prey. Which is more or less what I was expecting. Lights out, and listen everyone: don't go showing too much of yourself at the windows."

Even as he spoke there came flashes of light and the snarl of submachine-gun fire. It caught up with Herr Gruber as he ran across the night square with his hands fluttering. He cried out and lurched one more pace, then lowered his hands and fell flat on his face.

"Like rats in a compost heap," Trask rasped as Ian Goodly put the lights out. "And those people out there have their orders: to shoot any rat—*any* damn one—who tries to leave. So if we want to live we have to defend this place. You two techs, Alan and Graham, take your crossbows upstairs, the back of the hotel; watch the car park. If we're ever going to get as far as Schloss Zonigen we'll need our vehicles. And don't worry about friend or foe: we have to play their game now. Anything at all, if it moves out there, shoot it! Frank, where are you?"

Trask was speaking to the spotter Frank Robinson now, but the room was full of shadows and his eyes were still adjusting. "Are you getting anything? These hunters outside: are there any wild talents among them?"

"I feel nothing," Robinson replied out of the darkness. "I think they're just 'ordinary' killers."

"Okay," said Trask. "You and Paul get upstairs, keep watch from the front of the building."

"Wait!" came Agent Hauser's voice, sounding much steadier, controlled now. "Please, Ben, I shall go with Frank. I feel the need to . . . to hit back!"

Trask wasn't too sure. "You're certain you'll be okay?"

"*Bestimmt!* I mean, absolutely."

Trask nodded. "Okay, then go!"

Then Paul Garvey spoke up. "I'll do the back, downstairs," he said.

"And I'll go with him," said David Chung.

"Right," said Trask. "So, Millie, Ian, you're with me, and we're staying right here. You've got your weapons? Good. Knock out that other round window and keep watch. It could get to be a very long night . . ."

37

Outdoors at Scott's place in London, after a very warm day it was still muggy, breathless as the dusk came down. Sitting in a deck chair in the garden with a cool soft drink—frustrated and feeling wasted, with nothing as yet on which to expend his energy and his anger—it dawned on Scott how quiet Shania was and how she'd been that way for quite some time now. Wolf, too, sniffing about in the bushes with his tail down, oddly anxious and occasionally whining; both of them tense, uneasy.

Narrowing his eyes and sitting up straighter, Scott put his drink aside and watched Shania with a new, knowing intensity where she moved distractedly among weed-grown borders, her forehead lined with concentration. And suddenly, without reading her mind—respecting the privacy of her thoughts—still Scott knew that it was going to be soon. In fact:

"It's now, isn't it?" he said. And when she looked at him but didn't answer he knew he must be right, sat back again and remembered what she'd told him when he'd asked her if there was any way to find out when the Mordris would act. Yes, she'd told him, there was, but it would be very dangerous . . .

"It will involve one of two things," she had said. "I can either try to contact their minds from here, try to spy on the minds of the Mordri Three themselves—which of course carries the risk that they might detect my probe and attack me telepathically, three deranged Shing't minds against my one—or we can use the localizer one last time, go to Idossola under the Alps, and see what we can learn from the people there. We will have to be there eventually . . ."

And while Scott had considered what she'd said:

"That, too, has an element of risk," Shania had continued, "for a good many of the village people were already in the service of the Mordri Three the first and last time I was there, and there are certain to be more of them now. Also, since the Mordris are sure to maintain at least partial mental access to the people they control, it could be that through them they'll discover us . . ."

And finally:

"In the second case the risk is fairly small but it does exist. And since I'm loath to put you in danger—first because I love you, second because you've accepted that you've been endowed and I don't want to move against the Mordris until you've learned how best to use your powers—I think the first option is the safest: I should attempt to infiltrate one of the Mordri minds, perhaps in the dead of night when they're asleep, and so learn whatever I can. In which case I must also avoid the Khiff companion of whichever mind I choose. Alas, unlike the Shing't, the Khiff only rarely sleep."

That had been the basis of their first and what might yet prove to have been their last argument, for Scott wouldn't hear of Shania placing herself in danger. "Then we'll have to wait a while longer," he'd told her, "maybe until there's little or no time left at all! And as for using my so-called powers, if they exist, and if I really do have them: one of them makes my flesh creep, and the other"—he shook his head—"well frankly, it just baffles me. For one thing my math isn't *that* good, and for another I don't have any coordinates . . ."

At the time—it seemed like ages ago but was just a few days—that had been that: Scott wouldn't for a single moment consider any plan that would put Shania in direct contact with the Mordri Three. He'd lost one love that way and without even knowing how or why. But now, this momentous evening—here and now in the garden, with the quiet and oppressive warmth threatening thunder—the simple fact that Shania hadn't answered him threatened a different, far more deadly kind of thunder. For it told Scott that indeed this was it.

Shania read his mind and said, "Dusk is settling in and we should go inside. By now it's dark in Idossola; perhaps you can shield me as I scan the area more deeply—but just the village itself—to see what I can discover."

Wolf, no longer limping, now a handsome creature, soft and clean to the touch yet still feral in his yellow eyes and great sharp fangs, came loping like a night elemental from the dusky shrubbery, his tongue lolling.

Certain pleasures are gone out of my life, he said. *There are no rabbits here I fear, not that my nose can sniff out, and I'm forbidden to scavenge for chickens! A pity. But so have the dangers—some of them, the old dangers—gone from my life, and I have found my One and even my Two. I find it . . . comfortable; and yet I miss the excitement and can't help looking forward to new adventures. I heard you talking, and I want to help. I know how to issue silence, to cover my scent in empty thoughts. That is how I confused the hunters in the hills in my father's land.* He nuzzled Scott's hand, and licked it with a wet tongue. *Also, I know directions. Only let me scent these enemies, in my mind, and just as I always know where you are, and Shania—also Zek, Jazz, and my father—I shall also know where they are, always. And no matter where they go, I shall find them. Directions, yes . . . I think it must be a wolf thing. Anyway, it's my thing.*

Scott nodded, patted Wolf's head, and said, "Of course it's a wolf thing, but you have it like no wolf before you—not in this world, anyway. And we'll be glad of your help, if and when it comes to that . . . but what the heck, it seems it *has* come to that!" And looking at Shania: "What makes you think it's now?"

She came to him as he stood up. "Don't be angry, but these last few days, I have on one or two occasions scanned Idossola. Also Schloss Zonigen. I'm sorry I kept it from you, Scott, but I had to try."

"You what!?" He took her by the shoulders. "But haven't we already discussed that? How dangerous it could be?"

"I was in and out as quickly as that!" she protested. "It wasn't as if I was searching out the Mordris—I wouldn't have dared—or even that I was doing any deep scanning in the village. I promise you, I was simply getting the *feel* of the place. I didn't endanger myself, Scott. Of course I didn't, because to do so would have been to endanger you."

Scott hugged her, then put an arm around her and walked her back to the house. Wolf came alongside, so close that his flank brushed Scott's legs. And as they went indoors: "So then," said Scott resignedly, "what did you see, hear, sense that makes you think it has to be now?"

All three, they sat down in the study. And Shania said, "I sensed such terror radiating from the village, but only silence from Schloss Zonigen. The Mordris have the high crag blanketed, closed to all telepathic transmissions. They no longer feel the need to look outward and won't allow me or anyone else to look in. Why else would they do that if not to ensure the utmost secrecy and security in these last few days or even hours? What's more, your friends at E-Branch have fallen silent, too. From time to time I've tried scanning them and there has always been something: a tensing, an awareness, faint echoes of their presence. But now . . . nothing. It's more than possible that they, too, are making their move."

Scott shook his head in something approaching defeat. "Our 'great plan,'" he said wryly, "if we can continue to call it that, was to go in guns blazing and wreck *their* plans, the Mordri Three's plans, at the very last moment. At first, after I'd found out about Simon Salcombe, I wasn't much concerned that it might mean my life, not as long as it meant his. But since then—while I still want him dead, and those other Shing't lunatics with him—there's been you. Now I do care about my life, about *our* lives, and that's weakened me. Yes, I know we must do this, because if we don't that's *definitely* the end of things, for us and everyone else . . . but damn it, we still don't know when The End that the Mordris have planned is coming, and even if we did know we don't have any guns to blaze with!"

"As to when, I *will* find that out!" Determined now, Shania jumped to her feet. "And as for guns, I can get guns."

"Just like that?" said Scott. "I mean, now?"

"That's the easy part." She nodded. "Just wait a moment."

She used the localizer, disappearing in a suck of air and a swirl of dust motes, and in a count of ten was back carrying a pair of double-barrelled shotguns and a large box of shells.

"From a sports store in the city," she explained. "I took its coordinates a long time ago."

Scott was no longer surprised or astonished by her coming and going in this manner—he had experienced that himself, and in more ways than one—but his confusion was steadily mounting. As he unloaded the weapons from her arms and placed them on his desk, he said, "But didn't you and your Khiff say that from now on we wouldn't be using the localizer? That we had to limit its use or something?"

"Absolutely!" she replied. "Indeed, I dare use it for just one more long, multi-passenger trip; then for short trips only. But as long as it contains even a spark of energy it will suffice to sustain my Khiff. So then, it will carry us to Idossola, yes, but it won't return us. After that—if there's to be an after that—I shall use it only under advice from my Khiff."

And before Scott could ask any more questions: "Now we'll need to prepare," she continued. "You'll be wanting to arm the weapons, and dress in dark clothing, and . . . and—"

"—And say my prayers?" Scott snorted. But already he was snapping a shotgun open, squinting down the barrels, and shoving shells into the breach.

"Prayers?" said Shania. "Well yes, of course. That, too, if you believe. I have already said mine."

"I've a power hacksaw in the garden shed," Scott mused. "I could cut these down in no time at all."

"Cut them down?"

"So that we can conceal them more easily," he explained.

At that she smiled, however tightly. "So then," she said, nodding. "Finally you are ready."

"I've been ready for some time," he answered, "ever since I learned that Simon Salcombe killed my Kelly, but we've a ways to go yet."

The nighttime is my time, said Wolf. *I am a shadow among shadows! When do we go?*

Shania answered him. "Not until I've taken one final look at Idossola. You and Scott will cover, shield me?"

"And what about your Khiff?" said Scott, seating himself beside her on the edge of the couch. "Won't it—I mean she—won't she also be helping?"

"Of course, as always!" said Shania. "No need to ask. She is constant. And if we were to meet up with a Mordri Khiff—"

I would be there to ward him off, said her Khiff, in their minds. *I would try to draw off the evil in him. I would cleanse him—or he would pervert me—one or the other.*

"He, or she," said Shania. "Don't forget, my Khiff, Mordri One is female. And anyway, we shall try to avoid the Mordri and their crazed creatures."

I forget nothing, my Shania, said the Khiff. *He or she, it makes no difference. And of course we shall try to avoid them.*

Then Scott and Shania clasped hands over Wolf where he sat between them, and Shania closed her eyes in concentration.

It took a moment, a dozen heartbeats at most. Scott felt his mind go out—he *sent* it out—to accompany Shania's and Wolf's; man and creature shielding the woman, as truly a woman as any Scott had ever known, where her psychic probe went winging to Idossola. A dozen heartbeats, no more than that, but she "heard" more than enough in that small amount of time. And man and wolf, some of it passed through her to them:

" 'Xavier!' " Scott gasped. "He's there, and in trouble!"

"Others from E-Branch, too," said Shania breathlessly. "I sense them . . . they no longer shield themselves . . . too busy to try even if there was a need . . . which there isn't because they are discovered! They are under attack, not from the Mordris but their servitors: men in the pay of the Mordris, and certain others in their sway, who dare not disobey them!"

"It's already started," said Scott, "and we're not in it!"

Shania's mind veered, and different thoughts came through; dark, evil thoughts . . . from Schloss Zonigen.

Ahhhh! said a female "voice," far off, yet as clear as day where it met with Shania's probe. *Shania Two! And will you also invade us? Beware, Shania Two. Your human friends hold no power over the Mordri Three.*

"Gelka Mordri!" Shania gasped. "Poor mad creature!"

Mad? Mad? said a different, twittering voice: Mordri One's Khiff. *Do you wish to see real madness, Shania Two? Then by all means come here, to Schloss Zonigen! Oh, ha-ha-ha!* And that was more than enough.

"Get out of there!" cried Scott, leaping to his feet and grabbing Shania by the shoulders. And shaking her, he shouted, "Get out now—before she, it, whatever—before she follows you back here!"

Only let her dare! growled Wolf, baring his fangs.

But Shania was already out, and soon in control of herself. And with a final shudder: "So now we know," she said.

"And yes, it is now. But don't worry, she won't—they won't—come here. Shing't telepathy to me is like . . . it's like words to you: all in the way they are spoken. Or rather, like facial expressions, displaying a person's emotions. I *felt* Gelka's anxiety! And as for her Khiff: its challenge gives the game away. It invites us to Schloss Zonigen because it knows they may not come here, and *that's* how close we are! They're preparing to leave! We have to go there, Scott, and now. First for the sake of your world, but also revenge for the death of Shing and those other worlds, and not least for the loss of your true love. Now we must dress for the night, and you've yet to prepare our weapons. How long will that take you?"

"Ten minutes, maximum," he answered, heading for the door. And when he hurried out to the garden shed an excited Wolf went with him, his eyes like yellow lamps in the deepening dusk . . .

In Idossola Ben Trask and Ian Goodly had turned a pair of massive oak tables onto their sides and positioned them against the heavy, locked double doors that led out front. Now any bullets from outside must either spend themselves or pass through four inches of tough timber before finding their way into the foyer, but sporadic bursts of machine-gun fire from across the square continued to speak of the enemy's determination.

Even more determined, however, were the agents of E-Branch in their defensive positions, upstairs and down in the Gasthaus Alpenmann. And in the frantic half hour gone by since the onset of hostilities, they had made excellent use of the advantage of cover that the hotel afforded them; an advantage that spoke for itself in the outlines of half a dozen crumpled corpses in both the square and on the outer perimeter of the car park.

To those agents of the Mordri at the rear of the building, death had come quietly, with barely a whisper of disturbed air, a meaty thud of nailed flesh, or on one occasion the *splat!* of a bursting eye as a bolt passed through, wrecking the brain and shattering the skull at the back. Three of them lay still where they had fallen, victims of Alan McGrath's and Graham Taylor's deadly accuracy.

But at least three more were still out there, making fleeting movements in the deep shadows but no longer coming into the open. Now and then a chattering stream of bullets would trace a line across the wall or shatter a window, but that was all. The true beauty of the situation was this: that while the defenders could see the flashes of gunfire whenever shots were fired, the attackers saw only the dark, deadly vacancy of apparently empty windows.

Similarly, at the front of the building:

Trask had taken out one man who had come so close to one of the shattered circular windows that he could put the muzzle of his weapon right through it . . . but that was as far as he'd got. Trask hadn't given him enough time to squeeze his trigger, and the anonymous would-be killer had known nothing of the hot lead that traced the angle of his weapon's barrel back to him, smashing his hands, ruining his face, and blowing half of his head off.

And in a room upstairs Norbert Hauser had kept a wary eye on a figure behind the trunk of a tree standing central in the square; and when finally that one had leaned out and trained a gun on the front of the building, then Hauser—a marksman with his own special arms—had spent just one round of 7.62 ammunition to shoot him through the heart.

As for the spotter, Frank Robinson, only the fact that he was inexperienced with the Swiss weapons kept him from killing several of the enemy. They weren't ESPers, no, but still Robinson's knack for picking them out in the night was unerring. And sensing what he could only describe as "something" in bushes on the periphery of the dark square, he'd sent a stream of bullets to riddle a man's body from chest to groin.

That last kill had been all of ten minutes ago, and while the enemy was still out there in some force they had obviously been taking stock of the situation, calling for reinforcements. For three sets of vehicle headlights could now be seen descending the hairpin bends from Schloss Zonigen.

During the quiet spell Trask had sent Millie Cleary creeping through to the rear of the hotel to see how Paul Garvey and David Chung were doing: a weak excuse to get her out of what he considered the danger zone at the front. And she knew it was so because she had already contacted Garvey—briefly, telepathically—to check on his and locator Chung's situation. But still Trask had insisted that she go and "relieve" one of them.

Which as it turned out was just as well. For no sooner had she found the pair in a room at the rear than Chung reported an "occurrence" that left him all excited. And despite that it was strategic folly to leave two telepaths together, he had hurried through the dark hotel to Trask in the foyer.

And now he made his report:

"It's this," he said, taking Scott St. John's paperweight from his pocket. "It's warm—well, to my touch anyway. And I think I know why. He's here, boss! St. John is here somewhere, and close!"

The eyes of all three ESPers, Chung, Trask, and the precog Ian Goodly, had now more nearly adjusted to the hotel's gloom. But as Chung finished speaking Trask saw Goodly give a massive start, staggering where he stood close to one of the shattered windows. For one awful moment Trask thought his old friend had been shot through the window, but then the precog steadied himself and said, "Yes! Oh, yes!"

"What is it, Ian?" said Trask. "What did you see?"

"It was like . . . a series of pictures . . . brief, kaleidoscopic," said Goodly. "But promising, oh so very promising! It was Schloss Zonigen, Ben, and we were there. But by God, there were monsters there, too, and dead men, fighting and screaming! It was like bedlam! And there were creatures that weren't even human, whose very touch is death or worse: instantaneous mutation and hideous disfigurement. Scott St. John was there, and a beautiful woman, and even a dog—no, a wolf!—his partners!"

Ducking low to cross the floor behind the upturned tables, Trask took hold of the precog's arm. "But what about that other thing you've been forecasting? The 'cosmic disruption,' or whatever? Isn't that more important?"

"That, too," said Goodly, with beads of sweat on his brow. "I saw that, too, Ben. Or rather I sensed it: a colossal blast that makes a nuclear explosion look like a Chinese firecracker! And yet . . . and yet . . ."

"Yes?"

"I also saw us. Dirty, dishevelled, bloodied. But we were there, Ben, we were there!"

Trask gripped his arm tighter still. "Before or after this Big Bang?"

But the precog could only shrug apologetically. "Ben, I'm sorry, but as I've said it was kaleidoscopic, all utterly confused, disordered. As to what came first, I just don't know . . ."

And before Trask could question either the precog or the locator further—

Coming from the steep stairwell between the reception desk and the door to the dining room, a burst of gunfire sounded and the clatter of chaotic movement. Frank Robinson appeared, staggering backward down the stairs, directing a continuous stream of fire up onto the landing. But as his weapon's fire failed he fumbled for a spare magazine, tripped, and flew backward, shouting, "Jesus Christ! Oh, my good God!"

Following him in no great haste, seeming to float down the stairs—and yet with paradoxically jerky or spastic movements of stick-thin limbs—came a weirdly tall, willowy figure with deep-sunken eyes, a long neck, and a long head, wearing his hair in a silvery comb that overlapped his pure white kaftan's laid-back cowl. It was Mordri Three, also known as Guyler Schweitzer, but it was not his now completely alien appearance that momentarily paralysed Trask and his E-Branch friends. No, it was what he was guiding or leading alongside him, like a dog on a leash, with the wand-like, foot-long fingers of a foot-long hand sunk deep in one of its ears.

And because no other description could adequately or immediately describe it, all three who saw it, however dimly in the foyer's shadowy gloom, could only properly think of it as "some sort of thing."

A thing indeed! But on looking closer—and as the horrifying fact sank in—there could be no denying that *this* thing's agonized, silently shrieking face . . . *was that of special agent Norbert Hauser!*

38

Shania used the localizer, and she and Scott arrived in Idossola at the place she knew best there, the *Gasthaus* on the main street, no longer in use and dark. But still they arrived with all due caution, Scott with Wolf draped over his shoulders and a sawn-off shotgun in his hands, aimed forward, with his finger on the triggers.

They were in the foyer—dusty, and cobwebbed in its ceiling—where just a little moon and starlight came filtering in through high, fly-specked windows. As Shania released Scott he crouched down, backed up to the dust-layered desk, and let Wolf kick himself free of his shoulders.

Undignified, said that one, jumping down, *but comfortable.*

"Speak for yourself," said Scott. And then to Shania, "The place is completely empty, deserted?"

She nodded. "This is where I stayed, but when I scanned it I could detect nothing, no one. There are several other places I could have brought us to, but this building gives us immediate cover."

"Except now we have to get out of here," said Scott, "and I don't know Idossola. I won't be able to find my way around."

"Perhaps we can help you there," said Shania.

"We?"

"Me and my Khiff." When she spoke to her Khiff Scott heard what she said. *My Khiff, do you remember that place high in the foothills under the crag? We climbed there once, until we dared climb no higher?*

Of course I remember, my Shania, her Khiff at once replied. *Mordri thoughts lay heavily on the air, so that we feared to be discovered. And now? Would you go there again?*

If my localizer has retained sufficient power, yes. Shania held the device to her forehead, and in a moment:

Three or four very short multiple-person trips remain possible before the localizer is spent, the Khiff at once reported.

Shania's face at once fell. *Only three or four more trips? Are you sure? Is that all?*

At which Scott came in, "Now hold!" And looking completely baffled, frowning his confusion: "Shania, what's going on here? I mean, for quite some time now you've been more than a little worried, concerned that your localizer is going to burn itself out—which has caused me to worry, too. Yet now you seem to be saying there's still a handful of trips left in it? I mean, can we or can't we trust the thing? Also, why is it I've been kept in the dark as to just exactly what the score is?"

"Ah . . ." Her face fell farther yet. "Perhaps in my efforts to spare the localizer, perhaps in the interests of economy—"

"—You've been a bit too economical with the facts of the matter?" Scott finished it for her, stood back from her, stared hard, and waited for her answer.

"But if I had let you believe that the localizer was inexhaustible," Shania began to protest, "you might have tempted me to use it more adventurously or recklessly, and in so doing put yourself in more danger! Also . . ." She paused.

"Yes, also?"

"Please remember that when all of the trips are used up—and when my localizer is utterly depleted—then my Khiff will also be . . . used up. Scott, I could never let it go that far. I have been trying—*had* to try—to keep something in reserve."

And remembering all that she had told him about her Khiff, about their lifelong relationship, he sighed, relaxed, and said, "Of course you've tried. I'm sorry I was so insensitive."

My Shania, time is wasting, said the Khiff. *And in order to understand what is happening you still need to see the village from your lofty vantage point of old. Wherefore you should now note these coordinates . . .*

As Shania's Khiff gave coordinates, Scott took Wolf under one arm. Then Shania wrapped her arms around his neck, her slim fingers moving deftly on her wrist device, and:

There came darkness, and almost immediately a lesser gloom in which—

—They stood in the faint light of the stars on a scree-littered hillside under Schloss Zonigen.

"Look!" said Shania, her head tilted up at a sharp angle. Scott followed her rapt gaze, his eyes narrowing at the frenzy of coruscating lights—like so many Christmas tree illuminations blazing on and off but in no particular sequence—in the high walls of the cavern-riddled crag.

"The Mordris are monstrously busy," said Shania, a slight tremor in her voice. "They use—they *mis*use—their powers to threaten and chastise those who serve them. They feel the pressure. Obviously the work has not gone well, or it has gone too slowly and now they feel the need to hasten their workers. But oh, those poor people, their hostages!"

"How do you know about them?" said Scott, now scanning the village hundreds of feet below.

"What?" she said, looking at him. "But can't you *feel* the horror seeping out of that place? I know you could if you would open your mind to it."

I feel it, said Wolf, trembling however slightly where he leaned against Scott's legs. *That is a very bad place.* Then, as his gaze joined Scott's on the village down below: *And there go the hunters in their vehicles! Oh, I know their minds well, for I am a wolf of the wild who was once hunted. So if anyone knows them, I do. They are horrid killers!*

"Your minds must do as you see fit," Scott told them. "Me, I've no time right now for horror, though I'm sure it's coming. Instead I'm concentrating on what I can see: those three cars, for instance. Yes, Wolf, you're right. First they were clearly in convoy; now they're splitting up, moving apart as they come to a halt in the narrow side streets around that building with the small square in front. And now, see—they've dimmed their headlights."

Hunters, yes! said Wolf again. *But they don't hunt rabbits or chickens—they hunt men!*

"That place is . . . is a small *Gasthaus*," said Shania, with her eyes closed and a hand to her forehead. "That is where your E-Branch people are trapped under siege." And opening her eyes, glancing to one side: "Look there: another vehicle, bigger, and with yet more people—"

More hunters! Wolf cut in.

"—descending from Schloss Zonigen."

"We have to join up with E-Branch," said Scott. "They knew about me, tried to help me. Now we have to help them."

"Yes of course." Shania nodded. "We must."

Scott's eyes narrowed as he trained them on the coach that negotiated the hairpins down from the high crag. Its motion had slowed to a creep where it approached a sharp bend with a sheer cliff face on one side and a drop of some five hundred feet on the other. And to Wolf: "Hunters? You're sure?"

They have weapons, that one growled in Scott's mind. *Their thoughts are full of blood. These are truly bad men!*

"Take us to that bend!" said Scott, hoisting Wolf with one hand and grabbing Shania with the other. "Can you do that?"

"If I can see it," she answered, her fingers on the localizer, "I can do it."

She did it, and they were there!

The driver saw them in his headlights as he came around

the bend: a man, a woman, and a dog, just standing there in the road. No, not *just* standing there. The dog was crouched, eyes aflame, snarling—and the ones he was with were aiming weapons!

Squeezing her eyes tight shut and firing blindly, Shania jerked on both of her shotgun's triggers. Twin blasts shattered one of the coach's headlights, and the tire immediately beneath it disintegrated into chunks of rubber. The weapon's recoil unbalanced Shania, causing her to fall backward on the road. The front of the coach lurched to one side, jolted against the face of the cliff and glanced off, but somehow the driver managed to retain partial control. And fighting the steering wheel, deliberately targeting the three figures on the road, he brought the coach trundling forward again.

Knowing little or nothing about shotguns, still Scott had learned something from Shania's mistake. Aiming at the driver's window and squeezing off one barrel, he saw the man hurled backward in his seat, hands flying to a face mangled with shot and shards of glass. And without pause Scott aimed and fired at the other front tire.

The coach came on, skidding on the rims of front wheels that threw off showers of white sparks. And as Scott moved to scoop Shania up from the road, with Wolf snarling and skittering this way and that, so the coach hit the safety rail, tore it loose, and tilted over into a void of night air. There were faces at the windows—pale, shrieking, terrified faces, their eyes and their mouths wide open, disbelieving—and then they were gone.

It seemed a very long time before an explosion like a bomb going off sounded from below, its echoes bouncing from wall to wall of the valley, gradually fading.

"So much death!" said Shania in Scott's arms.

"Yes, but less than a world of death," he answered as he reloaded the shotguns with shells from his pockets. "And hell, all of those bastards together were less than Kelly!"

"Yes, I agree." Shania nodded. "Of course I do. But there are at least three more carloads of them down in the village,

surrounding your friends. What do you think? Can we perhaps be of more help to E-Branch on the outside?"

"I think you're right," said Scott. "Do you see that open
space surrounded by trees—maybe a park or kids'
playground—just two side streets this side of the *Gasthaus*?
I saw the last of those cars parking on the far side. If you
can take us there so that we come up behind them, maybe
we can do a lot more serious damage."

And no sooner said than done, they were there in the
playground, creeping forward.

I smell hunters up ahead! said Wolf.

"Then go as quietly as you can," Scott answered him in a
whisper, forgetting for a moment that he was able to use
Wolf's own telepathic medium. But in the next moment he
remembered and said, *Take us to them. Point them out.*

With never a sound, quickly merging with the shadows,
Wolf went on ahead . . .

At that precise moment, in the foyer of the Gasthaus Alpenmann, Ben Trask, Ian Goodly, and David Chung were still
emerging from their moments of shocked paralysis and
Frank Robinson was lying on his back at the foot of the
stairs, scrabbling away from the alien creature who bore inexorably down on him.

As Guyler Schweitzer came, he cast aside the veritable
caricature of the man that had been Norbert Hauser—now
a loose-limbed, scarecrow thing with useless tentacle arms,
welded lips, and tatters of clothing hanging from what had
been a sturdy and entirely human frame. Set free, Hauser
flopped in a heap on the stairs, then tumbled like a bundle
of rags to the bottom.

"Sh-sh-*shoot* that f-fucking thing!" Robinson was shouting, pointing a trembling finger at Mordri Three while dig-
ging out a spare magazine with his other hand and trying to
fumble it into the housing of his weapon. "Jesus Christ,
shoot it!"

Locator Chung and precog Goodly, closer than Trask to
the stairwell, needed no second bidding. Triggering their

weapons, they blasted off single shots that would have stopped any ordinary person dead in his tracks, heard the *splat! splat! splat!* sounds that punctuated each shot, sounds of hot metal impacting on flesh. Schweitzer staggered a little as an uneven pattern of dark holes appeared in the chest and trunk of his white kaftan; he staggered, yes, but scarcely seemed concerned. And with his long arms reaching, he continued to bear down on Robinson.

The spotter had reloaded, but his weapon had jammed! Somehow struggling to his feet, he threw the SMG at Schweitzer, who simply batted it aside in midair. Then, as Chung's and Goodly's magazines emptied and their gunfire stuttered to a halt, so the alien spoke, his voice booming in the ringing, cordite-tainted air:

"We were curious to see who threatened us," his words rang out. "For we thought to discern something new and different—a *Presence* in the psychosphere—and we wondered if perhaps some god had come to the aid of your loathsome, degenerate planet in these its final hours. But no, your gods are false gods, as are *all* gods, and you are only men, albeit cleverer than the majority. But these talents of yours: they are nothing; neither your talents nor your weapons. Compared to the Shing't, or perhaps I should say the Mordri Three, you *yourselves* are nothing! Ignorant god-lovers and 'true believers,' your flesh is weak, and so very, *very*... malleable." Smiling monstrously, he came on.

Babbling to himself, completely unmanned, Robinson had managed to back off out of Schweitzer's way. But now the alien was moving faster, his spindly arms reaching for Chung and Goodly.

"Don't let him touch you!" Robinson screamed at them. "For God's sake don't! He touched Hauser and I saw what happened. We didn't see him come—maybe I sensed him at the last moment—but he was suddenly there behind us. He took hold of Hauser for just a few seconds, and ... and ..."

"And this!" said Schweitzer, his neck outstretched and his spidery hands descending eagerly toward Chung and Goodly.

But then Ben Trask was there, shouldering the pair aside, one hand on the grip of Hauser's flamethrower, the other on its trigger; and the weapon's pilot light flaring, hissing a chemical threat. "So if bullets don't impress you," Trask grated the words out, "how about this?"

Mordri Three jerked to a halt, his arms seeming to shrink back as if they were elastic, as fire roared from the nozzle of Trask's terrible weapon. The long flame was blue in its sheath, white in the middle, invisible in its core, which was where its heat was concentrated. Trask spilled liquid fire on Schweitzer, setting his kaftan ablaze and sending the stick-like figure who wore it reeling toward the stairs, his arms thrashing, beating uselessly at the flames. A stench was at once apparent: that of roasting flesh. And Mordri Three was shrieking!

When Trask took his finger off the trigger, he and the men with him saw a pillar of fire, the last of Schweitzer's kaftan, blazing to the ceiling, while the creature it had covered continued to shriek and back away like a seared slug. Its flesh on one thin flank was black and visibly shrivelling, and its head jerked to and fro in an agonized frenzy. Finally, with a shriek that was louder and shriller yet, it fumbled its long hands together and in the next moment appeared to implode!

The flames at once went out, and Trask and his people were left staggering, coughing in the smoke and the stink. And there was no sign of Mordri Three.

"What the hell . . . ?" said Trask when he could speak. "Where did he go?" Then, turning to Robinson, "Frank, what happened up there?"

"I . . . I don't know," Robinson answered, from where he was backed into a corner of the room. "He, it, that bloody thing—whatever it was—came out of nowhere. It just appeared out of nowhere, behind us in that room! I barely had time to sense its presence before it was standing there. And it was strong! Damn, it knocked that gun out of my hands like it was a toy and I had to scramble for it! But I saw it touch Hauser, and then . . . and then he . . . he started to change!"

Trask put down the flamethrower on the reception desk, ran at Robinson, and grabbed his lapels. "Frank, listen," he snarled. "I need you to get a grip on yourself, and now! Okay, so things are happening that we don't understand, things that are outside our previous experience; but isn't that what we're all about? I *need* you, Frank, so start acting like a fucking man!"

"Christ! Oh, Christ!" said the other, his face like death where Trask held him upright against the wall. "But you weren't there . . . you didn't see!"

Trask might have struck Robinson then, but from out in the night came new sounds that drew him back to the shattered circular windows. They were dully booming blasts that came from the near-distance, but by no means automatic or semi-automatic gunfire. "What?" said Trask, squinting out into the darkness from one side of his window. "Shotguns? Do I hear shotguns? But how can that be? Four shots in short order, almost simultaneously?"

"Shotguns, definitely," said Chung, feeling psychic vibrations and the sudden unnatural warmth of a certain heavy object in his pocket. "Two of them, and double-barrelled. So if these people haven't started fighting themselves, it has to be Scott St. John and his girlfriend. There's no longer any doubt in my mind. I *know* that it's them—and they're here!"

Even as he spoke two more booming explosions sounded, but closer this time. And out in the night there were cries, curses, shocked shouting, and screams of pain. But in the darkest corner of the room Frank Robinson was still babbling to himself:

"I can feel them, sense them. Two more of them, maybe even three. They're close and coming closer all the time, and one of them's a real power! Oh, God, *he's a real power!*"

"Get these lights back on," Trask snapped. "We have to

be able to see what we're doing." The precog found the switch and flooded the room with light, and Trask went on, "As for Frank: it seems to me he's out of it. But on the other hand we should take heed of what he says. He's hypersensitive to psychics, so if he says they're coming, then—"

At which the door to the dining room creaked open!

Millie Cleary stood there looking out at three armed men, and all of their weapons trained on her! Blinking in the light, she said, "What?" And Trask breathed a sigh of relief.

"Millie." He moved toward her. "What are you doing here?"

"I keep asking myself that same question," she said, shakily. "I just had a message, that's all."

"You what? A message?" Trask knew she spoke the truth but failed to understand. And frowning he asked, "What do you mean, 'that's all'? From whom?"

"A woman, I think," said Millie. "But her telepathy . . . I never experienced anything like it. It was as if she were standing right beside me! Anyway, she says to hold your fire."

"They're coming!" Robinson screamed from where he crouched in the corner. "Oh, Jesus, they're coming *now!*"

Even as he spoke the three sets of chandelier lights went berserk, almost strobing as they flashed on and off, while the chandeliers themselves danced on their cables and fixings!

Then in a sudden rush of displaced air, three more beings were in the foyer—and Chung, Millie, and Scott St. John were shouting in unison, "Hold your fire! Hold your fire!"

In the silence that followed the locator David Chung shook his head dazedly and murmured, "Good God, but just a moment ago I could have sworn that it . . . I mean it felt just like . . . like it was Harry Keogh himself coming in!" Then, as his almond eyes opened wider: "No, it's him, Scott St. John. *He* feels just like Harry!"

And Trask, knowing Chung spoke the truth or what he saw as the truth, stepped forward and asked Scott outright, "Is it so? I mean, impossible or no—in whatever shape, form, or reincarnation—are you the Necroscope, Harry Keogh?"

Scott shook his head and crouched down to let Wolf off his shoulders. "Not a bit of it," he said. "I'm just me."

But then his companion stuck out a grimy hand to Trask and said, "Well actually, it's possible that he's just a little bit more than him. Myself, I'm Shania, and I'm very pleased to meet you . . ."

39

Almost without thinking, Ben Trask took Shania's hand, released it just as quickly, then stared hard at her and her companions: Shania and Scott St. John . . . and Wolf of course. But where the latter looked fairly pristine—a handsome animal, and far more wolf than dog—the two human figures were anything but. Clad in black track suits (Shania had thought well ahead), carrying sawn-off, double-barrelled shotguns and wearing determined expressions on faces smeared with greasy soot from the fireplace in Scott's living room, there could be no doubt but that these were soldiers on a mission. And it was Ben Trask's instinct as much as his talent that told him they were his allies.

Meanwhile, as their arrival's effect on the electrics wore off, and as Shania brought her heightened psychic energies more properly under control, the lights had stopped their gyrations. Also, it had dawned on Ian Goodly that if any of the enemy had taken the opportunity to creep closer to the building, then he and his E-Branch colleagues—not to mention their new friends—would make excellent targets in the now well lit foyer. And ever aware of the future's unpredictability and devious nature, the precog said, "We should move well away from the windows."

Scott told him, "That's good advice—er, 'Xavier'?—but there's maybe five or six of them out there who won't be bothering you anymore."

Still Trask told Chung and Goodly, "Get up on a table

and take some of those bulbs out of the chandeliers, all but one or two." And seeing Millie Cleary pinning pages from a Swiss broadsheet over the circular windows, but yet leaving narrow gaps at both sides through which the defenders were able to observe and shoot if that should once more become necessary, he nodded his approval.

Then he turned back to Scott and Shania. "So then, those blasts we heard were your shotguns, and you've taken out maybe half a dozen of those people out there?"

Scott nodded. "Yes. I don't think we got them all, but we certainly scared off any who we missed! They weren't expecting trouble from the rear."

"And those?" Trask indicated a pair of fragmentation grenades dangling from Scott's ex-army web belt. "What, you raided an armoury or something?"

Glancing down at his belt, Scott replied, "Oh, those! No, I took them from one of the men we shot. That was probably his next move: to toss them in here."

Trask nodded. "Then we're lucky, and we're very grateful."

Dozens of questions crowded Trask's mind, but right now he had other things to do, and anyway he didn't know which ones to ask first! Shaking his head, he looked again at Scott, and took an even longer look at his companion. Despite the black finger stripes of soot on her face, this was obviously a lovely woman. In face and form . . . why, hers was an almost unearthly loveliness! On considering that last thought, Trask was only a little surprised to find himself frowning . . .

Looking this way and that, familiarizing herself with her surroundings, Shania had seen the unnaturally crumpled shape of Norbert Hauser at the foot of the stairs. Her hand at once flew to her mouth, and she asked, "What? Were the Mordri Three here? Did they actually leave their refuge to risk coming here?"

"The Mordri Three?" Trask repeated. "Is that what you call them, those shape-changing bastards up in Schloss Zonigen? Well, *one* of them was here, yes." He grimaced and added, "That's the result," meaning Hauser. "He wasn't one of mine—thank the Lord, but he was a friend. As to why that murderous thing came: if I remember correctly he was looking to discover some sort of god-figure? But he was also trying to kill us, and it seemed to me he was as mad as a hatter!"

Shania glanced at Scott and said, "They've felt your presence, enhanced by my own and Wolf's." Then she hurried over to the collapsed form of Hauser and went down on her knees to lay her hands on his transformed body. It was far too late for him, however, and shaking her head sadly, slowly she stood up again. "He's gone and I can't help him. I'm sorry . . ."

Just for a moment as she had laid hands on Hauser, a pair of small lightbulbs in the central chandelier—the only ones Chung and Goodly had left secured in their sockets—had begun flickering and jolting again. Having noticed this, Trask had at once associated it with the electrical chaos that had ensued as this disparate trio first arrived. Now, as the lights steadied up, he said:

"You can't help him? But surely there's nothing you could do that could possibly have . . . helped . . . him?" Pausing for a moment as suddenly he knew the truth of it, Trask felt himself stiffening up a little, frowned, and said, "You're one of them, aren't you?" But it was more a statement than a question.

"No, she isn't!" Scott rasped, half crouching, his weapon pointing at the floor but in Trask's general direction. "Shania is one of us, so don't you go jumping to any wrong conclusions, or start making any serious mistakes!"

"Take it easy," said Trask at once. "I didn't mean it like that." Well, perhaps he had, but not entirely.

"Of course you didn't," said Shania. "Anyway, you're right to be suspicious, for your lives are at stake." She crossed the floor to Trask. "But tell me: which one of them was it, and how did you beat him off? Bullets wouldn't have been much use."

Trask nodded, took her to a small table near the reception desk, and showed her the flamethrower. "You're right. He was hit maybe a dozen times at close range, and any one of those shots would have stopped a man stone dead. But not him, he kept right on coming. This is what finally stopped him." He rapped his knuckles on the weapon's dully glinting casing. "He didn't like this one little bit!"

"A fire weapon," she said, nodding. "Oh, yes, that would do it. He would fear that. Even self-repairing flesh will get eaten up by fire. So who was he, Mordri Two or Three?"

Frowning, Trask shook his head. "I don't know how they're numbered," he replied, "but this fellow was thin as a lath and all of seven feet tall. His hair was silver and worn in a sort of stiff coxcomb. I believe his name is Guyler Schweitzer."

"The last and least of them," said Shania. "Mordri Three!"

David Chung spoke up, the tremor in his voice showing how his nerves were beginning to play him up. "Well, if that was the least of them," he said, "I can certainly do without seeing the worst of them!"

"You won't," Shania told him with a shake of her head. "At least, not down here. Not if Mordri Three went back to the high crag displaying burns. Gelka Mordri—or Mordri One—won't be taking any more chances with her subordinates, not now that she knows you have a fire weapon."

From out in the night came the screech of tires on tarmac; and from the window where Millie was squinting through a gap in one of her broadsheet "curtains," she reported: "I can see headlights moving—one set anyway—lighting up the road back to Schloss Zonigen. It seems some of them are pulling out."

"It's pretty much the same at the back," said Paul Garvey, having returned from his vigil at the rear of the hotel and now standing framed in the doorway to the dining room. As he spoke, footsteps sounded on the stairs where Techs McGrath and Taylor, the final members of the team, descended into view.

"Aye," McGrath agreed, emerging more fully into the light. "There were just one or two o' they left, and as they made for their car Graham here sent a bolt through another scrawny neck. Their losses hae been heavy, which may . . ." He paused as he saw the newcomers, then continued: ". . . Which may or may not be why they've suddenly decided tae leave us be. But what's all this? Is it no a couple o' new recruits ah can see?" He eyed Scott's and Shania's weapons appreciatively.

And Trask didn't hesitate to reply, "Yes, it most definitely is. Or if not recruits, reinforcements certainly."

Hurried introductions all round followed, and soon Millie reported a second vehicle's headlights lancing the night on its retreat up the precipitous zigzag road to Schloss Zonigen. This had to be the last one or two members of the group that McGrath had reported.

And now Trask and his crew were able to relax a little and begin asking questions of the newcomers in earnest. The locator David Chung was barely able to contain himself.

"Scott," he said, when Trask okayed it. "So you're not the Necroscope, Harry Keogh. Okay—but I have to say you felt very much like him, and—"

"I *felt* like him?" Scott cut in. "How do you mean?" But in fact he knew what Chung meant. It was just that he still tended to back away from it.

"Ah!" Chung fingered his chin. "How do I mean? But how can I explain? Let me try. You see, I have this knack, and—"

And now Shania cut in: "David is a psychic sensitive," she said as she read Chung's mind. "He's a locator. Which means he can find things, including people. And because people—especially gifted ones—have individual auras, their own feel, he's able to remember them. David remembers how Harry Keogh . . . well, how he *felt,* that's all."

"Yes." Chung nodded, looked puzzled. "That's it exactly. I couldn't have put it much better myself . . ." And then he continued: "But then again there's this other thing, the way you *came* here—and not only you but also that Mordri creature—which must have been via the Möbius Continuum. So if you're not Harry Keogh or . . . or some *kind* of Necroscope, then what are you? And what are these Mordris? Because it's obvious that they used the same route."

Shania answered him. "You must be aware now that the Mordris are, well, alien to your world, extraterrestrial. They come from a race called the Shing't, most of whom they have murdered along with their planet. They are evil, insane. The scientific achievements of the Shing't are far in advance of your own, but fortunately for you—for all of us—Shing't weapons technology, at least on a small-arms scale, is nonexistent. They have no enemies and wage no wars; therefore there are no sidearms—and in any case the Mordris would not care to use such. So they rely on dupes, mercenary men such as the ones you've fought off tonight, to fight for them. As for the way they move from place to place . . ." She looked at Scott, who now took it up:

"It isn't the Möbius Continuum," he said. "And yes, having been there I know about the Continuum; but Mordri teleportation isn't it. As Harry may have explained it to you, what he called the Möbius Continuum is of the mind: it's metaphysical, and can only be conjured using weird maths. But what the Mordris do is science, pure physics. That's how they became space-travellers, and for short distances they use the same principle on a smaller scale."

"You're saying it's a mechanical, scientific thing?" said Chung.

Shania held out her localizer where they could see it. "It can—or could—take me anywhere I wanted to go in this entire world. Now it's almost all used up. After just a few more short trips it will be finished, useless. But up there in Schloss Zonigen, the Mordri Three are building a much bigger machine, what you would call a spaceship: in fact, a large man-carrying device for surfing gravity waves. And when it is energized . . . but no, we can't *allow* it to be energized, for not only would that give the murderers their escape route, it would also mean the total destruction of your planet!"

Trask was beginning to understand things. Looking at Shania he said, "These Mordris murdered your race, an entire race?" His expression showed the depth of the sympathy he felt. "Well, that surely explains why you're here."

Shania nodded. "Call it revenge if you will, but I call it justice. With Scott's help—and Wolf's, and now yours—I'll stop them if I can."

With Wolf's help? That made twice Shania had mentioned the animal in this way. But Trask let it pass, turned to Scott, and said, "I think we know your reasons well enough."

"Mordri Two is my reason," said Scott, gruffly. "You probably know him as Simon Salcombe. He killed my wife."

"Yes," said Trask. "When you boil it down that's why we're here, too. If it wasn't for you, your loss, we might never have investigated in the first place." Then he looked at the precog and said, "Ian, if I've ever seemed to doubt you—"

"It isn't a problem," said Goodly, smiling one of his oh-so-rare smiles. "But if we get out of this with our skins intact you can treat me to the best lunch money can buy. Yes, and Anna Marie English, too." And turning to Scott and Shania, he said:

"We couldn't join forces with you at the beginning of this thing because we didn't want to jeopardize your part in it. You see, I knew that you—both of you, in fact all three of you—would be the prime movers in whatever was coming. Any interference on our part might take the initiative away from you, might destroy your effectiveness."

At which Shania said, "And we couldn't let you in on what we were doing for the very same reasons. If we had alerted you, with all of your special talents, it might have meant alerting the Mordris, too. For they must have known of you as surely as I did. You and your talents, you stir the psychic aether."

"And so you kept your shields up," said Paul Garvey.

"As best we could." Shania nodded.

"And so did you," said Scott. And then he grinned, albeit ruefully. "You know, you people gave me quite a rough time!"

They once were your enemies, said Wolf, who until now had kept absolutely quiet while sizing up the situation. *Or so you thought. But as it now turns out they are your friends?*

"That's right," said Scott out loud, without thinking.

Millie Cleary and Paul Garvey gave massive starts, staring at Wolf where he cocked his head on the side, one ear bent in a querying attitude. *Oh?* he said. *Did you think you were the only ones who could talk inside your heads?*

Now Millie and Garvey stared at each other, and their jaws fell open. Seeing their astonished expressions, Trask was immediately alarmed. "What now?" he asked.

"Eh?" said Garvey, his eyes on Wolf again. "Oh!" The telepath finally got a grip on himself. "What's wrong? Well, nothing very much. It's just that this fellow here"—he indicated Wolf—"is unusually clever."

"He's what?" said Trask.

"He's not only clever," said Millie. "He's a telepath!"

"Damn!" said Trask, as once again the truth, if not quite the whole truth, struck him. "Zante—Jazz and Zek—and Wolf! Zek's wolf from Sunside/Starside! We've wondered about that."

"No." Scott shook his head. "That's Wolf Senior, and this is Wolf Junior. A wolf of the wild, born here, and one hell of a fellow in his own right. He makes up our Three Unit."

"Your what?"

"Don't worry about it," said Scott. "It isn't important."

"But about Wolf—" Trask was frowning again, for something wasn't quite right here. He turned to the precog. "Ian, don't I recall asking you to contact Zek about this?"

"You did," said Goodly, "and I didn't."

"You what? You lied!?" Trask could scarcely believe it.

"What, to you?" said the precog. "Quite impossible! Fortunately you never mentioned it again, so I didn't need to lie."

"But . . . why?"

Goodly sighed, and said, "Because I wasn't about to—"

Trask finished it for him: "—To compromise anyone? Yes, I can see that now. And even if you didn't follow orders, once again I owe you one." But the precog simply shrugged it off.

Mystified by much of what they'd heard, the techs had gone to the windows and were peering out into the night. It was full night now, and up in the hollow crag the lights were still coruscating in a frenzy of activity. Graham Taylor turned from his window and called out, "Has anyone taken a look at what's going on up there recently? A few fireworks is all that's needed, and then it would be like some kind of crazy aerial carnival!"

At which Shania joined the techs and looked out and up at Schloss Zonigen. As Scott, Trask, and the others followed her to the windows, she said, "Yes, the Mordri Three are in a passion, allowing their energies to run wild. Now might be the time I've been waiting for—my last opportunity—to discover their best-kept secret."

"Using your telepathy?" said Paul Garvey, who understood.

"Yes."

"Their best-kept secret?" said Trask.

And Goodly answered, "When they intend to launch, searing our world with their exhaust."

Shania started to nod, then shrugged and said, "Well, not quite, but close enough."

Scott took her elbow. "Not again." He shook his head. "You can't be serious about trying to contact them. They may be mad, but it's still three minds to your one."

"Not really," said Millie. "There's also myself, Paul, and Wolf. Yes and you, too, Scott. E-Branch was right about one of your talents at least: your telepathy."

But Shania had already put an arm around Scott's waist and was reassuring him. "No, I won't try to probe the Mordris; and certainly not Gelka. She's quite obviously in a state with herself; who knows what she'd do if she sensed me trying to enter her mind? But what about all of those other people up there—the ordinary people—surely they must know at least something of what's going on? It's their minds I have to probe. But I'll need all of you to give me cover."

"You've got it," said Scott, "as long as you'll promise to leave those mad devils well alone."

Whenever you are ready, said Wolf.

And Paul and Millie nodded in unison, which was sufficient in itself. But then, accepting Trask's authority as usual, they looked to him for his approval.

"Very well," he said. "Let's do it. But first: Graham, and David. We still need to keep a watch. You two take the upstairs rear; it's a good vantage point. Alan and Ian, upstairs here at the front. The rest of us stay here, and if we need it I'll fix up a watch roster later. Where's Frank Robinson?"

"I . . . I'm here, boss," said that one, coming out of the shadows in the farthest corner of the room. "I . . . I feel like a bloody fool, a rotten coward."

"Well don't," Trask growled. "Because this isn't over yet, not by a long shot, and I'm still going to need you. You're our spotter, remember?"

"I . . . I got a terrific shock, that's all," said Robinson, "It . . . it sort of unsettled me."

"I'll say!" Trask nodded. "But how about now? You've settled down again?"

"Yes, I think so."

"Okay, what's past is past." Trask turned to Scott, Shania, and the rest of his crew. "Those of you who are taking part, we should get you seated around a table. And then when we've calmed down a little, let's get on with it . . ."

40

And so with four of Trask's team continuing to keep watch from upstairs at the front and rear of the *Gasthaus,* Scott, Millie Cleary, and Paul Garvey—and Wolf, even that one, in a chair of his own with his paws on the table—sat in something of a circle, throwing a mental shield around Shania where she sent out her telepathic probe to Schloss Zonigen.

Scott and Shania flanked Wolf, their hands on his clawed paws. Millie and Paul were seated opposite, connected to each other by touch, and also to Scott and Shania. And much like a seance group they were the souls of concentration, as if they conjured other souls—those of the dead, a notion that indeed gave Scott pause, so that he must put it right out of his head—but all five of them concerned now with the living, aware of the danger in what they were doing, and no one daring to relax his or her mental effort for the smallest fraction of a second.

"Schloss Zonigen!" Shania breathed the words like a curse, her eyes closed, her still camouflaged forehead deeply creased, her Khiff—as yet a secret ally, unknown to Trask and E-Branch—lying by no means dormant in her mind but ready at a moment's notice to spring to her defence. And:

"Schloss Zonigen," Shania said it again, but just a little louder. "I have to seek out the ordinary people, those who live in fear: the captives, hostages, and injured people, the workers who bend to Mordri threats. Some of these must surely know when it's going to be, and the fate of the entire world hangs in the balance of that knowledge."

Keeping guard by one of the circular windows—occasionally craning their necks to watch the flickering lights in the ice castle, but more often with their eyes glued on Shania and the other telepaths—Trask and Robinson were both well aware of the importance of the moment. The latter, however, with the nightmarish nature of what he had seen continuing to cloud his mind, remained more than a little dubious of the situation, of the newcomers, and of almost everything else.

"That woman, Shania," he said very quietly, making sure he wasn't overheard by those at the table. "She's a whole lot more than she seems."

"I know," said Trask.

"Yes, but she's even *more* than you know," the other insisted. "I can feel it, it's what I do."

"Yes, I know," said Trask again. "Weren't you listening to what she told us?"

Silent for a moment, finally Robinson admitted, "Actually, boss, I don't think I was listening to much of anything! I was right out of it, in a complete funk, and I'm really very sorry. I feel I've let you down. And now . . . well, perhaps I'm trying too hard not to let you down again."

"I'm sure you won't," said Trask. "So get over it. Anyway, St. John says Shania's on our side, and she certainly has good reason to be."

"Perhaps, but what about St. John himself?" Robinson still needed convincing. "David Chung is right. When St. John—when they—were on their way here, just a split second before they arrived, I felt them coming. It was like . . . I don't know, some kind of mental tsunami! It was *that* powerful! And the only time I've ever felt anything like that before was at the Necroscope's place in Scotland, the night we razed his house to the ground."

"Oh, really?" said Trask. "Well you know something, Frank? That's truly excellent news, because that's precisely the sort of power we may need to see this thing through."

"You do trust them then? I mean, completely?"

Staring straight into Robinson's eyes, Trask said, "Every word that St. John and Shania have spoken since they first got here has been true or what they believe to be the truth. And I do mean *every* word they've spoken."

The other nodded. "Fine. But have they spoken every word?"

Instead of answering him, Trask looked at the group around the table, held up a quietening hand, and said, "*Shh!* Look, something's happening!"

For suddenly Shania's back was ramrod-straight against the back of her chair, as if she strained against it. Her eyes were still closed but her mouth was half open, her face turned up at an angle—looking not at the ceiling over

Trask's and Robinson's heads but through it—"looking," in fact, at Schloss Zonigen.

"Those poor people!" she whispered, drawing Trask back to the table the better to hear what she said. "They are in pain, tortured, terrified! And the guards, the trustees and soldiers, many of them criminals: the things they've done, despicable and unbelievable cruelty! And many of them lusting still! The workers—the lies that they have been told—all frantically busy, putting the finishing touches to the Mordri Three's vessel. For they think that when the grav-ship departs they'll be set free, their loved ones returned to them whole again in body and mind. No, they don't *really* believe the Mordris will keep their word, not all of them, yet at the same time they daren't *not* believe! They *have* to believe in something. But in all of the prisoners, hostages, and workers, the uppermost emotion is hatred! Given a chance, one decent opportunity, and they would fight, even some of the trustees. Alas, but until now they've had no chance, and the Mordri Three's punishments are severe . . ."

As she paused, Trask spoke to her from close at hand. Not wanting to break her connection with the thoughts of the people trapped in Schloss Zonigen, however, he spoke almost as quietly as Shania herself, asking the all-important question: "But when is it going to be? When, Shania, when?"

"The Mordris have accelerated things," she said, without seeming to speak to Trask directly, as if she simply continued to transcribe the thoughts drifting outward from Schloss Zonigen. "It appears they're afraid; perhaps they begin to feel the hatred and the sheer energy of the talents ranged against them. And so they have brought the time of their departure forward—not just once but on two or three occasions—until now it's going to be . . . it will be . . ."

"Yes?" said Trask.

At which a ragged cry sounded from the stairs: "Ben! It's going to happen at dawn!" Holding on to the bannister and still almost falling, Ian Goodly came staggering into view. "At dawn, Ben—it *will* happen at dawn!"

The group at the table immediately broke apart, and starting to her feet Shania cried, "Yes, he's right! They've planned their departure for first light. As the sun rises, then they'll leave. And unless we stop them your world will go with them!"

Trask hurried to the foot of the stairs to offer his support to the precog, who was plainly shaken. "What did you see?" he demanded. "Damn it all, Ian, tell me what you saw!" And assisting Goodly to a chair, he helped lower him into it.

"What did I see, Ben?" said Goodly then, choking the words out. "Oh, I saw and felt more than enough! First, dawn's light: a crack of silver, dazzling on the eastern peaks. And a beam of purest energy lancing upward from the roof of Schloss Zonigen. Then I was inside a great cavern, where a trench of gold became liquid, burning in the fires of an electrical storm! But it was *real* liquid gold, Ben! Gold that flowed, then smoked, evaporating and turning into blue-grey sand! The essence of the gold—some unknown property of it—was being leeched off, sucked out of it along that beam of pure energy that poured through a hole in the cavern's ceiling. And tons of gold, quite literally *tons* of it, being converted in this manner, while the cavern's electrics went insane! Then it was done; there was nothing but this blue-grey spoil in the trench, and all the lights were out . . ."

"And?" said Trask. "What then, Ian? Don't tell me that was all you saw, because I *know* there was more to it than that!"

Of course Trask knew—as anyone who knew Ian Goodly would have known—if only because of the lost, hopeless look in the precog's eyes. And:

"More than that?" he finally groaned, a rare sound indeed, considering Goodly's usually high-pitched voice. "Oh, yes, there was something more, but I felt it rather than saw it:

"An incredible disruption of space-time. A massive blast,

followed by an irresistible suction—as if a great black hole had suddenly come into being. It was everything that Anna Marie and I told you about when we were working on it together at the HQ. Except that this time . . . this time . . ."

"Tell it, Ian," said Trask, gritting his teeth. "You have to tell it, because we have to know."

Goodly stared at him blankly for several long seconds and finally said, "Yes, yes of course you do. You have to know . . . but believe me you don't *want* to know."

"Go on," Trask urged. "After the blast—the disruption, Big Bang, or whatever else you want to call it—what then?"

"A vast erasure," Goodly answered, in the merest ghost of a voice. "Ben, I can't describe it any other way. It was . . . it was like everything we ever knew being shut down at once, wiped out, removed, erased. Until nothing was left but darkness."

Trask's throat was suddenly dry as chalk; it caused him to croak a little as he inquired, "Beyond which?"

"Beyond which there was nothing!" said the precog, shaking his head and slumping down in the chair . . .

For all that Ian Goodly's reputation was something of a legend in E-Branch, Trask hadn't been willing to let it go at that. A fighter to the very last, he'd immediately made himself responsible for bolstering morale, reminding his team that the future can be a very devious thing. Rallying to him, they had seen him sit down, behaving as nearly as possible as if nothing much had changed, and deliberately make out a watch duty roster. And now he continued to make plans, inviting suggestions from everyone around him.

"We should eat," said Paul Garvey. "We should have already eaten, but with everything that's been happening . . ."

"You're right," said Trask. "In the dining room there's a whole lot of food going to waste. It went cold a long time ago, but what does that matter? We should bring some of the choicest and most easily digestible cuts in here. And we can brew tea or get some fresh coffee on the go in the kitchen."

At which Millie Cleary said, "Leave the kitchen to me."

"Okay"—Trask nodded—"but there's something very unpleasant in there, and—"

"It's all right," she assured him. "It can't be any worse than what we've seen upstairs, or what happened to poor Norbert Hauser." The latter's body had been moved to a broom closet out of the way, undignified but very necessary. When Millie made to head for the kitchen Wolf went padding along with her; with his keen nose he knew there was death back there, but with any luck there should also be some fresh meat of a more acceptable kind. A wolf of the wild no longer, he'd now settled for a life with his human friends and that was that . . .

In something less than half an hour jugs of hot coffee and plates of food had been delivered to the four on duty upstairs, where Robinson had replaced Ian Goodly at the front of the *Gasthaus*. As for the latter: it appeared that his latest experience had completely exhausted him; the precog was asleep in the easy chair where he'd collapsed, and Trask had thrown a blanket over him.

While things had been settling down, Trask had also found time to order his thoughts. Now as the group in the foyer ate, he began to outline his simple plan:

"We can't get up there tonight," he began. "They know the place and we don't. Right now, up there on that esplanade, you can bet your life—you *would* be betting your lives—there's a fully armed welcoming party just waiting for us. And it'll be the same in the morning, but by then they should at least be as tired as we are; maybe more so if we can get some sleep tonight. And we will if we stick to the watch roster. So let's make that an order: if you're not on watch you're asleep, and your weapon is right there alongside you! We can never be too sure."

He paused to look at his watch, said, "Almost 9:30. Doesn't time fly when you're having fun?" And turning to Scott: "Any idea what time the sun comes up around here?"

Scott shook his head. "Never thought to check it out."

"Neither did we," said Trask.

But Shania said, "Even though it's summer here, dawn isn't as early as you might think. Your precog said the Mordris would depart when a crack of silver appeared on the eastern peaks. It seemed like dawn to him, and as far as this valley is concerned you might well call it dawn, but in fact it's about 6:15, 6:20 when the sun begins to clear the peaks."

Trask nodded. "You've done your homework."

"Not really," she said, "but I have been here before when I was trying to find out what they were up to, and it was about this time of year. I simply remembered it, that's all." In fact, it had been a very close friend—indeed a perpetual friend of hers—who remembered it. But then that was one of her Khiff's main functions.

"So then," said Trask, "if we're to get up there at all it will have to be before 6:15; let's say 5:30. That means we'll have to be out of here by . . . oh, five at the very latest."

"You'll be driving straight into the teeth of hell!" said Scott.

"I hope not," Trask replied. And to Shania: "Didn't I hear you say there was enough power in that thingumajig of yours for another two or three short trips?"

"Three more, I think," she answered. "Maybe even four, but that's just guesswork. Any small spark of energy retained after that wouldn't be enough to take anyone anywhere."

"But at least you and Scott will be able—"

"—To get up there ahead of you?" said Scott. "To reprise our previous attack, get behind them and take Schloss Zonigen's defenders by surprise? Yes, we can do that. I have to tell you, though, that after that you'll probably be on your own. I know what's important to you, Trask—and to everyone, of course—but I have my own agenda, too. If we're all going to die I want to be sure that at least one of those bastards is going to hell ahead of me."

"Simon Salcombe?"

"The same."

"Very well," said Trask. "I can't argue with you, for if I were in your place I'd feel the same. And without you we'd never stand a snowball in hell's chance of getting up there anyway!"

"That's it then?" said Scott. "Is that all there is to it? That's the deal?"

"Unless you've got something to add?" Trask looked at him. "Or you?" He turned to Shania. "Or any of you?" He glanced from face to face of the others. But only Wolf answered:

I go with my One and my Two! he growled, rising up on his hind legs and planting his paws on Trask's thighs. Then, fixing the Head of E-Branch with an unwavering feral glare, he said it again, *I go with Scott and Shania!*

Trask couldn't hear him, but the four telepaths could. And aloud Scott answered Wolf: "Certainly you're going. We'll doubtless be needing that nose of yours to sniff things out."

And now, understanding what had passed between them, Trask nodded his consent. "Yes, of course you'll go with them, Wolf." And dryly, "Let's face it, you're one of their Three Unit."

"Just one thing," said Scott then.

"Oh, and what's that?" said Trask.

"I can't find my name on your watch roster. Neither Shania nor myself. What, we're not accepted as part of the team?"

"You must know it means no such thing," said Trask. "It's just that you'll need to be at your best tomorrow morning. And anyway there are eight of us: techs, a spotter, a locator, telepaths, and a precog—well, when he wakes up! We're more than adequate to the task. And then there's Wolf, who I'll bet is a better watchdog, er, watch-wolf, than all of us put together. So you two get your sleep and let us do the rest."

"Ben is right," said Ian Goodly, stirring in his chair. "I saw it a very long time ago, or so it seems now: you two in the thick of it, and the whole world in the balance. So if you want to be strong tomorrow you should sleep tonight."

"Oh?" said Trask. "So there'll be a tomorrow, will there?"

"I suppose there's always hope," said the precog. "And

anyway, you should never try to second-guess the future. You would think I'd know that by now, because in my experience the future always finds a way to do its own thing no matter what."

Trask nodded and said, "Okay, let's leave it at that then. And now go back to sleep."

"I will after I've eaten," said the precog, getting to his feet and stretching.

"Very good," said Trask. "And *then* go back to sleep."

Goodly crossed to a small table heaped with the remainders of the team's meal, and taking a sandwhich, he asked, "Ben, why are you so eager for me to sleep?"

"Because you're on watch at the midnight hour," said Trask with a sour grin. "I'll bet you didn't see *that* coming!"

But the precog only sighed, then bit into his sandwich . . .

41

Appearing on a backdrop as black as interstellar space, impossible numbers, equations, and evolving formulae flickered on the screen of Scott's mind, scrolling up his dreaming field of vision as if some hugely powerful computer was attempting to solve the most complicated mathematical problem; and while Scott knew that he'd witnessed this before, still he couldn't understand a single line of what he was seeing.

It seemed to go on for a very long time, and when finally Scott recognized a part of the sequence—its resolution?—then the cosmic screen where this constantly mutating math was being written split open like the doors of an elevator, showering space with disintegrating decimals, fragile fractions, and all the scrawled paraphernalia of higher, highest, and totally towering mathematics. Except that it wasn't a pair of doors at all but a single Möbius door, and from behind it stepped . . . a boy.

Scott knew the boy at once, because he'd been places, done things with him before. And:

"You," he said, almost in a groan. "Wouldn't you just know it? It's the Necroscope Harry Keogh. And just when I thought it was safe to go back to sleep!"

The apparition, however, didn't seem to be in the mood for jokes of any kind; and taking Scott's arm—Scott's boy's arm—he walked him through another door and out again onto that same Scottish riverbank where they'd dangled their feet in the water during an earlier visit. This time, however, it was the dead of night; and standing back from the riverbank perhaps one hundred yards away, an old house was blazing like a bonfire and sending up smoke, flames, and showers of sparks to a starry sky.

"That was my old place," said Harry then, as a sort of sad shadow crossed his face. "My last vestige on Earth—and that's what my friends did to it when it was my turn to fail. *Huh!* But it didn't stop me trying, fighting for them, and that's why I'm here." He grasped Scott's arm that much tighter, almost hurting him. "Because this was my life, my world . . . but now it's yours, and you're letting it slip away!"

"I'm what?" Scott answered, tugging himself free. "Letting it slip away? Are you kidding? I'm trying as best I can to save it!"

"Hey!" Harry snapped. "A small part of me is part of you, remember? But even a small part of me is one hell of a lot more than you! So don't go trying to justify your actions—or lack of action—by telling any half-truths to me! You might as well try lying to Ben Trask! It simply doesn't work, Scott."

"You really fancy yourself, don't you?" Scott narrowed his boy's eyes at his visitor. "What, you're calling me a liar? You want to get it on with me? Well just say the word. I mean, what do you think I'm doing here, or there, in that Swiss hellhole? Do you think it's some kind of holiday I'm having?"

"It's not what I think, it's what I know!" said the Necroscope. "Didn't you tell Trask that he'd be on his own after you go looking for Simon Salcombe? Yes, you did. But that's *not* why you got my dart, Scott! That's like me: only a small part of the reason. The Big Part is my world, mankind, humanity itself! I showed you the Möbius Continuum—and what have you done with it? Nothing! I've given you deadspeak, and have you used it? No way—in fact, you're avoiding it! What's wrong with you, Scott? Do you think you have nothing to live for? And what about Shania? Isn't she worth living for? Man, you're loved by an amazing woman and a beautiful animal, by *two* creatures now! Do you want to be the ultimate loser? Better listen to me, Scott, because I know what it's like to lose, and believe me I would rather have won!"

I'm talking to myself! Scott thought. *I know I'm dreaming, and in my dream I'm talking to my stupid bloody self!*

"To a *part* of yourself," said Harry, but more calmly now. "Okay, so explain yourself. But make it quick, because I can't stay here much longer; there are deserving cases elsewhere, and I go where I'm told to go. So what's your problem, Scott? Don't tell me you still don't believe."

"No," said Scott. "I believe. How can I do otherwise when the proof is piled six feet deep all around me? I believe, yes, but I'm *not* the Necroscope! I can't do the things you did."

"Why not? You have the power."

"But not the skills, and not the humility. The dead loved you because you were humble. Oh, you were hard, but at the same time you were humble. Me, I don't know how to talk to the dead! I mean, maybe I'm afraid to; it's not . . . not natural! Natural? God, what am I saying!? And anyway what good can it do? I don't *know* the dead, and even if I did I couldn't call them up out of their graves . . ." And pausing, Scott wondered how he knew about all that.

"You know about it because I'm *in* you!" said Harry. "Part of me, anyway. And as for not knowing the dead: well maybe not, but they know you. You're the warm one, Scott, and you have the power! If you call on them, they'll answer you."

Not wanting to even think about it, Scott changed the subject. "And then there's this Möbius Continuum thing. Even if I could break into it—"

"Conjure it," Harry corrected him.

"—I wouldn't know how to use it. Coordinates? I know a few. My place in London; places I've worked; embassies in Japan and other countries where my father worked when I was just a boy . . ." He glanced down at himself. "This boy, in fact! But to try going to any of them would be meaningless now."

"And what about Schloss Zonigen?" said Harry.

"I don't *know* any coordinates in Schloss Zonigen!" Scott protested.

"But you will, in just a few hours' time. And since we're talking about time, I don't have too much of it left myself."

"A few hours?" said Scott. "You think I can learn a whole lifetime's worth of maths—assuming I had that kind of mind—in just a few hours? Now who's joking?"

"I seem to remember," said Harry—his figure beginning to waver like the air over a hot summer road, so that the fires of the burning house along the river showed through him—"that I was once in a similar fix. I'd lost the knack, I couldn't deadspeak and my maths had deserted me. But I didn't let it stop me. I had friends among both the living and the dead who were there to help me out."

"I don't have any dead friends," said Scott. "And not even a great many among the living."

"You have me," said Harry, wavering again. Then he sighed, and said, "I had a feeling this was going to happen. That's why I called in a marker or two, favours I'm owed. I don't know for sure if they're able to help out, or even if they'll get to you in time. But at least I tried. Which is more than I can say for you. Damn, Scott, but I've put really big money on you! A whole world's worth. It comes hard now to have to admit that I picked a loser."

Breathing hard, muttering to himself, tossing and turning on a hard floor under a thin blanket, Scott was angry now. "Why don't you fuck off and let me be, Harry?" he said.

"I've really had it with you calling me a liar and a loser. So now I'll give you fair warning, *don't* do it again!"

"Oh?" said Harry, suddenly as thin as a ghost, because he *was* a ghost, or at least a revenant. "So now you're a hard man, eh? But why do you want to fight me when the really bad people are up there in that hollow crag? Wake the hell up, Scott! You can't lash out at what's not physically there, only at what *is* there—you loser!"

At which Scott did in fact lash out; he launched a blow at the suddenly grinning Harry, a blow that passed through him and took Scott with it! Such was the force behind his swing that he would have gone over the edge and straight down into the river, if a door hadn't opened before he could hit the water—

—And if Ben Trask hadn't given him another shake, saying, "Wake the hell up, St. John! And whoever it is you think you're fighting, quit it now!" And there he stood—the shadowy figure of the Head of E-Branch—looming over Scott in the dim light, and holding Scott's balled fist in a white-knuckled hand.

For a moment Scott remained disorientated, then he relaxed and slowly fell back off his left elbow until he felt the floorboards under his back again. "I was . . . I was nightmaring," he muttered then, as his eyes adjusted to scan the gloomy dining room in what light came in from the foyer where the door stood slightly ajar.

"Oh, really?" said Trask, and from his tone of voice Scott knew he wasn't the least bit fooled. "Well whatever, but in any case it's time you were up."

Close by, Shania stirred in her blanket and yawned, and in another moment Wolf came nuzzling. *I slept a little,* he whined, *but the night is too strange, too still. I went out with one of the men people into the darkness to smell things out, to listen and see what I could see. Those lights in the mountain peak are quieter now, but I smell danger in the air. Things are again in motion, and bad minds are set against our minds.*

Scott stood up, Shania, too, and four others who Trask

had awakened. "You've got fifteen minutes to freshen up and do your thing, whatever needs doing," said Trask. "Then we get together in the foyer for our last O-Group. Questions? No? Then get to it, ladies, gents. I'll see you all in fifteen minutes . . ."

Scott and Shania freshened up in a hotel staff rest room on the ground floor at the rear of the building . . . and having done so immediately "dirtied up" again, daubing their faces with greasy soot and ashes from a small jar they'd filled from Scott's open-hearth fireplace. But on their own in the hotel's echoing emptiness and eerie stillness, as Shania was about to apply one last black smudge to her nose, suddenly she stiffened.

"What is it?" Scott stared at her intently.

Half closing her eyes, concentrating, she held up a finger and said, "Listen!" And then, "No, listen *with* me, in here." And she tapped Scott's forehead.

Scott "listened" and nodded. "What was it Wolf was saying? Things are moving again? Well, something's moving for sure! But where?"

"You felt it?" said Shania. "That sly, creeping sensation? Something moving, yes, but all shrouded in a thick, threatening fog. I think I know what it is. Mordri minds are at work covering some sort of covert activity!"

Again Scott nodded. "Didn't Wolf say something about that, too? About minds set against our minds? But I'll ask you again: where?"

"I don't know," said Shania. "But come, let's hurry. For I think I know someone who can help us find out."

The locator David Chung was already in the foyer when they got there, likewise Trask and Millie Cleary, and both of the techs. Paul Garvey followed fast on their heels, bringing a large urn of coffee from the kitchen, and behind him Frank Robinson with a huge rack of hot toast and a bowl of warm butter.

"Okay, we're a little early," said Trask, "but that's all to the good. Breakfast is served and we have time to talk, sort out what's what."

As he spoke the rest of the team appeared: the precog Ian Goodly rising up from a long, wide shelf that he'd cleared off under the desk, and Wolf from the kitchen, gnawing on a bone.

Then Scott spoke up. "Trask," he said, "before you begin. We think something is happening and it could be urgent. Shania has sensed some sneaky activity, and so have I. If we can work with Chung, maybe we can find out what it is and where."

Glancing at his watch, Trask nodded. "Very well, but you'd best make it quick. We're okay for time—maybe fifteen minutes to the good—but very little to spare."

Chung seated himself between Scott and Shania at the table they'd used last night and clasped hands with them, and as they grew still and concentrated the locator closed his eyes and let their psychic probes guide him. It took only a moment before he gave a start, letting go their hands and jerking back away from them.

"Well?" said Trask anxiously. "What is it?"

"*Wow!*" said Chung. "I've never before got anywhere as fast as that in my life!" He looked at Scott and Shania in awe. "You two are really something! Are you sure you needed me?"

"I can locate," said Shania, "but I'm far from accurate."

Aware that time was fleeting, Trask was impatient. "Well?" he said again, looking at Chung. "What the hell is it!?"

"It's to the east," said the locator. "And I wasn't simply locating just now; I actually *saw* it, and clearly! A sprawling, two-storied, chalet-style building with a fancy balcony, standing all alone on a shallow slope. It's something a little over a mile, maybe a mile and a half away."

And Ian Goodly said, "Ah! Do you remember on our way here, as we drove up that last spur? There was a reentry on the other side, with a ski lodge tucked away in the foothills."

Trask snapped his fingers. "You're right! And at the back of the ski lodge I saw a cable-car station. And the cars—"

"—Go up around the back of the spur to Schloss Zonigen," said Chung. "And what goes up can come down!"

"As you and your agents drive up the mountain road," Scott joined in, "or maybe even before then, they're planning to send men down behind you—behind us—cutting off any retreat."

Tech Graham Taylor was at one of the circular windows. Now he called out, "Hey, boss! Come and look at this."

Trask and the others joined him where he gazed through his binoculars at the crag. "The approach road," said Taylor, handing Trask the binoculars. "Take a look at the approach road."

Trask looked, adjusted the focus, and said, "Damn! They've blockaded the road! One large coach, and two minibuses, slewn across the road at the highest bend. And I see people, movement in and around the vehicles. Well, we knew it wasn't going to be an easy job getting up there, but now"—he looked at Scott and Shania—"thank God for you two!"

"What about the ski lodge?" said Scott. "Why do they want to cut off our retreat? You'd think they'd be happy just to see us leave, because surely from their point of view nobody is going to get out of this alive and we're all dead meat anyway!"

"It isn't just that they're eager to get off this planet," said Frank Robinson. "Yes, they want to destroy it, but that's not all: they'd like to be absolutely sure that *we* are finished before they go!"

"No, not you particularly," said Shania in a hushed voice. "It's me. I'm the one that Gelka Mordri wants dead. She doesn't know that I'm powerless to follow her—as I followed her here—and so wants *me* finished before they go, to make sure I can't possibly follow her!"

Trask looked at her and said, "You're probably right, but it doesn't change the fact that if we don't stop them we're all dead. On the other hand this blockade does make a difference to our plans, or rather my plan, which in any case was a bit iffy. It's no longer a case of simply blasting our

way up there; but hell, I'm not sure that would have succeeded even without this blockade! And we don't know
what the situation is up there. We don't know what else is
waiting for us behind the blockade, or how many defenders
there are in total, or their locations. And that's a hell of a lot
of things that we don't know! I hate to admit it but the
whole thing is looking more and more problematic."

"Ben," said Chung . . . then hurriedly corrected himself:
"I mean boss: I think maybe we can find those things out."

"Call me Ben," said Trask. "Let's face it, this could well
be the last chance you get! Okay, what do you mean?"

"But don't you see? Scott and Shania might not be accurate locators, but they are powerful ones. I didn't just locate
that ski lodge, I actually saw it! So maybe we can do the
same—"

"—With Schloss Zonigen?" Trask finished it for him.

But Shania, who had returned to her place at the table and
had her eyes closed again, murmured, "A cable car is on its
way down from Schloss Zonigen. It's crammed with armed
men. They no longer have Mordri Three cover, which makes
it easier for me to read their minds. And their minds are full
of murder! The Mordris can't be too worried about us now;
they think they're safe, and they're concentrating on preparing their departure and the destruction of your world—
which is little more than an hour and twenty minutes away!"

Millie and Paul Garvey at once joined Shania at the table,
and almost as quickly Garvey said, "She's right. And these
men in the cable car are actually in the pay of the Mordris:
dupes, true mercenaries, dumb, stupid, murderous bastards
who have no idea what's going on here and don't care what
they're doing—but determined to do it anyway!"

"Listen," said Scott. "Maybe we should give them something to think about, show them we're still fighting. We've
hurt them once, caused them to retreat, beaten them back. I
think that ski lodge should be an easy target, and it will only
take minutes."

"You want to take out the ski lodge?" said Trask.

"And the cable car." Scott nodded. "With these." He indicated the grenades attached to his belt. "It's a shame I'll have to use them for they're all we've got, but—"

"—Hold on there!" cried Tech McGrath. "Me and Wolf were oot in the nicht earlier." He dipped into a shoulder pack, came out with four more grenades. "Ah took these frae a dead'yin who doubtless intended them for use on us. So go right ahead, Scott, Gi' 'em hell, lad! And these beauties are all yours when ye get back."

"If we're going to do it we'd better go now," said Shania, checking that her shotgun was loaded.

I'm going, too! said Wolf, jumping up onto the table, which made it easier for Scott to hoist him onto his shoulders.

Trask looked at Scott, Shania, and Wolf, all three of them together, and just for a moment seemed hesitant; until the precog reminded him, "This is how I saw it, Ben. And it's how it's going to be."

"Very well." Trask finally nodded. "Let's do it. And good luck. We'll be waiting here for you, but not for long. You have ten minutes, no more than that."

"Just one thing," said Scott. "What I said to you before— about my own agenda—forget it. Whatever you need, if we three can deliver it, we will. Simon Salcombe will have to wait until we've stopped all three of them. And then with any luck it will be my turn to stop him personally."

And right then it seemed as if something or someone whispered inside Scott's head, *I knew that I'd get through to you in the end, Scott. I just knew it!*

42

With only one hour and sixteen minutes to go before Idossola's false dawn, Shania used her depleted localizer and transported herself, Scott, and Wolf to that location east of Idossola remembered by her Khiff from their psychic "visit" of just a few moments ago.

By no means instantaneous, still the trip was as fast as a lightning flash, the blink of an eye, a radio transmission; and yet in that single instant of darkness, still Scott was able to think, *I am moving faster than any man ever moved before!* Which wasn't quite true, because Harry Keogh and those of his friends who had experienced the Möbius Continuum had moved a great deal faster, as fast as thought itself. And that was a thought that had crossed Scott's mind previously:

When a thought is conceived, born, and comes into existence, is it everywhere? But surely it must be. An immaterial addition to the universe, as soon as the parent mind has conjured it, it simply IS without spacial and temporal limitations except that the one place where it may *not* exist is in the past. And Harry Keogh had used the word "conjured" in connection with the Möbius Continuum. Was that then a definition of the Continuum? Was that what it was: an incredible thought or series of thoughts, issuing from the mind of—but of what? Of a Father, a Creator, a God?

The darkness passed; going to one knee, Scott helped Wolf down from his shoulders; the three stood on a dirt road in the predawn gloom before the once-inviting, now menacing frontage of the ski lodge. Wolf set off at a lope, a grey shadow skirting the building but sticking close to its walls. And silently, half crouching, Scott and Shania mounted wide wooden steps to the doors.

There were surprisingly few windows to the front, or perhaps unsurprisingly. The mountains and the ski lift were to the rear and this would have been the preferred view when the lodge was in use. The double doors were unlocked, so whoever occupied this place wasn't expecting visitors. Scott and Shania entered, closing the doors quietly behind them. From somewhere within—from the rear—came the muted rumble of machinery in motion.

"Three minds," Shania whispered, in the even deeper gloom of the lobby. "Two are full of murderous thoughts, but I think the third is frightened. They're all three at the back, two on the landing stage, and one other . . . I'm not sure where he is."

"I know," Scott answered, his own telepathic probes reaching out before him. "I can read them, too. And at least two of them are would-be killers, murderers for money and for someone else's insane cause. Mercenaries and dupes . . . Lord, I find it hard to believe that such as these are human beings! But three of them? Well, what else should I expect? Three against three? Always that same fucking number!"

"Don't curse!" she admonished. "It only serves to detract from your concentration, your ability to rationalize, which has to have an adverse effect on your judgment."

Scott nodded and replied, "I know. I haven't forgotten." *I should think coldly, without anger, pain, or passion.* And though he couldn't see it he sensed Shania's response—her smile, however brief, tense, and nervous—as they crept forward into and through the lodge.

It was a big place: dining rooms, corridors, stairs, passages, all in wood, pine-panelled and -ceilinged; and in a large central area a pine-columned modern barroom where a lone light burned over the long bar and the white walls were still decorated with crossed skis, photographs of skiers, and various trophies. Scott could almost hear the clink of glasses and the small talk of holiday-makers, tourists, and thrill seekers out of the past. But that past was some four years ago, and the room wore a fine coat of dust now and cobweb veils in the corners of the ceiling.

But still, that single bar light was on. And:

Look, said Shania. *On the bar near the door there.*

Scott looked where she directed. Three bar stools, grouped together against the bar; two beer steins, a wineglass, and an ashtray on the bar itself. And on a nearby table a plate with a few crusts of bread and what looked like bits of cheese rind.

Also, there on the floor, said Shania.

But Scott had already seen: three makeshift beds, with the covers thrown back. *The caretakers,* he said. *The rearguard.*

We have to hurry. Shania's "voice" was anxious. *The cable car is halfway down.*

They moved on out of the barroom into the dim grey light

of a large glass-walled and -ceilinged observation lounge
whose central area was a conservatory with benches in a
delta arrangement, so positioned to look out on the mountains and especially the rising pylons and gently looping cables of the aerial tramway. Steps opposite the forward
section of the delta climbed to the floodlit landing stage, and
as Scott and Shania arrived at the foot of the steps they heard
excited German-language voices coming from overhead.

Only two of them, said Scott. *But where's the third?*

He's down here, came Wolf's answer at once. *He's on
watch, prowling the area. Now he looks in—he sees you and
is startled—he raises and points his weapon—and I attack!*

Now, even through the strengthened glass of the
panoramic windows, Scott and Shania heard the guard's
outcry: "Halt! *Wer sind sie? Was tun sie hier? Halt, oder ich
schiessen sie zusammen!*"

The pair "heard" all of what he said, especially the last
part: "Halt, or I'll shoot you to pieces!"

But the guard and the cable-way operator up on the landing stage had heard it, too, as had Wolf, who was already
snarling, launching himself out of the shadows!

Now, crouching low and turning on his heel, Scott saw
the man outside and at the same time heard the stutter of automatic gunfire. Pushing Shania aside and down and lifting
his sawn-off shotgun, he saw as in slow-motion the
prowler-guard struck from the side by a wild grey shape and
sent reeling off balance as a tracery of stars shaped themselves where they climbed the glass wall; then the feral
shape detached itself to go bounding away from the distracted guard. And as things speeded up again and a section
of the glass wall crashed to the floor in shards, Scott saw the
guard staggering and beginning to aim his weapon in the direction that Wolf had taken. And yanking on both of his
gun's triggers he saw the guard hit by the double blast,
hurled backward out of sight.

Booted feet clattered on the metal steps. The beam of an
electric torch cut the cordite-tinged air. Behind the torch, a
black shape loomed and metal dully glinted. *"Was ist? Was*

ist?" the second guard shouted. Then came a curse and the crazed chatter of gunfire as a stream of bullets lanced down, striking hot white sparks from the steps.

Scott had broken open his weapon, was loading cartridges into the breech when the torch beam fell full upon him. *Damn it to hell!* he thought, for that was probably where he was headed. But Shania only said:

Not ever, and certainly not yet! And with that she hurled herself down on the steps close beside him. Then:

The sound of her triggering off a single barrel so close to Scott was deafening, but he'd never heard a sweeter sound in his life. As for the guard descending the steps: he didn't hear it at all; but as his body went tumbling past them like a scarecrow blown off its pole in a storm, they saw the raw red blotch that had been his face and head.

Oh! said Shania then. *All this killing!* And Scott felt her pain.

Yes, that was ugly, he said, snapping his shotgun shut and keeping as low a profile as possible as he went headlong up the steps, *but a lot worse if he'd fired first! In fact, he did fire first, and if you hadn't shot him I wouldn't be alive.*

I know, she answered. *But, Scott, that one up there on the landing stage—the last of them, the operator—he's so very frightened, and I don't think he's armed at all.*

Wolf went racing past her, past Scott, too. *Let me test the way for you,* he growled. *I'm much faster than you, and this man may fear my snarling visage.*

He disappeared from view, and moments later:

"Nein! Nein!" came a hoarse cry from above. "Oh, *Mein Gott in Himmel! Was fur ein Hund ist dieser Geschopf?"*

"He's my *Geschopf*," said Scott, emerging from the steps to prod the small, fat, white-faced cable-car operator in the gut, backing him up against the throbbing boxed-in cable gear. "He's my creature, and if you so much as twitch he'll rip your throat out!" Wolf was there, of course—muscles bunched, jaws slaverering, crouched as if to spring—and indeed he looked the very essence of a nightmare, a hound from hell.

"English?" said the operator. "You English?" Sweat rivered his face, gleaming in the landing stage's neon lighting. "Don't shoot me. *Bitte, nicht schiessen!*"

Shania touched Scott's shoulder. "He's scared to death. He isn't one of them . . . or he is, because he's helpless to be anything else."

"I have *ohne Waffe,* er, no weapon." The man began to lower his trembling hands, until Scott prodded him again.

"So what are you doing here?" But Scott knew it was a dumb question the moment he'd asked it. Reading this poor man's mind was like reading a large-print book! He was here because he had no option. "You've got family up there, up in Schloss Zonigen, right?"

"*Jah, meine Frau.* My wife is a prisoner. And those animals have done things to her—*will* do things to her if . . ."

"I understand," said Scott, lowering his shotgun.

"Look!" said Shania, lifting her chin and gazing into the gloom. Emerging from behind a high spur, the lights of a cable car had just this moment come into view, the car itself like a softly glowing phantom ship of the air. "In a few more minutes they'll be here."

"Maybe not," said Scott grimly. "Maybe they'll be scattered all over the scree at the base of that spur." He took the grenades from his belt.

"What do you do?" cried the operator.

"What I have to do," Scott answered. And to Shania, "Take him downstairs. Wolf, go with them."

"But those . . . those *monsters* up there," the operator protested. "You don't know them! They'll come down on you, on all of us!"

Scott turned on him, shoved him roughly toward the steps, said, "They already came down on me! Is your wife still alive? Yes? Well mine isn't!"

And taking the stumbling, terrified man away, Shania told him, "We're here to try to save your wife, to save all of them, up there in Schloss Zonigen."

"What? Just two of you?" His jaw had fallen open. "That's *unmöglich*—impossible!"

"There are several of us," she said, taking his arm, "and we are strong. Come with me."

"But . . . but . . ."

But Shania shook her head and led him away down the steps.

And arming the grenades, Scott tossed one of them into the gearbox, hung the other on the travelling cable, and paused for a single moment to watch it swing out toward the first pylon no more than the length of a cable car away—

For a single moment, yes.

—But on a count of five he'd followed Shania part of the way into the lodge and was lying flat on his face halfway down the metal steps. And on a count of six . . .

There were two distinct explosions coming in rapid succession, followed by a continuous, frenzied whipping sound and the spatter and clang of concrete and metal shards where the debris of the gearbox and its container bounced or ricocheted off this or that surface. Dust, smoke, and the smell of cordite and burning came wafting down the steps from the landing stage, and its neon light went out in a sputter of sparks and a rain of splintered glass tubing.

In just a matter of seconds, when the tinkling and twanging ceased, Scott got to his feet and ran up the top five steps to the landing stage. Now in near-darkness, still he could make out the shattered gearbox housing where frayed strands of cable made the whipping sound as a snapped length continued its whirling revolutions around a buckled, eccentrically spinning shaft. Out in the gloom the closest pylon was mainly intact except for the gear in its upper gantry, destroyed in the explosion; Scott could hear broken cables snaking and clattering, snatched along the stony ground first by contraction, the release of tension, and second by the weight of the swaying, sagging cable car.

Scott didn't understand the mechanics of the thing; he had hoped to stop the cable car one way or the other, and knew that the most merciful scenario would be just that: that the car was brought to a halt. But on the other hand the people in that car were killers; one of their masters had murdered his wife coldly and cruelly, without a single moment's regret ... which was why Scott had also accepted that he might be sending the men in the car to their deaths. And in fact he'd told Shania that was precisely what he intended to do.

And now he had done it. The fate of a world—perhaps more than one—was hanging in the balance, but in these frozen moments that was a thought far from Scott's mind ...

There were safety blocks—brake shoes—that would snap shut on a broken cable in the event of its failure, but the designer hadn't reckoned on an act of sabotage or the catastrophic failure of *both* cables. The blocks had snapped shut, only to be snatched piecemeal from their pylon housings by the impetus and sheer weight of frenziedly lashing steel.

One hundred fifty yards away and one hundred fifty feet above the rocky scree slope, the cable car sagged, dipping its nose like a sinking ship. Its lights flickered low, brightened momentarily, and Scott saw figures milling at the windows. Then a knotted tangle of cables and brake shoes hit the gear on the pylon closest to the cable car with all the force of a runaway truck! The pylon shuddered; twin *cracks!* like pistol shots signalled the snapping of two of its girder legs; the other two bent over like strands of spaghetti as the pylon toppled toward the car. But as quickly as the pylon fell, the doomed cable car fell faster yet. Now standing on its nose, its tail pointing at the dimming stars, it dropped like a stone and its lights went out.

Watching, Scott gritted his teeth, felt his shoulders drawing in toward his neck, squeezed his eyes to slits. This wasn't the same as when he and Shania had blown a coach full of people off a mountain road. *That* had been desperation, all part of the action; *this* had been planned, the result of a very deliberate, destructive act. Scott found it hard to justify. And:

"Oh!" said Shania again, from behind him.

"Don't go trying to read them," Scott hoarsely warned

her, unable to disguise a shudder as he turned her face away. For he could already "hear" the screams of the doomed men . . . suddenly shut off as the sound of shattering glass and plastic and metal and flesh and bones came like a roll of thunder out of the predawn gloom.

"Mein Gott!" said the small fat man, wringing his hands at the top of the steps.

"Now we'll be leaving," Scott told him. "You might like to wish us luck because we—yes, and your wife, too—we'll need all the luck we can get!"

"Wait," said Shania as she turned her questioning eyes on the fat man and in the next moment spoke to him: "Have you ever worked up there in Schloss Zonigen?"

He nodded, his jowls wobbling, his eyes wide and terrified. *"Jah.* For almost two years. But I didn't want to. I *had* to, for my wife's sake!" He backed stumblingly away from Shania.

She shook her head, took his arm. "It's all right. I'm not blaming you. But listen now: did you have the run of the place? Do you know its layout?"

"The run of the place?" the man replied. "Yes, I suppose I did. I ran messages for . . . for *them*, for the Three."

"And you remember?"

"Of course. How could I ever forget?"

Meanwhile Scott had started to display his impatience, his anxiety. Glancing at the eastern peaks, silhouetted now against the first faint glow of the coming day, he said, "Shania, do we really have time for this?"

"Oh, yes, we really do," she replied. "This is exactly what we need to know!"

"But we have to get back to the hotel," said Scott. "Questioning him and extracting all of his knowledge, that could take hours!"

"For you, yes," she answered. "But not for my Khiff!"

Scott read her mind, nodded, grabbed the fat man, and half dragged him down the stairs into the lodge. And in the barroom he sat him in a chair, blindfolded him, and said, "Now we want you to tell us all, everything."

"Yes," said Shania, "tell us about Schloss Zonigen. Simply think about it: everything you saw there, the routes, the rooms and places where prisoners are kept, the workshop where they've built the machine. It must have access to the skies, that machine, so tell us about it. Just *think* about it."

While she talked her Khiff had emerged from below her ear, transferred to the fat man, slid into his head. Jerking in his chair, he said, "What was that? Something touched me!"

"Do as you're told," Scott told him, prodding him with his shotgun, "or something really will touch you, and hard!"

"Schloss Zonigen," said Shania. "Think about it. Just let your thoughts flow . . . let them flow . . ." For she knew that her Khiff would find the source and learn everything. And:

Done, said Shania's Khiff as it emerged, smiled its sweet, no longer entirely innocent smile, and reentered its host.

They took off the fat man's blindfold, and Scott told him, "We have to leave you here. You're free to go wherever you can, wherever you wish."

And Shania said, "You can walk into Idossola if you like. If we're successful, then sooner or later you may even see your wife there."

But the man only said, "I'll go and sit in the open on the landing stage. Right now, I don't quite know what else to do."

They went part of the way with him, watched him step carefully over the guard with the raw red face—which was turning black now—and make his way unsteadily up the metal steps.

But then as Scott took Wolf up onto his shoulders and they prepared to return to the hotel:

You fucking bastard! someone said close by; a male "voice" that only Scott could hear.

"What?" Scott gave a massive start, crouched low, and spun on his heel. And glancing this way and that, finally he stared at the dead guard.

Wide-eyed, Shania grabbed his elbow. "Scott, did you hear something? What happened just then?"

He continued to stare at the dead man, who said, *You*

*lousy shit, you or someone with you killed me! I had a life,
for what it was worth. Now I have nothing.*

Scott's blood ran cold, and the short hairs at the back of
his neck stood erect. Finally he found his voice. "But you
were about to kill me and mine." His words were deadspeak, of course. For at last the Necroscope's "talent," that
dark seed that he'd planted in Scott's metaphysical mind,
had blossomed into being.

Of course I tried to kill you, said the other. *It's what I do,
or did. And I would again if I could!* But deadspeak is more
than mere conversation, and Scott sensed the murderous
lust and psychotic menace behind the dead man's words.

Then, at the back of his mind, he thought he heard someone whisper: *An eye for an eye, Scott.* It wasn't the dead
man this time—or perhaps it was *another* dead man—but in
any case it was now a part of himself. And so:

"Fuck you, too!" he told the dead guard, and turned away.

Shania asked no further questions, because she didn't
need to. She could feel something new in him, and it was a
very powerful something: a Harry Keogh something.

A stream of obscenities that only Scott could hear followed, fading to nothing as he and Wolf joined with Shania and she performed a transference back to the hotel in
Idossola . . .

43

Their reappearance in the foyer of the Gasthaus Alpenmann
was no less spectacular than the previous one. Trask and his
crew, however—as familiar as they were with weird and unusual occurrences—were more relieved than startled. And
even before Scott could stoop and help Wolf from his shoulders, Ben Trask was asking:

"How did it go? Were you successful?"

"We were," Scott answered, nodding grimly. "The cable

car . . . it fell. And there's no longer anyone at the ski lodge who you need worry about. I could explain but that's something that can wait till later—if there's to be a later. Far more importantly, we've learned all of Schloss Zonigen's ins and outs; or rather, Shania has learned them, and I've yet to get them from her. But she knows the place's layout: its levels, passageways, rooms and caverns, places that the Mordri's soldiers could most easily defend. And now she has to share that knowledge with you and your team—and with me, of course."

"She what?" said Trask, turning his head to stare at Shania. "You've been gone mere minutes, done a lot of damage, and still had time to learn all that? I don't understand. But I do know that we don't have time to start drawing maps and committing them to memory or anything like that!"

"That won't be necessary," Shania replied. "All I require is your trust. You see, the Shing't have the means to transfer memories mind to mind. In any suitable dark place, you and your people can learn all that I've discovered of Schloss Zonigen in a matter of moments."

"Moments?" said Trask.

She nodded. "Less than a minute."

"All of us?"

"Indeed. Scott, too, and even Wolf."

"And it's safe?"

"Of course, or I wouldn't offer."

Trask, being Trask, knew she was telling the truth. "Okay, I'll go first," he said. "There's a cubbyhole of a room behind the desk there that the *Gasthaus* staff must have used for safekeeping. It's smaller than a broom closet but I suppose it will do."

"Boss," said Frank Robinson, beckoning Trask to one side.

"What now?" said Trask. "But make it fast."

Keeping his voice low, the spotter said, "I told you there was more to this woman than meets the eye."

Trask nodded. "More than meets the eye, but it still can't avoid the skill of a spotter, right?"

"That, too. So, do you still trust her? She is after all an alien."

"The way I see it," Trask replied, "I don't have a choice. But let's turn that around: do *you* trust her? If not, don't accept her offer. As for me, I definitely want to know what we're going up against in that hollow crag up there. And, Frank, what you need to remember: I have a talent, too."

"I know," Robinson answered, and offered a helpless shrug. "Actually, our talents don't conflict. I knew that she was more than she appears, that's all. You agree, but you also point out that whatever she is she's definitely on our side. So I suppose I'll just have to go along with it. It's simply that I wouldn't be doing my job if I—"

"I understand," said Trask. "Keep doing your job."

On the other side of the room Shania smiled tightly, withdrew her telepathic probe, and said, "Well, now that that's all sorted out can we please get on with it? Time is very short . . ."

In as little time as she had indicated, Shania's ability— more properly her Khiff's ability—was proven. And in the darkness of the tiny room behind the desk the benevolent creature's near immaterial presence remained a secret . . . except from Robinson, who now *knew* that Shania was more than Shania. But then, he had the same feeling about Scott St. John. But whatever it was about these two, Robinson no longer feared it. No, for there were far more fearful things abroad than a telepathic wolf and an incredibly gifted man and his "woman" (however alien the latter), who were obviously on the side of everything human, right and righteous.

And now in the minds of Trask and his team the memories of a man who had actually lived and worked in Schloss Zonigen were in flow as if they themselves had walked and worked there; they knew almost every inch of the place and were as well acquainted with it as with the towns and cities where they had been born.

"Fantastic," said the precog Ian Goodly. "While I've often glimpsed the future, I've never before had such clear and unobscured access to a place where I've never been! I even know the places where I would set up ambushes . . . er, that is, if I were on the other side."

To which Trask added, "That was the whole idea. And now St. John can get to those places first. Or some of them, maybe. But right now there's no more time left to worry or wonder about it. We have to get up there, and I do mean now!"

As he turned to Shania and Scott, the latter preempted him and said, "We'll clear the way as best as possible, yes—starting with that roadblock—but first you'll need to create a diversion. If you set off now your movements will be seen from their high vantage point. From then on, all eyes will be focussed on you, your vehicles, which will give us the element of surprise when we arrive on the road above and beyond them."

"But you'll need more than an element of surprise to shift those vehicles blocking the road," Trask replied. "And I've got just the thing, or things. You were gone only four or five minutes, but we weren't simply twiddling our thumbs back here. The techs were out counting bodies; actually, they were seeing what they could find. They found guns, and also these."

Producing three more ugly-looking grenades from his overcoat's generous pockets, he handed them to Scott. "These should do the trick."

Scott hung the grenades from his belt and said, "I'm sure they will—but there's something else I would like from you."

"Oh?"

"The flamethrower." Scott glanced at the weapon where it lay on the desk. "Since it's more than likely I'll meet up with the Mordris first, and since we know for sure that fire is something that will stop them . . ."

Trask nodded. "Take it," he said. "And may your flame burn brightly—and as hot as hell!"

With something a little less than sixty-five minutes to go, the techs brought the rented vehicles from the car park at the rear of the hotel; at which Trask and the rest of his team came into the open and quickly took their seats.

The predawn light was less gloomy now; the misty air was still and felt cold in the nostrils and lungs of all ten people and one wolf and seemed to have a silvery tinge to it. Poetically, it was "brightening;" likewise the faint, soft glow that silhouetted the darkly looming eastern mountains. While in the near-distant northwest, gauntly towering, the great crag that was Schloss Zonigen looked for all the world like a futuristic artist's castle, where mist spilled from its esplanade and its lights, though muted now, continued to flicker and dance.

But there were other lights on the access road. A coach's internal lights indicated a place where men were keeping themselves warm; every so often one or the other of the blockading vehicles would switch on its headlights, and torch beams would lance here and there, sweeping the road in a searching pattern.

When the techs started up their motors, switching on their own lights, it was an absolute certainty that the people at the blockade saw them. Which was exactly what Trask, Scott, Shania, and Wolf wanted them to see.

And as the cars started out of Idossola toward the foot of the crag, Scott St. John's Three Unit crept out of the Gasthaus Alpenmann to stare at the precipitous access road and the sudden burst of activity there, indicated by the abrupt shutdown of all but one or two darting beams from hand torches . . . also to say (or think) the meaningless things that people say and think at such times, which were anything but meaningless:

I love you, said Shania. *I think of you as my man—but I don't expect you—*

I love you, too, Scott cut her short. *And when this is over you can not only expect me to go on loving you but rely upon it. I think of you as . . . yes, as my "woman," Shania, and you can't any longer be my Number Two. You're my partner and my equal; in fact you're a lot more than me!*

But I'm sure I'd still love you even if you were just you. I will love you, just for you.

And Wolf said, *I love both of you. But what's all this sadness? I don't like sadness. And it isn't as if . . . as if we are going to . . . going to . . . is it?*

But it could be, said Scott. *Do you know about death—for yourself, I mean?*

I had siblings, said the other. *Yes, and I saw one of them afterward. Death is cold, a shrivelling, a stench, immobility. I don't like death.*

But Scott, who now knew that death wasn't quite like that, or not entirely, said, *You don't have to come with us. Why not stay here and wait for us?*

No, said Wolf. *I was nothing before you and would be nothing without you. I would be dead by now. So where you go I go.*

And it's time to go, said Shania, wrapping her arms around Scott. *Look! Look at the cars climbing toward the roadblock.*

Scott looked—saw the lancing headlight beams of the cars where they swung around the hairpins, climbing up and up—and said, "Very well, I'm ready. We can go. But first there's something I promised Trask." And turning back, aiming the snout of his flamethrower into the Gasthaus Alpenmann's foyer, he first ignited the pilot light, then hosed shimmering fire at the carpets, the pine walls and ceiling, any and everything flammable, until the entire foyer was an inferno and the hotel itself was doomed. And:

"There," he said, "it's done . . ."

As Trask's team in their two vehicles reached the eighth of the dozen sharp bends in the narrow access road directly below the roadblock situated two hairpins or one level higher, so certain of those above opened up with sporadic gunfire. Because of the near perpendicular range and the overhanging cliff, this was in the main a fruitless effort, which at best revealed the anxiety of the crag's defenders. They were

aware of the fate of many of their colleagues who had tried
to attack the E-Branch agents in the Gasthaus Alpenmann;
it was possible they had also learned something of the catastrophe that had overtaken a coachload of that group's
would-be reinforcements. Also, because the cars' headlights
were now on dipped beams—which the mist cascading
from on high more than half obscured—they were in any
case shooting at shadows.

But having safely rounded that bend and the next one,
halfway along a contour-hugging stretch of road that was
gradually curving as it climbed, and which soon must bring
them into view and weapons range of the roadblock, suddenly the telepath, Paul Garvey—a passenger in the lead
vehicle, along with Chung and Trask—gripped the latter's
shoulder from behind and shouted, "Stop!"

Alan McGrath was driving; slamming on the brakes, he
said, "What the bleddy hell . . . ?"

Fortunately their speed at this point was little more than a
crawl—due first to the gloom and the misty air, and second
to the proximity of the roadblock—for the car behind at
once shunted into them. It was no more than a bump, however, and now both vehicles were stationary.

Trask had already wound his window down in anticipation of sounds of battle, explosions from up ahead; so far he
had heard nothing. Now he looked back at Garvey. "Well,
what is it?"

"It's Shania!" said the other. "God, she could even be in
the car with us, she's that clear!"

"And?" Trask snapped.

"She says we're to creep forward—literally creep—until
just one of our headlights is showing. And then we're to fire
a shot or two."

Trask nodded, jabbed McGrath in the ribs, and said, "Do
it! They need another diversion, in order that St. John—"

"—Can plant his grenades, yes," said Garvey, finishing it
for him.

Their car edged forward around the curving rock wall.
From somewhere close in front a torch beam lanced along

the road and found them, then half a dozen more beams, slicing the gloom and the mist. Jerking the car to a halt, Mc-Grath switched his headlights to full beam.

Trask was out of his door in a moment, cocking his weapon, firing a burst of shots in the direction of the torches. There was shouting, the harsh stutter of returned fire, and hot lead sent a spray of sparks flying from the car's bumper, shattered its windscreen, and reduced a headlight to so much scrap. Other bullets zipped, spanged, and ricochetted off the cliff face, but McGrath and the others had already left the car and were sheltering in the shadows and the hollow of the cliff.

"And there's your diversion, St. John!" Trask muttered to himself, wincing as a hail of fire continued to pour along the road. But then—

Barely discernible as separate explosions, the deafening blasts of sound from the detonating grenades came precisely as fast as Scott had been able to yank their pins, lob them under the blockading coach and the minibuses where they were positioned diagonally across the narrow road, and fling himself back into the protective shadows of a roadside crevice, where Shania and Wolf waited for him. One, two, three, the explosions came, building to a thunderous roar that shook the ground. And accompanied by a waft of hot air and cordite stench—also by gouting fire, roiling smoke, and the screams of wounded and dying men—the explosions brought rills of smoking dirt and a hail of pebbles clattering from on high.

Even before the debris had stopped flying, Trask and his people—all of his people, from both cars—were moving forward, their weapons chattering, picking off the reeling figures of men where they were silhouetted against the blazing inferno of a shattered minibus, the only vehicle of the three that was still on the road. As for the coach and the second minibus: a trail of sparks and scraps of burning fabric came billowing up through smoke and thinning mist, aerial flotsam from a pair of fireballs, one large, one small, that twirled end over end into the abyss. As they bounded in seeming slow-motion from ledge to winding road to stony outcrops, the thunder of their collisions echoed up from their descent into total ruin . . .

"Scott!" Trask shouted across the rubble and the carnage at the rim of the devastation. "Scott St. John, are you okay?"

"We're okay," Scott called back, coming into view from the shadows with Shania and Wolf. "Now we're moving on. You'll have to shove that wreck over the edge yourselves. Can you manage?"

"Don't worry about us," Trask answered. "We'll manage just fine. You get on and . . . and do your thing. Good luck!"

But on Scott's side of the wreckage, Shania drew him back into the shadows of the cleft in the cliff and said, "Before we can move on there's something I must know." And while Trask and his agents began the grisly work of clearing the cratered road, she backed deeper into the shadows and pressed her localizer to her forehead.

My Khiff, she said. *Please test the localizer. For on that last jump I sensed its weakness. Is its energy such that we may safely continue to use it?*

In tune with Shania—in telepathic contact—Scott waited for her familiar's reply, which it seemed to him took longer in coming than was usual. But then:

Oh, yes, my Shania, said her Khiff.

And after the next jump, she went on, *the localizer won't be completely exhausted?*

There followed another long pause, until: *It will still be operative, however weakened.*

Now Scott sensed Shania's frown, so that even before she spoke again he knew she was concerned about something that she appeared to be keeping from him. Eventually, however: *My Khiff*, she said, *is something amiss? Could it be that you're not quite yourself? Your answers seem strangely deliberate, hesitant, and perhaps even contrived.*

I have seen other minds, (her Khiff sounded thoughtful and introspective) *I have learned new things, gained understanding beyond yourself, myself, our spheres.*

And Shania said, *My Khiff, I may not hide my thoughts from you, but you find it the very simplest thing to keep yours from me. Now I feel you shielding yourself, something that you never did before unless it was on my behalf. Surely you would not lie to me, my Khiff?*

Her Khiff at once replied, *I have only ever—I would only ever—work on your behalf, my Shania. And perhaps on behalf of those you love.*

Shania's concern was now very obvious, but Scott was glancing at the luminous dial of his watch and tugging at her arm. "We have to be on our—" he started to say, only to freeze in midsentence.

For now the conversation between Shania and her Khiff was being smothered, suddenly drowned out by a growing body of far, faint calls that grew louder moment by moment in his mind. And they were calls that only he could hear:

Haaarry! Necroscope! Is it you, Haaarry? And:

Haaarry! We feel your warmth. Is it truly you, Necroscope, come to avenge us, come to release us? And:

It can only be him! It must, it has to be him! (Now they, whoever they were, were talking among themselves; their voices—their deadspeak voices—rising to a babble.) *It is the Necroscope, Harry Keogh!*

I feel him there in the darkness.

Haaary! Only speak to us, Necroscope.

We've waited such a very long time.

Come to us, Harry.

Speak to us.

Comfort us.

Haaarry!

Haaaarrry!

Haaaaarrrrry!

Such pain, such torment in those voices.

But now, suddenly, such excitement and hope renewed, growing and burning bright in those dead voices from on high . . . but never from heaven. "I'm not Harry," Scott answered them at last, his voice husky, shaking his head and shaken to his soul, reeling there as Shania's attention left her Khiff to focus on him.

"What?" she said. "Scott, what is it?"

"We have to go there," he said, not looking at her— looking through her—as if his eyes, now as vacant-seeming as hers were beautifully alien, were seeking the source of those aching dead voices. "I can't . . . can't refuse them."

"Them?"

"Them," he replied simply as the deadspeak tumult continued to sound in his metaphysical mind: the pleading of the dead in the frozen catacombs of the high hellish crag called Schloss Zonigen. "All of those blameless ones." His head lifted and his gaze turned upward, as if to penetrate even the towering cliff face, the aeon-scarred rock. "All of those dead ones up there, where they're waiting for me."

Then—

He felt Shania shivering in his mind, and even Wolf's grey fur bristling. But the way was set now, and no turning back . . .

44

As Scott St. John's Three Unit stepped out from cover onto the blackened and cratered road, Trask and his agents brought their cars forward and began using them to nose the wrecked minibus through the twisted remains of the safety barrier and over the cliff. But it wasn't Scott's intention to watch their progress for there were other things on his mind now—and within it.

"I can't refuse them," he said again. "I have to go there, to that ice tunnel that I read of in their minds."

"Also in the mind of the cable-car operator," said Shania. "I have the coordinates. But, Scott, these are *dead* people that you're talking about!"

"I know." Scott nodded.

"And we have a mission. This can only interfere with what we're sworn to do."

Scott was gazing at her with that strange new look in his eyes. "No, I don't think so," he said. "For just like the cable-car operator the dead have things to tell us. They'll be privy to things that the living can't ever know."

"Yes! *Yes!*" came Trask's cry, startling them, as the minibus teetered on the rim and finally went crashing over, leaving the narrow road open.

My Khiff, said Shania then. *What of the localizer?*

And her Khiff answered, *Its energy . . . will suffice.*

Shania nodded. *I worry only for your sake, my Khiff.*

I know, said that one. *And I for your sake, and Scott's, and this world's.*

"Can we go now?" said Scott, taking up Wolf and cradling him in his arms. By way of answering him, Shania took Scott in *her* arms, and in another moment—

—They materialized from their jump in Schloss Zonigen's cryogenics tunnel, where Shania continued to shiver, but from the cold rather than the implications of Scott's now fully emerged macabre talent. The black track suits had been a good idea, but even under parkas commandeered from the belongings of the Swiss specials, who no longer had any use for them, still the air in the ice tunnel was freezing, causing their breath to plume.

Scott approached one of the frost-rimed cylinders in its deep niche, jammed the muzzle of his shotgun into its glittering, icy handle, and gave it a yank to free it. If he had used his naked hand, he had no doubt but that the contact with the cold metal would have welded his fingers to it and torn their skin off. And slowly he drew the unit out on its skids, until its convex cover came into view. The seals on the lid had been broken and a three-inch gap was visible where the cylinder had been opened up. Below the gap, darkness.

Now Scott used his shotgun again, inserting the butt into the gap and applying his weight until ice that had accumulated at the hinges shattered and the cover sprang open.

Shania's hand flew to her mouth and she took an unsteady pace to the rear. Wolf, up on his hind legs at Scott's
side, at once got down and backed off, hackles rising. As for
Scott himself: he no longer knew horror, only sadness,
compassion, as he stared at the contents of what now must
be considered a frozen tomb.

It was, or had been, a girl or young woman. But now—

The flesh on the face of the surgically gowned figure in
the unit was as brown as old leather streaked with grey
mould, with shrivelled lips drawn back in a rictus grin—
more properly a snarl—from brilliant white teeth. Her hair,
seemingly luxuriant despite that it glittered with ice crystals, flowed from her head to lie in tight curls on her thin
shoulders. But the fingernails on the hands lying folded on
her sunken chest were more than two inches long; and
curved like the claws of some prehistoric thing, they were
brown with dried blood!

Scott couldn't know it, but this was the girl that Mordri
Two—Simon Salcombe, his mortal enemy—had "touched"
in his necromantic fashion, whose waking instinct it had
been to reach out and rake the scientist, Herr Roberto
Stein's face. Released from Salcombe's hideous talent,
however, she had soon degraded, returning to her former
condition. And now:

Is it you, you monster? she wondered to herself. *Oh, I've
heard talk of a warm one, the Necroscope—but I've also
known the touch of a cold one, of a devil, of a fiend! Has he
come to torment me again? Or is it, can it be, that this is
truly Harry Keogh?*

She was terrified, but her deadspeak thoughts were as
good as spoken words to Scott St. John. And his heart and
his warmth went out to her: "No, I'm not this Harry Keogh
who you've heard of," he said, so that Shania could hear
him, too, "but Harry is, or he was, a friend of mine." (How
else to explain? How to even *begin* to explain that a small
part of Harry—or perhaps even a big part—was now a part
of him?) But deadspeak often conveys more than is actually
said, and even Scott's thoughts were deadspeak now. And:

Ahhh! said the dead girl. *Now I feel it! Your warmth! Your living, breathing warmth!*

"Tell me about yourself—" said Scott. "About all of these people here—but as quickly as you can, because my friends and I now have things to do. Things to put right."

Immediately recognizing the urgency of his situation, her deadspeak thoughts began to flow more rapidly; it was more akin to the Shing't transference of thoughts than an actual conversation:

To begin with—right from the start—we've been wronged, cheated, robbed, she said. *This cryogenic thing: there was very little chance that we could ever return, but we believed. Since when a great many of us have been tormented, tortured, and reduced to what you see before you. Now there is no chance at all, for the systems which once kept us deep-frozen—literally suspended—have been turned off. And the generators which powered our cryogenic units: now they power something else. A monstrous something!*

"But how can you know these things?" said Scott. "I mean, lying here, divorced from the living, and—"

—And dead?

"Yes."

But you are the Necroscope! At the very least you are like him. So surely you must know how we talk among ourselves? After all, it was another such as you who showed us the way.

"But I'm not that one," said Scott again, knowing that she would sense the deadspeak shake of his head. "I'm not the same, and I'm sort of new to all this. Let's just say that I'm gradually remembering things, which I hope will soon return to me."

In any case I'll tell you, said the girl, who was quickly becoming the spokesperson for the teeming dead. *When the first of us came here we were suspended in these units. We were dead, yes, but not gone into corruption. Our bodies, with our organs intact, had been saved. But even then there were faults in the system. When certain of us did go into corruption—a lingering process in this icy place, more a shrinking or*

*mummification—then the dead in Idossola's graveyard were
there to comfort us. As more of us succumbed, those who had
gone first were able to greet and comfort them. Some of our
number, however—of which I was one—were still suspended:
not "alive" as such but perhaps capable of life, if or when the
infant and inexact science of cryogenics should come more
properly into being . . . but that was when the monsters who
now run Schloss Zonigen first arrived here.*

*Then, as their vile works proceeded, so they required
more and more power and the energy of the generators was
diverted to their needs. Which meant that we—*

"That you more surely 'died,'" said Scott.

But that's not the worst of it, she sobbed, causing Scott to
"feel" the impossible deadspeak shudders wracking her
emaciated body. *For these terrible creatures have power
over flesh—even dead flesh!—provided it has not gone into
total dissolution, decay, or dust. Their touch, which could
bring life, more often brings death and nightmarish mutation. And they have used that miraculous touch to play with
us, like grotesque mad children with their puppet toys!*

Scott felt the short hairs at the nape of his neck prickling
as he remembered why he was here: to avenge Kelly's death
from just such a "touch." But the dead girl was continuing
her story:

*I myself was called up, given flesh, my lungs filled with
air.* (Now Scott looked again at the broken seals on her
cryogenic tube and remembered how the lid had been left
partly open.) *Coming awake, I lashed out! I can't say for
sure that these instinctive waking efforts of mine caused the
creatures who would have tortured me pain, but I do hope
so. In any event they went away, leaving me to the cold and
the dark again.*

"You're very brave," said Scott. "Others might have
begged for mercy. You fought, lashed out. And you did succeed; there's blood under your fingernails. But what if some
benevolent being had come to you, perhaps a cryogenic scientist who was attempting to revive you? I mean, how could
you know it was one of the Mordris?"

But the dead in this place have learned things, Necroscope. For one, we've learned to fear a certain tread—that of these Mordris—and for another, we fear their chill. When our cylinders seem to grow colder still, then we know they are near. For where you are warm, the Mordris are like the ice in this frozen tunnel.

At which something prompted Scott to ask, "Can you show me what you saw when these creatures awakened you? If I'm to go up against them, I need to know what they look like."

You intend to destroy them? She saw that it was so. *Then I must certainly try to show you what I saw.*

It was as if Scott looked through bleary eyes; he realized that her eyes had been . . . well, less than accustomed to seeing. But as the dead girl focussed on her memories—however startled and frightened she had been—slowly but surely the picture they conjured sharpened up. The face closest, which was the one she had raked, was just about as human and normal a face as any Scott had ever seen. Normal but terrified! Surely this couldn't have been one of the Mordris? But behind and to one side of the face of Roberto Stein was another which, as it came into focus, Scott recognized at once.

"Him!" Scott said, the single word exploding from him. For there could be no mistaking Simon Salcombe's black-marble eyes, his sallow, sunken cheeks, his waxy mask of a face under a long, domed, almost acromegalic head. All these things were precisely as Scott remembered them; but Mordri Two's sick, leering grin as his small mouth opened and revealed his little fish teeth, that was something new. And no matter where or in whom that look was seen, it would surely be recognized as a sign of total madness!

I hurt the wrong one! said the girl.

"That wasn't your fault," Scott told her. "But what *he* did to that man—like a cat playing with a mouse—that was very deliberate. I saw it written in his eyes."

He's your enemy, then? said the girl.

"He's just one of them"—Scott nodded—"but from my

point of view the very worst of them; and I'm going to kill him, yes. After that . . . well, all three Mordris have to die."

Scott, the girl said then, reading his name from his mind, *let us help you. Many of them here, they've danced like puppets for the Mordris. Now let them dance to another's tune.*

Yes, let us help! The cries of the Great Majority were as a wind, keening in Scott's mind, but a wind that blew from all sides at once. *We need this as much as you do, Necroscoooope!*

"But how can you possibly help?" said Scott, despite that he knew the answer; and knowing that answer, feeling the short hairs on the nape of his neck stiffening up again, he stepped back a pace.

Please, said the dead girl. *Don't turn away from us like that, Scott! We accept that you aren't Harry Keogh, but you do have the power. You ask, how can we help you? Simply ask us to help you, Scott. Simply ask us!*

Then . . . it was as if some other answered for him. And: "Will you help me?" he said. And as the answers came—

Yes!

Oh, yes!

Of course we will!

"—But first let me help you," he said.

And striding along the ice tunnel, he wrapped his hand in the sleeve of his parka and began yanking their cryogenic units out of their niches, using the butt of his shotgun to smash the few remaining seals that were still unbroken.

Enough! the dead cried out, seeing what he was doing. *You have done enough, Necroscoooope. Time for us to help ourselves.*

Hearing the lids on the cylinders beginning to crack open with pistol-shot reports one after the other, Scott returned to where Shania looked small and pale in her parka, and where Wolf whined and cringed down into himself, his tail between his legs and his ears lying flat to his skull.

"Try not to be afraid," Scott told them then, in a voice that perhaps wasn't quite his. "We're with friends here."

"Friends?" said Shania, with only the smallest shiver in her voice, as the lids on the cylinders began to hiss open and their occupants to creakingly dismount. "Yes, whatever you say—but still, it's time to move on."

"What about your Khiff?" Scott sounded a lot more like himself now. "Even though we're inside the crag, we still need the localizer. But I know your Khiff draws sustenance from it, and so I wondered . . ."

"I know," said Shania, looking along the ice tunnel, where dead people—literally mummies—were now freeing their colleagues from the long row of caskets. "Let me inquire." And:

My Khiff, she started to say—

But her familiar creature, well aware of all that was happening, said: *I know, my Shania. And the answer is yes, you may still use the localizer.*

"But, my Khiff, I know that by now its power must be nigh exhausted!" she protested. "Also that you may not exist without it."

And after a moment's pause: *For me the merest trickle will suffice, my Shania. Have no concern for me.*

But Shania was torn two ways. No longer convinced that her Khiff spoke the whole truth—believing that she was listening to lies, however white—she turned in her agony of indecision to Scott. "I fear for my Khiff! I think my Khiff is contemplating some sort of personal sacrifice! But is it necessary? What of the Möbius Continuum?"

Scott could only shake his head, however regretfully. "At school, I never got past fractions, decimals, a few simple simultaneous equations," he said. "I'm no dunce, but as for Harry Keogh's numbers: forget it. I would need a photographic memory to remember half of what he showed me."

I have just such a memory, said Shania's Khiff, taking the initiative and speaking in their minds. *But in this case even I am dubious of my memory, else I would have mentioned it before.*

Shania's jaw dropped. "I'm a simpleton!" she said. "For of course my Khiff was *with* you—with me, or with us—when Harry Keogh showed you the way!" And then, to her familiar creature:

My Khiff, why have you not mentioned this before? It could be our salvation!

Alas, my Shania, the other answered her, *but it could also be your destruction.*

"How so?"

I shall try to explain, said her Khiff. *But time is fleeting and I may not have the words. However . . .*

And after a moment's pause: *The Necroscope's numbers,* the Khiff began. *Well, I doubt if even he fully understood them. He knew where to bring them to a halt, in order to form his doors, but I sensed other doors that were lost in that numerical maze, a great many of them. There were doors to everywhere and everywhen, but some of them were by no means as malleable as Harry's doors. For example: you know that I issued from a gravity abyss on Shing to become one with you; of course you do. But I sensed gravity wells behind some of those hidden doors. Also, I sensed that several of those secret doors were one-way events; one may enter but may not return. What if I made a mistake and took you into a past when this world was molten—or a future where its atmosphere has evaporated—or deep into some enormous gravity well which would reduce you to atoms, and then strip your atoms to their basic elements? I could never risk that.*

Shania was angry now, or perhaps simply upset. "And so you have risked yourself instead! I *know* that the localizer must be all used up. It has to be by now!"

Not quite, my Shania, the other replied. *In this place the distances are so small that the energy requirements are negligible. We can still use the localizer; it is not yet exhausted, not quite.*

"But one more jump and it will be—and what of you then?" Without waiting for an answer she turned to Scott, and her look was pleading. "Scott, we'll just have to take our chances with the Möbius Continuum."

Glancing at his watch he answered, "Whatever we're going to do, we'll have to do it now. We've got thirty-three minutes left, and that's it." Then, realizing what he'd said: "Damn it to hell—that number again!"

"Oh!" said Shania, pulling him out of the way—with Wolf skittering after them—as the shuffling, frozen dead began to file past them, ice crystals like diamonds spilling from their near-rigid joints, their shrivelled, shrouded bodies. Only the dead girl paused to speak to Scott one last time:

Whatever the outcome, know this: that the dead of Schloss Zonigen will never forget you. And now we go to do whatever we may.

Scott looked at her—her ravaged body and twig-like arms; her withered eyes, sightless and filmed over, that yet "looked" back at him in their fashion—but in her *mind* he saw only how she had been: a lovely young woman, her smiling teeth and still beautiful hair. Bad enough that she'd died young, *terrible* that she should have been tortured in her bitter tomb!

"Yes," he told her, "and I shall never forget you. And you may believe me that we, too, shall do whatever we can do."

And with that the dead marched on . . .

"Where are we going?" said Shania, surrendering to the fact of her Khiff's warning and accepting that they must use the localizer one last time.

Adjusting the strap of the flamethrower around his neck, then checking to make sure his shotgun was loaded in both its barrels, Scott answered, "Eventually we're going to that central cavern, the place of the machine. But it's too risky to go there directly; we daren't simply appear there without knowing what may be waiting for us. Do you have the coordinates of the approach tunnels, especially the one that contains those cells where the Mordris torment their hostages?" It was just another stupid question, but everything was happening so fast now.

She nodded. "Like you, I have all Schloss Zonigen's coordinates. And so does my Khiff."

"Then that's it," said Scott grimly. "The approach tunnel with those cells, that's where we're going."

And as soon as he had gathered up Wolf, just as quickly as that they went there . . .

45

To the one man who was aware of it, their arrival out of thin air in the prison tunnel was an event of bone-jellying terror brought about by the certainty of what must surely ensue: his own slow and excruciating death! For the first thought to form in his mind was that this pair—Scott St. John and Shania—must be previously unseen Mordris. Who or what else could they possibly be, to suddenly appear in that fashion and at such an inopportune time? They must know what he had done and had come to punish him; this much at least was obvious. But as for the dog, or wolf, or whatever it was . . . !

The reason Scott had chosen this specific destination was because he knew that in Schloss Zonigen's labyrinth this tunnel, its immediate annexes, connecting tunnels, natural cavelets, and caverns were "out of bounds," restricted except to a handful of especially perverse guards and/or trustees whom the Mordris had seen fit to reward with certain "special privileges." This was knowledge that derived from Shania's Khiff's probing of the cable-car operator. Scott had reasoned, therefore, that the area would be deserted: the ideal vantage point from which to launch any assault on the nearby central cavern, the Mordri vessel, and the Three themselves.

And but for the presence of Direktor Gunter Ganzer and one other, it would have been deserted. The one other was—or had been—the simian trustee Erik Hauser. Indeed he still was Erik Hauser, but no longer that living, breathing pig that he'd once been. For he was now very dead, and at the moment Scott's Three Unit had emerged, Ganzer had been frantically busy dragging his corpulent body with its crushed skull into the cramped recesses of a dark crevice in the wall of the tunnel.

Scott had seen Ganzer just a moment before Ganzer saw

him, literally a split second's difference after Ganzer had felt the sudden brief rush of displaced air on his sweaty neck and glanced over his shoulder. As for what Scott saw:

Apart from his twisted lower limb and reversed left foot, where the toe of a black shoe pointed to the rear, the Direktor looked as normal a specimen as Scott might have thought to find in a place like this. Approximately five-eight in height, going prematurely bald, with a round wet face, bulging terrified eyes, and a twitching mouth, he was neatly, even *too* well dressed for the place and occasion. Under his open overcoat he wore a white shirt, a tie, waistcoat, and roll-collar jacket. Never a waiter, still he might easily be the chief steward of some large hotel; or as the case was, ostensibly, the manager of Schloss Zonigen. Only the guilty, frightened look on his face—along with what lay on the floor at his feet: a heavy spanner, gleaming red and wet, with a tuft of black hair stuck to it—spoiled the illusion.

The moment of mutual awareness, however frozen, was brief. Then:

"Nein! Bitte nein!" Ganzer cried out loud, falling to his knees. But at the same time his eyes had narrowed and Scott saw him reaching for the sidearm in a holster on the dead trustee's belt.

Scott paced forward, kicked at Ganzer's hand, and sent the automatic pistol skittering. And handing his shotgun to Shania, he grabbed the collar of Ganzer's overcoat, hauled him upright, and was about to strike with the heel of a rock-hard hand when Shania caught at his arm.

"Stop!" she said. "He's not one of the Mordris' men." She had read Ganzer's mind and found only fear there, and maybe the aftermath of a rage that was dying now, replaced by terror, the realization of what he had done.

Backed up against the tunnel wall, Ganzer's gaze went from Scott to Shania—then to a snarling Wolf—and finally back to Scott. His starting, rapidly blinking eyes took in their camouflaged faces, their dark clothing, and the weapons they carried, "What?" he gasped. "Who? But . . . you are British?"

Scott looked back at him, then at the corpse half in, half out of the crack in the wall. For several seconds, until he had shut it off, his deadspeak had made him privy to the dead man's shocked queries: his astonishment—not knowing where, when, or how he was—knowing only the sudden cold and Stygian darkness.

"You killed him?" said Scott, making it a statement rather than a question proper.

"But . . . but I didn't mean to!" Ganzer's voice was shrill, rising dangerously.

"Quietly!" Scott snarled, then added, "And don't go lying to me! I don't much care that you killed him, not if he was one of theirs."

"Oh, he was!" said Ganzer, beginning to control his trembling and hoarse, heavy breathing. "Oh, yes, most definitely. *Und was fur ein Schweinhund!*"

"In English, if you can," said Scott. Not that it mattered a great deal because his telepathy was now switched permanently on. He could have switched it off, but in the current situation it made good sense to continue scanning the immediate vicinity, so ensuring that he and his team weren't taken by surprise. "So why did you kill him?"

"For my poor wife, for myself, and for everything I cannot any longer bear! He had come here for my wife—to be with her—in that cell there. He *told* me what he would do to her; what he has done, and more than once! He is Erik Hauser, a so-called trustee. And of all the Mordri henchmen he was the worst. But I knew that in any case I was doomed, and so I followed him here. When he went to loosen the bolt on my wife's cell I could stand it no longer, and so I crept up behind him, and . . . and . . ."

"Yes, I know," said Scott. "So now calm down, pick up that gun, and tell me what you meant when you said that in any case you knew you were doomed."

As Shania went to release the bolt on the door of the cell in question, Ganzer did as Scott instructed, and said, "I meant precisely what I said. All three of the Mordris are insane, but the one who calls himself Guyler Schweitzer, he's quickly becoming the maddest of them all! Less than half an hour ago he told me that when their vessel departs, this entire cavern complex—Schloss Zonigen and all—will be destroyed and everyone in it killed! And whether he is crazy or not, I believe him! And so I had nothing to lose . . . well, except my life in a very terrible death!"

"Oh, you can believe him alright," Scott answered, nodding curtly. "But there's no time to go into all that now."

Even as he spoke there came a small, gasping cry—but of what? Relief? Disbelief?—from the open cell door. And then a small whimpering voice, calling, "Gunter? My Gunter? Is it your voice I hear? I'm coming, Gunter! I'm coming!" The spoken words were in German, which no longer made any difference to Scott's understanding of them. And:

"What?" said Ganzer, his jaw falling open. "My Hannelore? She is speaking, moving? She is *able* to speak, and . . . and . . ."

Shania came out of the cell; she looked shell-shocked; she could scarcely believe that even a deranged member of her race would think to transmute any living being as Ganzer's wife had been transmuted. All it had taken was a touch, a Mordri touch: the once healing, now crippling mutative touch of madness. But Shania was Shing't, too, and her touch was pure and untainted. What had been altered, disrupted, was far more easily and immediately put back to rights.

The tunnel's strip lighting had begun to flicker and spark shortly after Shania had entered the cell. Scott knew what that meant; but the effect was almost stroboscopic as a female shape emerged stumbling from the cell behind Shania, and Ganzer stood frozen, half daring to hope, half fearful, as the neons settled down again to reveal the woman's true form.

Then, with a choking cry, he lurched forward.

For this was not the rubbery octopus thing with the lower half of a woman that he had last seen and wept over in the hellhole of her cell. It was Hannelore as he remembered her, as she had been; it was the darling wife of his youth returned to him! Only her hair was different, where so many of her glossy chestnut locks had been displaced by prematurely grey ones. But what else could one expect? And it mattered not a jot.

Naked from the waist up, her skirt hanging in rags, Hannelore almost collapsed into Gunter's arms. At which Shania told Scott, *She's recovering, and quickly. My Khiff helped with the . . . the* terrible *psychological problems, while explaining everything to her. She knows what we're doing and what still remains to be done.*

Ganzer was unable to speak; his tears flowed, grew cold on his cheeks, as he shrugged free of his overcoat and wrapped his wife in it. She accepted the coat but then pushed him away, saying, "Gunter, now we have to help free the rest of them, all of them!" And without another word—still a little unsteady, but gaining strength moment by moment—she left him, went to draw the bolt on the door of the cell next to hers.

Ganzer would have followed her but Shania reached down and "touched" his leg. He at once fell to the floor, his lower left leg writhing like a crippled snake. And: "Ah . . . *Ahh!*" he said, his quivering hands massaging his leg. But the pain was gone in a moment, and now both of his feet faced front.

He stood up, at once spread-eagled himself against the wall of the tunnel, and stared in utter bewilderment at Shania. "But you . . . you're one of them!"

"No, she isn't," Scott told him. "She's one of us. So now get a grip and help us set the rest of these people free. Bring them to Shania. If any of them can't be brought, Shania will go to them. But as quick as you can, for our time is running out."

Probably faster than you think! said Shania, in his mind. *When I estimated the time of the sun's rising over the eastern range I deliberately brought it forward by some five minutes in order to allow us a little leeway. Even so, and if my calculations were correct, only a maximum of twenty-*

two minutes remain. Probably a minute or so less. So let's say twenty minutes to be on the safe side.

"Say what?" Scott wryly replied. "The safe side? There's a safe side to all of this?" Suddenly gaunt behind his striped, sooty camouflage, his eyes were now even less like the ones she knew. Coldly determined, they were also grim . . . but as grim as what? As grim as death, she supposed. Death, yes, with which he now seemed so familiar. And Shania shivered as Scott nodded and said, "Okay, twenty minutes. But we've still got to finish what we started here . . ."

It took only minutes, felt like hours, but finally the last few prisoners were freed; men and women alike, all of them returned as close to normal by Shania's "touch" and her Khiff's purging of their worst memories, and all crowding the immediate area of the tunnel's confines.

Which was when a heavyset armed guard came bustling around a bend from the direction of the main cavern.

Despite their telepathic skills—distracted by their work with the monstrously disfigured inhabitants of the prison cells—Scott and Shania were caught unawares. *They* were caught out, but not Wolf, not entirely. True, he had been unusually slow to pick up on the guard's approach, but what with the sensory assault of these new, mainly unpleasant odours from the cells, not to mention the weird smells from unwashed bodies as they underwent the process of reversed metamorphosis . . . well even a wolf has his limitations! Thus Wolf excused himself.

But finally that sensitive nose and those delicate ears of his had detected someone's approach; at which, and with no time to spare or alert his One and Two, he had loped to a spot close to the bend in the tunnel and there backed himself into a niche in the carved rock wall.

Now he alerted them: *Scott, Shania. Someone has come!*

Central in the crowd of ex-prisoners, the pair of would-be avengers heard Wolf's call and began moving through the crush—only to pause as they saw the guard where he, too, came skidding to a halt. But now their telepathy was fully back in play, and they focussed it directly on him.

Damn, she was right! he was thinking. *That weird bitch was absolutely right to think that something was going on back here. But whatever this is I'll soon put a stop to it!* The picture in his mind was that of Gelka Mordri, Mordri One as he'd last seen her: a raging, frenzied creature as thin and angular as a stick insect, with flying hair, snapping jaws, and gesticulating, taloned hands: Gelka, as she had been just a minute or so earlier, when she'd sent him from the central cavern after she'd thought to detect something of Shing't energies in play back here.

Scott was in motion again. As he broke through the forward edge of the crowd the squat guard saw his shotgun and flinched, his eyes narrowing to thin slits. Then, elevating the muzzle of his own weapon, he thought, *Well, whoever you are, fuck you! And as for the rest of you fucks, you can all have some of this!*

He squeezed the trigger . . . but just a moment too late.

For reading his intentions, Wolf had sprung from cover to crash into his shoulder, his black jaws closing on the guard's flabby neck under his left ear. Shrieking from shock and pain, lurching off balance, the man's aim was deflected upward, his weapon's crazed chatter gouging at the rotten rock of the ceiling and bringing down streams of dust and pebbles.

Hanging on and biting deep, Wolf heard his One's command: *Wolf, get out of there!* And knowing what was in Scott's mind he released his grip and dropped to the floor on all fours. Before the guard could recover, Scott triggered off a single barrel of his shotgun. At close to point-blank range the narrow spread of the blast hammered into the guard's chest a little left of centre, shattered his collar bone, ripped half of his throat away, and hurled him backward. As his weapon went flying he hit the floor stone dead.

What? What happened? the dead man said. But the Necroscope Scott St. John simply ignored him. And coming forward, stooping to gather up the fallen weapon, he handed it to one of the male ex-prisoners.

"Now it begins in earnest," said Shania, hurrying forward to clutch Scott's arm. "In the cavern of the grav-ship they've surely heard the shooting, and others will be on their way here even now. We'll be completely outnumbered!"

"For the moment, yes." Scott nodded. "But let's hope it's *only* for the moment. What the hell has happened to E-Branch?"

As he broke open his shotgun to reload the smoking, empty chamber, and before anyone could even begin to consider what to do next, there came a sudden flurry of displaced air that made swirling vortices in the drifting blue gunsmoke. And blurring into being, three figures materialized as if from nowhere. The two to left and right of the central figure were heavily armed guards who looked deadly dangerous in their own right, but the one they flanked was by far the most menacing. For she was the crazed leader of the Mordri Three, Gelka Mordri herself! And:

"Ahhh! Shania Two," she said, her voice a grating squeal, as painful on the ears as chalk on a blackboard or a shovel in cold ashes. "So I was correct and you are the author of my displeasure." With her head thrust out in front she moved forward, her incredibly long arms and taloned hands reaching. "Well, an end to that, Shania, for even the healing touch of the Shing't cannot repair that which is *utterly* sundered!"

Still moving forward, grinning or grimacing hideously in the renewed strobing of the lighting, she reached for Shania's face and shot instructive glances at the guards flanking her.

As one, they immediately opened withering fire . . .

Twelve minutes earlier:

Ben Trask and his team had raced their cars up the final, narrow stretch of access road onto Schloss Zonigen's esplanade. As the vehicles bounded from the steep slope to the level area, the tech drivers had waited just a second or two—

enough time to scan the complex's car park and looming facade with its huge glass and aluminum doors—before turning off their headlights. This had not left them totally blind,
for while the esplanade's perimeter lights were switched off,
secondary illumination from the facade, the high turrets, and
the reception area beyond the glass doors continued to provide sufficient light to see by . . . which meant that in their
turn they, too, could be seen.

And as their cars fishtailed across the icy surface, so a
pair of searchlights blazed into life, their beams lancing
down from rock-hewn balconies to crisscross the false
plateau. Then came a barrage of automatic fire from the
same vantage points, and as the techs drove for cover behind
a line of parked, nose-to-tail supply trucks, so a hail of bullets spanged and sparked where they struck metal surfaces.

"Bloody hell!" Trask swore in the lead car, crouching low
in his seat as the canopies on the supply trucks were shredded and searchlight beams lanced through the bullet holes
and torn, fluttering canvas. "Wasn't St. John supposed to
deal with such as this?"

"Aye," Tech McGrath replied. "But if we're sufferin' this
oot here, what's St. John goin' through in there, eh? Scott
and that bonnie lassie—aye, and that smart grey yin o'
theirs—up against who knows what in bleddy Schloss
Zonigen!"

"Out of the car," Trask snapped. "Take cover behind the
wheels of these trucks, where you'll be able to shoot back if
anyone tries to creep up on us across the esplanade. And
pray that none of these shooters—poor marksmen though
they seem to be—gets a notion to aim at the petrol tanks!"
And turning to the telepath in the backseat, "Paul, can you
reach Millie? Tell her the same thing: to get out of the car
and take cover. God knows I don't want that kid's blood on
my hands! And likewise the rest of the crew."

"It's done," said Garvey, opening his door. "Funny thing,
but she wanted to know if you are okay, too!" And as he got
out of the car, Trask asked him:

"Oh, and what about you? Are *you* okay now?"

"One h-hundred percent," the telepath grunted, his hoarse voice giving him the lie as he followed locator David Chung out into the misty, gradually brightening predawn air. "Why, it's just like old t-times!" But yes, Trask knew he would be okay.

And with the ground mist wreathing their legs, the eight took cover as best they could, wincing at each buzz and whirr, every *zip!* and *spang!* of ricochetting bullets.

"You techs," Trask called out. "These weapons of ours—even this Swiss stuff—they aren't much good over a hundred, maybe a hundred and ten feet. They're not accurate enough. But what about your crossbows? I'm thinking if we can take out the searchlights . . . ? It probably won't help much, but it will give these snipers something to think about, let them know they're not beyond our reach up there on those balconies."

No sooner said than a pair of ghostly figures hurried to position themselves one at the nose of the supply trucks, the other at the rear. And not ten seconds later—

There sounded the soft *whirr* of a bolt in flight. And:

—Glass shattered as a searchlight beam blinked out and a yelp of shock and outrage echoed down and across the esplanade. A moment later and there came a stream of curses as the lens of the second searchlight splintered, its beam instantly fading.

Except this time the cursing didn't stop but changed to a series of questioning shouts, a terrified babbling, and finally a massed, hysterical screaming. And despite that the clamour of automatic gunfire had suddenly picked up to a furious pitch—a veritable fusillade—it was no longer directed toward Trask and his people, no longer rained down on the esplanade.

Along with Garvey and Chung, Trask ran half crouching to join Tech McGrath at the front of the parked trucks. The hard-as-nails Scotsman's crossbow dangled loosely from his hand; his heavy jaw had fallen open; he was staring in disbelief at twin, jutting rock balconies over the cavern complex's entrance. This was where the searchlights had been located. But as for the men who had worked them, and others who had fired bullets down the paths of the sweeping beams—

—All but one had mysteriously vanished, and the one who remained was even now cartwheeling down the face of the facade, screaming as he fell, his machine pistol flying. And behind the balcony's chunky dry-stone wall, a group of grotesque, tattered scarecrow things stood severely silent, their eye sockets glowing with bioluminous corruption, their white teeth clenched in bony jaws under less than half-fleshed faces!

It was the same on the second balcony, on various ledges, and in openings all along the hollow facade of the crag: these *things* of leather and bone and shrivelled flesh, nightmarishly revitalized.

Despite that Trask knew what he was looking at, still his legs trembled as he stepped out from behind the truck into full view. With eyes that couldn't see, *still* they saw him; and with hands that shed their fingers, shreds of sinew, pieces of mummied muscle, they beckoned him and his team on!

Standing behind Trask, Garvey laid an unsteady hand on his shoulder, causing him to start, and said: "Well, and what did I t-tell you? It's just like old t-times, right, boss?"

"Right," said Trask, his throat dry, his flesh creeping.

And David Chung sighed and said, "So now you know what St. John has been up to. Scott St. John—Necroscope! I wasn't mistaken about him after all . . ."

46

Ben Trask could well imagine what it must be like in the reception area of Schloss Zonigen right now: the horror and insanity of the situation. *He* knew where these dead people had come from—the only place they could have come from—and how, by whom they had been brought back to pseudo-life. He and E-Branch knew these things, for they had known and "understood," as best anyone and even extraordinary people such as themselves might ever understand, the terrible talents of the original Necroscope. He and his team knew, yes, but as for the crag's defenders . . .

Had they believed, he wondered, that they'd seen all there was of terror and madness in the labyrinthine levels of Schloss Zonigen? The physical *abnormalities,* the malformations and mutations that the Mordri Three had visited upon their hostages: had these been considered the ultimate objects of revulsion, repulsion? Scarcely, for many if not all of the female prisoners, no matter how grotesquely mutilated, had been very badly and sexually used; even some of the males.

And having witnessed or—God help us!—*experienced* such atrocities, had it then been believed that every nightmare fantasy was made known, that there was nothing left of malevolence and its effects that might damage or even dismay the "sensitivities" of those who had seen and even partaken of such evil?

Well, and if so, by now they knew how wrong they had been. Not that the dead were evil, not where Trask was concerned, but as for Schloss Zonigen's defenders—

—Oh, yes, he could *well* imagine it:

Those crumbling creatures, dead people, not all long gone into corruption, but some so desiccated by failed or neglected cryogenic systems and the resultant ice in their veins and organs that they were literally breaking up; those vengeful revenants, impossible to stop and impervious to bullets that passed right through their bodies; those *zombies* slow-marching to the attack, shuffling inexorably on, silent and utterly relentless, their skeletal arms reaching.

And now several of the dead were up there on Schloss Zonigen's rock balconies, urging Trask's crew forward with flapping rags of arms and bony, beckoning hands . . .

Within the hollow crag the sounds of shooting and screaming had slackened off, and as a silver rim began to

form on the eastern peaks Trask's thoughts snapped back
from macabre reverie to the current situation. This one battle
appeared won, but not the war. And time so very limited now.

Turning to his half of the team, he said, "Back into the
cars—now!" And raising his voice he shouted along the row
of parked supply trucks to where the precog and his people
waited for his orders: "Ian, do you see what's happened?"

"Yes!" came the high-pitched answer. "Good Lord, yes!"

"Then get back into your car," Trask yelled. "We're going
to crash those doors!"

With the defensive gunfire from Schloss Zonigen effectively at a standstill, there was nothing to stop E-Branch's
tech drivers as their vehicles broke cover, accelerated out
onto the frozen esplanade, and went skidding and fishtail-
ing toward the doors. In an explosion of twisted aluminum
and disintegrating safety glass, the cars took the buckled
frames and a shower of flying shards with them into the reception area.

There the techs brought the cars to a sliding, screeching
halt and the team piled out. Crouching, half closing their
eyes in the dimly flickering, strobing lighting, they spread
out and scanned the area for danger. But while near-distant
gunfire was clearly audible, nothing seemed to be happening here.

As the electrics continued to sputter and flare, Trask
spied behind the desk a white-faced, slack-jawed man with
frantically swivelling eyes. Dressed in the grey uniform of a
guard where he stood spread-eagled, trembling against the
wall, he was no longer a threat. His machine pistol lay on
the desk directly in front of him but he made no effort to
reach for it. That was because a pair of dead men were with
him, flanking him, waiting for him to make a move . . .
which eventually he did when his legs gave way under him,
and his eyes rolled up, and gurgling in the back of his throat
he slid down the wall out of sight.

When the lights steadied up a little Trask's agents took in
a scene of utter mayhem. Grey-clad corpses were every-

where; they sprawled where they'd fallen, in deepening pools of their own blood, and it was obvious that the walking dead had turned their own weapons against them. Indeed, as the sounds of continued shooting echoed from somewhere deep within the complex, and near-distant shouting and screaming gradually faded away, so Schloss Zonigen's *first* victims—victims of hope and lies and greed—made themselves apparent.

They had been waiting in the shadows but now came creaking forward, forming a gauntlet that narrowed toward the arched-over portal of a major passage to the central areas. And there they came to a halt, let their commandeered weapons fall, and stood facing inward toward Trask and his crew. Silent and severe in countenance, still they were by no means threatening. Some were shrivelled, as dry as dust; some were wet with melting ice; and others . . . were simply wet.

But as one they lifted dusty, damp, or rotting arms, pointing out the route that Trask must take.

"Yes, I know," he husked. "And I thank you. We can't thank you enough." Then, finding his own true gravelly voice, he told his team: "Let's go!"

Within the passage—a great ribbed natural conduit, more like a lava run than a tunnel proper—the floor had been levelled and tracks laid. A pair of open-sided bogies, like the cars on a roller coaster, stood with their motors humming however unevenly. Two more dead men from the cryogenic level stood watch, and there were several more bodies beside the tracks where fleeing Mordri guards had been brought to a permanent halt.

The corpses stepped back as Trask's team boarded the cars and the techs operated the simple controls. Looking back as the vehicles lurched forward, Ian Goodly saw the dead men slump and crumple to the floor. Their work here was finished.

And it was the same in the reception area. The Necroscope Scott St. John's fifth-columnist warriors had now rejoined the Great Majority; they lay where they had surrendered once again to the darkness and the chill of Death's embrace, but at least they would know something of peace now . . .

While in a different tunnel, and closer to the central cavern:

Three things had happened almost simultaneously as Mordri One commanded her personal bodyguards to open fire on Scott and the people he had freed. First: Wolf had crouched low, snarled, and leapt straight for Gelka's throat in an attempt to distract her from Shania. Second: a renewed and vengeful Gunter Ganzer, Shania, Scott, and the ex-hostage to whom he had given a weapon, they'd all commenced firing in their own right. And third: several small explosions, a sudden uproar of shouting and curses, and the inexplicable but undeniable sounds of discharged firearms and close-quarter fighting had been heard echoing from the direction of the cavern of the machine itself.

Then . . . it was as if everything happened in slow-motion.

Scott was hit; he felt no pain, only surprise and disappointment, and a blow as from a huge fist, as the bullet passed through his shoulder under the collarbone and took him off his feet. People to left and right of him—it seemed like a great many of them—were being taken out, blown away, some of them mouthing their shock, their pain, as they drifted to the floor.

Dazed and beginning to hurt, Scott had lost his shotgun; his fingers were numb where a second shot had snatched it from his hand. But at the same time, as he came down on his backside on the dusty floor with his legs spread wide in front, he felt a jolt as the butt of his flamethrower thumped down behind him and the weapon rebounded and swung around in front on its sling. He caught at it automatically with his left hand, and his numb hand sought the triggers. Where the hell were they? One trigger for the pilot light, the other for the searing, cleansing fire.

But everything was happening oh so very slowly. And there was Gelka Mordri, no more than nine or ten feet away from him.

Torn by hot, flying metal, Mordri One's henchmen had been gunned down. Gelka, too, had been hit, as witness several dark, spreading stains on her kaftan. Nothing vital had been damaged, however, and she showed little or no concern about these presumably "minor" injuries. For after all she was Shing't; she could heal herself. But she *was* concerned about Wolf where his weight was throwing her off balance. He had sunk his fangs deep in her scrawny shoulder and was swinging from her like an erratic pendulum, twisting and turning with her every movement.

Scott found himself wondering, *Where's Shania?*

I'm here! she answered, from the rocky niche to which she had transported immediately after firing off both barrels of her shotgun at one of Gelka's bodyguards. *I used the localizer to jump to safety—or rather, my Khiff took control of my mind and* made *me make the jump . . . and thus is now doomed. For the device is finally drained!*

Scott gritted his teeth, felt rage flaring, and answered, *It's empty, dead? And without the localizer your Khiff will die, too? Well, she won't be going alone. This Mordri bitch is going with her!*

But he couldn't use the flamethrower because now Gelka had torn Wolf free of her shoulder and was employing Shing't paralysing power to hold him in front of her like a shield. And what was more—from the demoniacal look on her face and the way her taloned fingers were vibrating— Scott knew that she was using the touch on him!

"Hah!" she cried, throwing the howling animal in his face. Now, however, her expression changed to one of fear. She'd seen the flamethrower, the pilot light flaring as Scott squeezed its trigger. But before he could find the second trigger she issued a mad wild cry, backed off, and used her localizer. Swirling up from the floor, a dust devil filled the space where Gelka had been . . .

"My Khiff!" said Shania, hurrying through the shocked, frightened crowd and going to her knees beside Scott. "My poor Khiff! For now, for a time, she lives on but must slowly fade and die. And you . . . how badly are you hurt?" She slid her slender hand inside Scott's parka and his tracksuit jacket—and then slid a finger into the hole in his shoulder!

"What in the . . . ? *Damn!*" said Scott, reacting to her touch and instinctively snatching himself away from her. But already the pain was receding, and he was reminded of what she was and what she could do.

Altered flesh is easy, malleable, she told him. *But badly damaged flesh is more difficult. I can only start the healing, take away the pain. The rest is your body's business. But you are healthy and you'll come to no harm. I shall never let you come to harm!* And she hugged him fiercely.

"Look after these others," Scott said, carefully freeing himself and getting unsteadily to his knees. "Especially him." He meant Wolf.

What . . . what's happening to me? said that one from where he lay curled close by. *What is this . . . this pain, this terrible hurting? Even on my father's island when I was cut, cold, wet, and starving, I never knew anything like—like— Argh! Arrrgh!*

Wolf's cries of agony were mental *and* physical, his howling tore the air! He convulsed; his back arched; his tail grew stiff, bending up and over to lie flat along his back. And his dark anus began to split wide open, showing a pink interior as the inner flesh slowly curled back on itself!

Shania cradled him, stroked him, and Scott could almost feel the alien energies she expended. In another moment Wolf's howling ceased; he writhed in Shania's arms and then lay still, panting. The grey-furred flesh at his rear curled back, closed in on itself, and he was healed. Scott took him in his arms.

It is as I've demonstrated, said Shania, instantly turning to one of the human wounded, a young woman. *Altered flesh is easily corrected—what has been put wrong by the touch can be put right—whereas torn or mangled flesh can be helped but must take its own course. None of these wounds are fatal; they* will *heal, but until they do these people must be cared for.*

"You stay here and see to them," Scott told her then, as Wolf freed himself and struggled shakily to all fours. "And you women—" Scott spoke to the freed female hostages, "—stay with Shania, look after your wounded. But as for you men, listen—" Climbing achingly to his feet, he held up a finger. The sounds of hand-to-hand fighting from the central cavern were growing louder, more frenzied: shouts, screams, gunshots!

"That's where we're needed," Scott continued. "Because if that's not an uprising, I don't know what is! So grab a hold of these fallen weapons—my shotgun there, and Shania's, too—and let's be on our way. And remember, it's not just our lives we're fighting for, it's our world!"

Without waiting to see if they would follow his lead, he took his flamethrower in both hands, ignored the throbbing in his shoulder, and headed for the bend in the tunnel. Wolf went loping alongside him, whining and limping just a little. While behind them—

Grim-faced and determined, the ex-hostages looked at each other, then took up the guns and followed in Scott's tracks . . .

In the cavern of the alien vessel all was confusion, chaos.

Word had gone out among the workers, the forced labourers, that the now functional machine was much more than a spaceship; that it was also a colossal bomb. Certain trustees—as witness Gunter Ganzer—and even a handful of guards had heard the rumours and now believed that the Mordris had lied. There would be no share-out of precious gold among the dupes and hirelings, no freeing of hostages or righting of the wrongs worked upon them. Instead there would be death and destruction on a massive scale and for all concerned.

And even now these facts were being promulgated, broadcast from an observation shack on a ledge in the cavern's rock wall.

It was the young electrician Hans Niewohner who was shouting into the Tannoy system's microphone, his slob-

bered, sucking words reverberating even over the din of
battle; red-haired and once fresh-faced Hans . . . now gaunt
and hollow-eyed, whose face dripped crimson from the
long slash of the razor he had used to open his sealed
mouth, and his mouth itself full of blood where he'd sliced
the tip of his tongue free from the hard palate. He thought
he would probably die from loss of blood, but not until he
wreaked something of revenge on these loathsome Mordris.

"Fight them!" he yelled into the mike, slopping more
blood and nipping shut the blowhole in his cheek in order to
increase the volume of his words. "Cut them down—the
guards and trustees alike, and any who won't join us—but
keep away from those three monsters. Their touch can kill!
And that vessel, which we helped build . . . we *must* find a
way to destroy that machine, for if we don't it will surely
destroy us! So fight! Fight for your lives! Fight for all you're
worth!"

The machine, the Mordri vessel, yes. But the question
was: *how* might they destroy it? Because since late last
night it had been protected by an alien energy screen that—
in combination with the awesome presence of the Mordri
Three themselves—was the source of all the wild fluctua-
tions in the complex's electrics.

The cylindrical grav-ship and the entire tangle of cables
and conduits connecting it to its various servicing adjuncts
on the workbenches—including the benches themselves—
all these things were visible through a pulsating glow that
sheathed them in a swirling, sickly green mist some two or
three inches deep. Even the main power cables from
Schloss Zonigen's generators in another part of the complex: they, too, were affected, shimmering under this constantly writhing warp of energy where they snaked over the
cavern floor from the mouth of a service tunnel to the
workbenches and the alien vessel.

Yet paradoxically, and in one respect at least, the green
glow could be said to be advantageous; for it added a finishing touch to the alien appearance of the great cavern and
loaned an element of substance to the whispers that had

brought about the uprising. Moreover, its weird appearance emphasized the fact—though it no longer required emphasis—that these Mordris were utterly inhuman and their intentions pure evil.

As Gelka Mordri blurred back into being on the dais of the black disk, this is what she saw:

Her trustees and guards, under armed attack from the slave workforce in the greenly illumined cavern! And her lieutenants, Mordris Two and Three, where they also occupied the dais: their mouths were hanging open, their gaze rapt on the milling crowd. Struck dumb, apparently immobilized by what was happening, they seemed rooted in position, swaying this way and that apace with the toing and froing of the hand-to-hand fighting. For the spontaneous revolt—which had commenced only moments after Mordri One had departed to investigate for herself the disturbance in the prison tunnel—had taken them completely by surprise.

As to how it had happened:

Hans Niewohner, ever the rebel, had heard the rumours and passed them on. He had noticed a degree of unease in several of the trustees—people like Gunter Ganzer, with members of their families held hostage in the prison tunnel's cells—and taking a fearful chance had approached them with a plan scribbled on a scrap of paper. Some of them agreed that if he started the riot they would follow suit; others made no promises, but no one any longer seemed entirely against what he proposed.

The actual plan was basic; indeed, it seemed the very essence of simplicity if only on paper. Hans intended to approach and kill one of the more brutal guards, a thug whose duty station was in a secondary service tunnel. Taking the guard's machine pistol, Hans would then sneak it into the great cavern and turn it on other guards, hopefully a group of four who usually located themselves close to the dais. Their weapons could then be commandeered by other rebels, and so on, until everyone who opposed the uprising had been taken out.

As the riot got under way, Hans would then climb the

ladder to the observation shack, produce a number of Molo-
tov cocktails that he had already manufactured, and hurl his
bombs down onto the workbenches and perhaps even the
dais and the Mordri Three. Having seen the terrible damage
done to Guyler Schweitzer—by whom or what he couldn't
say—he already knew the effect that fire could have on
these beings; why, it was even possible that the blasts and
the heat from the kerosine explosions might also disrupt the
alien force screen protecting the spaceship!

In a nutshell that had been the plan; most of which, with
the exception of any injuries to the Mordri Three or damage
to their force screen, had proved successful. As for Hans's
self-mutilation: he considered that worth it. He loathed the
Mordris with every fibre of his body and would do whatever
was required of him to see them brought down. He had not
believed his warped flesh would ever be put back to rights,
and he would rather die in an act of retaliation than face the
last few minutes of his life as a freak.

Now, spitting blood and hatred into the Tannoy's microphone, stained crimson down his front and starting to feel
waves of dizziness, it was gradually dawning on Hans that
his ridiculously simple scheme might actually succeed.
Schloss Zonigen's insurgent slaves were winning!

Or they could be, or they had been. But now—

—Mordri One had returned, her angular mantis-like figure materializing just a moment ago on the dais of the
black disc!

47

For all the world like a great stick insect, Mordri One thrust
her head forward on its long neck and looked up at the observation shack—or "The Watchtower," as the captive
workforce had long since dubbed it—and screwed up her
face in rage. "Hans Niewohner!" she snarled out loud. "It's

him up there. Hans the troublemaker. Oh, but I should have dealt with that one a *long* time ago!" Then:

She looked at her lieutenants and her fury was redoubled. *What?* She raved at them in their shocked minds. *I leave you to your own devices for a minute—perhaps two at most—and this is the result? You idiots! One of you get down among them, use the touch, put an end to this . . . this uprising! You, Guyler—get down there now. And you, Simon—use your localizer, go to the observation shack, and hurl that troublemaker down!*

Snapping her rage, she gazed in disbelief at the melee in the cavern, the furious hand-to-hand fighting. *What? Have they gone completely insane? Or is it simply a desperate attempt to jeopardize our departure?* Hah! *Do they believe it's even possible?* But then, as suddenly a terrible doubt crossed her mind: *Or should I ask,* is *it possible? No, of course not. But in any case we must put an end to this. Now move, you great fools!*

Mordris Two and Three looked at each other—then looked away—and moved not at all. Gelka jerked upright to her full height; her hair stood out from her head as if electrified and she stuck her face into theirs, one after the other. Then, out loud in their own Shing't tongue, once again she cried, "What? Are you both suddenly brain-dead? Or could it be that my mentalism has failed me? Well perhaps, but I'm sure you can't also be deaf! So now . . . will you please be so good as to *get about your tasks!*"

Mordri Three, known as Guyler Schweitzer, was by far the most deranged of the three; but even Guyler—not only mentally but also physically impaired, burned up his right side from his narrow waist to his thin shoulder, and feeling the incredible agony of it—even he was not entirely insane. "Gelka, I *cannot* obey you," he said, lurching to and fro. "I'm employing my powers to heal myself! Using the touch will only deplete me further and so delay my recovery. We'll have to rely on Mordri Two."

"You'll have to *what?*" Simon Salcombe rounded on his One and Three, his look scornful, even contemptuous.

"You'll do no such thing! Rely on me? My localizer is running close to empty and I can't recharge it except from our vessel's drive when it is enabled and operational!" And then, turning to Gelka Mordri herself: "Would you have me exhaust my localizer on some frivolous trip to the observation platform to kill someone who shall in any case soon be dead, along with this entire world? I think not! Nor will I climb that ladder, because for all I know Hans Niewohner has more incendiary bombs that he would be delighted to rain down on me—which is something I can well do without! Surely we have enough on our plates with *one* badly burned, utterly ineffectual member without risking more and possibly worse setbacks."

"Ineffectual!" cried Mordri Three, fidgeting and favouring his right side where his ribs were tender under scorched flesh, and great blisters wept yellow fluid through his kaftan. "Meaning me? How dare you!"

"Not only ineffectual," Simon Salcombe repeated his accusation, "but a grave liability to boot! Did you really believe, Guyler, it would escape our notice that it was you who brought about this uprising? You, tormenting the hostages with details of our best kept secret? For they now *know* that they are going to die, which is what this revolt is all about!"

Gelka at once turned on Mordri Three. "What? Is it so? And have I been so busy with the vessel's computer that I failed to notice? You mad thing! You truly *insane* thing!" And then, questioning Salcombe: "Why didn't you inform me of this before?"

"Because I've only recently learned of it myself," her Two answered. "I heard it from a concerned guard who in turn had it from a hostage he went with. I repeat, from a hostage! They *all* know—hostages, trustees, even the most gullible of the guards—each and every one of them knows or at least suspects!"

"Well, and what of it?" said Schweitzer, his arms flapping and his face twitching. "They're only animals. They can't do us any real harm."

"Oh, really?" said Gelka, showing him the red splotches

on her kaftan, and pointing a shaking finger at the yellow ones on his. "And what pray is all of this if not harm? To some extent, however insubstantial compared with your own injuries, I, Gelka Mordri, have suffered depletion! And if this rabble wasn't busy engaging the guards—if we bore weapons in our own right with which to shoot back—I am sure that even now they'd be firing at us! All because of you, Guyler!" She fell silent, for a moment lost for words.

Then with a grimace, throwing up her hands, she continued. "Enough! Enough of this arguing which achieves nothing. Time is growing short; indeed we are down to minutes, and I must enable our vessel's systems. You two shall remain here and ensure that the energy screen suffers no interference, thus protecting the ship as best possible."

But as she went to use her localizer, Simon Salcombe said, "Gelka, wait! Wouldn't it be safer if we all entered the vessel together?" Suddenly alert, he was obviously suspicious.

"No," she answered him. "First you'll see to it that nothing occurs to prevent our departure. And then when all is ready I'll call you aboard. Be reasonable, Simon, and do as I say, or it's possible that none of us will get out of this place!"

Before he could argue further, Gelka used her localizer to enter the grav-ship. Almost immediately the force screen around the ship and its many adjuncts intensified by a factor of four, and the energy field began to throb that much more urgently; so that it was at once apparent to Mordris Two and Three that even if they used their localizers they couldn't enter the ship now. In fact, if a localizer so much as touched any part of that enhanced energy field it would instantly explode, self-destruct!

But while as physical beings Gelka's lieutenants couldn't enter the ship, their bodiless thoughts could. And:

Gelka, what are you doing? said Salcombe, nervously.

Testing the systems, she replied.

But it seems to me you've locked us out!

Don't be ridiculous! she answered, shielding her innermost thoughts. *I am simply protecting this vessel, which is what you should be doing. And now perhaps you'll obey me, get down among these animals, and give them something extra to worry about!*

Is that a command? said Mordri Three, sniggering involuntarily, then groaning from the additional pain it caused him.

No, it is a necessary requirement, said Gelka. *I shall require you to do certain things—for the good of us all, you'll understand—just as you, soon or eventually, shall require me to do certain things. Each action in its turn, of course, dependent upon the preceding action. Now then, are we in agreement?*

Absolutely, Gelka! Mordri Two answered at once. *Naturally we're in agreement.*

But he, too, was now shielding his innermost thoughts . . .

It was then, as Guyler Schweitzer and Simon Salcombe came down from the dais to do Gelka's bidding, that Scott St. John, Wolf, and the freed hostages entered the cavern and the fighting. And since a majority of the trustees—or at least those with clear consciences, with nothing in the past to cause them to fear for the future—had now joined forces with the rebels, Scott and his group might well have made an immediate and overwhelming difference. They *might* have, but Mordris Two and Three were already wreaking havoc, lashing out indiscriminately where they used the terrible Shing't touch on friends and foes alike. Even Guyler Schweitzer—completely mad now, no longer wholly intent upon healing himself—lurching like a grotesque mannequin among the fighting horde, touching left, right, and centre. And everyone he touched suffering near-instantaneous, crippling transmutations.

Long-striding Simon Salcombe, too, moving jerkily, erratically through the furiously battling ranks, extending twig-thin arms to touch faces, limbs, straining bodies; and never pausing to watch the ones he touched crumple, as if their legs had been scythed from under them. And he was laughing; with his Khiff on his shoulder he laughed until he cried, as the twin delights of murder and madness built up in him and the crowd thinned before him ... until suddenly he and his Khiff came *faces* to face with someone or something else.

It was a young girl, but one that he recognized from somewhere. And as it dawned on him where *precisely* he knew her from—and when her tattered aspect confirmed the fact that she was dead—then Salcombe concluded that he was now as mad as Mordri Three! For she was so very nearly fleshless that it was obvious she wasn't here by virtue of any Shing't touch. No, for corpses require muscles and ligaments to dance and cavort, and this one had none of those. Yet here she stood, upright and reaching for him! And reaching out in his turn—if only to loan credence to his crumbling senses, or perhaps corroborate his insanity—he allowed a trembling, long-fingered hand to make contact with her skeletal paw.

And however inadvertently, he administered the touch.

Except that this time it was very different. This time he sensed his power being *leeched* from him; not driven by his will but drawn out by this dead girl's, perhaps to be turned back on him. And he knew at once that having been called up by a powerful Other, hers was the greater will!

Snatching his hand away and beginning to gibber, Salcombe turned and fled; his Khiff, too, an obscene jelly-thing, melting away into his ear and leaving a single crimson orb to peer out. Daring to look back only once, he saw the dead girl's eyes dripping pus as she came lurching after ...

After the Necroscope Scott St. John had called them from their icy coffins, the dead people from the cryogenic level had split up into two parties. The larger group had gone to Schloss Zonigen's reception area in order to assist Trask and his E-Branch agents, while this smaller handful had taken a longer route and finally found their way here. Now, as best they were able, they were taking part in the last of the hand-to-hand fighting. And that was where they came into their own.

For they *were* dead and couldn't die twice. Cut them down, cut them into pieces, and even the pieces fought on! The dozen or so remaining die-hard guards and Mordri cronies were aghast. Low on ammunition—driven back by their once-captive workforce and vengeful, triumphant ex-hostages—even as they abandoned their weapons and turned to run they were swept under by a tide of death, by dead men and their crumbling or rotting remains.

Meanwhile Shania had done with her healing of wounded and/or altered men, women, and children in the prison tunnel and had come to seek out Scott and Wolf. Upon entering the central cavern, however, where even more healing awaited her, Mordri Three had at once spotted her and recognized her for what she was. It was her Shing't aura, which at close range she could never have disguised from one of her own kind.

Now, even in his madness, Guyler knew why his One had been so determined to get into their vessel—*her* vessel now—and understood what she'd meant when she said it was possibile that none of the Three would get out of this place. Gelka had discovered something of the forces ranged against her and had decided to cut and run! But . . . without her Two and Three? Would she do such a thing? Would Guyler Schweitzer in her place? Oh, absolutely!

Now, too, Guyler noticed a grim- and grimy-faced man heading in his direction, a man with just such a fire weapon as had burned him in the Idossola *Gasthaus*!

Suddenly panic-stricken, he called out: *Gelka, is the ship enabled? Will you power down the screen and take me aboard now? Won't you* please *take me aboard now!?*

But apart from a definite *quickening* of the pulsing of the energy screen and an audible *increase* in the throbbing from the grav-ship's drive, there was no answer . . . and the man with the flamethrower was closer. Guyler sensed concerned thoughts pass between the man and Shania Two: they were lovers; they were the ones who had caused the dead to rise up and join this rebellion against the Mordris. And moreover, they were the ones who Gelka Mordri feared!

All very well for Gelka, who was safe now, but as for Guyler: now he must protect himself . . . except he didn't know how!

My Khiff, he said, *what can I do?*

Aha! his familiar at once replied. *Now you call on me. Me, who you've so often suppressed, denying me my special needs!*

Because you were mad, Guyler answered, *and have made me no less mad. But now we are both endangered, for if I die you die!*

This is not necessarily so, said the other. *Do I feel your pain, the delicious agony of your burns? No, not if I choose to ignore it. And anyway, you are merely a host . . . one host.*

One host? What do you mean? Now Guyler was sore afraid.

Nothing, said his Khiff. *Take no notice of my raving. I am mad, as you yourself have so rightly pointed out.*

The man with the flamethrower was much closer now, but he was moving toward Shania Two, not Guyler Schweitzer. And hiding behind a knob of rock in the shadowed wall of the great cavern, Guyler thought: *He hasn't seen me, doesn't know I'm here!* Then, to his Khiff: *Well, can you help me or not?*

But haven't I always helped you? said that one. *Of course I can help you. Quickly now, take Shania Two hostage. For since she is one of the driving forces in what has happened here, she may yet be our salvation.*

And believing that he understood his Khiff's motives, Guyler came out from his hiding place and went lurching toward the unsuspecting Shania . . .

Having fled back to the dais and climbed its steps, Simon Salcombe had scanned the littered floor of the great cavern for any sign of his grotesque pursuer. Not as simple a task as it might sound, for she was just one of several of the walking dead, and they were milling with a crowd of some dozens of dazed but *living* survivors and walking wounded. But just a moment ago he had spotted her where she came on . . . and then had shouted aloud his relief as a Mordri henchman, dying in a pool of blood, used his final ounce of strength to lift his machine pistol and empty its magazine into the dead girl's legs. Down she had gone into the splintering remains of her lower limbs; following which she was only able to crawl, dragging her shattered legs behind her. And many an obstacle to block her way.

Salcombe was left with no time to savour the respite, however, for Wolf had sniffed him out and at once knew his foreign nature: that he was of the same sort as that female whose touch had caused him so much pain. Well, and so was or had been Shania, but where she radiated good these creatures stank of evil!

Now he came snarling up the steps of the dais—harassing Mordri Two, trying to trip him—but at no time getting within range of his deadly hands; no, for he'd learned better than to do that! And Salcombe whirling, staggering, his body and limbs and thoughts flying in all directions, so that he wasn't fully in control of any of them. But still he controlled his Shing't touch, and if he could only get hold of this skittering, snarling . . .

He lashed out with a foot to Wolf's black muzzle, sending him yelping, skidding, almost flying from the rim of the dais. And as the animal teetered there, so Salcombe reached for him. Wolf saw the alien's long-fingered hand descending, snapped at his wrist, and tasted something metallic between his jaws. Then the linked strap on Mordri Two's localizer came apart and Wolf took the device with him as he went toppling from the dais.

Landing on all fours, and having realized what the localizer was—knowing that Shania had one, and how she used it—Wolf turned to race away, instinctively bounding high over one of the deadly energy conduits. In midflight he felt a wrenching pain in his mouth; his jaws cracked audibly, snapping open from the shock as the localizer reacted to the proximity of an energy source that was infinitely more powerful than its own. And the device fell out of Wolf's mouth. The blast that followed hurled Wolf head over heels, left him sprawling and dazed but otherwise unhurt. As for the localizer:

As Salcombe had informed Gelka Mordri, his device's power cells had been in need of recharging. So that when its sensors had detected a Shing't power source, the localizer had automatically attempted to ascertain the source's compatibility. This had been the initial contact that had driven Wolf's jaws apart, causing him to drop the thing. But when the localizer had come down on the energy conduit . . . that had been the equivalent of trying to charge an electric torch battery from a small town's power grid! And all that remained of the localizer was a glittering cloud of dust, swirling over the greenly pulsating glow of the energy field . . .

From the dais Simon Salcombe had seen what happened. Now he howled his rage—*and* simultaneously realized his impotence! Until now there had existed a possibility, however remote, that Gelka would reduce the energy screen and thus allow her Two and Three to board the vessel using their localizers. But one thing was certain: now that the vessel was powered up, and time being so short, she would *not* be amenable to switching the screen off in its entirety!

Now without his localizer, the only way Salcombe was going to board the vessel was via a manual hatch—which was also out of the question. Even reduced to a minimum the screen was utterly impenetrable by any physical object—and that included him!

His mind went in several directions, each one bringing him up against a dead end. *His* dead end!

Except . . . perhaps there was a solution even now.

His plan would involve persuading Mordri One to reduce the power to the energy screen, of course—that was an unavoidable necessity, and it might not be easy—but if he could convince her of its benefits . . . After all, Gelka would not want to go on alone, would she? What, the lone survivor of her once dedicated Three Unit? Surely not.

So why not a Two Unit?

But the plan, the plan!

Fighting his panic, Salcombe focussed his teetering mind. His localizer was lost, disintegrated, that was true . . . but it wasn't the last available device of its sort in this place, now was it? And so, sweeping the floor of the cavern with his eager eyes, Mordri Two searched for Mordri Three. And why not? For it seemed to Salcombe that his plan was only right and just. After all, it was Guyler Schweitzer who had brought all this trouble down on their heads in the first place, wasn't it?

Now then, where was he? Ah yes, *there* he was. But . . . what was the lunatic doing?

Shania Two was kneeling beside a very badly wounded man, applying her healing version of the touch, when Mordri Three came up behind her. At the last moment she sensed his presence—would have detected it far sooner if she wasn't so intent on what she was doing—but too late now as she came upright, began to turn, and felt his spindly arms closing around her and his paralysing power beginning to freeze her in place. She could and did fight it, yes, but they were equal in this respect and only cancelled each other out, held each other in stasis.

Where physical strength was concerned, however, Schweitzer had the advantage: the strength of a lunatic. Numb from head to toe, Shania couldn't break loose. And:

I have her! Mordri Three told his Khiff, totally unnecessarily, as he managed to position Shania between himself and the oncoming Scott St. John. *What now?*

Now we deal with her Khiff, that one answered.

Her Khiff? said Mordri Three anxiously. *But why her Khiff? And what about me? This man has a fire weapon!*

Her Khiff empowers Shania Two, the other replied. *Even as I empower you. As for this man's fire weapon: have no fear. He won't risk burning this Shing't bitch . . . he loves her! When I have dealt with her Khiff, and when he comes to her assistance, then you may use the touch upon him.*

Yes, I see, said Schweitzer. *But . . . how may we deal with her Khiff?*

I shall see to that, said the other. *Now be on your guard, for the man is here.*

Seeing that his Khiff was right, Schweitzer clasped Shania more tightly yet, exposed her throat by yanking on her hair and pulling her head back, and shrilled at Scott, "Come no further, or else I shall harm her!"

Scott skidded to a halt less than ten feet away and aimed his weapon to one side lest he inadvertently apply pressure to the trigger. And from there he stared in horror as Schweitzer's Khiff emerged in all its semi-solid loathsomeness, bloating out of the mad creature's ear. It resembled a diseased second head, like a bubble of grey-green, blood-tinged pus from a huge boil, and its small crimson eyes were wicked as sin where they fixed on Shania. And then without pause, Schweitzer's Khiff extended a pulsing pseudopod toward her ear!

Scott paced forward, but Shania said: *No, Scott! Stop! He is attempting to lure you within reach. Also, his warped Khiff is trying to force its way into my mind, but my Khiff will now block its efforts—at least for a while.*

And indeed her Khiff came out onto her shoulder—a beautiful thing in its way, the opposite of the other's ugliness—and fended the pulsing member off.

Scott stared at Schweitzer, at his silvery hair in a comb that was ragged now, and glared his hatred, his loathing. Then what Shania had said registered, and repeating her, he made it a question: *For a while? What do you mean?*

With my localizer dead my Khiff is weakening, she replied. *And if Mordri Three's Khiff wins, then I could become as warped and evil as he is!*

Scott was torn two ways. If he rushed forward, Mordri Three would be sure to use the touch; and Shania, held captive, would not be able to heal him. But on the other hand, if he did nothing, Shania's sanity was in jeopardy.

He was stalled and cried out, "What can I do?"

Standing close by, and having heard the deadspeak thoughts that accompanied Scott's words, a dead man replied, *Call up the others, Necroscope.*

"What others?" Scott stared at the scarecrow thing.

The trapped ones, said that one. *The devolved ones. Those who are lost to the eternal darkness of the black disk, on the dais there, under that great blasphemous cross!*

And because deadspeak, like telepathy, frequently conveys much more than mere words, or even thoughts, Scott knew exactly what the dead man meant . . .

48

Scott turned to look at the black disc atop the dais, and asked the devolved ones, *Can you hear me?*

You and no one else, came the answer from at least a dozen trapped souls. *Now that you are near to us, we who for long and long heard nothing hear you! Yes, and we feel your warmth.*

Scott turned again to the fretted dead man. *But what happened to them? How did they come to this?*

It was of course the Mordri Three, said that one, *who have the power to reduce living matter to a black, lifeless solid in the shape of that disc. These poor souls "transgressed" against Mordri rules. Now they pay the price—now they are* truly *dead—incapable even of communication with their fellows, with us, by reason of this hideous, stony entombment! This knowledge was had from others who witnessed the way in which their colleagues were . . . reduced.*

And they can help me?

I can't say, said the dead man, slumping to the cold stone floor. *But if anything remains of revenge in this place, surely . . . they . . . deserve it?* With his work done, he fell silent and lay still.

Looking at the disc on the dais, speaking out loud, Scott said, "If you're able to help me, then help me. I call you up!" As before, his words were deadspeak. And they were answered.

It was as if a great sigh filled the cavern, but that was only in Scott's metaphysical mind. In the more solid, physical world, however, a sighing wind *had* stirred the air, and caused those who were still able to look up and seek its source.

On the dais, the black disc was dissolving, crumbling, and breaking apart. A swirling cloud of black dust rose up. Taking the shapes of men, it swirled, spiralled, and the dust figures mingled, passed through each other, came out on the other side unimpaired or only slightly so, re-forming like miniature, colliding galaxies. And with their dusty, insubstantial arms reaching, their sighing turning to a shriek of rage in Scott's mind, as one they swept toward Guyler Schweitzer.

He saw them coming and in his terror released his hold on Shania. His Khiff withdrew its probes and shrank back into him. The whirling dust figures closed on him as if to suffocate him, and barely in time he used his localizer to make a jump to the dais, which was as close as he could approach the pulsing grav-ship.

Gelka, take me in! he screamed. And when Mordri One failed to answer him—mad creature that he was, to the very last—he tried to hurl himself across the space between the dais and the alien vessel. He struck the screen and his localizer exploded, throwing him up and back onto the dais, and onto that circular stain where the disc had been. Broken and crippled, Guyler lay there under the cross, until the devolved ones came for him.

They surrounded him, swarmed *into* him—into his gaping mouth, straining nostrils, his every orifice—and told Scott: *Now, Necroscope! Now return us to the darkness. For other than pain there's no longer anything here for such as we are become.*

With Shania in his arms again, Scott understood what they intended and said, "Your work is finished here, but know this: you will never be forgotten." And then, nodding his gratitude, he let them go, saying, "Be as you were."

The dust that they were at once began to settle, and the

broken form of Guyler Schweitzer settled with it. Both him
and his loathsome Khiff—caught up in the devolution, sep-
arating into scarlet pieces that broke down in a moment,
their liquids like fruit in a blender—turning as black as the
dust of the vengeful dead as the disc reshaped itself and
they became part of it . . .

Simon Salcombe, on his way across the floor of the cavern,
had seen everything. Mordri Three was dead and his localizer disintegrated. Now there was no possible way he could
gain entry to the enabled ship without Gelka's help, and he
had nothing with which to bargain. Shania Two would be in
possession of a localizer, true, but the man with her was
armed with a fire weapon! Also, there were forces at work
here that were beyond Mordri Two's far less than coherent
powers of understanding.

Still, he must do what he could, try "reasoning" with the
creature he had used to call his One. And keeping low,
moving as close to the ship as he dared, Salcombe used his
mentalism to cry, *Gelka, don't leave me! Reduce the power
and let me in. We can go on together! I can still be your
Two, your Mordri Two!*

And she answered, *What, I should risk my own life to
save yours? You insubordinate creature!*

But, Gelka—

We searched for a god to defy him, she cut him off. *Well,
and perhaps we have found one . . . or if not a god a*
POWER *that serves a god. I mean this man who calls up
dead things. And he does it not by the use or misuse of any
sort of Shing't touch—which as we employed it was cold and
brought only terror to its victims—but by the love they feel
for him, the debt of gratitude they feel they owe him. And, Simon, if that isn't akin to godliness, then tell me what is.*

And again he cried out: *But, Gelka—*

And again she cut him off. *We vowed that if we found
such a one we would face him down and defy him. Very well,
you shall have the honour. So face him down, defy him.*

Gelka, have pity! Mordri Two was on his knees now.

Pity? she answered. *Ah, no. For that, too, is the province of benevolent gods, and so beyond my range. But, Simon, think on this: if gods really do exist, then so must devils. And if that is the case then you will* surely *meet with them—in hell!*

It was her final word on the subject. Then:

The ship's drive throbbed more powerfully yet, and a beam of blinding light shot from its prow and up through the yawning hole in the ceiling, where only a moment ago the last stars had blinked out. For the sun was up, a scarlet blister on the eastern peaks, its light falling on Schloss Zonigen's crag. And now the alien vessel lifted free of its cradle, surged forward, and began to accelerate as it climbed the beam.

Which was when Ben Trask and his people entered the cavern—in time to shield their eyes against the brilliant glare, the throbbing green, and the molten gold. Real gold! Because a long canvas cover on a shallow trench behind the vessel's cradle had suddenly burst into flames, charring from the heat of the treasure lying beneath it: the precious metal that the Mordri Three had amassed to fuel their journey.

And now the beam of light issued from both fore and aft of the ship, the one guiding it out into space, the other speeding it on its way. And with a sudden rush of air the ship departed, leaving a trickle of dust from the ceiling, and a thousand bars of gold, golden statuary, and other once-precious items melting together in the alien furnace of the trench. But while the grav-ship was gone the energy screen persisted, defying interference with a scene that was set, a disaster that now seemed inevitable.

And as for Simon Salcombe: he was nowhere in sight. Under cover of the blinding glare, he had taken his departure . . .

"Too late!" Trask groaned, after all the horrors and the alien wonders of the great cavern had revealed themselves: the dying and the dead—especially the *previously* dead, all but one of them returned now to death—and that dazzling shaft of light spearing out into space, slowly converting the gold and powering Gelka Mordri's vessel. "We're too late. The ship has gone. And yet"—he stared at the precog Ian Goodly— "*we* are still here, still alive and kicking. So where's your Big Bang, your 'nothing'? Maybe it isn't all over after all!"

Nearby, Shania was hurrying from one wounded person to the next, spending longer with some than with others. She had heard what Trask said and answered him, "No, not yet. But soon. Gelka Mordri rides the beam to a far place. And beyond the solar system, five times farther than the radius of the blast, where she considers it safe, there she'll send back a signal to transmute the bulk of the gold into Mr. Goodly's Big Bang. After that . . . then she'll ride the resultant massive gravity wave to her next destination, wherever that may be."

"What?" Trask's brow creased in a frown. "Beyond the solar system? But even at the speed of light . . . I mean, just how far *is* 'beyond the solar system'?"

And Ian Goodly answered him, "Pluto is—I'm not entirely sure—but maybe six billion kilometres away on average? Which means that even at the speed of light it would take her, oh . . ."

"At least five and a half hours to get there," said Scott, coming up on them, his math—or perhaps someone else's, someone inside?—immediately springing to his aid. "And five times that would be—"

"Something more than a day," said Trask.

"No, two," said the precog. "One day for her to get there, and at the speed of light another for her signal to get back to this cavern."

But Shania shook her head. "No, you can put aside all your laws of physics; they only apply to *this* level or parallel, and Gelka is harnessing the energies of a sublevel. She moves much faster than light, and by now many times faster."

"How many times faster?" said Trask.

"Gelka will be at her true launch point in just a few minutes," said Shania. "And it is the nature of the converter beam that her signal will return just as quickly."

Looking bewildered, Trask said, "But at that kind of speed . . . why would she need a gravity wave?"

"Because by comparison what Gelka does now is at a snail's pace," Shania answered with a shrug. "While riding on a gravity wave . . . she can cross the light-years in seconds."

"Good God!" said Trask. But Scott—with that strange look in his eyes again—shook his head and said:

"No, God can do it even faster." Then turning to Shania he said, *We have to try the Möbius Continuum.*

And unheard by the others, Shania's Khiff said, *I approve, for it appears we must. And as for myself, why not? I no longer have anything to lose. Scott, I will go with you.*

Wolf came limping. *Me, too,* he said. *For without me—*

"I know," said Scott. "We could never find the way."

It's this nose of mine, said Wolf. *Yes, and my directions. This Gelka person touched me—she hurt me—and I shall always know her scent. Wherever she goes and no matter how far, I will always be able to find her.* And lifting his muzzle to sniff the air, he went on: *Even now, I know where she is!*

Almost as one, Paul Garvey and Millicent Cleary looked at the animal, frowned, and said, "What is he talking about?" And: "Is someone shielding his or herself? What's going on here?"

"Don't worry about it," Scott said. "And don't worry about what happens next." Turning to Shania, he clasped her and said, "We have to do this, and you have to let her go."

"My Khiff!" she said, her eyes filming where tears formed. And in desperation, to her Khiff: *But the numbers and formulae: you said you couldn't remember them. At least you weren't sure!*

I have been practicing, said her Khiff, emerging from the hollow of her slender neck and transferring to Scott. *I believe I remember them now.*

And if you don't?

"Then what does it matter?" said Scott. "Shania, it isn't as if we have a choice."

She clung to him. "But even if you should find her vessel, and if you can get inside it, what then? She has the touch!"

And so do I, said a very different, deadspeak voice that, despite that it spoke to Scott alone, Shania heard "echoing" in his metaphysical mind: the voice of the single remaining member of the dead from the cryogenic level, a girl whose leather and bone legs had fragmented, broken away below the knees, causing her to crawl. *I have their monstrous touch!* she said again. *Or if not the Shing't touch, something very much like it. That is why I held on here when the others let go, because I believe I can offer yet more help. Now tell me, Necroscope: do you remember the beast-thing who tortured me?*

"Oh, yes," said Scott, grimly. "I'll never forget him! In fact, I can't wait to see him again."

Crawling closer as Trask and his people backed off— then rearing to her knees, clutching Scott's hand for support—the dead girl managed a nod and said, *But when he touched me again it didn't work. The power that called me up—your power—is superior to his and his touch came close to rebounding on him! Alas, because I am slow-moving he was able to make his escape. But as for this dreadful Gelka creature, if or when I confront her in her vessel . . . where can she run?*

As Scott took the girl up she wrapped her bony arms around his neck; which caused Trask—despite that he knew more than most about the Necroscope's powers—almost to gag as he said, "Can someone tell me what the hell is happening here? And what was that . . . that *thing* I saw passing between the two of you?" He looked from Shania to Scott and back again.

Scott took no notice. He could smell the girl; a very dry and musty smell, but one that he didn't find at all offensive. Indeed there was a definite familiarity about it, as if he (or someone else?) had known that smell before, and frequently.

But Shania told Trask, "What you saw wasn't a 'thing,' Mr. Trask. It was a life-form—a familiar creature, if you wish—that has lived in me since I was a small child. And *she* is our very last chance."

She turned to Scott. "I want to go with you!"

"No." He shook his head. "What good would that do? You've got your work to do here. It's *our* work that's out there."

"But—"

"Our time has run out," said Scott. "So if we're going at all it has to be right now." He sensed that Shania's Khiff had already set the thing in motion; and as he shrugged the flamethrower's strap from his shoulder and put the weapon down, then stooped to grab up Wolf, so Möbius's incredible, evolving math began to scroll up the dual screen of his and the Khiff's metaphysical minds. Mutating symbols, equations, esoteric formulae flowing and fluxing, until suddenly Scott recognized a certain pattern.

Stop! he said. But no need, for Shania's Khiff had seen it, too. And a Möbius door formed out of nowhere!

My Scott, said the Khiff. *Is this the one, do you think? Is this the door we need?*

"Only one way to find out," said Scott. And Shania, Trask, and his E-Branch team saw him take a single tentative step forward, and disappear as if he'd never been there at all . . .

In the Möbius Continuum they spun head over heels, but only for a moment, until Scott steadied them up. For he knew how; it was as if he had *always* known how, and for him there was nothing to fear in this place.

But Wolf's yelp was deafening!

Don't do that, said Scott. *Don't be afraid, and don't bark or howl. For even thoughts have weight in the Möbius Continuum, and a shout or a bark is like a bomb going off!*

But . . . where are we? said Wolf, and Scott felt the beginnings of a small, bewildered whimper.

Anywhere we want to be, he replied. *But we only want to be where Gelka Mordri is. Now tell me, can you find her?*

First I must find my . . . my directions, said the other, as his unique mind settled to analysing and aligning alien orientations. But then: *Ah, yes!* he said, "pointing" in Scott's mind. *She is that way, but such a very, very long way!*

Then that's the way we're going, said Scott as he set them in motion. *And no matter how far, it makes not the least bit of difference . . .*

In Schloss Zonigen, Trask asked Shania, "What now?"

"Now we wait," she answered. "But we won't wait for long. Minutes, at best—or worst. And meanwhile I must work."

As she went to seek out more of the wounded, Alan Mc-Grath came running. "That trench back there, where it's is-suin' this beam: it's full o' gold! Molten gold! But the gold is changin'. Even through that green glow you can see small patches of grey ash formin'."

Hearing him, Shania looked back from where she assisted a wounded man who had come staggering, gasping, bleeding from the artificial mouth he had cut himself. It was Hans Niewohner, who now gave himself up to Shania's ministrations so that she could lay her healing hands on him. And she called out, "Mr. McGrath, Ben Trask, the process of transmutation, from gold into energy, is slow right now because it powers Gelka at her current speed. But after she initiates a more powerful gravity wave, then the gold will be consumed that much faster. In other words—"

"Mr. Goodly's Big Bang," said Trask.

"Yes," Shania answered, "which either occurs here or—if Scott is successful—far out in space at Gelka's location. We must hope for the latter." And she continued with her work.

"Well then, let's do more than just hope," Trask muttered, leading his agents toward the poisonous-looking, pulsating glow from the trench. "In fact, it might be a good idea if we were to start praying . . ."

Out in deep space, more than twenty-five billion miles from the rim of the planetary solar system, Mordri One's vessel had come to a halt. At its rear, a seemingly solid beam or tube of white light reached all the way back to the cavern in Schloss Zonigen. Seated at a monitor screen, Gelka Mordri

watched the countdown, one hundred to zero, to the opti-
mum moment when she would issue the vocal command to
trigger Earth's demise. Mere moments after that her ship
would automatically drop into a gravity sublevel and hook
up on the wave emanating from what had been the innermost planets of the solar system.

But outside the ship, stationary now in the Möbius Continuum: *This is the place,* said Shania's Khiff. *I sense her
Khiff, very close and very erratic, insane, bent once again
on murder. The death of an entire world. But in order to fix
Gelka's precise location—*

She transferred from Scott to Wolf, becoming one with
his mind, and said, *Ahhh! Now we have her!*

Another transference, but this time to the dead girl. And:
We go, said Shania's Khiff.

I'm sorry it ends like this, said Scott, with his emotions—
his feelings, for an utterly alien being—wrenching at his insides. But:

Perhaps it doesn't end like this, said Shania's Khiff. *Who
can say? Perhaps there's life after death even for my kind.
For after all, Necroscope, you've proved that it's so for your
kind. And now farewell. Take care of Shania and be her One
always.*

Then conjuring a door of her own, and taking the dead
girl with her, the Khiff transferred to Gelka's vessel . . .

The changing Shing't numerals on Mordri One's monitor
screen had counted themselves down to thirty when suddenly she felt a waft of disturbed air and sensed a presence.
There on her left in the cramped ship's interior, in a curved
chair that should have been Guyler Schweitzer's—

—Was something she just couldn't believe!

"Gah!" she said, throwing up a claw-like hand as the
dead girl reached for her. And their hands—claw and fretted paw alike—met.

It was Gelka's immediate instinct to apply the touch with
all the force she could muster . . . a deadly touch, and a fatal

instinct. For no sooner was the power flowing *from* her than it reversed and flowed back *into* her—but with redoubled, trebled, and even quadrupled force. And:

"*Gah!*" she said again, as the irreversible change commenced. Her stick-thin arms shrivelled and her spindly legs began to bend sideways and up from the hips, tearing open her kaftan. As she sank deeper in her chair, her over-long neck concertinaed and her head shrank down; while in her nether parts she gaped open as if she were giving birth, her flesh curling up on her to expose inner organs that dangled like the weird appendages on a crimson nudibranch . . . one of which was not so much an organ as a hideously altered Khiff, a shuddering, poisonous blob that collapsed into loathsome liquescence even as the dead girl's jaws cracked open to smile an awful, vengeful smile.

Thus, in mere seconds, Gelka's evagination was complete, and she was left a gory, dripping, *truly* alien cucumber thing as finally the inverted flesh closed over her head.

Lolling there in her curved seat she quivered helplessly, utterly incapable of issuing any destruct command, and the timing on her monitor screen was down to ten.

Now you can go, Necroscope, said the dead girl in Scott's mind.

But what of you? Scott asked of Shania's Khiff.

In your world and without the localizer I would only feel myself fading away, said that one. *That would be painful for my Shania. Here I'll feel nothing at all. So here is better, where I shall abide with my new friend.*

Go now! said the dead girl.

And of course Wolf knew the way home . . .

In the Möbius Continuum:

Scott and Wolf felt their motion brought to a halt. *What?* said Scott. For even Harry Keogh in his time had known nothing like this. Then, out of the timeless nothingness of the Continuum, a dozen, a hundred, ten thousand golden darts sprang into existence. And Scott (or something in him) said, *You're just a little too late. It's over. And anyway what kept you? What? So many of you, and you couldn't get here in time?*

Thousands of us, yes, one of them answered him. *The smallest handful of our kind. But in this universe alone our worlds number billions, and the parallel places are countless! Anyway, we haven't come to help you. Only to clean up after you. So now go home. You still have work to do, and then we'll do ours . . .*

In the cavern in Schloss Zonigen the gold in the trench turned to ashes. It happened in a moment: a complete collapse of elements, a transmutation of metal into raw energy.

The pulsating green glare switched itself off; the beam of light from the trench contracted, gave the illusion of shooting up through the gaping hole in the ceiling, and was gone. Normal daylight flooded down from the same hole, finding Trask and his E-Branch agents wincing and holding their breath as one person. Until Shania, in the smallest possible voice, said, "We win!"

And from behind them where they stood at the edge of the trench, Scott St. John said grimly, "Only one thing left to do. But where is he?"

You had better ask me, said Wolf as Scott put him down. *My jaw is still aching from the jolt his device gave me. But I have his scent and he's not very far away. Not very far at all.*

Scott nodded, and with Wolf loping at his side went to recover the flamethrower from where he had left it . . .

In the cryogenics tunnel, Simon Salcombe frothed and gibbered. He had thought to threaten the frozen ones—use the touch to bring them back to a hideous half-life, offer them hope of last resort with lies and promises he could never keep. They were to have been his personal bodyguards, protecting him from whatever threats the future might bring. Except . . . their bitter coffins were open, empty, and there was no one here.

Searching the full length of the icy, glittering tunnel— from its root in the heart of Schloss Zonigen to its mouth

that gaped high in the precipitous face of the crag—Mordri
Two had scrabbled among the cryogenic units, desperate to
find the dead people who he and his Mordri colleagues had
so often tormented. But no more.

Now he stood on the rim of the cave with nothing out
there but a brand-new day, a risen sun and rising breeze,
and a dizzy drop to the scree thousands of feet below. Alone
of his kind in this place and afraid now, he communed with
his familiar creature: *My Khiff: what can I do?*

Flee, my Mordri! said that one. *You must flee this place, and
at once!* Salcombe's rage flared up anew, because his Khiff,
with its useless advice, appeared to be laughing at him!

Do you mock me? he said. *What is it that so amuses you?*

*Why, your fear, my Mordri! Your terror, which feeds me. I
enjoy it as much as anyone else's!*

You mad thing! Salcombe cried. *You advise me to flee, but
there's nowhere to go!*

Then stay here. I like *it here, where I can drink in your
nightmares for ever and always—or perhaps not for always—
for see . . . even now another nightmare approaches!*

Hearing the hum and throb of an electric motor, Salcombe looked back along the tunnel to where an open car
had arrived at the end of the track. In its prow stood a man,
and Salcombe recognized him from the central cavern. This
was the one Gelka Mordri had been afraid of, the one she
had run from, the **POWER** she had told him to confront.
He was carrying his fire weapon. And now the man—along
with a wicked-looking grey quadruped—now they were
stepping down from the car and coming toward him, coming *for* him.

Scott triggered the pilot light on his weapon and called,
"Simon Salcombe, it's the end of the road for you."

Salcombe showed his sharp fish teeth in a snarl, crouched
down, and came unsteadily forward. Emerging from his ear
onto a narrow shoulder, his Khiff told him: *It is time I took
my leave of you, for now I spy another mind to madden.*

Ungrateful thing! said Salcombe. And to Scott, "Why do

you do this? What have I done to you?" A delaying tactic, for still he crept forward.

Scott, too, pacing inexorably forward, and answering, "You murdered a woman in London, England. Her name was Kelly—Kelly St. John."

"Ah, the reporter bitch!" Salcombe cried. "I remember her. But what was she to you?" He made as if to spring; likewise his familiar creature, bunching itself on his shoulder.

"She was my *wife*!" Scott choked the words out, and without pause triggered his flamethrower.

A shimmering lance roared out and in a single moment half melted Mordri Two's insubstantial, suddenly shrieking Khiff to his shoulder. Trying frantically to reenter Salcombe, the creature oozed its seared, bubbling mass back in through his right ear—which caused him yet more excruciating agony! And hosing Salcombe head to toe with a near solid jet of heat, Scott grimaced as the stink of roasting flesh hit him. It was so terrible that he might even have relented—but in his mind: *An eye for an eye, Scott*, someone or thing said, and so he kept his finger on the trigger.

Simon Salcombe's kaftan had gone up in flames. His pallid skin was blackening, crisping, beginning to peel from him. And backing off, dancing like a fiery puppet—with his thin knees jerking high and his pipe-stem arms beating in vain at the fire that consumed him so mercilessly—in another moment he skittered on the rim of the abyss.

His Khiff came blundering out of him through his right eye and forced the eyeball out with it. Sightless, seared, the dislocated orb hung there for a moment before melting like candle wax and running down his cheek along with the liquefied Khiff.

Utterly relentless now, Scott applied yet more pressure to the trigger. And over the edge Salcombe went: a shrieking fireball pin-wheeling down the face of the cliff, flying apart into several flaming pieces as they spun and bounded from one jagged outcrop to the next, all the way down.

And finally it was done.

Then Scott released the trigger, letting the flamethrower fall to the floor. And apart from himself and Wolf, it was the only warm thing in the entire ice tunnel . . .

Meanwhile in Schloss Zonigen and elsewhere, indeed in a great many places, a host of—but of what? Forces, powers, superior intelligences? Golden darts? God's little helpers? But in any case a host—had commenced putting the finishing touches to what *must* be put right lest the world have cause to believe in an utterly hostile universe; which runs contrary to the facts. For the Mordris were the exceptions that prove the rule, and fear of strangers and the unknown is the fuel that drives the wheels of war . . .

In the central cavern, assisted by Trask and his people, Shania had done all she could of ministering to the physically and mentally wounded. Now she stood aside with Trask and the precog Ian Goodly and waited on Scott's return.

It was obvious from Trask's drawn features, however, that he was still very uncertain about what was happening here. And turning to the precog he said, "You know, I still can't work it out! What I mean is: you are what you are, and you do what you do, and you've never once been wrong, not that I can remember. Oh, the future has played its weird tricks on you—or on us—but the outcome is always as close as never mind to your predictions. Yet this time you predicted a Big Bang, and—"

"—And it *has* happened, or is happening," Shania cut in.

"Not here but out there. Once the process reached its critical stage there was no stopping it. How may I best illustrate it? Ah, yes! What would happen if you were to arm a hand grenade, then fail to throw it?"

"It would blow me to bits," Trask answered.

And Goodly said, "Or in that Gelka creature's case, to her elemental gases?"

Still Trask wasn't satisfied. "Okay, but unless my memory is playing tricks with me you also said that after the Big Bang there would be nothing. You said the Big Bang would be followed by a Big Nothing, right?"

Goodly sighed, shrugged, shook his head. "Ben, you know as much about all this as I do. I'm at a loss as to how to explain it. And so I'm obliged to agree with you—that maybe this time I was wrong."

"Oh, I'm not saying you were wrong," said Trask. "But I am concerned that you might yet prove to be right!"

The precog frowned. "Come again?"

At which Trask queried, "Ian, now tell me: is the future a devious thing, or isn't it?"

"It definitely is," said Goodly.

"In which case," said Trask, nodding, "mightn't everything depend on the nature of 'nothing'?"

The precog's frown deepened, but right then, in the moment before he could answer Trask, the NOTHING they had been talking about happened . . .

And at that same "moment"—if time has any meaning at all in the universe men think they know—Scott and Wolf arrived back in the great cavern to a scene that was scarcely believable.

Shania, her mouth and gorgeous eyes wide open in astonishment, moved, flying into Scott's arms; but apart from Wolf and Scott St. John himself—oh, and a myriad golden darts—Shania was the *only* flesh and blood creature, indeed the only thing, that moved at all! And all around the three, hurtling at such astonishing velocity that their trails filled the cavern with a crisscross weave of warm golden light, the darts sped from person to person and mind to mind, doing what they'd said must be done: "cleaning up" after the work that Scott's Three Unit, Ben Trask and his team, and the vengeful dead from the cryogenic level and the disc on the dais had done here.

But as for everything and everyone else in the cavern: They were frozen in time. Time itself was frozen! Smoke from the pit of ashes that once contained gold hung in the air as if painted there, the beam of daylight from the ceiling hole held dust motes in stasis, and while the air for everyone else was solid—its molecules unmoving, as if set as in invisible concrete—still Scott, his Two, and his Three breathed freely. Then something inside Scott said, *Time to go home.*

"But Trask and his people, and—" he began to reply.

Don't concern yourself, said the voice from inside; that familiar voice, of a boy, then a man, then more than a man, and now a revenant. But a different kind of revenant, one who knew that death isn't like that.

"But what's happening?"

You don't understand? The voice seemed surprised. *Shania's Khiff understood. Why, we might even say that she supplied the solution!*

And now, too, Scott understood. "You're saying they won't remember all of this? You've taken it away from them? But why? Was it all for nothing?"

And so the voice explained:

How other races would one day find their way here, perhaps even Shing't survivors like Shania Two, who were off-world when their planet was destroyed. But if or when they did—how would the peoples of Earth greet them if what had happened in Schloss Zonigen was known by all or even by any?

Well, it would be known by some, but only by a small, very small deserving few—say three?—but no more than that. And:

I can't wait around much longer, said the voice. *There are other places I need to be. So now, use the Möbius Continuum for the very last time, Scott, and go home.*

Scott looked this way and that. The weave of golden light continued its frenzied activity in this otherwise timeless cavern. People and things were vanishing—the dead, Ben Trask and his crew, the ashes in the trench—and the hole in the ceiling was resealing itself!

"Okay," Scott said breathlessly, "we'll go home. But first I'd like to know why you're allowing us to see this, why we get to remember."

But isn't that obvious? the dart answered. *When the others come—which they will, eventually, for there are a great many races out there in the stars—they may need someone* like you, Scott, and especially Shania, to vouchsafe them. We understand, of course, that it may not happen in your time, but then again it may. And something else . . ." (now the dart hovered over Wolf). "Not all of the species out there are bipedal. Not very many of them, in fact. That's just one more reason why your Three Unit makes perfect sense to us!

Scott looked at Shania, who said, "We should go home now."

Scott nodded, conjured a Möbius door, and took his Two and Three home with him. On their way, instead of performing an instantaneous transfer, he paused to say: *Suddenly I'm reminded of something. When Harry showed me future time there came a point when everything stopped. But as we now know, everything hasn't stopped. What do you make of that?*

And Shania answered, *Gelka Mordri was intending to hook up to the enormous sublevel gravity wave caused by her explosion. Perhaps the sublevel she chose had a connection to the Möbius Continuum.*

You're saying that maybe her Big Bang caused a disruption here in the Continuum, too?

Possibly, she replied. *Or there again, perhaps when those dart intelligences stopped time in the great cavern, it stopped here also. They do after all use the Continuum. Maybe they're a part of it, with a measure of control over it.*

So time stopped for everthing else, but not for us? Still Scott was baffled, and the smallest part of him that was Harry Keogh scarcely seemed interested, was gradually fading from his no longer metaphysical mind.

Ah! said Shania. *But time's a funny thing. Maybe it didn't stop at all but we simply speeded up! I'm sorry, Scott, but my knowledge of the sciences—and especially metaphysics—isn't all that it should be.*

Oh, really? he said. *Then what does that make me?* And then he laughed, but silently, of course . . .

As the trio emerged from the Möbius Continuum in Scott's study, Harry Keogh's golden dart—his sentient remnant—

left Scott and hovered at eye level in the early dawn light coming through the windows. And a second dart, which might have been its twin, issued from Wolf. There they hung in midair, turning on their axes, first this way then that, as if choosing a direction. But at the last moment—

A third dart—smaller, the merest sliver—split off from the side of Harry's dart, and turned to point its sharp prow at Shania. And she gasped, clinging to Scott as a small but oh-so-well remembered voice said, *And so we do go on. Good-bye my Shania.*

And then indeed they *were* gone—all "three," of course—passing out through the unbroken pane and disappearing over the misted garden . . .

That night—or perhaps the previous night, or possibly a night some time previous to that, time *not* being what it is—on the flat roof of E-Branch HQ in the heart of London: Ben Trask, his principal ESPers and techs, even the Minister Responsible, sat around a blazing brazier sipping from thin-stemmed glasses or simply warming their hands. On a table close by, several bottles of wine stood mainly empty. The fire in the brazier consisted of—

"What?" said Trask, leaning forward as a thick file burst into flame. "What are we burning here?"

"Old stuff," said Paul Garvey.

"Out-of-date stuff, I think," David Chung added. "It was a good idea of . . . of yours, boss?" The locator seemed uncertain as he glanced through the leaping flames at Trask.

"Yes, your idea, definitely," said Millie Cleary, smiling prettily. "And I think a celebration is perfectly in order."

"But a celebration of . . . ?" said Trask, feeling that there was something more than a little *out* of order here, but unable to say what it was.

Seated next to Trask, the Minister Responsible beamed and said, "Why, of my getting your funding doubled, of course!"

As another file went up in flames, Trask tried to read its title off the card cover but managed only a single word or name—"Scott," or maybe just "Scot"—before the card blackened and curled up on itself. "Scotland Yard," maybe? Most probably. But in any case . . . " he shrugged and let it go. And raising his glass, he said, "Very well then, here's to us, and here's to E-Branch!" But turning to the precog and seeing his forehead wrinkled in seeming concentration, "Oh?" Trask queried. "Well, my gloomy-looking friend, what is it now?"

"Eh?" The precog gave a start. "I'm sorry, I was . . . somewhere else entirely!" He looked at the glass in his hand. "This must be very good stuff. It's quite taken me out of myself."

"But you're sure there's nothing troubling you?" Trask was still trying to allay that small, nagging suspicion of his own, that something wasn't ringing entirely true here.

"No, nothing," Goodly shook his head. "Nothing whatever—not that I know of."

"Just a Big Nothing, eh?" Trask tilted his glass, pausing a moment to look at the stars.

"Right," said Goodly, smiling a rare smile. "Just a great Big Nothing." For whatever it was that *had* been bothering him, it was there no longer. And not surprising, really, for being the precog it was the *future* rather than the past that concerned Ian Goodly. It was the *future* that was devious—

—Usually.

But as for the immediate or close future:

The brief gamma-ray burst that was recorded by scientists a little later, which had its source in the Cassiopeian region of the sky, was believed to have been a) the faint echoes of a supernova at the outermost limits of space, or b) some smaller cosmic catastrophe closer to home, possibly the collision of a comet or mass of "dark matter" with a wandering black hole.

As for how close to home—

—"The world would never know . . ."